## Her brow arched.
## "So, this is our first date?"

"I'm not sure it started out that way, but that's how I would like to end it." [...] fingers along her cheek. [...] casual. I wasn't sure if I [...] more. But I am."

"Are you sure about tha[...]

He nodded. "Casual doesn't have the appeal it once did. I'm ready for something serious. Are you willing to take this to the next level, Vicki?"

It felt as if hours went by as she studied him, but it was only a few moments. Finally, she said, "So, how do you usually end your first dates?"

The smile that stretched across Jordan's face was so wide it made his cheeks hurt.

"It's been a while since I had a first date," he said. "But if I remember correctly, it usually ends like this."

He dipped his head and connected his lips to hers. The minute their mouths touched, Jordan was bowled over by the sheer softness of her lips, the sweetness of her delectable kiss. It had been so damn long since he'd felt anything even remotely close to the feelings racing through his blood that he had to slow himself down before he attacked her mouth with the passion suddenly coursing through his veins.

## Books by Farrah Rochon

### Harlequin Kimani Romance

*Huddle with Me Tonight*
*I'll Catch You*
*Field of Pleasure*
*Pleasure Rush*
*A Forever Kind of Love*
*Always and Forever*
*Delectable Desire*
*Runaway Attraction*
*Yours Forever*
*Forever's Promise*
*A Mistletoe Affair*

---

## *FARRAH ROCHON*

had dreams of becoming a fashion designer as a teenager, until she discovered she would be expected to wear something other than jeans to work every day. Thankfully, the coffee shop where she writes does not have a dress code. When Farrah is not penning stories, the *USA TODAY* bestselling author and avid sports fan feeds her addiction to football by attending New Orleans Saints games.

# A
# *Mistletoe*
# *Affair*

## FARRAH ROCHON

**HARLEQUIN**® KIMANI™ ROMANCE

For my aunt, Gail Becnel.

She looks well to the ways of her household
and does not eat the bread of idleness.
—*Proverbs* 31:27

Recycling programs
for this product may
not exist in your area.

ISBN-13: 978-0-373-86381-5

A Mistletoe Affair

Copyright © 2014 by Harlequin Books S.A.

For questions and comments about the quality of this book please contact us
at CustomerService@Harlequin.com.

**HARLEQUIN®**
www.Harlequin.com

**Printed in U.S.A.**

Dear Reader,

Have you ever wondered why love stories at Christmastime are so enduring? Year after year, bookstore shelves overflow with yuletide tales of love, laughter and sometimes even a little heartache. As I was writing *A Mistletoe Affair,* I finally figured out why these stories are so popular. It's because the holidays and love go hand in hand. As you embark on this journey into the fictional seaside town of Wintersage, my hope is that the magic of the Christmas season touches you as deeply as I was touched while writing this story.

I would be remiss in not thanking fellow contributors to the Wintersage Weddings series, Harlequin Kimani authors A.C. Arthur and Phyllis Bourne. Bringing the town of Wintersage to life with the two of you was an amazing experience.

Blessings,

Farrah Rochon

# Chapter 1

Stealing a brief moment to decompress after a hectic morning of back-to-back-to-back customers, Vicki Ahlfors closed her eyes and inhaled a healthy lungful of rich, pine-scented air.

God, she loved this time of year.

The delicate perfume of tea roses in spring was lovely, but it couldn't compare to the crisp freshness of balsam fir. The fragrant scent filling Petals, her floral-design shop, was a telltale sign that her favorite time of the year was finally upon her.

She snipped a wayward thatch of pine needles from the thick spray, then draped the nine-foot garland across her custom-made chest-high worktable. She gathered sprigs of deep red hypericum berries and, using floral wire, attached them to the garland in perfectly measured six-inch increments. She knew how precise Mr. Wallace liked his floral arrangements, and she would not give that old curmudgeon a single opportunity to complain about the treatments she'd designed for his front door this year.

"Oh, my goodness! It smells amazing down here."

Vicki lifted her head to find Sandra Woolcott-Jacobs, one of her partners in crime in the Silk Sisters event agency, rounding the newel post at the base of the winding staircase. She walked over to Vicki's workstation, leaned over the garland and pulled in a deep breath.

"I love this time of year," Sandra said with a satisfied sigh. "Laurel Collins was hanging Christmas lights around the window of her gift shop when I walked past there this morning. I nearly broke out into 'Jingle Bell Rock.'"

Vicki arched a brow in knowing amusement. "That may be the case, but for some reason I don't think it's *just* the time of year that has you singing these days."

Sandra dipped her head, a coy grin lifting the corners of her mouth. "There may be another reason," she admitted.

Vicki burst out laughing. "Sandra Woolcott-Jacobs, is that an actual blush forming on your cheeks?"

"Oh, stop it," Sandra said, the blush deepening.

If that wasn't a sign that Sandra had undergone a radical change since reconnecting with the love of her life, Vicki didn't know what was. Isaiah Jacobs had swooped back into town and swept her girlfriend right off her feet.

"You've got that special newlywed glow," Vicki said. "It looks really good on you."

She denied the slight twinge of envy that pinched her chest, refused to even acknowledge its existence for fear that it would show on her face. She was thrilled for her friends. Truly, she was. Both Sandra and Janelle

Howerton-Dubois, the third member of their trio, had found love in the past few months, and Vicki could not be happier for her two best friends.

But happiness and envy weren't mutually exclusive. She was a multitasker; she could feel both.

"I can already tell that my first Christmas with Isaiah will be magical," Sandra said with a look that could only be described as dreamy. "If you're not booked solid already, I may have you put together a wreath for our front door."

"You know I'll make time for you," Vicki said. "What about a tree?"

Another of those soft, faraway smiles graced Sandra's lips. "I think we're going to decorate that ourselves. It'll be our first tree as a family."

Vicki could barely contain her own wistful sigh. In the epic battle between happiness and envy, envy was winning by a landslide right now. There was no doubt about it, decorating her tree at home, once again by her lonesome self, would suck even more this year.

"I will, however, have you order our tree from the supplier you usually use," Sandra said, finally coming out of her it's-a-wonderful-life-with-Isaiah-induced daze. "Have you ordered the tree for the Victorian yet?"

Vicki nodded. "It's being delivered later today. I was able to find the most gorgeous twelve-footer for the front parlor. It should fit perfectly in the curve of the staircase."

Petals inhabited the majority of the first floor of the three-story Victorian she, Sandra and Janelle owned in their New England hometown of Wintersage. Dubbed the Silk Sisters since their high school days at Wintersage Academy, the three had gone into business together soon after college graduation. Swoon Couture,

Sandra's dress boutique, was on the second floor, and Janelle's event-planning business, Alluring Affairs, occupied the third.

"The place looks great so far," Sandra said, gesturing to the gathering room, which served as the lobby for all three businesses. The room's focal point, a pillared, carved wooden mantelpiece, was festooned with silver ribbon, ice-blue glass ornaments and glitter-dusted seashells to bring in the essence of their seaside town.

"If you need help decking the halls, just give me a ring," Sandra said.

Vicki waved off her offer. "You've got enough on your plate with getting Swoon Couture Home off the ground."

Sandra and her new husband were starting a new venture, marrying her design business with Isaiah's family's furniture business.

"Only if you're sure," Sandra said.

"I'm sure. Besides, I get a bit territorial when it comes to holiday decorating."

"Don't I know it," Sandra said with a snort. "One piece of tinsel out of place and the girl goes crazy."

Vicki pointed her pruning shears at her. "If you even *think* about bringing a string of tinsel in here…"

"No tinsel! I promise." She laughed, raising her hands in mock surrender. "I'll leave the decorating to you. I can't wait to see the finished product." Sandra started up the stairs, but stopped on the second step and called, "The Quarterdeck at seven?"

"I'll be there," Vicki returned.

Even though the Victorian served as their home base, it was rare for the three of them to be in one place at one time. Even when they were all here, they were so busy with their respective businesses that there was never much time for idle chitchat. Years ago they made a pact to meet on Monday nights for dinner, drinks and girl talk at the Quarterdeck, a landmark eatery on Wintersage's waterfront.

They were in for some serious chatting tonight. These past couple of months had been a whirlwind of activity, with life-altering events happening for Sandra and Janelle.

After witnessing the transformation in both her friends' lives, Vicki had decided it was time she undergo a few changes herself, on both the professional and personal fronts. She had sensed for quite some time that she was in a rut, but as far as ruts went, hers had been comfortable.

Honestly, what did she have to complain about? At twenty-eight years old she owned her own business, her own home, and had family and friends who loved her. She was blessed.

But she wasn't happy. At least, not as happy as she wanted to be. As she *deserved* to be. Witnessing both her friends enter into that much-sought-after world of wedded bliss had brought what was missing in Vicki's own life into stark relief.

So she'd taken matters into her own hands, undergoing a radical makeover. Okay, not entirely radical; it wasn't as if she'd dyed her hair purple and gotten a nose ring or anything.

But for quiet, reserved Vicki Ahlfors, a chin-length pixie haircut and a closet of new cleavage-revealing blouses and dresses were pretty darn drastic. By the slew of new male clients Petals had garnered over the past week, the results of her transformation could not be denied.

She was Wintersage's hot new item.

"Whatever," Vicki said with a snort.

She had definitely caught the eye of several men around town, but instead of being flattered, Vicki found herself just a tad pissed off. She'd lived here her entire life. Why in the heck had it taken a makeover for all of them to finally notice her?

Despite the umbrage she'd taken over her admirers' obvious shallowness, Vicki wasn't entirely blind to the romantic opportunities that her newfound popularity had created.

There was just one problem: not a single one of the men who had come calling in the past week held an ounce of appeal. She found their overaggressiveness off-putting, and for the few who'd strolled into her flower shop as if they were God's gift to the female population, Vicki had taken great pleasure in knocking the wind out of their overinflated egos.

Talk about egos! What about her own? After all her bellyaching over being single, she now had the nerve to play hard to get.

"Damn right," Vicki said.

Not only did she refuse to settle for the first guy who walked into her flower shop and offered to buy her a dozen roses, but she planned to make sure that any man she dated was worthy of her precious free time. Life was much too short to waste it on a relationship that was going nowhere. She wanted to find what Sandra and Janelle had both found.

*So why are you still dragging your feet?*

Setting down the shears, Vicki walked over to her laptop and flipped it open. Inhaling a fortifying breath, she logged on to the online-dating profile she'd created after she'd got home from Sandra's wedding this past weekend. The message sitting in her inbox seemed to pulse with a life of its own. She'd read over it at least a dozen times since it had arrived, had attempted to hit Reply more than once. Yet there it sat, staring at her, goading her into donning the new, confident, vivacious mantle she was determined to wear.

The new Vicki.

Was she *really* going to take this step? As popular as online dating had become, Vicki could never bring herself to try it. She'd held steadfast to the romantic notion of meeting her Prince Charming the old-fashioned way. They were supposed to spot each other across a crowded room, fall madly in love, start a family and live happily ever after.

Blah. Blah. Blah.

The old-fashioned way hadn't worked for her. The old-fashioned way had her still single, while her two best friends were now both married and living their happily ever afters. She was done waiting for things to happen the old-fashioned way.

Especially after accepting the harsh reality that the one man she'd been waiting on—the one whom she'd carried a torch for so much longer than she would ever admit to anyone but her own foolish heart—would apparently never see her in that way.

A dull ache settled in her chest, but Vicki quickly tamped down the gloominess before it could take hold.

She was done pining for what would never be. It was time to move on.

Ignoring what felt like a million butterflies flittering around in her stomach, Vicki replied to the date request from a handsome E.R. doctor who, according to his profile, was an attending physician at Tufts Medical Center in Boston. The moment she hit Send, a weight seemed to lift from her shoulders.

There. That hadn't been so bad. And it was yet another step on her journey to finding the new Vicki.

Maybe she should give her new journey a name—something along the lines of The Reinvention of Vicki?

She rolled her eyes as she closed the laptop.

That was something the *old* Vicki would do. The new Vicki would not be so lame.

The rumbling of a truck engine had her dashing toward the front door. All morning she'd been anticipating the arrival of the Christmas tree she'd ordered. It was the final piece required to transform the bottom floor of the Victorian into the picture-perfect New England seaside Christmas escape.

Vicki stepped out onto the gabled front porch and stopped dead in her tracks.

"What is this?" She pointed to the truck bed. "I ordered a twelve-foot Fraser fir. This tree isn't even eight feet."

"This is what they gave me, lady," the deliveryman replied in a thick Boston accent. He rounded the truck and pulled the tree out by its thin trunk.

Vicki shut her eyes against the thumping that instantly started up at her temples. With a full slate of projects lined up, hassling over the tree farm's obvious mistake was exactly what she did *not* need today.

But she'd had her heart set on that Fraser fir. She'd purchased the most amazing hand-painted ornaments from a gift shop on Main Street, along with a crystal tree topper that would bring the entire ensemble together.

Dammit, she'd *paid* for that Fraser fir, not this scraggly little pine that looked as if it was a reject from *A Charlie Brown Christmas* school play.

The old Vicki would just accept the tree and move on. The new Vicki wasn't standing for it.

She stomped down the porch steps and blocked the deliveryman's path. "Sir, would you please bring this... this thing," she said, pointing to the tree, "back to the lot and return with the tree I ordered?"

"Come on, lady. A tree is a tree."

Vicki folded her arms over her chest. "I want the tree I ordered," she annunciated in a clipped tone.

The man let out a grunt. He shoved the tree back onto the truck bed and mumbled something unintelligible under his breath.

"Thank you," Vicki said with a curt nod. She marched up the steps and walked inside, closing the door behind her. She fell back against it, covering her hand with her chest.

"Holy crap," she breathed. A grin curled up the corners of her lips. "I think I'm going to like the new Vicki."

Vicki buried her chin deeper into her scarf as she braced herself against the brisk wind coming off the water. She could have taken her car, but with the Quarterdeck so close to Silk Sisters, it felt unnecessary, even in the misty, frigid weather. Besides, she could not fully appreciate the holiday decorations adorning the businesses on Main Street from behind the wheel of her car. Even the shops that were closed—now that the tourist season was over—were bedecked with festive lights.

She entered the Quarterdeck and headed straight for the table she, Sandra and Janelle usually occupied.

"Sorry I'm late," Vicki said as she came upon them, planting a kiss on Janelle's cheek. She hadn't seen her at all today. "There was a mix-up with the Christmas tree. I'm convinced the driver took extralong delivering the correct one just to be difficult."

"That just means that you'll have to play catch-up with me and Sandra," Janelle said. She signaled a waiter, who was at their table in an instant.

His pen poised over his notepad, he asked, "The usual?"

"Yes," Vicki automatically answered. Then she thought better of it. "Actually, no. I'll have a vodka martini with two olives."

The waiter's brow shot up. "Okay, then. Coming right up. I'll have that fried calamari appetizer out in a minute, ladies."

Vicki looked across the table to find both Janelle and Sandra staring at her with their mouths open.

"What?" she asked.

Sandra put her hands up, her eyes wide with shock. "First the new hair and makeup, and now a vodka martini instead of a white-wine spritzer?" She slanted Janelle a questioning look. "Can you tell me what's happening with our girl over here?"

"I'm not sure, but I like it," Janelle said.

Even as she waved off their teasing, Vicki could feel a warm blush turning her cheeks red. She knew these changes were a shock to her friends. They were used to her being demure, staid.

Dull.

The fact that a simple change in her drink order could elicit that kind of reaction from them was as telling as anything.

As they snacked on crisp calamari tossed in a sweet ginger sauce, Sandra filled Vicki and Janelle in on the plans for her and Isaiah's belated honeymoon in Paris in a few months.

"It just makes sense to wait. We're both looking forward to several art exhibits, and I'll have the chance to check out Fashion Week. Besides, we can do what we're going to spend most of our honeymoon doing right here in Wintersage," she said with a wicked grin. She batted her eyes and added, "Wink. Wink."

"Subtle," Vicki said with a good-natured eye roll. She laughed, but deep down it was hard not to feel the tiniest bit jealous. Of the three of them, she was, by far, the romantic at heart. She was the one who had always believed in one true love, happily ever after, the whole nine yards. Yet she was the one who was perpetually single. Both Janelle and Sandra, cynics to the core, had found love. Where was the fairness in that?

Vicki squelched a groan. When had she turned into such a complainer? She was beginning to work on her own nerves with all this bellyaching.

The waiter came over to take their orders. Vicki bypassed her usual Caesar salad in exchange for the almond-crusted cod in a lemon *beurre blanc* sauce, garnering yet another pair of baffled looks from her friends.

Seriously? Was she *that* predictable that they could be so surprised at her ordering fish instead of a salad? It looked as if the decision to become the "new Vicki" couldn't have come fast enough.

The discussion around the table soon segued from Sandra's honeymoon plans to Vicki's plans for the float she'd entered into the Wintersage Holiday Extravaganza Day float competition. Her submission had yet to be accepted, and now Vicki was starting to regret ever telling her friends about it. If Petals wasn't chosen as one of the businesses to contribute a float to this year's extravaganza, it would leave some serious egg on her face.

"Building this float won't interfere with the decorations you're putting together for the Kwanzaa celebration, will it?" Sandra asked.

"Absolutely not," Vicki said.

The Woolcotts' Kwanzaa celebration had become an institution in Wintersage. As had been the case for the past few years, Janelle had been hired as the event coordinator and Vicki was, once again, in charge of decorating. Janelle set her fork on the edge of her plate and folded her hands. "Speaking of the Kwanzaa celebration." She paused for a moment, and then continued, "Things were a bit, well, strained at the dinner table this Thanksgiving when my dad asked if Alluring Affairs was still involved in the planning of your parents' party."

"Because of the election?" Sandra asked. "Does he expect you to give up a job you've taken on for years just because of this thing with Jordan?"

A few weeks ago, Janelle's father, Darren Howerton, had claimed victory in a statewide election against Oliver Windom, the candidate Jordan had campaigned for. The ensuing fallout had caused much tension between their families.

"Can you blame him? My dad should be celebrating his victory as the new state representative and preparing to head to the legislature. Instead, there's a huge cloud hanging over the election now that your brother has called the results into question."

"You can't put the entire blame on Jordan," Sandra retorted.

"Who else is to blame? He's the one who won't let this go."

Vicki held her hands up. "I thought this topic was off-limits? We're Switzerland, remember?"

"You're right," Janelle and Sandra murmured in unison.

"I'm sorry," Janelle continued. "We did agree not to talk about it, but I do wish Jordan would drop this."

"I know." Sandra blew out a frustrated sigh. "I don't see that happening anytime soon, though. Jordan took an extended leave of absence from the law firm. He was so confident Oliver Windom would win the election and would need Jordan to work on his transition team."

"So should I tell my dad that Jordan plans to be a pain in the ass until he returns to practicing law?" Janelle drawled.

Sandra shrugged as she tipped her wineglass to her lips.

"It sounds as if he needs something to occupy his time now that the election is over," Vicki said.

"*I* think he needs to get laid," Sandra said.

Janelle pointed the lime wheel from her cosmopolitan at her. "Bingo. Has he even been on a date since his divorce? It's been long enough."

Sandra waved her hand. "His pat response is that he's too busy to get involved with a woman, but Jordan's not fooling anyone. He could find the time to go on a simple date if he really wanted to."

"What about his wife?" Vicki asked.

"*Ex*-wife," Sandra stressed. "And let's not even go there. I don't know the last time Jordan spoke to Allison, and as far as I know, she's made no attempt to contact him, either."

"Not even about Mason?" Janelle gasped. "That's ridiculous. I don't understand how a woman could leave her baby and not even bother to see how he's doing."

"Especially a sweetie pie like Mason," Vicki agreed.

A smile broke out across Sandra's face at the mention of her nephew. "He is the most adorable child on the face of the planet, isn't he? He takes after his auntie Sandra."

"It's a good thing he doesn't have his auntie Sandra's attitude," Janelle said with a laugh, and then laughed harder when Sandra flipped her the finger.

As the two went back and forth trading good-natured barbs, Vicki's mind remained stuck on Jordan.

No surprise there.

How often had just the mention of his name prompted a long spell of daydreaming about what could have been? If only Jordan had any idea that she'd been crushing on him like a lovesick fool since the age of fifteen.

Actually, it was probably better that he *didn't* know. The only thing worse than Jordan discovering that she'd been clutching so tightly to this torch she'd carried for him all these years was for him to discover it and then pity her because he didn't feel the same way.

*Oh, God.* A rush of heat swept across her skin just at the thought of how mortified she would be if that ever happened.

Her chagrin quickly turned into annoyance, along with a healthy dose of self-disgust. She would not allow thoughts of Jordan Woolcott to turn her back into the starry-eyed romantic she'd been just a week ago. The new Vicki wasn't spending her days hoping that Mr. Clueless would finally notice her.

Yet despite her anger over his obliviousness, Vicki couldn't help but feel sorry for Jordan's current predicament. The madness following the state representative race had caused such turmoil. After Darren's victory over Oliver Windom, Jordan had demanded a recount, claiming that there must have been some sort of tampering.

His accusations had driven a wedge right between

the Howertons, Woolcotts and Ahlfors. It all must be weighing heavily on Jordan's peace of mind, knowing that so many people were against his dogged determination to contest the election. Vicki hated that he was at the center of the friction currently rubbing their families raw.

Of course, if she was making a list of the things she hated regarding Jordan, she had several other items she could add. Like the fact that he'd settled for such a cliché when he'd married his now ex-wife. Sure, Allison Woolcott was beautiful and vivacious, but that was *all* she was. The woman had no substance.

Another item on the list would be how much she hated that Jordan had never bothered to see her as anything other than a friend of his little sister. After all these years, Vicki still felt like nothing more than an acquaintance in his eyes.

Getting past this long-held obsession with Jordan should be at the very top of her priority list. If she was to fully embrace this new outlook, she could not continue to pine over a man who had never shown even the slightest romantic interest in her. It was time for her to move on, to concentrate on all the changes she was ready to make in her life.

*New Vicki. Think new Vicki.*

"I've got some news," she blurted.

Janelle and Sandra both stopped talking and looked at her expectantly.

Oh, great. Now that she'd put it out there she would actually have to share some news. She should have considered that before she opened her normally not-so-big mouth. A lesson for the new Vicki.

"So?" Sandra raised an expectant brow.

Vicki sucked her bottom lip between her teeth. "I,

uh...I signed up for an online-dating website. Just before I came here tonight, I accepted a date with a guy that contacted me a few days ago."

"What!" Janelle and Sandra both whooped, high-fiving each other.

"I told you our girl was breaking out of her shell," Sandra said. "Who is it? Have you been talking to him through email? Have you two had a phone conversation yet?"

"Slow down," Vicki said with a laugh. "His name is Declan James. *Doctor* Declan James. And yes, we've shared a couple of emails. I haven't talked to him on the phone yet. He seems nice," she finished with a casual shrug, as if it didn't feel like she had a million butterflies doing an aboriginal rain dance in her belly.

"So," Janelle prompted, circling her hands in a give-us-more motion.

"He suggested dinner," Vicki continued. "But then he said if I wanted to take it slow and start off with a coffee date he would be okay with that, too."

"I take it you two are going out for coffee?" Sandra asked.

An impish grin tilted up the edges of Vicki's lips. "Dinner. And dancing."

"Ooh," both Janelle and Sandra said.

"I'm scared of you, girl," Janelle said.

"So when's the date?"

"Tomorrow," she said. She hunched her shoulder. "I know a Tuesday night isn't your typical date night, but he's on call a lot at the E.R. Tuesday is his only night off this week."

"Who cares what night," Sandra said. "All I know is that the men of Wintersage had better watch out. Vicki Ahlfors is on the move."

## Chapter 2

"Don't be an idiot," Vicki murmured around the piece of twine she'd stuck between her lips. "You know better than this."

Even though she *did* know better than to try to balance on the wobbly, backless stool, she remained standing on it. If she fell and broke her tailbone it would be sufficient punishment for forgetting to bring the stepladder she'd taken from the Victorian to hang the new artwork in her living room at home. As far as punishments went, maybe a broken tailbone was a *bit* harsh.

"But you don't have to worry about that," she said as she tied that last bit of twine around the garland, fastening it to the molding that framed the front door. She hopped off the stool and slipped back into her heels. Then she took a couple of steps back and observed her handiwork.

"Perfect," Vicki said.

"I'd say so."

Vicki whipped around, spotting Jordan Woolcott walking up the walkway. Sixteen-month-old Mason toddled alongside him on legs that still didn't quite have that whole walking thing down yet. Vicki smiled as the chubby-cheeked sweetheart fought for his independence, trying to walk ahead of his father.

She stood on the top step and waited patiently while he slowly climbed up to meet her. She scooped Mason into her arms, plopping a kiss on his too-adorable-than-it-had-a-right-to-be face.

"How're you doing today? You and your daddy coming to see your auntie Sandra?" She looked up at Jordan, who remained at the base of the porch steps, a tired smile tilting up the corners of his lips.

"Hello, Jordan," she said.

"Hey there, Vicki."

There went her idiot heart, doing that stupid fluttering thing it did whenever she saw him. Goodness, how pathetic that at twenty-eight she still had the same reaction to him that she did as a teenager. No, it was more than just pathetic, it was downright pitiful, because never once had anything in Jordan's demeanor suggested that he felt anything even remotely similar toward her.

Yet when she'd sat in that salon chair last week and told the stylist to glam her up, it was with the intent of seeing Jordan's reaction to the finished outcome.

Pathetic.

If the man hadn't caught a clue in all these years, he certainly wouldn't notice her just because she'd cut her hair.

"Is my sister up there?" he asked, gesturing to the

building's second floor with the hand that held Mason's diaper bag.

"She sure is." Vicki looked down at Mason. "You want to get out of this cold and see your auntie Sandra?"

Jordan joined them on the porch, but before Vicki could turn toward the door, he stopped her.

"What exactly did you do here?" he asked, motioning at his own head.

"You mean my haircut?"

"Yeah. The light brown color you added to the ends, too."

"They're called highlights."

He nodded. "I like it. It suits you."

"Thank you," she answered.

She was *not* going to blush at a simple compliment.

Dammit, she was *so* blushing. She could feel the heat climbing up her cheeks. Her fair skin hid nothing, so in a matter of seconds Jordan would see it, too.

With Mason in tow, Vicki quickly turned for the door, leaving him to follow her inside.

"Wow," Jordan said once they'd entered the building. "You all are really getting into the holiday spirit, huh? There are more flowers in here than at the Rose Bowl parade."

"Well, it *is* a floral-design shop," Vicki noted with a laugh.

"A busy one at that," Jordan said, pointing to various arrangements in different stages of completion. They covered every available surface.

"When it comes to flowers, the Christmas season is second only to Valentine's Day. Although, to be honest, I've been a bit busier than usual this week."

Jordan peeled Mason's puffer jacket off while the

baby was still in her arms, and then stuffed it inside the diaper bag.

He gestured to her feet. "You don't normally wear fancy shoes to make flower arrangements, do you? Is this something special you're doing for the holidays?"

Vicki's eyes narrowed. "Are you trying to be funny?"

The blank look on his face gave her his answer even before he said, "No."

"I'm wearing fancy shoes because I have a date," she said.

"Really?" Jordan's head reared back slightly. He took Mason from her arms and the baby immediately started to fuss. "A date?"

Vicki couldn't see past her irritation over Jordan's apparent surprise at the news that she had a date. It both stung *and* pissed her off.

"Is it so hard to believe that someone actually wants to go out with me?" she asked.

"No," he said with a hasty head shake. "It's just that I didn't know you were dating anyone."

Not that *that* should come as a surprise, either. When had he ever taken interest in whom she was dating?

Vicki held no illusions about where she stood as far as he was concerned. She had never been in Jordan Woolcott's league. For that matter, she had not always been in Sandra and Janelle's league, either.

Unlike her two best friends, Vicki hadn't been born into money.

She and her three brothers had spent the majority of their formative years in the public school system, not moving to Wintersage Academy until her sophomore year of high school, once her father's business had taken off.

Ahlfors Financial Management's success secured

her family's place among Wintersage's elite, but their wealth didn't reek of "old money" like that of the Howertons and Woolcotts. Although her friends never made her feel inferior, Vicki never let herself forget that one difference between them.

When it came to Jordan, there was no denying that they were different.

He had been several years ahead of her in high school, having already graduated from Wintersage Academy by the time she'd started there. Vicki had developed the most ridiculous crush on him from the very first day she'd gone over to the Woolcotts' to study with Sandra one afternoon. It had taken her years to accept the fact that, if not for her being one of Sandra's very best friends and their families knowing each other for years, Jordan wouldn't know she existed.

Well, that wasn't entirely true. Wintersage was a small town. He would know she existed—in the same way he knew Jocelyn Cornwell, who ran the realty office on Main Street, or Agnes Ripple, the owner of the corner bakery, existed.

That thought annoyed her to no end. And when she thought of how long she'd pined over Jordan, it irritated her even more.

Vicki returned to her worktable, picking up the stem cutters and attacking the stubborn stalks of the lilies that had just been delivered by one of her suppliers. But as Mason's crying intensified, she walked to where Jordan stood struggling to get the baby to calm down. The minute she lifted him out of Jordan's arms, Mason's cries quieted. Vicki bounced him softly, running her hand up and down the baby's back and whispering soothingly into his ear.

"I don't know what's going on with him today," Jordan said. "I usually don't have a problem getting him to calm down, but he's been more agitated than usual."

"Maybe he can sense that you're—" she started, but then she stopped.

"I'm what?"

Vicki bit her bottom lip, but then she stopped that, too. The old Vicki would keep her mouth shut to spare his feelings. She was no longer listening to the old Vicki.

"Uptight," she finished. "You've been rather uptight lately, and I think Mason can sense that."

He rubbed the back of his neck and grimaced. "You're probably right."

The sheer exhaustion on his face quelled the ire that had risen within her just moments ago. Vicki couldn't help but feel sorry for him.

Jordan cocked his head to the side and looked down at his son. "The problem is I can't seem to unwind because he constantly has me on the go. I get agitated, and then *he* gets agitated. It's a vicious cycle."

"You need some rest, Jordan."

"You're not telling me anything I don't already know. But I don't see rest anywhere in my immediate future, not with this little rascal who wants to get into everything these days," he said, pinching the baby's chubby leg through his cute corduroy pants.

Vicki took a moment to consider the suggestion she was about to make before she asked, "How about I watch Mason for you so you can get some rest?"

Jordan's neck stiffened with shock. "Really?"

She nodded. "Sure."

"I can't ask you to do that."

That was what his mouth said; the naked hope in

his eyes, on the other hand, said that he was dying for a little help with the baby.

"It's not as if it would be a hardship," Vicki reasoned. "How could I pass up the opportunity to spend time with this little heartbreaker?" She kissed the baby's chin. "And while I do, *you* can get some much-needed rest."

Jordan's shoulders sank with relief. "God, Vicki, that would be wonderful."

"I'm happy to do it. Just not tonight," she said.

"Yeah. You have a date," Jordan said. He lifted Mason from her arms but remained standing there, his gaze trained on her.

"What?" Vicki asked. After several moments of his staring, her self-consciousness ramped up to skin-tingling levels.

He shook his head as if to clear it. "Nothing." He gestured toward the staircase. "We'll go up to Sandra's."

"Okay." She leaned forward and gave Mason a little baby wave. "See you later."

"When?"

Vicki's head popped up at Jordan's question. "Excuse me?"

"When will you see us?" He shook his head. "Him? Mason. To babysit?"

She hadn't thought that far in advance, but it was obvious Jordan needed to rest as soon as possible. "What about tomorrow, maybe around seven?"

"Tomorrow is good. It's great, actually."

"Okay, well, I guess I'll see you both tomorrow, then."

"Good." He gave her another of those tired, grateful smiles before he started up the stairs. After he'd climbed a couple of steps, he stopped and turned. "Vicki?"

"Yes?" She felt her face heat after being caught still staring at him.

"You really do look nice," Jordan said. "I hope this guy you're going out with tonight realizes how lucky he is."

The instant warmth that traveled across her skin from his simple compliment was embarrassing to say the least.

"Thank you," Vicki said. "I'll see you tomorrow."

She fingered the wispy end of a lock of hair and grinned as she returned to her workstation. Her stylist would get a very nice tip after her next haircut. Even though she no longer cared whether or not Jordan Woolcott noticed her, apparently the pixie cut had gotten her just the result she'd initially hoped for.

"Anybody home?" Jordan called as he arrived on the second-floor landing of the huge Victorian where his sister's dress shop was located.

Sandra turned from the glittery ball gown she was adjusting on a mannequin and smiled.

"Well, look who's here." She walked over to them and reached for Mason. "Give me my nephew."

Jordan handed the baby off and plopped into an empty chair. The exhaustion of the past week had him on the verge of both mental and physical collapse.

"So what brings you two here?" Sandra asked, taking the chair opposite his and bouncing Mason on her lap.

Jordan shrugged. "Just thought we'd get out for a bit. He doesn't understand that it's too cold for the beach or the park, so I've been taking him other places. We just came from the dry cleaners."

"Such party animals," Sandra said with a snort. She snapped her fingers. "I know exactly where you should take him—the children's museum in Dover. I saw something on TV about a special exhibit they have going on for the Christmas season."

Sandra turned the huge computer monitor around to face her and grabbed the wireless keyboard from her desk. As his sister searched the web, Jordan pitched his head back and let his eyes fall shut. He tried to shake off the edginess that had his skin tingly. The weird vibe had settled over him after his exchange with Vicki, and hell if he knew what to make of it.

She had popped up in his head more than once this week, creeping into his thoughts and setting off memories of how shocked he'd been when he'd noticed her standing on the beach at Sandra's wedding. The new haircut and that curve-hugging dress had been something to behold.

Jordan couldn't remember if he had ever once noticed what Vicki wore. Of course, he'd noticed *her*—no man could deny that Vicki was gorgeous in her own right. He just had never looked at her in *that* way.

She was just…just Vicki.

She was the quiet one; the one who, if Sandra or their other best friend, Janelle, ever got into trouble, would get them out of it. She was steady. Reserved. She wasn't the type that normally produced the prickle of awareness that climbed up the back of his neck when he'd spotted her standing on the porch in sexy leopard-print heels.

"What do you think about that?" Sandra asked.

Jordan blinked. "Huh?"

His sister stabbed him with the most aggravated look. "Are you even listening to me? I just listed every special exhibit going on at the children's museum in

Dover. Or maybe there's something in Portsmouth the two of you can do."

"Maybe." Jordan shrugged. "I need to find something to keep him occupied. It can get boring sitting around the house. Makes me wonder what Laurie does over there all day," he said, speaking of his housekeeper.

Sandra started on the tirade Jordan knew was forthcoming. "Oh, let's see. She takes care of your son, keeps the house impeccable and cooks dinner."

"I meant besides all that," Jordan said, his mouth tipped up in a smile.

He saw the moment that Sandra caught on to his teasing.

"You're such an ass," she said.

"Not true. You're just an easy target," he said with a laugh. "Don't worry, I know exactly how indispensable Laurie is, especially now that she's away on this extended Christmas vacation. I haven't done the best job at keeping up the housework since, and when it comes to dinner Mason and I have tried just about every takeout place within twenty miles of Wintersage. He likes gyros. Who'd have thought?"

Sandra shook her head, a pitiable look on her face. "I'm almost tempted to tell you to hire a temporary nanny to cover for Laurie while she's away, but that won't solve your problem."

"I don't have a problem," he said.

"You most definitely *do* have a problem. You have no life. And yes, I know you've been taking care of Mason full-time since the election ended, but that's not the life you're used to living. Maybe you should just go back to work. Maybe you'd be less irritable."

Hadn't Vicki just accused him of the same thing?

"Why does everyone think I'm irritable?" Jordan

asked. "I'm just tired. Besides, I can't go back to the firm. I took an extended leave, remember? I thought I would be working on Oliver's transition team right now."

Sandra rolled her eyes. The election was a sore subject for everyone in his family, especially his sister.

When he spoke, Jordan kept his voice low. "Hey, Sandra? The fallout from the election, it hasn't caused any friction, has it? You know, between you three?"

"What do you think, Jordan? You accused my best friend's father of trying to steal an election. Do you think things would be all sunshine and roses around here? The three of us decided that when it comes to the election we're Switzerland, but things are still a bit awkward."

"Switzerland?" he asked.

"Completely neutral."

"Oh. Well, I wish I had that luxury."

"You do." Sandra reached over and clamped a hand on his forearm. "The election is over. You can accept the results and move on."

Jordan shook his head. "I can't. I know something—"

She lifted her hand and held it up, stopping him. "Switzerland. I don't want to know."

"That's too bad," Jordan said. "I'm pulling the 'sibling in need of an ear' card, because I need to talk this out with someone."

Sandra blew out an aggravated breath. "What is it?"

"I heard from the election commissioner this morning. According to Massachusetts's election laws, only the candidate can officially file for a recount, so they can't go forward unless Oliver requests it."

"Oliver has already conceded."

"I know. I told him he was making a mistake, but he

refused to listen to me. I just don't understand how he can sit back and do nothing."

"Maybe he wants to be gracious in his defeat and move on with his life," Sandra said. "Just as *you* should move on."

Jordan shut his eyes and pitched his head back again.

"I wish I could," he said. He straightened in the chair and looked at Sandra. "Something fishy happened with that election. My polling data was solid."

"Well, if the commissioner's office refuses to go forward with a recount, none of that matters, does it? You need to just put this election behind you."

Jordan pressed his palms together and tapped his fingers against his lips. "I hired my own investigators," he finally admitted.

Sandra groaned. "Okay, Jordan, I'm just going to say it. This election has driven you right off the deep end."

"I'm only doing what I think is right," he said. "If I just rolled over and played dead the way Oliver has, then it's like admitting that my polling was wrong, and I know it wasn't." He put both hands up. "If I don't find anything before Darren takes office in January, then I'll drop it. But until then, I'm going to search for the proof I know is out there."

"Can we please stop talking about this election? You're giving me a headache."

"Fine," Jordan said. He picked up what he could only assume was some kind of dressmaking thing from a nearby desk and twirled it around his finger. "Are you and Isaiah planning to hang around until after the Kwanzaa celebration?"

"Of course," Sandra answered, balancing Mason on her lap while he bounced up and down. "This is Isaiah's first Christmas in Wintersage in years. He wants to experience it all again—the big extravaganza and Christmas parade, and our family's annual Kwanzaa celebration. We'll likely spend Christmas Day shuttling between Mom and Dad's and his parents' place." She glanced over at him. "What about you guys?"

Jordan shrugged. "We'll be at Mom and Dad's."

"What about spending Christmas with *his* mom?" She nodded toward Mason. "Have you heard from Allison at all?"

"No," Jordan said. "Subject closed."

"Jordan—"

"Subject *closed*," he repeated. He ran his hand down his face. "I'm sorry. I'm just not in the mood to talk about Allison."

"After I just had to listen to all that election crap?"

"Do you really want to use your 'sibling in need of an ear' card on talk about Allison?"

"Whatever," Sandra said. "Why did you come over here in the first place if you don't want to talk about anything but that election?"

"Maybe I wanted you to spend time with your nephew, but if you don't want to we can leave." Jordan made as if he was about to get up. His sister shot him an evil look.

"Sit down," she said.

He grinned, knowing that would get under her skin. He took his seat, picked up the shiny tool again and resumed twirling it around his finger.

"Would you put down my eyelash curler?"

"Your what?"

She gestured to her eyes. "Eyelash curler. You know, to extend my lashes."

Jordan tossed the thing on the desk as though it had

suddenly caught fire. He blew out another weary breath and stretched his legs out in front of him.

Folding his hands over his stomach, he said, "I saw Vicki downstairs. She looks nice today."

"She has a date."

"Yeah, that's what she told me. She offered to baby-sit Mason so I can get some rest."

"I hope you took her up on her offer. You can use it. You look like a reject from *The Walking Dead*."

"You do know how to flatter a guy," Jordan said with a snort.

She sent him a saccharine smile. "I try."

"So," Jordan asked, picking up a pencil from Sandra's desk and tapping it against his thigh. "Do you know the guy she's going out with tonight?"

The moment the question left his mouth Jordan wanted to take it back. *Why* had he just asked that? Especially of Sandra.

His sister's eyes narrowed. "I haven't met him," she said. "Why do you ask?"

"Forget it."

Her brow arched. "No, why don't you tell me, Jordan? Why the sudden interest in Vicki's dating life?"

Just as he was about to tell Sandra to drop it, Mason threw his head back and started to wail. Not since his first moments of life in the delivery room had Jordan been so grateful to hear his baby boy cry.

"I hope your mother appreciates these," Vicki said as she handed Samson Cornwell his credit card. "It's sweet of you to buy her a dozen roses just because."

"I thought it would be nice to brighten her day," Samson said. "And you do such an amazing job, Vicki. These roses are just amazing."

"I can't really take the credit. I just arranged them. Mother Nature did the hard work."

His roaring laugh echoed against the walls. The effort it took for Vicki not to roll her eyes was downright admirable.

"Did you have this sense of humor back in high school?" Samson asked, wiping tears of mirth from his eyes. "Who knew you were so funny?"

Vicki hunched her shoulders in a "who knew?" gesture. She pushed the vase filled with blush-colored Antique Silk roses and baby's breath toward him, hoping he'd take the hint and leave. He didn't.

Sam rested an elbow on the counter and leaned in close. "When did you get interested in flowers?" he asked. "You know, I read somewhere that there are over twenty different species of roses. That's amazing, isn't it?"

"Try nearly two hundred," Vicki said.

His eyes went wide. "Really? Two hundred? That's amazing."

She wondered if he would be offended if she threw a thesaurus in with his dozen roses. That was the fifth *amazing* since he'd walked through the door.

The phone rang. Vicki decided then and there to give whoever was on the other end of the line a free centerpiece for their holiday dinner table.

"I have to get this, Samson. Thanks again for utilizing Petals for your floral needs. I hope your mother enjoys her roses."

"Oh, I know she will," he said. He winked at her.

It took everything Vicki had in her not to groan. She answered the phone. "Petals."

It was Declan. As she listened to his apology and explanations for canceling their date tonight, her spirits deflated. Well, there went her big plans. Maybe she should run outside and stop Samson before he drove away.

The door swung open and Samson rushed back in. She immediately regretted the thought she'd just had. She so was not going out with Samson Cornwell. She didn't care how *amazing* a date with him would be.

"My wallet," Samson said, retrieving it from where he'd left it on the counter.

Vicki walked him to the door, then turned and spotted Sandra, Jordan and Mason marching down the stairs.

Sandra pointed to the door as she reached the landing. "Let me guess, another new male customer who suddenly has a penchant for flowers?"

"Samson Cornwell," Vicki said. "You remember him?"

Sandra pulled a face. "That fool who nearly blew up the chemistry lab at Wintersage Academy?"

"The very one."

"Don't tell me he asked you out."

"I didn't give him the chance," Vicki said.

Jordan stood there with Mason, his gaze volleying back and forth between her to Sandra.

"The men of Wintersage have developed an amazing interest in flowers this week," Sandra explained to him.

Vicki groaned. "Please don't say the word *amazing.*" Sandra's forehead dipped in question. "Don't ask," Vicki added.

"Anyway," her friend said, turning once again to Jordan, "one came in yesterday and bought a bouquet for his dentist. His *dentist.* It's ridiculous."

"Petals appreciates it," Vicki said. "Petals's owner, however, is so over it."

"Wait." Sandra frowned. "Why are you still here? Don't you have a date tonight?"

Vicki tried to keep the defeated sigh from escaping, but failed. "Declan had to cancel. He was called in to cover the E.R. Apparently they just got slammed with food poisoning from a birthday party."

"Aw, honey, I'm sorry."

"There's always a next time," she said, hunching her shoulders. She turned her attention to Jordan, who was now fighting to put Mason's jacket on him, a battle he was clearly losing. Vicki bit the inside of her cheek to stop herself from laughing. "Do you need some help?" she asked.

He held the jacket out to her and let out a relieved sigh. "Please."

Instead of taking the jacket, she took Mason. The little boy leaned his head on her shoulder and stuffed his thumb between his lips, and Vicki's heart instantly went the way of ice cream on a hot summer day.

Her heart did something all together different when she looked up again and found Jordan with his bottom lip between his teeth, concentrating hard as he threaded Mason's chubby arms through his jacket sleeves. She absolutely hated that everything he did looked so damn sexy on Jordan. And that she couldn't help but love it.

She suddenly discovered a bright spot to her canceled date.

"I'm free to babysit tonight," she said to Jordan.

His head popped up. "You sure? What if your date manages to get away from the hospital after all?"

"From the way things sounded, that doesn't seem likely. Besides, you look as if you can really use the rest."

"I told him he looks like shit," Sandra said.

Vicki covered Mason's exposed ear. "Not in front of the baby," she admonished.

"Don't waste your time," Jordan said. He hooked a thumb toward his sister. "I've already accepted that this one will teach my son every swearword there is by the time he turns three."

"That's what aunties are for," Sandra said, giving the baby a kiss on the cheek before heading back up the staircase.

"So are you really up for babysitting tonight?" Jordan asked. "Because if you are I won't turn you down. Sandra's right, I do look like shi… Crap," he finished.

"Saying *crap* isn't much better," Vicki said, unable to hide her grin. She jiggled Mason's chubby cheek. "Just wait until his grandma Nancy hears those swearwords coming out of his mouth. Then both your daddy and Auntie Sandra will have some explaining to do."

"Don't remind me," he said.

"Don't say I didn't warn you." Vicki laughed. She turned her attention back to Mason. "What do you think of me coming over, huh? We can play games, or watch a movie, or even make a snowman while your daddy gets a little rest. What do you say about that?"

The little baby teeth that peeked out as his face broke into a smile was hands down the most adorable thing she'd seen in months.

"I think he's okay with it," Jordan said with a grin of his own.

Her reaction to *that* smile was wholly uncalled-for. Maybe if she refused to acknowledge the flutter that swept through her stomach, she could pretend it didn't really happen. Because, seriously, how could a simple smile give her butterflies?

She could not wait until the day she was past this ridiculous infatuation—*if* she could ever move past it.

No. There was no *if* about it. When it came to her feelings for Jordan, the new Vicki was not going down the same road the old Vicki had traveled. She'd come to that decision after Sandra's wedding. It was the reason she'd signed up on that dating website: she was done pining for Jordan Woolcott.

Yet she'd just agreed to babysit for him tonight. What in God's name had convinced her to come up with that stellar suggestion?

She studied the look of exhaustion etched around his face and was reminded of just why she'd made the offer.

"Are you on your way home now?" Vicki asked.

"You done here?" he asked, gesturing to the refrigerated display case.

"Yep, Petals is closed for the day. I was supposed to be on a date, remember?" Vicki refused to read anything into the way his brows dipped at the reminder. "Just let me grab my purse and keys and I'll follow you to your place."

She retrieved her phone from the counter and sent Sandra a text message, letting her know she was leaving. When she went outside, Jordan was strapping Mason into his safety seat. A few minutes later, they were making their way along Seaside Drive, the stretch of highway that hugged the coastline that wrapped around Wintersage. Jordan lived on the opposite side of town, what locals called "below the bay."

Jordan's gray, single-story, shingle-style cottage, with its charming white shutters and walkway bordered by weather-beaten boulders from the shoreline, was, in Vicki's opinion, one of the most charming homes in this section of Wintersage. Though modest for someone of Jordan's means, it seemed to fit him perfectly.

He turned into his driveway and both doors of the double garage opened. Vicki pulled her car in alongside his. When she walked over to Jordan, he was holding a finger against his lips.

"He fell asleep on the drive over," Jordan whispered.

"Ah." Vicki nodded. She pointed to her car and mouthed, "Should I go?"

He hunched his shoulder. "I guess," he whispered as he unstrapped Mason. He took great care in lifting the baby from the safety seat, huddling him close to his chest.

Vicki waved goodbye and started back for her car, but her feet stopped at the sound of Mason's sudden wailing. She spun around and instantly took pity on Jordan's pathetic expression. He looked on the verge of collapse.

"I guess I'm staying after all," Vicki said, returning to Jordan's side. She lifted Mason from his arms. "It's okay, honey." She patted his back as she followed Jordan up the garage's steps and into the mudroom.

By the time they entered the house, Mason's wail was down to a soft whimper. Vicki carried him through the short hallway that led into the kitchen, but stopped short as she passed the threshold.

The place was a mess.

Plush teddy bears and plastic toys littered the floor. There were newspapers and empty coffee mugs strewn about the table in the breakfast nook. Dirty dishes and at least a half dozen sippy cups filled the sink.

"Uh, excuse the mess," Jordan said as he pushed aside an open box of animal crackers to make room on the counter for the baby bag he'd carried in from the car. He perched against the counter and folded his arms over his chest.

He looked from her to Mason and huffed out an exhausted laugh. "I don't know what you do, but I wish you'd tell me," he said. "I'm starting to believe you have some kind of magical powers when it comes to my son."

"I already gave you my theory," she said. "You're agitated, and I think Mason can sense that."

"I guess your theory makes more sense than magic. I have been wound pretty tight since the election results came in. I can't seem to relax."

"Have you tried?"

"Not really," he said with another weary chuckle. "I've never been good at it. Always seems as if my time could be better spent doing something more productive."

"Get some rest, Jordan. I'm sure some uninterrupted sleep will do you good."

He walked over to them and smoothed a hand over Mason's head. This brought him *way* too close to her for her peace of mind.

"Maybe you're right," he said.

"There's no 'maybe' about it," Vicki said, taking a step back to create some distance between them. "Put the election and everything else out of your head for a few hours and rest. This little one and I will be just fine."

He came over to them again and pressed a kiss to Mason's forehead. "Thanks again for doing this," he said to her, his grateful though exhausted smile setting off all kinds of sinfully delicious tingles in her belly.

Goodness, but she was pitiful when it came to this man.

"If you need me, just come in and wake me," he said

before walking through the arched entryway that led to the rest of the house.

Vicki remained standing there until she heard the click of a door closing.

She looked down at Mason. "The new Vicki needs to remember what she said about not acting a fool for your dad."

"Ball," Mason said, pointing to a multicolored ball on the table.

Vicki picked up the ball, along with several other toys scattered along the kitchen counter, and brought Mason into the living room. Lifting an afghan with a seaside lighthouse pattern on it from the sofa, she spread it out on the hardwood floor and set Mason on it, then she plopped down next to him and rolled a plastic ball toward him.

After several minutes of playing with the ball, Mason's mouth twisted in a frown. Seconds later, Vicki caught a whiff of something that made her stomach turn.

"Oh, you would do that *after* your daddy has gone to nap, wouldn't you?"

She scooped the baby up and went in search of diaper-changing supplies. Vicki opened several doors, including a linen closet and what had to be Jordan's home office, which was impeccable—a surprise—seeing as how the rest of the house was in shambles.

Finally, she came upon Mason's brightly colored bedroom. Unfortunately, she didn't find any diapers in there.

Vicki remembered the baby bag Jordan had brought in and returned to the kitchen where he'd left it on the counter. With the baby perched on her hip, she searched the bag but only came up with baby wipes and a small bottle of baby powder.

"Well, we'll definitely need these, but we're missing the most important thing."

She hated to wake Jordan up so soon after he'd gone in for his nap, but if this diaper didn't get changed soon the stench would probably wake him.

She went through the great room and down the hallway to the master bedroom. Tapping lightly on the door, she softly called, "Jordan?"

"Come in," came a voice that was much too robust to come from someone who should have been asleep.

Vicki pushed her way through the door and frowned.

Jordan sat up with his back against the headboard, his stocking feet crossed at the ankles. An open laptop rested on his thighs and a pair of reading glasses was perched upon his nose. Make that an astonishingly sexy pair of reading glasses.

She tried to block the sexiness from her head, otherwise her impending lecture wouldn't be nearly as effective as she needed it to be. She plopped a hand on the hip that didn't have a twenty-two-pound toddler on it and narrowed her eyes at Jordan.

"Seriously?" she said, jutting her chin toward the laptop.

"Yeah, I know." He grimaced. "I just needed to check one thing."

"You're supposed to be *resting,* Jordan, not working. Those are two very different concepts. It's easy to tell them apart."

He looked at her over the rim of his glasses and grinned. "Who knew Vicki Ahlfors was such a smart a—" He glanced at Mason. "Aleck," he finished.

No, no, no. Her cheeks would *not* heat up at his teasing.

"No changing the subject," she said, keeping her voice as firm as possible. "I didn't volunteer to watch Mason so you can work." The little boy shifted in her arms and Vicki caught another whiff of his aroma, reminding her of the reason she'd come in here in the first place. "Please tell me you have diapers," she said.

"In there." He pointed to the master bath.

Vicki cursed the deep flutter that traveled through her belly as she entered Jordan's bathroom. There was something way too intimate about this. The discarded facecloth hanging on the rim of the sink, the bottle of multivitamins, the razor—not an electric one, a classic manual razor, the kind that required control and a steady hand.

She briefly shut her eyes against the image that tried to crop up in her head. Thinking about Jordan and his steady hands was bound to get her in trouble.

At the far end of the long vanity sat a stack of disposable diapers, along with more baby wipes, lotion and powder. She grabbed a plush towel from the wooden towel rack and gently laid Mason on top of it.

She'd just pulled off his pants when she heard Jordan say, "I can do that."

Vicki's back stiffened. She'd been so busy with Mason that she hadn't heard him approach.

"I've got it," she called over her shoulder.

The tingle that raced down her spine was completely inappropriate, but wholly expected. Those tingles were par for the course when it came to being in close proximity to Jordan. The new Vicki was supposed to be done with those tingles, but apparently she hadn't gotten the memo.

Standing watch just over her shoulder as she efficiently went about changing Mason's diaper, Jordan said, "You handle that like a pro."

"Changing a diaper?" she asked.

"Yeah, especially with the way that one squirms."

As if on cue, Mason immediately started to writhe around on the vanity. Vicki caught his feet together in one hand and moved her hip to block him from rolling right off the counter.

"I see what you mean." She leaned over and nibbled Mason's chin. "But your cute little booty isn't getting away from me." She looked back at Jordan. "Goodness, is there anything more adorable than those two bottom teeth that peek out whenever he smiles?"

"Nothing I've found," he said with a laugh.

He finally backed away, making it easier for Vicki to get her breathing under control. His nearness was pure torture on her new quest to not be affected by him.

He settled in the doorway and leaned a shoulder against the jamb. "How'd you learn to change a baby's diaper?" Jordan asked. "You don't have any kids of your own."

Vicki snorted as she glanced over her shoulder. "Thanks for pointing that out."

"Damn. I'm sorry. I didn't mean for that to sound the way it did. I'm just impressed," he continued. "It took me a while to get the hang of diaper changing."

"I guess it's instinctual for some," she said. She gave the two pieces of tape a firm pat before pulling Mason's corduroys up over his fresh diaper. "There you go, sweetie," she said, tickling the baby's belly. He giggled and treated her to that wide, sweet grin that was sure to break hearts.

"So did you reschedule your date with the doctor?" Jordan asked.

Vicki's head jerked up. She met his eyes in the bathroom mirror.

"Uh...no," she stammered, caught off guard by the subject change. "He was already at the hospital when he called earlier. He didn't really have time to talk."

"Oh. Well, maybe you two can find a time that works later this week."

Hefting Mason into her arms, Vicki turned and faced him. "I doubt there will be any future dates with Declan."

"Really?" Jordan's brows rose. "So it wasn't anything serious, whatever it is you had with the doctor?"

Should she tell him the truth, that before it was canceled, her date with Declan would have been her first in well over a year? And that the last date she went on—with the cousin of a friend of a friend—was so unremarkable that she couldn't even remember the guy's name?

Vicki considered it for a moment, but decided against mentioning it. She had no desire to be pitied, especially by Jordan.

Instead, she said, "It's pretty obvious that Declan is too busy for even a casual relationship, let alone something more serious."

Still leaning against the doorjamb, he crossed his arms and cocked his head to the side. "And you're opposed to casual?"

"I wouldn't say I'm opposed to it. But it's not what I want." When it came to this particular issue, Vicki decided that being vague would do her no good. "I've done the casual-dating thing in the past. I'm ready for something more stable...something that has potential."

She fought against the self-consciousness brought on by Jordan's thoughtful, probing gaze.

Several long moments passed before he asked in a curious tone, "Does this have anything to do with Sandra and Janelle both getting married? Are you feeling left out?"

Vicki's head reared back. Had he really just asked her that?

"You do realize how insulting that is, don't you?"

He looked completely baffled. "Insulting?"

"Yes. Your question insinuates that I only want a serious relationship because my two best friends have recently found their soul mates. It's insulting."

He grimaced, bringing his hand up to massage the back of his neck. "Now that you put it that way…" When his eyes returned to hers, they were filled with contriteness. "I'm sorry if that offended you. I swear that wasn't my intention." He lifted his shoulder in a half shrug. "It's just that the three of you have always done everything together. With Sandra getting married so soon after Janelle, it just seemed natural that you would be next."

Vicki had to work hard not to release a deflated sigh. He was likely one of many who shared that same sentiment.

"It's okay, Jordan. Both Janelle and Sandra would tell you that of the three of us, I'm the one who they both suspected would be the first to marry." She gave him a wan smile. "Things don't always turn out the way we expect."

"Tell me about it," he said with a gentle smile of his own. His gaze shifted to the little boy in her arms. "But sometimes those unexpected detours in life turn out to be the best thing to ever happen to you."

The complete adoration in his eyes made her heart squeeze.

"A blessing in disguise," Vicki said.

"Ball," Mason said, pointing in the direction of the living room. "Ball, ball, ball."

She laughed. "We were playing with the ball before the diaper change became mission number one." She scooped up the towel she'd used to cushion Mason and tossed it on top of the overfilled clothes hamper before heading past Jordan on her way out of the bathroom. Her elbow brushed against his chest and a shudder went through her.

*Pitiful!*

"You *are* going to nap, right?" Vicki called over her shoulder. When he didn't say anything, she turned and scowled. "Jordan," she said in a warning tone.

"I will," he said, following her out of the bathroom. "I just need to finish rerunning some polling data."

"Seriously?" Vicki rolled her eyes. "You can't keep going at this pace. This election is going to drive you crazy."

"It already has." He ran a hand down his face, the exhaustion in his eyes becoming more apparent with every second that passed. The man was dead on his feet.

"Maybe I'm missing something here, but if Oliver Windom can accept the election results, why can't you? I don't understand why you're allowing this to consume you."

"Because I messed up, and I can't figure out what went wrong." He shook his head. "I've been racking my brain, but nothing makes sense. It doesn't matter how many angles I look at, I still don't see how Darren pulled it off." He pointed at the laptop. "According to my statistics, Oliver should have won."

"Polling isn't an exact science. No one really knows what happens when a person enters the ballot box except for that person."

"I know there are margins of error, and I know that this race was close, but when I look at the districts that Oliver lost, it makes me even more convinced that there was some sort of tampering. Those were the ones that he should have won by the biggest margin." He shook his head. "Maybe it's the math nerd in me, but I just don't see how I could have been so off with the data."

His pained expression was full of anguish. "I wish I could let this go, Vicki. I'm not oblivious to the rift this has caused between my family and the Howertons, and to a certain extent your family, too. I truly hope that it hasn't affected the relationship between you, Sandra and Janelle."

"We're Switzerland," she said.

"Yeah, that's what Sandra told me, but still, it can't be easy."

No, it wasn't. There had been an underlying layer of tension around the Victorian since the end of the election. Yet as much as she wished Jordan would drop this, Vicki couldn't help but be impressed by the way he'd held to his convictions, despite the enormous pressure he was obviously getting from all sides to let this go.

"I doubt anything is going to change with the numbers in the next couple of hours, so why don't you put that stuff away and get some rest?"

"You're right," he said. He lifted the laptop from the bed and set it on the tufted ottoman in the sitting room area. He turned to her and held his hands up. "I promise that I'll sleep this time."

"Good," she said with a firm nod. A blue-and-white pamphlet caught her eye as she passed the dresser on her way out of the room. "Do you work with Mass Mentors?" Vicki asked, referring to the mentorship program she'd been a supporter of for the past few years.

"Yeah," he answered. "I've been helping out there."

"It's a great program. I've brought in several of the kids to intern at Petals. They go out on deliveries and a few are even starting to learn floral design."

"I didn't realize you were involved with the program," he said. His voice softened with appreciation. "That's wonderful, Vicki."

Their gazes locked and held for several weighty moments. Jordan was the first to look away, picking up a pen from the lap desk on the bed and tossing it on the nightstand.

"Uh, we didn't discuss any kind of payment for the babysitting. How much…" His words trailed off and his mouth dipped in a frown. Probably because of the daggers she was shooting at him right now with her stare. "What?" he asked.

"Are you deliberately trying to annoy me?" Vicki asked, making sure her displeasure came through her voice. "I *volunteered* to watch Mason out of friendship. Don't you dare suggest paying me, Jordan."

"Sorry." He held his hands up in mock surrender once again. "It looks as if I've made a world championship sport out of offending you today."

"Yeah, well, you don't have to try so hard to sweep the medals," she said, wrangling a laugh from him. With Mason in tow, she headed out of the room.

"Vicki," Jordan called just as she reached the door. She looked back at him. "Thank you," he said.

She smiled. "You're welcome. Now sleep."

## *Chapter 3*

Jordan's eyes popped open.

He sprung up in bed, but quickly relaxed when he remembered that Vicki was here, watching over Mason so he could rest.

Vicki.

Jordan shook his head, still confused as hell over what to make of her. He'd dreamed of her while he slept, his mind conjuring images that would probably make her blush. But he couldn't help it. Vicki Ahlfors had burrowed her way into his brain, and he enjoyed having her there too much to let those delicious fantasies of her vanish anytime soon.

Jordan dragged his palms down his face.

He'd mulled over these feelings that had started swirling within him the night of Sandra's wedding and had decided to ignore them, but fighting thoughts about Vicki was more than his taxed mind had the ability to deal with right now. It was easier to just go with it and let the fantasies play out.

Jordan knew her dating status shouldn't matter to him one way or another, but damn if something akin to relief hadn't hit him when Vicki had confirmed that she wouldn't be rescheduling her date with the doctor. She'd said she wasn't into casual relationships anymore; he could respect that. He'd grown weary of carefree flings that were only fun for the moment, but left him unfulfilled. Now that he had Mason, his taste for meaningless relationships had soured even more.

He wanted substance. He wanted stability. He wanted someone who could appreciate the simple pleasures of a quiet night at home, someone who would value the absolute joy he found in raising his son.

But whether or not he was even ready to explore a relationship with a woman again was still up in the air. He'd been burned so badly by the last one that just the thought of exposing himself to that kind of hurt again scared the hell out of him. And that was nothing compared to how he felt when he considered bringing another woman into Mason's life.

Protecting his son was his number one priority. He would not allow his own needs to supersede those of Mason's.

Jordan glanced at the digital clock on the nightstand and did a double take. It was nearly 10:00 p.m.

*What the hell?*

He'd been asleep for *four hours?*

He hopped out of bed and rushed from the room. Finding the great room empty, he took off for the kitchen.

He crossed the threshold and stuttered to a stop.

The kitchen was spotless. Vicki had washed and put

away the dishes, swept and mopped the floors. She'd piled Mason's toys into one of the wicker laundry baskets from the laundry room and tucked it into a corner.

She looked up from the table she was scrubbing and smiled. "You're up," she said.

"Yeah," he replied with a sheepish grin. He rubbed the back of his neck. "I...uh, I'm sorry I slept so long. You should have been gone a long time ago."

"I didn't mind staying," she said. "You obviously needed the rest."

"More than I thought I did," he agreed. "Is Mason asleep?"

She nodded. "He actually fell asleep less than an hour after you did."

"You should have woken me, Vicki, or at least brought him in bed with me and taken off."

"I wasn't going to just leave without you knowing, Jordan. It's okay. As you can see, I found a way to occupy my time."

"I can see that." He motioned around the impeccable kitchen. "Thanks for doing all this. I've been meaning to clean since Laurie left but haven't gotten around to it."

"Have you been interviewing new housekeepers?"

Jordan frowned. "Why would I do that?"

"I thought your housekeeper quit."

"She didn't quit. She's just on an extended vacation, visiting her family in Toronto for the holidays."

"Oh, thank goodness, because you obviously need her," she said with a good-natured laugh. A devious smile tilted up the corners of her mouth. "Maybe I should have charged you after all. This kitchen was no small task."

He reached for the wallet he'd tossed on the kitchen counter earlier.

"I'm joking, Jordan."

"I'm not."

Vicki plunked a hand on her hip. "You'd better leave that wallet right where it is," she said in a warning tone.

He dropped the wallet and held his hands up in surrender. "Okay, okay. Don't hurt me," he said. He folded his arms across his chest and perched against the counter. "If you won't take money, at least let me pay you back with dinner."

The awkward silence immediately following his suggestion was deafening.

Where had *that* come from?

"Dinner?" Vicki asked, the dubious lift to her voice echoing her confusion.

Jordan was just as stunned as she was. He hadn't asked a woman to dinner—one who wasn't his sister, mother or a member of Oliver Windom's campaign committee, that was—in nearly two years. Not since Allison.

But now that he'd asked, he couldn't very well rescind it, could he?

An unexpected rush of adrenaline raced through Jordan's gut as he realized he didn't want to rescind anything. He wanted her to say yes. Later, when he had time to process it, he would have to figure out just why, after all this time, he was suddenly excited—damn near ecstatic—at the thought of sitting across a table and sharing a good meal and even better conversation with Vicki Ahlfors.

There was time to think about that later. At the moment, his main objective was making sure he secured an opportunity to see her again in the very near future. Tomorrow, if he had anything to say about it.

"Yes, dinner," Jordan continued. He pushed away from the counter and took a couple of steps forward. "There's nothing wrong with two friends going out for a meal, is there? It's the least I can do to express my thanks for everything you've done here this evening."

She looked up at him, and for the first time he detected the faint flecks of gold in her light brown eyes. How had he never noticed those before? Why had he never paid attention?

"You really don't have to, Jordan. As you pointed out earlier, I don't get the chance to hang around babies all that much. Mason has such a sweet temperament. I was happy to babysit."

Her words doused the excitement that had begun to flow through his bloodstream, reminding him that she had been here for Mason, not him.

He halted his advance toward her and hoped like hell that his disappointment didn't show on his face.

"In that case," he said, "let me at least follow you home."

"Be real, Jordan. You're not going to wake Mason and go through the hassle of bundling him up in his coat just so you can follow me home. I'm a big girl. I'm perfectly okay getting home on my own."

She gave the table a final swipe and folded the dishcloth. She hung it over the gooseneck faucet and picked her purse up from the counter, pulling the strap over her shoulder.

She held up a finger. "There's just one thing I need to do before I leave."

Jordan followed her to Mason's room. He stood in the open doorway and watched as she tiptoed to the crib and placed a gentle kiss on Mason's forehead. An odd feeling pulled at his gut. His son's own mother had not bothered to kiss him good-night in months. Seeing Vicki show him such attention—such affection—made the emotions stirring inside him intensify to unprecedented levels.

Why had he never noticed these things about her before? He knew she was sweet and quiet and kind. But she was also generous and giving and surprisingly funny.

And sexy. Even while wiping down his kitchen table she was sexy.

He followed her back to the kitchen, through the mudroom and to the garage. Jordan opened the garage door then went over to her car. Bracing his hand on the hood, he leaned in and asked, "You sure you'll be okay?"

"Of course, Jordan. It's not as if I have to drive to Connecticut, just to the other side of Wintersage." She closed the door but lowered the window. "Promise me you won't mess up your night by diving right back into work. Why don't you pull one of those novels off the bookshelf, or pop in a DVD? Anything but work."

"I'll think about it," he said, chuckling when she rolled her eyes and let out an exasperated sigh. He reached in and put a hand on her shoulder. "Thanks again for doing this, Vicki. I didn't realize how much I needed it."

The moment he touched her, things changed. Their gazes locked and held. Jordan didn't miss the way her chest rose with the deep breath she sucked in, nor could he miss the way *his* skin tingled with something he couldn't identify.

"It was my pleasure," she finally answered in a breathless tone.

His hand remained on her shoulder a second too long to be considered just a friendly gesture, but at the moment Jordan couldn't bring himself to care. He had no desire to stop touching her.

"Jordan, I should probably get going," she said.

Funny, he thought she should get out of her car and return to the house with him. At the moment, nothing would give him greater pleasure than to have her follow him into his bedroom so he could relive some of the fantasies he'd dreamed about a short while ago.

And that was when Jordan realized he needed to let her go.

Reluctantly, he withdrew his hand and backed away from the door. As she put the car in Reverse and pulled out of the garage, Jordan followed. He stopped at the edge of the garage and gave her a silent wave as she drove away.

Jordan brought his hand behind his head and tried to rub away the tightness in his neck muscles.

He was so damn confused. Hell, he'd been puzzled over these feeling for *days* now, and it became more perplexing with every day that passed.

He'd known Vicki for years. Why was he just noticing the slightly mischievous curve to her subtle smile? Or the way her eyes lit up when she laughed? Why was he suddenly feeling this bolt of electricity when she was around?

It was probably just the lingering effects of not being with a woman since Allison had left.

"That has to be it," Jordan said.

*You don't believe that.*

Jordan shut out the annoying voice in his head. If he

paid attention to it, he would be up for the rest of the night dissecting these new emotions Vicki had started to stir within him. It was a combination of exhaustion and horniness; he couldn't afford for it to be anything else.

The last time he'd allowed himself to get caught up in a woman, he'd been careless and had quickly found himself with a one-way ticket to fatherhood. He couldn't bring himself to regret it, not with Mason as the outcome of those less-than-stellar decisions he'd made a couple of years ago.

But that was why he had to be even *more* careful now. He had his son to think about. After the hard lessons he'd learned during his short marriage to Allison, he had to be more careful when it came to whom he exposed his son to. He couldn't allow his own baser needs to supersede what was right for Mason.

Though it wasn't as if Vicki would ever do anything to harm his son. She had a way with him—a special touch that seemed to calm Mason when nothing else could.

Jordan's spine stiffened, his back going ramrod straight.

Was *that* what this was about?

Were these feelings simply the result of gratitude over the compassion Vicki showed his son?

But a lot of women doted on Mason. On those occasions when Jordan had brought him over to Oliver's campaign headquarters, the females working on the campaign would get so wrapped up in Mason they would hardly get any work done. Why had he never felt his breath quickening or this low and steady burn in his gut toward any of those women?

He exhaled a frustrated sigh.

He didn't have the mental energy to deal with this

right now. His focus needed to remain on the election. The investigators he'd hired would need him to go over the information they uncovered—if they uncovered any—so that they could discern if there really was ballot tampering. He couldn't allow any outside forces to steal his attention away from what was really important right now.

Jordan returned to the house, locking up behind him. Despite the four-hour nap he'd just taken, he fell asleep as soon as his head hit the pillow.

The next day, after a morning of scouring the newspaper and web for any new news on the election and coming up empty, Jordan zipped Mason into his heavy coat and headed over to his parents. His father was likely at Woolcott Industries, but at this time of the day he had a good shot of finding his mother at home.

Jordan used his key to enter through the front door. His parents had never asked for the key once he'd moved out, and he never once considered giving it back. Even with a house of his own, this place was home.

He made his way through the massive house, finding his mother in the formal dining room. She looked up from the table, where she was replacing the silver cutlery with gold-plated ones. She put the mahogany box down and raced toward them.

"Well, hello there," she said, scooping Mason from his arms. "How are the two most handsome men in the world doing today?"

Nancy Woolcott was every bit the society wife, entrenched in her role among Wintersage's elite. But to Jordan's surprise, his mother was just as passionate in her role as a grandmother. She'd made her displeasure over his relationship with Allison known from the very beginning, and at first, Jordan thought she would project those feelings onto her grandson.

He should have known better. Mason was the apple of her eye.

"Do you have kisses for Grandma?" She peppered Mason's cheeks with loud pecks that had his son squirming and giggling in her arms. Turning to Jordan, she asked, "Why didn't you call to say you were coming over? I could have had something prepared for a late lunch."

"It's no big deal. We had a lazy morning, which seems to have stretched into a lazy afternoon. I figured I'd drop in and say hello." He pointed to the array of decorations adorning the twelve-foot dining table. "Getting the house ready for the holidays?"

"It's called tablescaping. Like landscaping, but for the inside of the house. I saw it on one of those home-decorating shows and knew I had to do it for the holidays."

His mother hired people to come in and decorate throughout the year, but when it came to Christmas she always insisted on doing things herself. Jordan doubted any outsider could ever put the amount of love and care his mother put into getting the house ready for Christmas.

"Have you picked out a tree yet?" she asked him. "You need to make sure they trim a good portion of the bottom limbs so that this little one won't reach them."

"I wasn't planning on getting a tree at all," Jordan said.

His mother looked at him as if he'd just confessed to armed robbery of an orphanage.

"What?" he asked defensively. "It doesn't make sense

to go through the hassle of a tree when we'll be spending Christmas Day here anyway."

Her chastising frown was a throwback to his days in elementary school after coming home with a note from the teacher for "bucking authority," which Jordan later realized was code for speaking his mind.

"Jordan, you have a baby now. This munchkin needs a Christmas tree. And it's more than just one day, it's an entire season. Get a tree," she stated in a tone that brooked no argument.

Jordan grunted, just as he used to do when those notorious letters arrived from his teachers, but he grudgingly accepted that, in this case, his mother was probably right.

He had never bothered with decorating for the holidays when it was just him, but now that he had Mason, he had to think about the kind of childhood he wanted his son to have. Some of his fondest memories as a boy were from Christmas. His parents went out of their way to make this time of the year special for both him and Sandra. He wanted Mason to have the opportunity to make those same memories.

"Okay," Jordan said. "We'll get a tree today."

His mother gave him a firm, regal nod, as if she never doubted he wouldn't do just as she'd requested. She turned her attention back to Mason.

"Now that that's settled, why don't we go into the kitchen? Grandma has a special treat for you."

"What's new about that? You always have a special treat for him," Jordan said as he followed her to the kitchen.

"Oh, hush," she called over her shoulder. "If I have to wear the title of grandmother, then I want to enjoy all the privileges, which includes spoiling my grandson."

She retrieved a package from the pantry. "I ran across these organic fruit chews the other day. I figured any healthy snack is a good snack. Let's just hope he likes them."

Perched in his grandmother's lap at the breakfast table, Mason took the dried fruit between his stubby fingers and immediately started to devour it. The smile on his mother's face stretched to the Massachusetts state line.

"Yes!" she said. "Score one for Grandma Nancy."

"I hope you bought a case. He's at this stage where he gets fixated on a certain thing and that's all he wants. Last week it was canned peaches."

"I'll make sure Millie picks up a few more boxes when she does this week's grocery shopping," his mother said, referring to the live-in housekeeper who had been with their family for years. "But you do know that you shouldn't let him have too much of any one thing, even if it is healthy. Not that I'm trying to tell you how to raise your son," his mother quickly interjected.

"I know," Jordan said. She made a point not to butt in, as she called it. Unless it concerned Christmas trees. Apparently, all bets were off when it came to proper holiday preparations.

Jordan walked over to the fridge and grabbed a can of soda. "I try to practice moderation as much as possible, but I've been somewhat lax these past few days. Mason's been fussier than normal lately. If I find something to appease him, I'm doing it."

"What's got you fussy, huh?" his mother asked, smoothing a hand over Mason's head.

"I don't know what it is," Jordan said. "Maybe he's missing Laurie? He's used to having her around."

"How long will she be gone?"

"Until after the New Year."

Jordan groaned just thinking about it. He appreciated his housekeeper/nanny, and paid her well because of it, but he didn't realize just how much she handled until she'd left for this extended vacation.

Maybe that was why he was feeling off-kilter. With Laurie gone and him stuck at the house all day, things seemed out of whack. He needed his life to return to normal.

"I'm thinking about maybe shortening my leave of absence," Jordan said. "I'm not used to sitting around the house doing nothing."

"You are not doing 'nothing,' Jordan," his mother said. She stood and brought Mason over to him. "You are enjoying the holidays with your son. Do you even realize how lucky you are? Your father would have loved to have weeks off around the holidays to spend with you kids, but it was a luxury he couldn't afford. He was always too busy with Woolcott Industries when you and Sandra were little."

His mother cupped his jaw in her soft palm. "Enjoy this time with Mason. Take it from me when I tell you that he's going to be grown and on his own before you know it. It's Christmas, Jordan. Enjoy Christmas with your son."

He nodded. "Okay, Mom. I hear you."

"Good. No more of this 'shortening your leave of absence' nonsense again. And when you *do* go back to the firm, you need to think about cutting back on your hours. You're a single father after all. This little one needs to have at least *one* of his parents around."

Jordan didn't miss the thinly disguised dig at Mason's *other* parent.

To say his mother wasn't his ex-wife's biggest fan

was an understatement that put all other understatements to shame. She'd somehow seen through Allison's facade from the very beginning. Jordan had been too blinded by his ex-wife's stunning beauty, vivacious personality and ridiculously hot body to pay attention to anything else. He'd ignored the warnings his mother tried to send him. And he'd paid for it. Dearly.

Water under the proverbial bridge.

He couldn't go back in time and change what had happened with Allison. He wouldn't even if he could. His son was worth every bit of the heartache and strife Allison had caused him.

Millie, who had been the Woolcotts' housekeeper for decades, came into the kitchen, and when she discovered Jordan had yet to have lunch, insisted on whipping up a quick meal. After demolishing the seared tuna over arugula that was worthy of a restaurant menu, Jordan patiently followed his mother around the house so she could show off the rest of her holiday decorations.

A half hour later, she followed them out to the car and strapped Mason into his car seat.

"You *are* going to get that tree this very instant, right?"

"Yes," Jordan said with an exaggerated groan.

"Good."

"Should I expect a surprise visit from you tonight to make sure I have the tree?"

"Your father and I have plans for tonight, but I expect you to text me a picture." She kissed his cheek before closing his car door and giving him a wave.

Jordan chuckled to himself as he rounded the circular driveway and drove away from his parents' home. As he pulled up to the stop sign at the end of the street, his cell phone trilled with the special ringtone he'd set

for the investigator he had looking into the election results. Jordan pulled over to the curb.

He answered the phone. "What do you have for me,
Mike?"

Several minutes later, he flipped his blinker to turn
left, back toward his house. The news he'd just received
was the most promising he'd heard in days.

Tree shopping would have to wait.

# Chapter 4

"Ouch!"

Vicki stuck her finger between her lips, sucking on the spot where the prickly holly leaf had just nicked her.

"Careful," her mother admonished. She looked up from the leather-bound organizer spread out before her on the marble kitchen island. "You don't have to do that, you know. I could hire someone to put those together."

"Very funny," Vicki said. She looked over the tall centerpiece and caught the glimpse of a smile tipping up her mother's lips. "If you want to pay me, go right ahead, but if I catch another florist within twenty yards of this house I cannot be responsible for my actions."

"I wouldn't dare." Her mother blew her a kiss. Vicki pretended to catch it and threw it back at her.

Her mother's shocked laugh echoed around the massive kitchen. "That was rude."

"That's what you get for suggesting bringing in another florist to decorate the house," she said, but then to show her mother that she knew it was all in good fun, Vicki walked over and plunked a kiss on her cheek.

Sitting with her legs crossed on the high-backed stool, Christine Ahlfors was the epitome of everything Vicki had thought she wanted to be. Physically, they were unmistakably mother and daughter, with their fair skin and naturally wavy hair. Her mother had thrown a fit when Vicki had chopped half of hers off, but when she'd arrived today to help ready the house for Christmas, Christine had remarked that the chin-length pixie cut was growing on her.

Vicki joked that she could give her the number for her stylist, but found that she was actually grateful when her mother laughed it off. Her new hairstyle was just one of the ways that she was finally starting to come into her own. She'd followed in her mother's footsteps in so many ways, being on the cheer squad in high school, majoring in the arts in college, serving on the boards of several philanthropic groups.

But as the years marched on, Vicki had begun to realize that they had different goals. Unlike her mother, she would never be satisfied filling her days with charity events and the other things that occupied her mother's time. Vicki needed more.

"I was thinking of a shopping trip in Boston this weekend. Why don't you join me?" her mother asked. "We could have lunch. I can even get us tickets to the Boston Pops' Saturday-night performance."

"I doubt I'll have time," Vicki said. "I have to drive up to a supplier in Scarborough to look at a few things for the Woolcotts' Kwanzaa celebration."

Her mother made a tsking sound. "That's going to

be one interesting party if this thing with the election isn't settled by then."

"You're still planning on going, aren't you?" Vicki asked.

Her mother looked at her as if she'd lost her mind. "I wouldn't miss it for the world. Who knows what's going to happen if Jordan is still accusing Darren of stealing the election."

"Let's hope this has all blown over by then," Vicki said.

"Speak for yourself. I'm looking forward to a little drama."

They looked at each other and burst out laughing.

As she returned her attention to the centerpiece, Vicki shot a surreptitious glance at her mother. She was trying to determine whether or not to tell her the other reason she would be too busy to frolic around Boston this weekend.

So far, Sandra and Janelle were the only people she'd told about her entry into the float competition. She had decided not to mention it to anyone else until she knew whether or not her submission was accepted. But this was her mother. She would be just as stoked over the possibility of Petals being selected as an entrant, wouldn't she?

"Mom, another reason I can't go with you to Boston this weekend is because I'm hoping that I'll be too busy working on a float for the Holiday Extravaganza Day Parade."

"Oh?" Her mother said, her attention still directed on the organizer. "Who are you decorating a float for this year?"

Vicki hesitated for the tiniest second before she answered, "Petals."

Her mother's head popped up. "For *your* business?"

She nodded. "I submitted an application for Petals to sponsor a float this year."

Genuine concern creased her mother's normally flawless skin. "That's a lot to take on by yourself, isn't it?" she asked.

"I won't be totally by myself. I have part-time employees."

"Those little kids from the high school that deliver for you?"

"They're hard workers, Mom. And they do more than just deliver. I'm also teaching them basic floral design. I haven't done so these past couple of weeks because of the holiday madness and their semester finals, but after the New Year I'm actually hiring two more students."

"But putting together an entire float? That's so much to take on, Vicki."

"You do realize that I have supplied the flowers for many of the floats that take part in the parade every year, don't you?"

Her mother stepped down from the stool she'd been perched on and rounded the kitchen island. She clamped her arms around Vicki's shoulders and gave her a gentle squeeze.

"It's not that I don't think you can do the work."

Judging by her reaction, Vicki wasn't so sure about that.

She knew exactly what her family thought when it came to her desire to be an entrepreneur. They didn't see Petals as the thriving small business that it was; they saw it as "Vicki's little flower shop." That was often how her father even referred to it, as if it was some hobby she played around with on the side, instead of a business that she'd poured her blood, sweat and tears into.

The fact that he had built Ahlfors Financial Management from the ground up should have made him even *more* proud that his daughter was following in his footsteps, but that had never been the case. And as supportive as her mother tried to be, Vicki knew deep down that Christine Ahlfors's expectations for her daughter were that she would get married and step into the role she was supposed to play—the society wife and mother. Becoming a wife and mother was one of Vicki's most cherished dreams, but it was not her *only* dream.

She was a businesswoman. She took her work seriously. It was time her family took it seriously, as well.

She turned to her mother. "If you think I can do the work, why were you so dismayed when I told you I'd entered the float competition?"

"I wasn't dismayed," her mother said. She gave Vicki a patient pat on the arm. "I just don't want you to be humiliated."

*Humiliated?*

The word knocked the wind right out of her.

Vicki managed to keep her expression indifferent, but on the inside her soul was breaking.

She shouldn't have expected anything different. Foolishly, she had. Which was why she only had herself to blame for being naive enough to think a new wardrobe and new haircut would change the way her family regarded her. They didn't see the *new Vicki,* they still saw polite, reserved, nonconfrontational Vicki. The Vicki who would rather keep her mouth shut in order to keep the peace, who never would have had the guts to even attempt to enter the float competition.

They still saw the Vicki she *used* to be. She would have to show them she wasn't that Vicki anymore.

She put the finishing touches on the centerpiece she'd created for the foyer, but that was all she was willing to do today. She had a float to design.

"I just remembered that the Buckleys want a second wreath for their guesthouse," she said. "I'll come back later to finish the decorations."

"That's fine, honey," her mother said, her focus once again on her calendar.

Vicki studied her for a moment, wishing she'd given Vicki the reaction she'd been hoping for when she'd told her about the float. Couldn't her mother have surprised her just this once? Couldn't she be proud, or even just excited? Why had her first reaction been to doubt that Vicki could pull this off?

She should have gone with her first instincts and kept this news quiet until she was sure her submission was accepted. If it turned out that she wouldn't have a float in the parade after all, she would have to hear "I told you so" for the next six months.

Yeah, she had no one to blame but herself.

Jordan braced his elbows on his kitchen table and ran both palms down his face. The longer he stared at this stuff, the less sense it made. For the past two days he'd pored over the data, running the numbers over and over again, trying to figure out just where the inconsistencies had come from.

When he'd gotten the call Wednesday from the investigator he'd hired, notifying him that he'd found a sharp decline in the number of voters for several counties in the western part of the state that normally had high voter turnout, Jordan thought he was on to something.

But the gap in voter turnout wasn't as wide as Jordan had anticipated, and there could have been a number of factors that accounted for it, including the weather in that part of the state on Election Day.

*Dammit.* Why couldn't this have been the break he'd been looking for?

He massaged the bridge of his nose. "You're driving yourself crazy," Jordan murmured.

"Crazy," came a little voice from around his feet.

Jordan looked down at Mason, who had started to climb up his leg.

"Did you just call daddy crazy?" He scooped his son up and sat his cushy bottom on the table. "What do you say we finally pick out that Christmas tree before Grandma Nancy comes over and murders Daddy, huh?" He tickled the pudgy rolls underneath Mason's chin. "You think you're up for that?"

"Crazy," Mason said.

"Great." Jordan groaned, then laughed. "Of all the words you could have picked up on, that's the one you go with?"

They went through the ten minutes of torture also known as dressing Mason for the cold. The temperature had dropped overnight, so Jordan broke out the heavier coats, along with scarves, gloves and an extra hat for Mason. When he strapped him into his safety seat, the only things visible were his eyes. The poor kid was going to bake under all those layers.

He'd put off buying the tree because it would just be an extra bother, but the more he thought about it, the more he began to look forward to bringing a little Christmas cheer into the house. It was a tradition that he wanted his son to have, memories he wanted him to cherish years from now.

Jordan tried to be mindful of spoiling Mason too much. He'd attended high school with a number of friends who were products of divorce. They had made manipulating their guilt-ridden parents an art form. Jordan never wanted to create that sense of entitlement in Mason, but giving his son the kind of Christmas he had enjoyed as a child wasn't spoiling him.

He remembered his mother's warning from a couple of days ago about trimming the low-hanging tree limbs so that Mason couldn't reach them. That brought about another concern: pine needles all over the floor. He was sure he'd read somewhere that some trees were more susceptible to losing their needles than others, and with the way Mason had of putting everything in his mouth these days, he needed to make sure he bought a tree that wouldn't have dozens of dead pine needles scattered about the floor.

What in the hell did he know about picking out the safest Christmas tree?

A slow grin lifted one corner of Jordan's mouth as a thought occurred to him.

He might not know much about trees, but he knew one person who did.

He didn't give himself time to deliberate before making a U-turn and heading toward Wintersage's main business district. As he drove toward the yellow-and-white Victorian that housed the Silk Sisters, Jordan tried to discredit the sudden quickening of his pulse. And the reason for it.

He wanted Vicki's expertise. She worked with this stuff for a living. She could give him advice on the safest tree, the one that would last the longest, maybe even the one that would look the best in his great room. That was all he wanted here—a little advice.

*She's going to see right through you.*

Yet he stayed on the same trajectory, because it didn't matter if she didn't buy his flimsy excuse. He hadn't been able to get her off his mind since she'd left his house Tuesday night. Scratch that, since Sandra's wedding.

Jordan still couldn't pinpoint exactly what it was that had changed about her that had him so intrigued. It couldn't be just because of her new look, could it? He wasn't *that* damn shallow, was he?

But what else could it be?

He had always viewed Vicki as just one of Sandra's friends. He definitely had never looked at her with romantic interest. But Jordan couldn't deny the current of electricity that had shot through him when he'd first seen her standing on the beach at Sandra's wedding.

A slow burn started low in his belly.

He could recall with incredible clarity the way his breath had caught in his throat. She'd stolen the air from his lungs, and turned the heads of more than a few of the single men at the reception. The fact that he had even noticed the attention that other men had paid to her that night should have been the first clue that something had changed.

He just didn't get it. Vicki Ahlfors wasn't his type. She was restrained and demure, while he tended to gravitate toward sassy and vivacious.

Jordan huffed out a sardonic laugh. His experience with Allison should have taught him something about his "type" and the trouble that it could lead to. The more he thought about it, the more he realized that he'd never had much luck with his usual type. Once the shine wore off, he found that he wasn't all that attracted to what was underneath.

Still, was Vicki the kind of woman he could see himself getting involved with?

"Hell yes," Jordan whispered to himself. If the excitement skittering across his skin just at the thought of seeing her again was any indication, hell *yes* he could see Vicki becoming much more than just a friend of his sister's.

The question was did *she* see *him* that way?

Jordan refused to believe he was the only one who'd felt the electricity that had sparked between them Tuesday night. He'd seen it in the way she'd looked at him, in the way her breath had caught. There had been interest in those beautiful brown eyes. Maybe she would be willing to see if there was anything more to the awareness that had ignited in those moments just before she'd left his house.

Jordan's chest tightened as he contemplated whether or not *he* was really ready to take that momentous step.

He sure as hell wasn't going to go the rest of his life without a woman. He loved women too much. He cherished the feeling of waking up with a soft, warm body snuggled up next to him. Relished the simple pleasures of sharing his life with another human being.

But Jordan would be the first to admit that his ex-wife had done a number on him. After the whirlwind that had been his love affair with Allison and the heartache she'd caused when she walked out on him and Mason, the thought of allowing another woman to get that close, of trusting another woman not to hurt both him and his son, was something he just didn't know if he could do.

The image of Vicki's sweet, subtle smile flashed before him, and the tightness in his chest eased ever so slightly.

Something about this felt right. Whether it was because of the way she treated Mason, or something deeper, he couldn't say yet, but Jordan had the suspicion that if he didn't explore these new feelings he would regret it.

He pulled up to the Victorian, unstrapped Mason from his car seat and started up the stairs. Even though clients were in and out of the Victorian all the time, he still knocked on the front door before walking in.

Vicki was in the front parlor, straightening a bow on the massive Christmas wreath that hung above the fireplace.

"Hi there, you two," she greeted.

If he was a betting man, Jordan would put his money on Mason being the reason her face lit up the way it did. But it felt damn good to pretend it was because she was happy to see him.

She hurried over to them and took Mason from his arms.

Yeah, that was what he'd figured.

Vicki tickled Mason's chin. He responded with that smile made to melt hearts. His son was such a flirt.

"Sandra isn't here," she said. "She had to meet with a client in Portsmouth."

"I'm not here to see Sandra. Actually, I'm here to see you."

Her pretty brown eyes widened. "Me?"

"Mason and I are going shopping for a Christmas tree. I figured I should probably get one." There was no need to mention that it was initially his mother's idea. "I was hoping you could give me some advice on the type of tree I should get. I don't want one that will shed pine needles. He loves putting things in his mouth."

"I noticed that Tuesday night," she said as she grinned

down at Mason. "When it comes to picking out a tree, it's more about how you maintain it than the particular variety. Needle retention is better in some, but honestly, as long as you keep it properly watered, any tree you get should keep its needles well past Christmas."

"Ah. Okay," Jordan said.

Her brow dipped in a curious frown. "Was that the only thing you needed?"

It suddenly occurred to him that if he'd wanted her to think he was just seeking advice, a simple phone call would have sufficed. Which made his trip here even *more* transparent.

Which begged the question, why was he being vague?

Over the past week, if his mind wasn't occupied with Mason or the election, he was thinking about Vicki. The more he thought about it, the more he realized that thoughts of Vicki had usurped the election.

What he felt for her was real. He wanted this. He wanted *her*.

And if he was going to do this—if he was really going to pursue Vicki, then he needed to *do* this. No more skirting around the issue.

"Actually," Jordan began, "I was...uh... I was thinking that maybe—if you have time, that is—that you'd like to come with us? If you have the time."

Well, that was as smooth as a porcupine's ass.

When had he become so inept at asking a pretty girl out? He wasn't even asking her *out* out just yet; he was only asking her to help him pick a Christmas tree, for crying out loud. How was he going to ask her out on a genuine date if he couldn't do something this simple?

"I know it's still pretty early." He glanced at his

watch. It was just after two in the afternoon. "I understand if you can't leave your flower shop just yet."

A delicate smile drew across Vicki's lips. Either she went for bumbling idiots, or she was laughing at him. Maybe both.

"You're inviting me to go tree shopping?" she asked.

"I'd appreciate an expert's opinion." He shook his head and blew out a frustrated breath. "That's not true," he said. "At least that's not the only reason."

He shifted from one foot to the other like a nervous schoolboy, which put the final stamp on this humiliating episode.

*Dammit, enough of this!*

It had been a while since he'd approached a woman, but he wasn't completely out of his element. Not to brag, but he'd won a few hearts in the past. He could do this.

"Look, Vicki. The truth is I really enjoyed hanging out with you the other night. Even though I slept most of your visit, the brief time I *was* awake it was nice to talk to someone—another adult who isn't my mom or Sandra or someone involved with the election."

He gestured to the topiary adorned in glittering gold-and-red foil ribbon.

"You're really into all this Christmas decorating and floral-design stuff, so I thought you'd enjoy tree shopping." He paused for a moment. "Now that I think about it, it was pretty presumptuous to assume that you'd just drop everything to help me pick out a Christmas tree. Maybe I'll come over another time, when you're not busy. I'll let you get back to what you were doing."

Feeling like an ass, he lifted Mason from her arms and started for the door.

"Jordan?" He looked back to find her staring at him, an amused expression edging up the corners of her lips.

"I would love to go Christmas tree shopping with the two of you."

His eyes widened. "Really?" Maybe she *did* go for bumbling idiots.

She nodded. "Yes, really. Give me a few minutes to lock up, and we can go."

Jordan tried to stop the huge smile from spreading across his face, but that wasn't going to happen. He would probably smile like this for the rest of the night.

# Chapter 5

Vicki cursed the nervous energy shooting through her bloodstream and the stupid butterflies fluttering around her idiot stomach. But how in the heck was she supposed to control them when Jordan Woolcott was in the parlor—not waiting to see Sandra, but to see *her?*

"Calm down," Vicki cautioned herself. Apparently, she was in need of a little refresher history lesson.

How long had she pined for this man?

For years, Jordan had never bothered to look her way. Yet all of a sudden, he was showing interest. What made him any different than the dozen men who'd strolled into Petals this week with a newfound appreciation for fresh flowers?

Because this was Jordan.

As much as she wanted to make him work for her attention, she just couldn't play hard to get when it came to Jordan. Because he was the one she'd always wanted.

Vicki's chest tightened with anticipation at the thought of him finally wanting her in the same way she wanted him.

She'd sensed a change in the air. Something about the way he'd looked at her on Tuesday, as if he was seeing her for the first time. She'd tried to disregard it, too afraid she was looking for something that wasn't really there. But the look in his eyes as he'd so adorably fumbled his way through that invitation to go tree shopping confirmed what she thought she'd seen before leaving his house the other night.

She paused for a moment and inhaled a deep, calming breath. She didn't want to get ahead of herself. It wasn't as if she was the best at reading men; she didn't want to think how foolish she would feel if she'd misjudged his intentions.

Vicki lifted her purse and coat from the coatrack and then shut down her computer. Just as she started for the foyer, the phone rang. She almost let it go to voice mail, but remembered that she was expecting a call from a fellow florist in Durham who possibly wanted to go in on a huge decorating job in Boston.

"Petals," she answered. "This is Vicki. How may I help you?"

"Ms. Ahlfors, this is Robin Tooney with the Wintersage Holiday Extravaganza Day Parade."

Her heart instantly started to thump a million times faster against the walls of her chest.

"Yes. Hello," Vicki stammered.

"Ms. Ahlfors, the committee has made its decision on the submissions that were entered for this year's competition." Vicki's heart jumped right up into her throat. "It is my pleasure to inform you that you've been granted a float in this year's parade. Congratulations."

"Oh, my," she whispered. Her capacity to think evaporated, but she quickly pulled herself together. "I'm stunned, and thrilled, of course. Thank you so much."

"The committee was completely charmed by your idea of Christmas celebrations from around the world. I know you've had a hand in creating several floats for other participants in the past. I can't wait to see what you create for your own."

"I'm looking forward to showing you. Thank you again."

Robin Tooney instructed her on where to find the newly updated guidelines for float building on the committee's website and filled her in on the deadline information.

After ending the call, Vicki just stood there for a moment in stunned disbelief. Then she threw her fists in the air and yelped.

"*Yes!* Yes! Yes! Yes!"

"I don't mean to pry, but I'm assuming you just received some good news?"

She whipped around to find Jordan standing in the arched entryway that led to Petals's retail area. Heat instantly flooded her cheeks, but she was too excited to try hiding her embarrassment.

His brow arched. "So?"

"I got in," Vicki said with a breathless laugh. "I can't believe I got in."

"In where?"

She pointed to the phone. "That was the head of the float committee for the Wintersage Holiday Extravaganza Day Parade. I submitted an idea for a float, and it was accepted! After providing flowers for dozens of other floats over the years, for the first time Petals will have its own in the parade."

"That's wonderful, Vicki. The Christmas parade is a pretty big deal. But that's also a pretty big undertaking, isn't it?"

"It is, but I think I can do it," Vicki said. She shook her head. "No, I *know* I can do it."

Wintersage Holiday Extravaganza Day had grown into a region-wide event, reaching far beyond the boundaries of their small New England town. And the parade had become the focal point of the entire day. Businesses from several cities stretching along the coast, and as far inland as Lowell, used the opportunity to promote their brands.

As the floats had grown more elaborate over the past several years, larger floral-design shops had begun courting the businesses. A number of those larger shops had managed to steal away several of her customers. One of her previous clients, a marina that catered to Wintersage's elite, had the audacity to take the design Vicki had created for them and bring it to a competing florist to actually produce the float.

And, like the pushover she *used* to be, she'd allowed it.

Not anymore. The new Vicki was not going to quietly sit back while others took all the glory. This year she had something to prove.

When her float took to the streets of Wintersage and held its own against the stiff competition she was sure to face, her family would be forced to see her as the serious, career-minded entrepreneur that she was, and not the owner of just a "little flower shop."

A mischievous grin spread across her lips. "I'm really going to do this," she said. "I'm going to put Petals on the map. I really, *really* wanted to get in. It feels amazing."

"You need to celebrate," Jordan said.

"Yes, I do. Luckily for you, Christmas tree shopping is exactly the kind of thing a florist does to celebrate." She sent him a cheeky wink. "Let's go."

Vicki was stunned at her own audaciousness, but she didn't care. She was much too giddy over the news she'd just received to feel self-conscious.

It didn't make sense to take separate cars, so she joined Jordan in his. As she sat ensconced in the supple leather seat, she closed her eyes and pulled in a healthy whiff of his scent. There was something about the combination of sandalwood and a man's unique essence that drove her crazy.

Of course, when that man was Jordan Woolcott, the sandalwood was optional. He drove her crazy merely by existing—always had.

"Have you thought about a theme for your float?" Jordan asked.

"Christmas from Around the World. I got the idea from my favorite ornament from when I was a little girl. It has Santa Claus dressed in traditional garb from various cultures around the globe. My mom used to tell me that Santa's clothes would magically change as the reindeer flew him to different countries."

He grinned. "And you believed that, huh?"

"I was five, of course I believed it."

"Do you still have the ornament?"

She nodded. "I've kept all of my ornaments. I buy a new one every year to add to the collection."

"So what's this year's?"

"I haven't gotten one yet." She stared out the window at the myriad boats hugging the harbor's shoreline. "I always try to find an ornament that reflects something significant that happened during the previous year. Maybe I'll find something to commemorate all the changes that have happened over the past couple of months." She looked over at him. "This is turning out to be a year that I'll want to remember for a long time to come."

"I know what you mean," he said in a quiet voice. "It's been memorable in more ways than one."

There it was again, that flicker of awareness she'd felt the other night. It started with a spark that turned into a slow burn, humming in the air around them.

"Do you have any Christmas traditions from when you were a little boy that you plan to pass on to Mason?" she asked.

He shrugged the shoulder closest to her. "Just being with family. That's always been at the core of the Woolcotts' holidays. Although I do like the idea of an ornament collection," he said. "Maybe I should start one for him."

Vicki looked over her shoulder at the baby. He was engrossed in a colorful plastic centipede with antennae that rattled.

"You should," she said. "He'll cherish them for the rest of his life."

She twisted back in her seat and caught Jordan staring at her, his gaze probing, penetrating. Once again, the air pulsed with energy, a tangible force that provoked all manner of interesting ideas to blossom in her head.

"You, uh, should probably pay attention to the road," Vicki said.

"Oh," Jordan said, quickly turning his head forward.

The flutter that had previously traveled around her belly returned with a vengeance. The awareness that had been a faint suggestion just a few moments earlier now saturated the air around them, flooding the space with a potent mix of something Vicki couldn't quite describe.

She'd thought about the spark of desire that had flashed between them Tuesday night at least a million times over the past couple of days, trying to decide whether it was real or just a figment of her wishful imagination. But she had not imagined the look in Jordan's eyes just a few moments ago, when his piercing gaze had captured hers and held it. He'd looked at her as if he was seeing the real her for the first time.

There was just one problem: she had yet to decide if this really *was* the real her.

As much as she loved her new wardrobe and haircut, she was still the same Vicki Ahlfors she'd always been on the inside. Quiet, sensible, reliable Vicki. How could she be sure Jordan was interested in more than just the aesthetics?

They arrived at a parking lot jam-packed with cars as the residents of Wintersage and its surrounding towns scoped out Christmas trees. Vicki unstrapped Mason from his car seat and waited while Jordan unfolded the stroller he'd just taken out of the trunk. The minute she tried to sit him in the stroller, Mason started to wail.

"I don't know what's up with him today," Jordan said. He took the baby from her and held him over his shoulder, patting him gently on the back. "Something has him fussier than usual. Hopefully the walk will calm him down."

They started for the entrance to the tree lot. Vicki pushed the empty stroller, just in case they were able to cajole Mason into sitting in it a bit later.

"Is this the only tree lot around?" Jordan remarked. "This place is packed."

"It's definitely the biggest for several counties," she

said. "And they have the widest selection. Let's just hope people haven't picked over all the good ones."

Vicki felt a familiar excitement building as they traveled along the rows of freshly cut trees. Christmas carols floated from speakers nestled throughout the vast lot, and the scent of pine and evergreen hung in the air. It encompassed everything she loved about this time of the year.

She was having a hard time keeping her active imagination at bay. It was all too easy to let her mind wander into the cozy yet dangerous territory of this being the real thing. She, Jordan and Mason strolling through the crowd of other young families made her long for things that were not a guarantee.

After contemplating several choices, they chose a balsam fir because of the low maintenance and its tendency to retain its needles.

After Jordan paid for the tree and for home delivery, he turned to her and said, "That was relatively painless. Now I guess the next thing I need to do is get some ornaments."

"You don't have ornaments from last year?"

"I wasn't really in the spirit last year," he said.

"Oh, right," Vicki said, feeling a bit like an idiot. His ex-wife had just left him to raise their young baby on his own around Christmastime last year. That would take the holiday spirit out of anyone.

"To be honest, this will be my first time putting up a tree," Jordan said.

Vicki's mouth fell open in horrified shock.

"Hey." His palms shot up in mock surrender. "I didn't kill an elf or anything. Not everyone gets into the whole stocking-and-tree rigmarole. My mom has always done more than enough at Christmas to make up for my lack of decorating." He shrugged. "I just never found it necessary."

"Well, you do realize that's changed now, right?"

He looked down at Mason, who had finally allowed Jordan to put him into his stroller about ten minutes ago.

"Yes. Like so many other things, he's changed the way I celebrate the holidays. He's changed everything."

"For the better," Vicki said.

"Absolutely," he said, his eyes still focused on his son.

Once they were in the car again, they headed back toward Wintersage.

"The guy at the lot said they would have the tree delivered no later than six o'clock. That will give me time to bring you back to the Victorian." He looked over at her. "Unless you want to help pick out some ornaments?"

His tone, the look in his eyes, the way his voice dipped ever so slightly… It all gave her the impression that his question was more than just an invitation to go ornament shopping.

"I don't think you need help picking out ornaments," Vicki said. "But if you don't mind the company, I would love to join you."

"You're right. Your decorating expertise isn't exactly what I'm interested in." His hands tightened on the steering wheel. "This is new territory for me, Vicki."

Her heart started to pound in her chest.

"What's new territory?" she asked.

"This uncertainty, the awkwardness." He blew out a heavy breath. "I'm not used to questioning myself—questioning my feelings—and that's all I've done since Tuesday night." He paused, and then he looked over at her, his eyes full of intent. "I don't want to question it anymore."

The pounding intensified, to the point that she thought her heart would burst right out of her chest.

"I'm enjoying your company," he continued. "And you can tell me if I'm way off base here, but I get the feeling you're enjoying this, too."

She swallowed deeply, then shook her head. "You're not off base," she managed to get out.

The slow smile that drew across his lips sent a swarm of tingles skittering along Vicki's spine.

"Then what do you say we do a little ornament shopping?" Jordan said.

As they browsed the department store shelves stacked high with glittering hanging ornaments, fake fur-trimmed stockings and tree toppers, Vicki came to her most shocking realization of the night.

Jordan Woolcott was utterly charming. *And* funny.

To hear Sandra talk about her brother, one would think he was an oaf with zero personality. *He's an attorney,* Sandra would always say, as if that explained it all.

But Jordan had no problem making a fool of himself in the middle of a crowded store, especially when it came to trying to get Mason to laugh. He grabbed a Santa hat from the shelf and plopped it atop his head. He put on a plastic Rudolph the Red-Nosed Reindeer nose that blinked like a beacon, then did an awful rendition of the beloved Christmas song, mixing up the words and skipping some lines entirely.

Vicki laughed until her eyes watered, but Mason's crabbiness only grew.

Jordan's shoulders sagged with defeat. "I don't know what's wrong with him. He woke up irritable and it's just gotten worse as the day's gone on."

Frowning, Vicki took the baby out of the stroller and pressed her lips to his forehead. "He's a little warm, but I can't tell if it's a fever. You wouldn't happen to carry his thermometer in his diaper bag, would you?"

He shook his head. "It's at the house, but I can get one from the pharmacy department."

"Do it. It doesn't hurt to have a spare, especially at his age. I'm going to bring him to the car and away from all this noise."

Jordan gave her the keys before going off in search of a thermometer. Less than ten minutes later, Vicki spotted him exiting the store's sliding doors, both hands burdened by several bags. He walked up to the passenger side and handed her a bag through the window.

"Can you open this up while I put these in the trunk?"

She hadn't bothered to put Mason in his car seat, so the task of opening the ear thermometer's hard plastic packaging wasn't the easiest. By the time she got it open, Jordan had slid behind the wheel. Vicki held the squirming baby in her arms as Jordan placed the thermometer in his ear. A second later it beeped.

"Ninety-nine point one," he said, looking at the readout.

"That's not bad as far as fevers go, but apparently that's enough to make him irritable," Vicki said. "Do you have a fever reducer at home, or do you need to go back in and get one?"

"I have some at home from the summer cold he caught back in August."

"I remember when he had that cold," Vicki said, pressing a kiss to the side of Mason's head. "I think he'll be okay in a bit, once we get a little medicine in him."

Jordan got out of the car and came around to her side.

"Let me get him strapped into his car seat, then we can get out of this cold."

He drove Vicki to the Victorian so she could pick up her car, but she insisted on following him back to his place to make sure all was well with Mason. When they arrived at his house, a Christmas tree wrapped in blue netting was leaning against the front door.

The tree, along with all of the ornaments, remained exactly where they were until after Jordan had given Mason some cherry-flavored syrup. Vicki carried Mason over to the sofa in the great room and watched while Jordan carted the bags of ornaments into the house.

Cuddling Mason to her chest, she folded her legs beneath her and pulled an afghan over the both of them. A satisfied sigh escaped her lips as she relished in the feel of the baby's soft weight against her, so close to her heart. She murmured a soothing lullaby into Mason's ear as she watched Jordan bring in the stand that had also been delivered with the tree. He set it up in the corner of the great room, and then he walked over to where she sat.

"Vicki, I don't want to keep you here any longer than you need to be," he said. "I'll hold Mason until he falls asleep, then I'll finish getting the tree up."

"Jordan?"

"Yeah?"

"Get the tree," she said.

His forehead creased in a frown. "Vicki, you don't have—"

"As someone whose job calls on you to read people for a living, you should be able to tell that I am perfectly content right where I am."

"Are you sure?" he asked.

"I'm sure, Jordan." With a brazenness the old Vicki never would have even contemplated displaying, she finished, "I can't think of anywhere else I would rather be right now."

That surge of electricity, the one she'd felt before leaving here Tuesday night, pulsed between them again.

"I can't think of anyone else I would want to be here," Jordan said in a voice so soft she could barely hear it, as if the admission both surprised and thrilled him as much as it surprised and thrilled her.

His eyes slid closed and he dropped his head, releasing a weary breath. He brought a hand up to massage the back of his neck before lifting his head and looking at her.

"What's happening here?" he asked.

"You tell me, Jordan."

She knew he was questioning his feelings again. She could tell by the confusion clouding his face.

He held his hands out, as if in a plea for her to understand. "I know what I'm feeling," he said. "I just don't know what to do about it. I don't want to give you mixed signals."

"Good, because I don't want them."

"I just need…" He shook his head again. "Can I take some time to figure this out? I feel what's happening, but I need to be sure."

"This doesn't have to be complicated, Jordan."

"That's the thing. From here on out, it will always be complicated."

Now it was her turn to look confused.

Before she could question him, he continued, "I accepted months ago that the choice to bring another woman into my life will never be an easy one. I'm more cautious now than I've ever been in the past. I have to be. I have Mason to consider." He put a hand up before she could say anything. "I'm not suggesting that you would ever treat Mason unfairly in any way. The way you are with my son, the care you take with him, I can't tell you how much that means to me, Vicki."

He paused for a moment. "But it's hard for me to drop my guard where he's concerned. His own mother refuses to put him first. I have to make sure I'm with someone who will."

"What makes you think I wouldn't?" she asked.

"I know you would," Jordan said. He shook his head. "But I still can't help but feel cautious when it comes to him."

"Here's the thing, Jordan." With the hand that wasn't cradling Mason, she reached out and captured his wrist. "Whether or not you decide that you have romantic feelings for me, I would still do exactly what I've been doing as far as Mason is concerned. This little guy wormed his way into my heart from his very first visit to the Silk Sisters." She paused for a moment before continuing in a softer voice. "But it's my heart that I'm thinking about right now. I don't want to be hurt."

"I won't hurt you. But I'll be honest. This scares me, Vicki. I trusted my heart the last time, and look what happened."

"Don't make me pay for her mistakes," Vicki said. "I'm nothing like Allison."

"No, you're not. I know that. But you also said you weren't looking for casual, that you want serious. A part of me thinks I'm ready, but another part—"

"I have an idea," Vicki said, cutting him off. Nothing good could come of him continuing to overanalyze his feelings like this. "Why don't we just enjoy the time-honored tradition of putting up a Christmas tree? We can think about casual versus serious and just what all of that means later." She pressed a kiss to Mason's soft head, then looked up at Jordan. "Right now, I just want to enjoy this time with you and Mason."

He shook his head, a grateful smile spreading across his face. "You have to be the most understanding woman I know," he said. "I promise I'm going to figure this out—"

"Jordan, get the tree."

He smiled again, then nodded. "I'll get the tree."

## Chapter 6

The moment Jordan left the room, Vicki exhaled the unsteady breath she'd been holding in. Not too long ago, she would have shied away from what was happening between them, too afraid to take a chance.

But things were different now. *She* was different. She was no longer willing to sit on her feelings. She was putting it all out there, and whatever happened, happened.

Vicki didn't even try to hide her amusement as Jordan struggled to get the eight-foot tree through the door. Back at the tree lot, she'd told him that he would be just fine with a small five-footer, but he had proclaimed that if he was going to get a tree, it would be a *real* tree.

He set it up in the corner of the great room and filled the stand with water, then turned to her. "This feels more significant than I thought it would," he said.

"Having a tree?"

He nodded. "It's yet another of those milestones,

you know? House, kid, Christmas tree. I'm gradually moving into this new phase of my life. At one time it scared me, but I'm beginning to realize that I've been ready for this for a long time now. I'm enjoying all of these new experiences."

She had been insanely attracted to him well before fatherhood had turned him into this insightful person who actually took the time to appreciate something as simple as decorating for the holidays. To see him embracing life's simple pleasures made him a thousand times sexier.

He clapped his hands together. "Now that I have the tree, I guess it's time to put stuff on it." He reached over and lifted Mason from her arms. "Let's see if my little man is feeling well enough to help out."

Vicki looked on as Jordan showed Mason how to hang the ornaments. Her chest swelled with emotion every time he put his hand up for a high five and Mason responded with an awkward little slap of his palm. This was all beginning to feel too domestic for her own good.

Instead of shying away from it in an attempt to shield her heart—just in case Jordan decided he really didn't feel the same way about her as she felt about him—Vicki decided to hold on tighter. She would enjoy this while she had the chance and deal with the consequences later.

"You know what this calls for?" she said, pushing up from the sofa. "Hot chocolate."

"That sounds great," he said.

"Will I find everything I need in the kitchen?"

He nodded and she turned toward the kitchen.

Vicki felt his eyes on her, following her as she walked out of the great room. Once in the kitchen, she had to brace herself on the counter and catch her breath. She was still getting used to dealing with the consequences of this new Vicki's boldness. Inviting herself into a man's kitchen to make hot chocolate was something she never would have done before.

A smile drew across her face.

She liked this new Vicki a hell of a lot more than the old one.

She searched around for the things she needed, grimacing when all she found was a box of instant hot chocolate mix. She should have known a man who had never bothered to put up a Christmas tree wouldn't have the real stuff. She was able to doctor it up with vanilla extract and cinnamon sticks; both were surprise findings in the pantry.

She carried two mugs of hot chocolate back into the great room, but stopped short when she discovered Jordan taking the ornaments off the tree. Mason sat on the floor a few yards away, playing with the packaging the glittery reindeer ornaments had come in.

"What happened?" Vicki asked.

Jordan looked over at her and gave her a chastising frown laced with humor. "I would have expected better advice from a person who does this for a living," he said.

Vicki lifted her shoulders in question, unsure what he was talking about.

His hands burdened with ornaments, he nodded toward the coffee table.

Her head flew back with a laugh when she spotted the boxes of Christmas lights. "Ah, yes. The lights go on first."

"I realized that after we'd already put about twenty ornaments on the tree."

"Well, why don't you sit and have some hot chocolate while I hang the lights? Then you and Mason can do the fun part."

Their fingers touched when she handed him the mug, setting off a torrent of tingles up and down her arms. Jordan undoubtedly felt it, too. Their eyes held over the steaming mug and Vicki's inner muscles pulled tight with need.

He set the mug on the coffee table, then lowered himself on the floor next to Mason, who remained mesmerized by the array of shiny plastic ornaments.

Vicki did her best not to feel self-conscious as she walked around the Christmas tree, stringing the lights on its full branches. She couldn't help but be hyperaware of every move she made, because Jordan's eyes remained on her the entire time.

"How did your interest in floral design come about?" he finally asked after some time had passed. "I doubt that was one of the majors offered at Nillson."

"No, it wasn't," she said with a laugh. "I majored in art history."

"So you've always had this artistic side?"

"I can't draw to save my life. Not like Sandra, for sure. But there is a certain artistry to floral design. It's all art, I just happen to create my pictures with flowers."

"According to Sandra, your 'art' has acquired a number of new admirers."

Vicki could tell by the inflection in his voice that he was fishing for information about those new admirers, but she wasn't taking the bait. Instead, she kept their conversation lighthearted.

"Don't get me started on Sandra. She and Janelle have had their share of fun at my expense this past week. However, they've been so supportive of my plans to participate in the float competition that I've pretty much forgiven them both."

The glint in his eyes told her that he saw right through her subject dodging. Thankfully, he didn't press her.

"It's unbelievable that you all have remained such great friends," Jordan said. "It must be comforting knowing you always have someone you can count on."

The envy in his voice caused a bit of sadness to tug at her heart. "You have people you can count on, Jordan."

"I know I do. But I also know that I've made a few enemies lately."

"If you're talking about the election—"

He held up a hand. "If you don't mind, I'd rather not get into all of that. Not tonight. I'm decorating my family's Christmas tree," he said, running a hand over Mason's smooth hair. "I want to enjoy this." He looked up at her. "Having you here with us is going a long way in making tonight special, Vicki. Thanks for sticking around."

"I said it before, but I guess it bears repeating. There is nowhere else I'd rather be right now, Jordan."

They shared a smile before Vicki went back to stringing the lights on the tree. As she continued to thread the multicolored lights through the branches, she wondered if she'd eventually convince Jordan to trust her, not just with Mason, but also with his heart.

She understood his hesitancy. At the height of Allison's treachery, a fair amount of the conversations over Monday-night dinner at the Quarterdeck had centered on the debacle between Jordan and his ex-wife. Sandra had kept Vicki and Janelle abreast of his ordeal and the toll it seemed to take on Jordan.

Suppressing her reaction to the demise of Jordan's marriage became harder and harder with every story

Sandra shared. She hadn't wanted to appear overly interested. Even though Sandra and Janelle were the closest things she had to sisters, Vicki had kept her feelings for Jordan hidden from her two best friends.

If even half of what Sandra had claimed Allison had put him through was true, Vicki couldn't blame Jordan for being gun-shy, but she had to think about herself, as well. She knew what she wanted out of life. As she caught glimpses of Jordan and Mason playing on the floor, she couldn't help but think of how much the scene resembled everything she'd fantasized about for herself.

If she dwelled too long on just how close it was within her grasp, yet how far, it would crush her mood. Tonight was about living in the moment and enjoying it for as long as she could.

Jordan tried to get Mason to resume their decorating duties, but the little boy was more interested in the cylindrical container the Christmas balls had come in than actually putting the balls on the tree. When it was time to place the pointy star on the very top of the tree, Jordan grabbed a two-step ladder from the utility closet and held it steady while Vicki climbed. After a brief wobble, she positioned the star in the place of honor.

"There," she said. "That looks pretty perfect to me."

"I agree," Jordan said.

She glanced over her shoulder and realized he wasn't looking at the tree.

"I was talking about the star," she said.

He lifted his eyes from her backside, a slight, sexy grin tipping up the corners of his lips. "Yeah, that, too."

As she gingerly climbed down from the stepladder, acutely aware of Jordan's eyes still on her, Vicki just knew her cheeks were flaming red.

"Where are the stocking hangers?" she asked once she was off the ladder.

That grin still on his lips, Jordan reached into one of the shopping bags and retrieved the hangers. He handed them to her, deliberately brushing his fingers over her palm.

"Do you remember what I said about needing time to figure this all out in my head?" he asked. Vicki nodded. "It's taking me a lot less time than I thought it would."

His words sent a rush of pleasure shooting through her veins, but she refused to allow herself to be overwhelmed by it. Despite how long she'd wished for this very thing, she knew she needed to be careful. Jordan was still "figuring this all out." Meanwhile, her heart was in this—had been in this for far longer than he knew.

She walked over to the fireplace and placed the brass-plated stocking hangers between framed pictures of Mason. Vicki refused to acknowledge the envy that streaked through her at the sight of Jordan's ex-wife holding an infant Mason in her arms. Allison was all smiles, yet judging by Mason's size, she had left Jordan and her new son only weeks after this photo was taken. Vicki still didn't understand how the woman could do such a thing.

But, in the most selfish way, she was happy Allison had. Because the thought of Allison here tonight, sharing in this wonderful evening with Jordan and Mason, made Vicki sick to her stomach.

"Let me see if he'll at least hang up his own stocking," Jordan said, going over to the couch where Mason now lay with his toy centipede clutched to his chest.

Jordan picked the baby up and frowned.

"Something wrong?" Vicki asked.

He touched Mason's forehead with the back of his hand and his frown deepened. "He seems warmer than he was even before I gave him the fever reducer."

Vicki quickly made her way to his side and pressed her lips to the baby's forehead. "His fever has definitely spiked," she said, gingerly lifting the baby from Jordan's arms. "Get the thermometer."

Jordan was gone before she finished the statement. He came back seconds later with the thermometer and stuck the instrument in Mason's ear.

The readout said 103.4.

Vicki's eyes shot to Jordan's. "That's a dangerous number. We need to get him to the doctor."

They quickly bundled Mason into his outerwear and were out of the house in less than three minutes. Jordan's thumbs tapped nervously on the steering wheel as he tested the speed limit of Wintersage's roadways.

Vicki reached over and covered his forearm.

"It'll be okay," she said.

He looked over at her, but he didn't respond—only nodded.

Less than ten minutes after leaving the house, they pulled into Wintersage Urgent Care. The twenty-four-hour medical clinic that had recently opened was closer than the area hospital. Their wait was brief but agonizing. Vicki could see Jordan's anxiety increasing with every second that passed. Mason, on the other hand, was quiet. Despite his high fever, his fussiness from earlier in the day had actually dissipated.

Once in the exam room, Vicki stood next to Jordan while the young doctor assessed Mason. She didn't even hesitate before taking his hand and threading her fingers through his. He looked down at their clasped hands and gave hers a squeeze. His grateful expression, mixed with the underlying worry over Mason, tugged at her heart.

"Just as I expected," the doctor said, wrapping the stethoscope around her neck. "This little one is cutting a few new teeth. He must be a late bloomer."

"He only got his first teeth a few months ago," Jordan said.

"It happens. Anywhere from six to sixteen months is normal. However, he also has an ear infection. Have you noticed him pulling on his ear or favoring his right side lately?"

"He's been doing that for the past few days," Jordan said.

Vicki nodded. She'd noticed it Tuesday night. She couldn't believe she hadn't picked up on that.

"They're prone to ear infections at this age," the doctor said. "I'm going to give you some drops. They won't be easy to administer, especially to a baby Mason's age. One of you will probably have to hold him down while the other inserts the drops, but it should all clear up in a few days."

"So that's it?" Jordan asked.

"That's it." The doctor nodded. "It looks as if those teeth will break through any day now. He'll be back to normal soon."

"Thank you," Jordan said. Vicki detected the faint catch in his voice and her heart swelled with empathy. The minute the doctor vacated the room, Jordan slumped back against the exam table, his entire body sagging with relief.

"Jordan, he's okay," she said in a soft voice.

He blew out a weary breath and ran both palms down his face.

"This is never going to get easier, is it?" Vicki saw

his throat move as he tried to swallow. "When he was eight months old he rolled off the bed and hit the back of his head on the hardwood floor. I rushed him to the E.R. Nothing came of it, just a little bump that went down in a couple of days." He looked over at her, his eyes filled with worry and pain. "I thought I was going to die when that happened. I felt the same way tonight." He shook his head. "I'm never going to not worry about the next time he bumps his head, or gets an ear infection, or any of that stuff, will I? This will never get easier."

"It won't," she said in a hushed tone. "But he's worth it."

"Yes, he is." Jordan looked down at the baby, who was now sleeping in Vicki's arms. "There is nothing in my world worth more than him."

Her heart pinched at the love in his voice. What she wouldn't give to become a part of that world, a world where Jordan and Mason were both a part of her everyday existence.

The old Vicki wouldn't dare to dream of it. As for this new version of herself that was slowly starting to emerge, the fantasy didn't seem out of reach.

Once in the car, Jordan slid into the driver's seat, but he didn't turn over the ignition. His hands gripping the steering wheel, he released another of those exhausted breaths and let his head fall forward.

"He's okay, Jordan," Vicki said.

He raised his head and aimed his eyes at the brick urgent-care building. In a voice that was terribly soft and filled with emotion, he said, "Thank you for being here with me, Vicki."

"You're welcome," she answered, her voice equally soft.

"I've never been a fan of the double standard that

says that women should be the automatic caregivers. If Allison had even bothered to ask for custody, I would have fought her on it. Being a single father isn't easy, but I know I'm the better parent." His eyes closed briefly. "But on a night like tonight, I'm grateful that I didn't have to go through this alone."

Vicki reached over and put a comforting hand on his arm. "You're an amazing father, Jordan, and despite what you may think, you didn't need me here tonight. You would have done just fine on your own."

Finally, he looked over at her, his eyes teeming with gratitude and something else, something that warmed every inch of her skin.

"I'm happy I didn't have to," he said.

Vicki didn't know how much time passed as they continued to stare into each other's eyes. It wasn't until Mason let out a loud yawn from the backseat that they snapped out of their daze.

"I guess that's our cue." Jordan chuckled as he started the car, but before backing out of the parking space, he turned to her and said, "You wouldn't let me take you out to dinner to thank you for babysitting Tuesday night, but this time I insist."

"We can't go to dinner, Jordan. You need to get Mason home and in bed."

"I know. I was thinking something more along the lines of takeout. Between the tree shopping and the trip to urgent care, I'm starving."

"I haven't eaten anything since noon," she said, making a point of looking at the time illuminated on the dash. It was after eight o'clock.

"Since noon?" Jordan put the car in Reverse. "It's no longer a question. You, Ms. Ahlfors, are joining me for dinner."

* * *

Jordan stared at the tapered candles in the kitchen drawer, debating whether or not to take them out. Who would have thought candles could be such a big damn deal?

But they were a big deal. Candles made all the difference. Candles turned a casual meal shared between two friends into a cozy dinner shared between two people who wanted to be *more* than friends.

Was he ready to become more than just Vicki's friend?

He took out the candles.

He found a couple of Waterford crystal candleholders in the closet that housed most of his and Allison's wedding gifts. They had been married long enough to keep the gifts without feeling beholden to send them back, but not long enough to unpack at least half of the stuff they'd received.

He ran across the wedding china and considered setting the table with it, but then thought better of it. He would not subject Vicki to eating on dishes meant for Allison. He would give that china to Goodwill the first chance he got.

Jordan was setting a match to the second candlewick when Vicki emerged from the back of the house where she'd just tucked Mason into his bed.

"Is he asleep?" he asked.

"He is," she said, a surprised smile slowly stretching across her face as her eyes darted from the candles to the wine chilling in the electronic wine chiller. "I checked his temperature again and his fever is already going down."

"Hopefully he'll sleep through the night," Jordan said. He snatched the baby monitor from the counter. "But just in case he wakes up…"

She walked over to the table and trailed her finger along the rim of one of the wineglasses. "This is…nice," she finished. "Very nice."

He lifted the bottle of wine from the ice. "Are you okay with Riesling? I like my wine on the sweet side."

"Sure." Her eyes followed him as he rounded the table.

"What?" Jordan asked.

She motioned to the setup. "This is just a little more… involved than I was expecting."

He paused in the middle of pouring his wine. "Look, Vicki, if it makes you uncomfortable, you can just consider this a thank-you for being there for me tonight."

There was a questioning lift to her brow. "Is there another way to consider it?"

Time stretched between them as they stared at each other across the brief expanse of the table separating them.

Jordan measured his words before speaking. "For me, this is more than just a thank-you," he said. "I've known you for years, Vicki, but I don't *know* you."

"We ran in different circles," she pointed out. "It's not all that surprising that we've never really gotten the chance to know each other."

"How do you feel about changing that?"

The words came out on a deep, husky whisper. Jordan's chest tightened as he awaited her answer. He couldn't deny the significance of it. Her answer would tell him whether or not she was willing to give this thing he felt growing between them a chance to blossom, or if it would dwindle and die.

After several long moments passed, Vicki finally said, "I'd like that."

The relief that tore through his body was strong enough to bring Jordan to his knees.

One corner of his mouth edged up slightly. "So would I," he answered.

Once seated at the table, Jordan dished up steaming noodles and chicken satay from takeout containers. Suddenly realizing how famished they both were now that the intensity of the urgent-care visit had worn off, they dived into their meal. As tasty as the Thai food was, it was the conversation, and particularly Vicki's musical laugh, that Jordan found himself enjoying the most.

In fact, they both laughed so hard that they had to remind themselves to quiet down lest they wake Mason. Vicki told him stories of some of the antics she, his sister and Janelle had pulled back in college, some so devious that Jordan teasingly threatened to tell all of their parents, even though years had passed since the pranks. He found himself wiping tears from the corner of his eyes several times.

He stopped Vicki in the middle of the story she was currently telling.

"Wait a minute." He held both hands up. "First, who came up with the idea to put pepper in the basketball team's jockstraps, and second, how in the hell did you all pull it off?"

"It was Sandra's idea, but I'm the one who got us into the locker room. My chemistry partner was a kinesiology major, so she had access to the locker room as part of her work study."

"I never would have thought you could be so Machiavellian."

Vicki mimicked his previous pose, her palms facing him. "Keep in mind that I was always roped in. They were never my ideas."

"Doesn't seem as if you regret it," he said.

A wry grin curled the edges of her sensual lips and she shook her head. "No, I don't. Those were some really good times." She took a sip of wine and asked, "How about you? Any regrets?"

Jordan laughed, but this time it didn't hold much humor. "If I had to go through the list, we'd be here until New Year's."

"It can't be that bad," she said.

"It's definitely not all good. Alienating lifelong family friends, marrying the most selfish woman in the world." He shook his head. "I have to remind myself not to say things like that. I don't want to get in the habit of talking bad about Allison, especially in front of Mason."

"Even though she deserves it?"

"She does, but I have to own up to the part I played, too," he said. Jordan moved his plate to the side and put both elbows on the table. He studied Vicki over his folded hands, contemplating whether or not he wanted to get into the morass of misery and frustration that he always fell into when he thought about his ex-wife. He decided that he didn't.

He reached across the table and took her hand. Running his thumb back and forth over her smooth skin, he said, "I don't want to spoil our dinner with talk of Allison. This is supposed to be about us, remember?"

"And exactly what are we, Jordan?" She slipped her hand away. She matched his recent pose, placing her elbows on the table and folding her hands. She rested her chin on her clasped fingers, her face serene.

"What's behind the candles and wine? What were you hoping to accomplish when you set them out?"

"What do you mean?"

"I mean I'm not interested in playing games," she

said. She gestured to the table. "The wine, the candles...
What are we doing here?"

It was not as if he hadn't expected the question. It
was not as if she didn't have the right to ask it. But Jordan had been dreading it all the same. Because he'd
asked himself the same question, and he still didn't
have an answer.

"I'll be honest with you, Vicki. I've been asking
myself that same question since you left here Tuesday night." He ran a hand down his face, then held that
hand out to her in a silent plea. "It's been a long time
since I've been with a woman, longer than I've ever
gone. I wasn't sure if that's what was fueling my attraction to you."

Her composure slipped for a moment, her eyes growing wide with outrage. "Excuse me—"

Jordan cut her off. "I know I sound like a jerk, and
maybe I am."

"Maybe?"

He reached across the table and took her hand. "The
more I thought about it, the more I realized that needing
a woman had nothing to do with why I'm attracted to
you. Shit," he cursed. "That sounds just as insulting."

Vicki nodded. "Yes, it does."

He squeezed her hand slightly. "Look, Vicki, I like
you. I like you a lot. You're great with Mason—"

"So is that what's behind this? Are you wining
and dining me in hopes that I'll become a convenient
babysitter?"

"No!" Damn, he was blowing this. Big-time. "I don't
have to tell you that Mason is the most important thing
to me," he continued. "Seeing how much you care for
him makes a difference, a huge difference. But when I
look at you, a caregiver for Mason is not the first thing

that comes to mind. I like you because you're sweet, and beautiful, and you have this dry sense of humor that comes out at the weirdest times. You're intelligent and giving and you have one of the kindest hearts I know."

Not letting go of her hand, he stood and walked over to her. Taking both of her hands in his, he lifted her from the chair and wrapped an arm around her waist, settling his hand lightly at the small of her back.

"The wine? The candles? They're here because I wanted to make tonight special. Not just to thank you for helping me pick out a Christmas tree or because you held my hand while Mason was being examined."

He looked into her eyes. "I wanted tonight to be special because for the first time in a very long time I'm sharing a nice meal and good conversation with a woman I find unbelievably attractive and funny and interesting. You deserve wine and candles and everything else that makes a first date special."

Her brow arched. "So this is our first date?"

"I'm not sure it started out that way, but that's how I would like to end it." He trailed the backs of his fingers along her cheek. "You said you didn't want casual. I wasn't sure if I was ready for anything more. But I am."

"Are you sure about that?"

He nodded. "Casual doesn't have the appeal it once did. I'm ready for something serious. Are you willing to take this to the next level, Vicki?"

It felt as if hours went by as she studied him, but it was only a few moments. Finally, she said, "So how do you usually end your first dates?"

The smile that stretched across Jordan's face was so wide it made his cheeks hurt.

"It's been a while since I had a first date," he said. "But if I remember correctly, it usually ends like this."

He dipped his head and connected his lips to hers. The minute their mouths touched, Jordan was bowled over by the sheer softness of her lips, the sweetness of her delectable kiss. It had been so damn long since he'd experienced anything even remotely close to the feelings racing through his blood that he had to slow himself down before he attacked her mouth with the passion suddenly coursing through his veins.

Jordan closed his eyes and focused on the breathtaking gentleness of her mouth as it became pliant underneath his kiss. He brought his hands up to her neck, his fingertips brushing lightly along her jawline as he held her steady. He hesitated for only a moment before he swept his tongue along the seam of her lips and had his first taste of what awaited him.

A groan tore from his throat the moment Vicki parted her lips and let him inside. She was sweet and spicy and warm and undeniably sexy. His tongue moved with determination, sweeping inside the silky depths of her hot mouth, claiming it, relishing in it. His fingers inched up to the back of her head and held her head steady while he explored every delectable crevice.

As one hand cradled her head, the other traveled down her spine, stopping in the shallow dip at the small of her back before lowering a few inches farther. Jordan smoothed his hand over the curve of her firm backside before cupping it and pulling her to him. He held her close, his body instantly hardening at the feel of her stomach against his groin.

As his tongue plunged in and out of her mouth, his thickening erection mimicked the motion.

God, how he'd missed this.

But it was so much more than just missing the feel of

a woman against him. It was *this* woman that he wanted, *this* woman that made it special.

"Damn, Vicki," Jordan whispered against her lips before swooping his hands underneath her thighs and lifting her up and onto the table. Her legs clamped his hips, and their kiss grew hungry.

Hands, lips and tongues all collided in the hottest, most intense kiss Jordan had ever experienced. His body ached with the need to tear her clothes off and take her right there on the table. The urge to bury himself inside her obliterated all thought from his brain. He couldn't think of anything else he wanted more.

And that was when he realized he needed to stop.

This was moving too fast.

Yet with every soft moan that climbed up from Vicki's throat, Jordan felt that it wasn't moving fast enough. She wanted this as badly as he did. They were two adults. They were attracted to each other. And, most of all, they both wanted it.

But he'd learned the last time that being swept away in a fit of passion carried a price.

Jordan moved back a step, his breaths coming out so harsh it hurt his chest.

"That was...um... That was way more than just a thank-you," he said.

Vicki's dazed expression, her full, just-kissed lips, had him on the verge of finishing what he'd just started.

"I agree." She nodded. "This is probably far enough for a first date."

Jordan stared into her eyes. "I'm not stopping on the second date, Vicki."

"Good," she said. "Because I won't let you."

# Chapter 7

Vicki measured out the dark blue ribbon that was threaded with gold, hoping she would have enough on the spool. Just under ten feet. She was cutting it close, but this was a last-minute job, so the customer would have to take what she gave them.

They'd better be happy she'd taken on the job at all.

Vicki could hardly choke back her resentment. The accounting firm of Crawford and Daniels had been one of her best clients. She'd provided weekly fresh flower arrangements for their lobby and decorated for several holidays throughout the year. Until last year, when they'd decided to go with a bigger florist in a neighboring town.

When the accounting firm's office manager had called that morning, frantic because their new florist had dropped the ball and wouldn't have their offices decorated in time for their yearly Christmas-card photo, a tiny, evil part of Vicki had wanted to turn down the job. It would have served them right for dropping her.

But she was a professional. And despite how satisfying it would have felt to be petty—and it would have felt *damn* satisfying, she had no doubt about it—she just couldn't sink that low.

They would pay where it counted, because, even though she didn't need the money, Vicki had tacked on a 30 percent upcharge for the rush job. She felt justified. She'd never given them reason to be dissatisfied with her work.

In a way, she owed Crawford and Daniels a huge thanks. The idea to enter a float in this year's Christmas parade had been planted after they'd pulled their business. She'd decided then to show them—to show everyone—just what Petals was made of.

"Thank you for your disloyalty, Crawford and Daniels," Vicki said into the empty florist shop. "It gave me the kick in the butt I needed."

She nestled intricately painted blue-and-gold ornaments around the gigantic wreath that would hang prominently on the wall at the accounting firm. They were lucky she'd had the pine garland on hand. It was for a Christmas party she'd been hired to decorate for that weekend, which meant she would have to make a special trip to one of her suppliers so she could replace what she'd used. Maybe she should change that upcharge to 35 percent.

Vicki heard the front door open moments before Sandra and Janelle both walked in.

"Hey," she called. "What are you two doing together? I thought you both had separate meetings."

"With the same couple." Janelle laughed. "The mother of the bride hired Sandra to design the dress and the mother of the groom hired me to coordinate the wedding. We didn't realize it until we all showed up at the restaurant together."

"Well, I hope you both told them which florist would be perfect to design the floral arrangements for the wedding," Vicki said.

"Don't we always?" Sandra said.

"When you have a minute we need to go over the list of floral arrangements we'll need for the Woolcotts' Kwanzaa celebration," Janelle said. "Nancy wants to make sure the centerpieces on the buffet tables are completely different from those on the tables where guests will be eating."

"That's Mom," Sandra said with a laugh. "Makes you wonder why she even hired you if she's going to stick her nose in every little detail."

Janelle waved her off. "I go through this every year with your mother. I know what to expect."

"Speaking of my mother," Sandra said, a sage smile lifting the corners of her lips, "Isaiah and I had her and Dad over for dinner last night and she said Jordan came to see her yesterday."

Vicki cursed her stomach for the flip-flop it did just at the sound of his name.

"Oh?" she said. It was the sorriest excuse for nonchalance she'd ever engaged in.

"Mmm-hmm," Sandra murmured. "She said Jordan could not stop talking about a certain florist. She said you two went tree shopping, then you helped him with Mason's trip to urgent care."

"What happened to the baby?" Janelle asked.

"Teething and an ear infection," Vicki provided without thinking.

"So you *have* been hanging out with my brother," Sandra said with an excited lilt to her voice.

"It isn't that big of a deal," Vicki said.

Although it was. Kind of.

Okay, it was a *really* big deal.

Over the past week she'd seen Jordan every single day. He and Mason had come over to her place for dinner, and on the nights they were not at her house, she was at Jordan's.

When the float builder had delivered the base for her float yesterday, Jordan had dropped what he was doing and had come over to the storage facility she'd rented to house the float while she worked on it. They'd gone over her sketches and talked out the logistics of what she planned to do. It had felt amazing to have him there with her, to see his excitement over her project.

Other things she did with Jordan felt amazing, too.

They had yet to take that next step, but the kisses they'd shared over the past week were hot enough to melt every bit of snow in Wintersage.

Vicki turned her attention to the garland twining up the banister so her friends wouldn't see the blush that was no doubt reddening her cheeks.

"So?" Sandra prompted.

"So what?" Vicki asked.

"So what's going on with you and Jordan? How serious is it?"

"It's nothing serious, Sandra. I babysat Mason and helped Jordan decorate for the holidays." *And nearly died when his hands crept up my stomach and over my breasts when he kissed me goodbye last night.* "Honestly, it's nothing to get worked up about," Vicki reiterated, even as she stood there as "worked up" as she'd ever been.

"Are you kidding me? I think it's great," Sandra squealed. "I told you that Jordan needs to get laid."

"Who said anything about him getting laid?" Vicki asked. Her cheeks were definitely red now. "I'm just helping him out with Mason. That's it."

"Are you sure that's it?" Janelle asked.

"Yes!" *No!* She was doing so much more than just helping him out with Mason. "Goodness, would you two stop it!"

"Okay, okay, we'll leave you alone," Sandra said. "However, let the record show that I have absolutely no problem with whatever it is that's going on between you and Jordan. Allison caused him a lot of heartache. He needs someone in his life who can show him that not every woman is like his ex-wife."

"But Vicki said there's nothing going on between them," Janelle said.

With another of those knowing smiles, Sandra playfully lifted her brows before going upstairs. Janelle started to follow her, but Vicki caught her by the wrist.

She waited for Janelle to look at her before she asked, "If there was anything going on between me and Jordan—not that I'm saying there is, but if there was—would you have a problem with it?"

"Does it even matter?" Janelle asked.

"It does to me," Vicki said.

Janelle's eyes softened with understanding. "I know we all agreed that we would remain neutral as far as the election goes, but I can't say that I'm not at least a little resentful toward Jordan. He's accused my father of cheating. I can't just pretend that I'm okay with that." She hunched her shoulders. "It's difficult, Vicki. My entire family is up in arms over the fact that I'm still coordinating the Woolcotts' Kwanzaa celebration."

"I'm so sorry this is all happening."

Janelle nodded. "I'm sorry Jordan is still petitioning the election results. Every person who adds their name to that online petition is like a slap in the face to my dad."

"Have you looked at it from his perspective? He has—"

"Don't." Janelle put her hands up. "Please don't stand here and try to justify Jordan's actions to me." Janelle blew out a weary breath. "Look, Vicki. Whether or not anything is going on between the two of you, I'll be happy for you, but I don't want to hear about how you think Jordan is right or that I should look at things from his perspective. I just can't."

Vicki nodded. "I understand."

Janelle looked down at her from two steps above and caught her chin in her hand. She smiled, and said, "Your face has had a bit of a glow this past week. If Jordan is the one responsible for it, I am grateful to him for that. You deserve to be happy."

"Thanks," Vicki said.

Janelle's smile dimmed just a bit. "I just want you to think about something."

"What's that?"

"What happens when things get back to normal?"

Vicki frowned. "What do you mean?"

"Once everything with this election is finally put to bed and Jordan returns to work. When Mason's nanny returns. What happens then, Vicki?"

"I don't know why anything has to change."

"What about if Allison comes back wanting to reclaim the little family she left behind?"

Vicki's head reared back. Where had *that* come from?

"Allison hasn't been around in months," Vicki said.

"What makes you think she would return making demands?"

"Stranger things have happened," Janelle said. "And you know what Sandra used to say about her. That Allison was like catnip for Jordan." Janelle raised both palms up. "I'm not trying to influence you one way or another. I just don't want you to get hurt." She patted Vicki's hand, then turned and headed up the stairs.

Vicki remained standing there, Janelle's words playing over and over again in her head. Thinking about Allison and the influence she'd once had over Jordan caused a bunch of Vicki's old insecurities to resurface.

Even more upsetting, she couldn't help but think that Janelle had brought up Jordan's ex-wife for exactly that reason.

She hated the thought of there being a rift between her and Janelle because of her blossoming relationship with Jordan, but she also had to respect his stance, as well. Jordan understood the strain his petitioning of the election results was putting on everyone, but he believed he was right. Who was she to tell him to disregard his belief just because it made things awkward for her?

Vicki just hoped she didn't have to choose between the man she could easily see herself falling in love with and one of her best friends.

"Mr. Jackson, I don't want you to think that just because the election is still up in the air that it will affect the promises we made to Mass Mentors one way or the other. No matter what the final results turn out to be, I will make sure the program is fully funded."

Even if he had to fund it himself, Jordan thought. His emails and texts to Oliver Windom regarding the program had gone unanswered, but Jordan wasn't allowing that to deter him.

"I made a pledge to your program, and I'm going to make good on it," he told the program director before ending the call.

Releasing an aggravated sigh, Jordan tossed the phone on his desk and ran both palms down his face. It wasn't supposed to turn out this way. According to the schedule he'd laid out in his head, he and the rest of the transition team should be well into preparation for Oliver to take office. Instead, here he was, stuck at home, waiting for even the tiniest bit of evidence from one of the investigators he'd hired to look into the ballot tampering.

As for the candidate himself...

Jordan didn't know what to make of Oliver's actions since the election. For some reason, the man he'd backed and had believed in so strongly was more than willing to roll over and play dead. It frustrated Jordan to no end! Why in the hell was *he* more upset over Oliver's loss than Oliver himself?

Jordan had tried to come at this from every rational standpoint he could, but it just didn't add up. His polling data couldn't have been off by so much. Someone had to have tampered with those ballots.

But what if no one had touched the ballots? What if he *was* wrong?

"It's not as if you've never been wrong before," Jordan said with a cynical, self-deprecating snort.

He swerved his chair around and grinned at his son, who was becoming increasingly frustrated with a wooden block that would not stay where he'd stacked it on top of another block.

Scooting onto the floor, Jordan said, "Mind if Daddy

joins you?" He picked up a block with a green *A* on it, but Mason reached for it.

"Mine," his son said with a frown.

Jordan raised his hands up. "Okay, okay. Looks like we need to have the 'learn how to share' talk when you get a little older."

As if Mason understood him, he picked up a yellow *Y* in his chubby little hand and held it out to Jordan.

"There you go," Jordan said. "You know how to share."

He stared down at his son with wonder, still amazed at how much his perspective had changed in such a short amount of time. It had been a whirlwind these past couple of years. He'd met Allison and had been swept right off his feet, marrying her only six months after they'd met, after she'd gotten pregnant with Mason.

He'd known from the beginning that when it came to children, her feelings were lukewarm at best. Jordan had hoped those feelings would change once Mason was born. He'd expected her to take one look at their son and fall in love, just as he'd done.

He didn't doubt that Allison loved Mason. She was just too selfish to give up her lifestyle in order to raise a child.

"I, on the other hand, can't imagine my life without you," Jordan said, placing Mason in his lap. He kissed Mason's chubby neck, thanking God for blessing him with this unbelievable gift. It was a gift he hadn't known he wanted, a gift that had come to mean everything to him.

Jordan's breath caught in his throat just thinking about the sheer terror that had hit him last week when Mason had spiked that high fever.

It hadn't been all that long ago that the only thing

that concerned him was getting ahead. He'd been on track to rise to the top of his law firm faster than any associate had done in the past. His career had been his only focus.

None of that seemed important anymore.

He recalled his mother's recommendation after he mentioned shortening his leave of absence, and realized she was right. What would he gain by returning to his law firm earlier than necessary? He had more money set aside than he could spend in a lifetime, and he sure as hell didn't need the stress of fourteen-hour workdays.

What he needed was to relish this time with Mason. In the blink of an eye he'd gone from a helpless infant to a fast-moving toddler ready to explore the world. Blink again and Mason would be in kindergarten, then high school, and then before he knew it, Jordan would be watching him move out on his own. He didn't want to miss a minute of the precious time he had with him.

Besides, he'd grown used to working shorter hours since joining Oliver's campaign. Although things had become hectic during the past few weeks of the election, for the most part, Jordan was home by six, as opposed to eight or nine at night. He had time to play with Mason instead of only going into his room and giving him a small kiss, careful not to wake him up. How was he going to go back to that when his housekeeper returned and they all went back to their old routine?

Simple. They weren't going back to the old routine.

Working those crazy hours had been okay when he was single and trying to climb his way to the top, but his priorities had changed. He didn't need the top. He had all he needed right here.

He kissed Mason's head, a gentle smile lifting the

corner of his mouth as he thought about the future that awaited them.

His cell phone rang.

Jordan sat Mason back on the floor with his blocks and picked the phone up on the third ring. He recognized Vicki's number and couldn't help the thread of excitement that coursed through him.

"Hello," he answered.

"Hi," she said. "How is Mason doing?"

"He's just fine as long as no one touches the building blocks his grandma Nancy got for him. He's a bit territorial when it comes to his toys."

Vicki's laughter flittered through the phone line, causing another rush of excitement to skate across Jordan's skin.

"Well, I wasn't sure if you two would be up for it," she continued, "but I was wondering how you would feel about taking Mason to see Bright Nights at Forest Park in Springfield. There's a big Christmas lights display there every year."

"I've heard of it, but I've never been."

"I went a few years ago and it was incredible. I heard they've added even more displays since then. I was hoping to find some inspiration for my float and figured Mason would enjoy all the lights. It's a two-hour drive, though. I wasn't sure if you would be up for it."

Jordan didn't have to think but for a moment.

"We'd love to," he said.

He heard the smile in her voice as she said, "Wonderful. Why don't I pick the two of you up in a half hour?"

"I'll see you then."

Jordan raced to get both himself and Mason ready. He opted to give Mason a quick wipe down with a damp towel instead of a bath. His mother had drilled it into his head not to give him a bath too soon before bringing him out into the cold.

Jordan had just finished packing some toys, animal crackers and juice boxes in a bag when he heard a car pulling up. Excitement shot like a lightning rod through his veins.

Now that he'd decided to fully own this attraction that had been building between him and Vicki, he could barely contain the pleasurable exhilaration that flooded his brain whenever she was around. He'd allowed the turmoil he'd been through in his first marriage to scare him off from getting involved with anyone else, but he was not going to let that happen this time.

Honestly, this was the first time he'd even *wanted* to get involved with someone since Allison left. Who would have ever thought Vicki Ahlfors would be the person to break down the wall he'd erected around his heart? How had he allowed her to fly under his radar for all these years? He felt like a shallow, callous fool for not recognizing just how attracted he was to her.

Jordan considered himself lucky that Vicki had even bothered to give him the time of day. She could have held it against him that he hadn't noticed her until after she'd gone through a complete makeover, but she hadn't.

And *that* was what he was attracted to the most. She was so unbelievably tender and giving, and she had a heart of pure gold. She was more than he probably deserved.

No, she was *definitely* more than he deserved.

"You better not mess this up," Jordan said.

The doorbell rang. He damn near ran at the speed of light to get to it. The moment he opened the door, one thing became crystal clear: there was no way in hell he could ever deny that these feelings were real. Just the sight of her warm smile had his skin tingling and long-dormant areas of his body coming to life.

"Hey there," she greeted with a smile that could make every unpleasant thought in the world melt away.

"Hey," Jordan returned, his body humming with energy now that she was near him again. He leaned over and captured her lips in a kiss so sweet it drew a moan from her. God, she tasted good.

"Well, hello to you, too," Vicki whispered against his mouth.

"You have no idea how much I love doing that."

"Mmm...I don't know about that. I think I have an inkling." That wicked smile tilting up her lips set off way too many naughty thoughts in his brain. A glimmer of shared desire flashed in her brilliant brown eyes before she said, "The feeling is mutual. And as much as I love doing that, I want to do more."

A delicious shudder cascaded down Jordan's spine.

It was obvious what they both wanted. A barrier had been crossed, a step taken. With those few words she'd just spoken, this new relationship they'd found themselves in had just moved to the next level.

"We don't have to see the Christmas lights," Jordan said.

If he called his mother right now she would be here in ten minutes, more than happy to take Mason for the night. He and Vicki could spend the rest of the evening exploring this new step in their relationship.

"Yes, we do have to see the Christmas lights," she said, her smile widening. She reached for Mason, taking him from Jordan's arms. "This little one is going to love them."

Jordan's chin fell to his chest. *So close!* He'd been so damn close to satisfying the fantasies that had overwhelmed him over the past two weeks. Instead, he was off to see Santa.

Jordan groaned. "Just let me grab Mason's bag," he said, sounding like a sulky teenager. He felt like one, too. A sulky, horny teenager who was being denied something he knew they both wanted.

"That's a good daddy," Vicki said. The amusement tinting her voice told Jordan that she was having way too much fun at his expense. "Can you bring a blanket, as well?" she called after him. "It's going to be cold out."

Jordan grabbed a blanket from the hall closet, and then met Vicki at his car. She was already strapping Mason into his car seat.

Jordan was once again struck by how right this all felt. She'd slid into place so seamlessly, as if she'd been a part of his life forever. It felt as if she belonged here, like she was the missing peg that fit so much better than his ex-wife ever had.

Jordan waited for panic to set in just at the thought of the word *wife,* but there was no panic, only a surprising sense of peace. It was crazy. Their relationship wasn't even two weeks old. Sure, he'd known Vicki all his life, but not in *this* way. What business did he have thinking in terms of a wife? Hell, they had yet to do more than kiss. Granted, they'd shared some of the hottest, most intimate kisses he'd ever experienced, but still, that was the furthest they'd gone.

*But they would go further.*

Jordan's hands tightened on the steering wheel.

If he'd read the signs correctly—and he was pretty damn sure he had—they would go a lot further. And soon.

The appendage behind his zipper responded to the

decadent thoughts flooding his brain, setting him up for what was sure to be the most uncomfortable two-hour drive of his life.

Before they even broke past the Wintersage city limits Mason had already fallen asleep.

"The car really is like a sleeping pill for him, isn't it?" Vicki said with a laugh.

"It's my go-to lullaby. Whenever he's having a hard time falling asleep, I strap him in and we take a ride. I should have known it was more than just crabbiness when he didn't go out like a light when we went tree shopping."

"Did you schedule a checkup with the doctor?"

Jordan nodded. "This coming Tuesday. She wants to see if the antibiotics are clearing up the ear infection. Of course, my mom thinks I should take him to a specialist in Boston just in case it's something more serious. She was never this nervous with us kids."

"But this is her grandbaby. I'm sure my mother will be the same way. Of course, at this rate, she doesn't think she'll ever have grandkids."

"You still have plenty of time to make her a grandmother."

Vicki shrugged. "All hope isn't lost, but I'm much closer to thirty than I am to twenty."

"Vicki, you have nothing to worry about. The right man is going to come to his senses and realize you're the perfect woman to share his life with."

The air in the car grew heavy with anticipation, saturated with desire.

"You think so?" she asked in a breathy whisper.

Jordan looked over at her. "He would be a fool not to." He took her hand and brought it up to his lips, kissing the back of it.

"Can I be honest with you?" he asked.

"Always," she said. "I refuse to have it any other way."

He glanced at her again, both surprised and turned on by her direct attitude. She knew what she wanted; it was *such* a freaking turn-on.

God, he wanted her.

Jordan blew out a heavy breath. "This scares the hell out of me, Vicki," he admitted. "I've spent the past year and a half trying to convince myself that feeling this way for a woman again was more trouble than it was worth. But you're proving that to be wrong. Every minute I'm with you, you chip away at the wall I built, and it scares me."

"You have nothing to fear, Jordan. I'm not your ex-wife. I'm nothing like her."

"I know you're not." He squeezed her hand. "You're so different that it makes me question just how I could have ever been attracted to two women who are the polar opposite of each other."

"Did you come up with an answer?" she asked.

"Yes," he said. "I discovered that substance is so much sexier than style. Not saying that you don't have style," he quickly interjected. "You're gorgeous, Vicki. And it has nothing to do with your hair or makeup or any of that other stuff. What makes you gorgeous, what makes you the sexiest woman I've ever met, is that beautiful heart of yours."

She leaned over the center console and kissed his cheek.

"Thank you for saying that," she said. Entwining her arm with his, she rested her head against his shoulder and, with a touch of playfulness in her voice, said, "But you don't mind the new wardrobe, do you? I treated myself to a nightgown that I'm pretty sure you would appreciate."

Jordan groaned so loudly he was sure he'd wake up Mason. "Please tell me I'll get to see it soon."

She looked up at him and grinned. "Seeing as I bought it yesterday with the sole purpose of seeing your face when I put it on, I would say that's a yes."

"Thank God," Jordan breathed. He put a bit more pressure on the accelerator. "Let's get through these damn lights so we can get back home."

## Chapter 8

Vicki spent the remainder of the drive to Springfield trying to talk herself out of telling Jordan to find the nearest U-turn so they could return to Wintersage. Now that they both knew what would happen when they got back home tonight, the desire to get there was more than she could stand.

However, all thoughts of rushing through their evening vanished the moment they arrived and Mason caught his first glance at the brilliant display of Christmas lights. The wonder in his wide brown eyes—eyes that looked so much like his father's—wrapped a ribbon of warmth around Vicki's heart. His little mouth formed a perfect O as they drove underneath the arched lit sign welcoming them to the annual Bright Nights at Forest Park holiday display.

As they pulled up to the attendant to buy tickets, they discovered that instead of driving through in their own vehicle, for a small fee they could take a horse-drawn carriage ride through a portion of the display.

"It's pretty cold out here. You want to?" Jordan asked.

"Absolutely," Vicki said. "We have a blanket, remember?"

"Is that why you told me to bring the blanket? You'd already planned this?"

"No, but I'll take credit for it anyway," she said with a cheeky wink.

After parking, she suggested that Jordan take Mason into the gift shop while she scheduled the carriage ride. She spotted them at the huge display of stuffed snowmen and reindeer.

Sidling up next to Jordan, she said, "The next carriage leaves in fifteen minutes."

"Uh-oh," Jordan said. "This one can do some damage in fifteen minutes. He already wants everything he sees."

"Me and him both," Vicki said as she browsed the shelves. She found several items for her float—a wooden train set that she could put under the tree with the American version of Santa Claus, and several angels that would look perfect with the Papa Noël from France.

"These are gorgeous," she said, picking up a set of jewel-toned wineglass charms.

"Check out the monogrammed ones." Jordan nodded to a nearby shelf.

"Oh, I have to get these for Sandra and Janelle," she said. "They're perfect stocking stuffers."

By the time she'd finished shopping, Jordan had to run back to the car to deposit their packages, which numbered too many to take on the carriage ride. Vicki had opted for a private carriage to take them through the winding tour instead of the shared one.

The horse hoofs clopped along the roadway as they passed under the arching lights of Seuss Land, which brought the stories of Dr. Seuss alive through Christmas lights. Vicki couldn't contain her laughter as Mason's eyes grew wide as saucers. He squealed with delight, reaching out and trying to touch Horton the Elephant from the beloved *Horton Hears A Who!* book.

"Please tell me you have all of Dr. Seuss's books and that you read to him every night," Vicki said to Jordan.

"I don't have them all, but you can bet I'll have the entire collection ordered by the weekend."

Mason's chubby finger remained in a pointing position as he oohed and aahed over *The Cat in the Hat* and *How the Grinch Stole Christmas!* done up in thousands of twinkling lights. The tour continued through the Garden of Peace, with its dozens of flowering blooms and angel wings. Vicki nearly gave herself whiplash looking from side to side at the gorgeous display.

She turned at the sound of Jordan's low chuckle.

"What's so funny?" she asked.

"You," he said, amusement coloring his voice. "You're as enthralled as Mason."

She felt her cheeks heat. "I can't help it," she admitted. "It's just so amazing to see what they've created with Christmas lights."

"You can create something just as beautiful with flowers," he said. "I've seen you do it before."

"So you don't think I'm wasting my time with this float?"

"Who said you're wasting your time?"

She shrugged. "My family. My father and brothers,

in particular, but even my mom to a certain extent. They think I'm going to make a fool of myself."

"Did they actually say that to you?"

"Not in so many words, but when I told my father and brothers about it over Sunday dinner this past weekend, they did everything they could to discourage me. I told my mom about it first, just to gauge her reaction, and she basically said the same thing. They think I'm going to be humiliated."

"Vicki, you have as good of a chance of winning that float competition as anyone else. No, you have an even better chance, because you want it more." He took her hand and gave it an affirming squeeze. "Forget what your family thinks. Don't allow it to cross your mind again. You're going to kick ass in that float competition."

"Thank you," she said, a gentle smile touching her lips. She held up a finger. "But don't use that language in front of Mason."

"Can I do this in front of Mason?" he asked before leaning to the side and capturing her lips in an easy kiss.

Their fingers remained entwined throughout the rest of the tour. The carriage meandered through Jurassic World, with its towering brontosaurus, triceratops and an exploding volcano. After Mason's reaction, it was obvious that a few toy dinosaurs would have to be added to the shopping list.

Once the carriage ride was over, they returned to the car and continued on the driving tour, viewing the Noah's ark display, Peter Pan and Captain Hook in Never Never Land and the charming Victorian Village.

After parking the car once again, they walked through Santa's Magical Forest to Santa's Cottage, where Mason took pictures on Jolly Ol' St. Nick's lap.

Following picture taking, they walked through the rows of trees, their twinkling lights imbuing Forest Park with a magical touch.

"Here we are. The arching reindeer," Jordan said, unfolding the blanket and laying it on the ground.

"What makes the arching reindeer special?" Vicki asked. Before he could answer, a teenager dressed in an elf costume interrupted them. The young boy carried a tray with two steaming paper cups and a basket of chocolate-chip cookies.

"What's this?" Vicki asked.

"I thought it would be nice to sit for a while underneath the stars, both the real ones and the thousands they've put here in the trees," Jordan answered.

Her heart melted at his thoughtfulness.

At the same time, her body hummed with anticipation of what was to come. The heated looks they'd shared across the carriage and Jordan's tender yet sensual little touches throughout the night had turned her body into a throbbing ball of nerves. She needed relief in the form of a release she was more than ready for Jordan to deliver.

Vicki's face heated to unheard-of levels. It felt heretical to have such erotic thoughts while surrounded by the innocent, festive Christmas lights.

The copse of oak trees provided a perfect spot for them to settle with Mason. Jordan lay on his back and held the giggling baby high above him.

"Wow, you're getting heavier every day," Jordan said with a laugh as his elbows started to buckle under Mason's weight.

"He is growing quickly, isn't he?" Vicki agreed. "You'll look at him one day and realize that your baby is gone. He'll reach those terrible twos soon, then the next thing you know it'll be time to start school."

"Don't remind me," Jordan said. "I've already missed so much time with him because of my work schedule." He paused for a moment before continuing, "I'm beginning to rethink my approach to this whole thing."

Vicki tilted her head to the side. "What thing?"

"This. Life. The future." Jordan placed Mason on the blanket between them and set several of the toys he'd bought at the general store in front of him. "A few times a year the partners bring in this consultant to talk about the work/life balance. I've always seen it as a load of crap, because even though they tell you they want all associates to have a healthy balance between work and family, everyone knows that the more time you give to the firm, the quicker you'll rise in the ranks."

His eyes found hers. "I'm not sure rising in the ranks is what I want anymore. I'm starting to learn that there are many definitions of success. Who's to say that raising a healthy, happy son doesn't make me just as successful as bringing in seven figures a year?"

"It's not as if you need the money," Vicki pointed out.

"It's never been about the money. It was always about winning. It's *still* about winning. I just think the prize has changed. I don't want the things I used to want in life. Those things aren't as important to me anymore.

"My mom said something to me the other day and it's been gnawing at my brain ever since. She said that my dad would have given anything to have more time to spend with me and Sandra when we were growing up."

"I'm sure he would have."

"If you'd asked me a few years ago—hell, a few *months* ago—if I felt neglected by my dad, I'd have called you crazy. But the more I think about it, the more

I realize that, in a way, I *did* feel as if Woolcott Industries came before me.

"Damn," he added with a low, self-deprecating chuckle. "Could I be any more of a whiner? It's not as if I have anything to complain about. My parents gave us everything we could have ever asked for."

"Look who you're talking to, Jordan. Do you know how many nights I stayed up past my bedtime, waiting for my dad to come home from the office so I could share the perfect grade I received on a test, or so he could read the remarks my teacher made on my research papers? Even though I knew he would be too tired to really pay attention to it. I started to resent AFM with a passion, yet at the same time I knew that without Ahlfors Financial Management, I wouldn't have the life my dad was working so hard to give us."

He stared at her. "You're right," he said. "I did resent it. Maybe, in a way, I even resented him." Jordan shook his head. "I don't want Mason to grow up resenting me. I don't want him to think that I'm putting anything ahead of him."

"Then don't," she said simply. She pointed to Mason. "That little boy is the center of your world. Do what you have to do to keep him there."

He smiled at her. "Good advice, Ms. Ahlfors. I think you may have missed your calling. Maybe you should have been a life coach, or whatever the heck those people are called."

Vicki laughed. "What do you know about life coaches?"

He rolled his eyes. "Not much, and I'm just fine with that. Allison thought a life coach was the answer to everyone's problems."

Vicki acknowledged the blend of emotions that rioted through her at the mention of his ex-wife. It was insane to feel even a drop of jealousy. Allison wasn't the one here with Jordan tonight. *She* was. Why would she still be jealous of his ex?

Yet even though she knew she would probably regret it, Vicki heard herself ask, "What about Allison? Do you have any contact with her at all?"

"She calls occasionally," Jordan said with a shrug. "As in maybe four times in the past six months. Her excuse is that she's dating some jet-setter and they're always traveling."

"That's no excuse. With all of the technology available these days, she can tell Mason good-night via video every night if she wanted to."

"You hit the nail on the head. She *could* do that if she *wanted* to. She doesn't. Allison's only concern is Allison."

Vicki reached out and covered his shoulder, giving it a gentle squeeze. "I'm sorry she isn't at least there for Mason."

"Allison didn't want to be a mother, I knew that. Hell, I wasn't all that sure I wanted to be a father. I hadn't really thought about it. But when Mason was born—" Jordan shook his head "—he changed everything. From the moment I first heard him cry, I wondered how I'd ever lived my life without him in it."

"You're so lucky to have him," she whispered, looking down at the baby with a wistful smile as he played with the plush toy snowman. She brought her eyes to Jordan's again. "You're lucky to have each other."

"What about you?" he asked. "Do we have you? Because that's what I want, Vicki. I want you in our lives."

That did it. Those few words, spoken in that velvety-soft voice, melted her heart.

"I want to be in your lives," she said. "There are no words to describe how much I want that."

He shook his head again, his eyes filled with wonder. "Why did it take me so long to see how amazing you are?"

"I've been asking myself that question for years," Vicki said with a wry grin. "Don't worry, I won't hold it against you. I'm just relieved you finally came to your senses."

She leaned over and they shared the kind the kiss she would love to come home to every single day for the rest of her life.

They sat underneath the tree's twinkling lights for a while longer. Jordan played catch with Mason, rolling the ball covered with fat snowmen that he'd bought from the gift shop along the blanket. After the temperature dropped to unbearable levels, they finally got into Jordan's car and headed back for Wintersage.

"Thank you for tonight," Vicki said, reaching across the console and covering his arm. "This is my favorite time of the year, and tonight you showed me just why that is."

"Thank you for inviting us to join you," Jordan said. "I haven't taken the time out to enjoy the holidays in years. I'm beginning to see just how special it is. I think this trip to Springfield will become an annual thing."

"I'll mark it in my calendar. If I'm invited, that is?"

He sent her a look that said she knew darn well that she was invited. The thought warmed Vicki from the inside out.

The snow began to fall in earnest as they drove along Interstate 291.

"I thought they said the snow wouldn't be here for

another few hours," Vicki said, pulling out her phone and checking her weather app.

"It definitely wasn't supposed to be this heavy," Jordan pointed out.

Vicki held the phone out to him. "Looks as if the forecast changed in just the past few hours."

By the time they arrived back at his house, the snow wasn't only falling, it was coming down in thick, heavy sheets and was accompanied by swirling wind that made the driving conditions treacherous.

Pulling into the garage, Jordan said, "It's a good thing you're not driving over the bay in this."

"I'm not?"

He glanced at her. "There's only one place you're going tonight. And the quicker I get you there, the more time we'll have."

Despite the excited shiver that ran through her at his words, Vicki couldn't allow him to get away with such arrogance unchecked. She waited until he rounded the car and opened her door, then asked, "So you just went ahead and made that decision all by yourself, huh? You didn't feel the need to consult me on it?"

"No," he answered without hesitation. "I already knew your answer. You've got a new nightgown you want me to see, remember?"

She crossed her arms over her chest as she waited for him to unstrap Mason from his car seat. "What if I decided on the drive back that hot chocolate under the stars is all I'm willing to give tonight? I know you're a Woolcott and all, but even Woolcotts don't get to have their cake and eat it, too."

Hefting the toddler over his shoulder, he turned to her and allowed his eyes to slowly roam the length of her body. "When it comes to what I'm planning to eat tonight, cake isn't on the menu."

Vicki nearly orgasmed then and there.

"Go put the baby to bed," she said, the words coming out in a husky rasp.

She followed Jordan into the house, her skin vibrating with every step she took. The time it took for him to tuck Mason in for the night gave her body the opportunity to cool down. She went into the kitchen and slid a bottle of wine from the rack. She heard Jordan approaching and turned, finding him standing in the entryway.

Vicki held up the bottle of wine.

"I know there's a snowstorm raging like crazy outside, but I have a feeling this wine would taste a whole lot better in front of the fire bowl on your enclosed deck."

Jordan's mouth pulled into a frown. "You want wine? Right now?"

"We both know what's going to happen tonight, but I expect to be romanced just a little before I give up my goodies." She nodded toward the glass-fronted cabinets that held the stemware. "Grab a couple of glasses, will you?"

"Really, Vicki? You want wine? Now?"

A smile curled up the edges of her lips. "Stop being so shortsighted, Jordan. Think of all the fun things we can do with the wine."

His eyes grew wide with interest, and he headed straight for the cabinet.

Ten minutes later, Vicki grinned as she eyed Jordan's surly expression from where she sat with one leg curled underneath her. The other was stretched out on the cushioned love seat glider, her toes inches from his thigh. His frown had appeared from the moment she poured the wine into the glasses instead of the more... interesting place he'd suggested.

Vicki moved her foot another few inches toward him.

He eyed her over the rim of his wineglass. "If that foot gets any closer I'm going to think you're trying to tell me something."

"I was trying to be discreet," she said. "But apparently you don't take hints very well. I guess I just have to come out and ask for a foot rub."

He set his glass next to the baby monitor on the side table and pulled her foot onto his lap.

Vicki let her head fall back as she released a soft moan. "That feels like heaven," she murmured. "Being on my feet at Petals all day is agony."

"You can't put flower arrangements together while sitting down?"

Vicki sent him a horrified look. "No," she said. "I need to walk around so I can see what I'm creating from all sides. There's no such thing as sitting for a florist. It's murder on my feet."

"On your hands, too," Jordan said. "I didn't want to mention it earlier, but when I took your hand in the car I think I nearly cut myself. Those things are brutal."

Vicki burst out laughing. "Yes, I definitely have florist's hands." She held them up in front of her, observing the many nicks and scratches.

"Be proud of them," Jordan said. "They're your own personal battle scars. You earned them." He took her hands in his and placed light kisses upon each and every mark.

A ribbon of desire curled through her belly. He was so tender, so unbelievably attuned to what her body craved.

"Vicki?" Jordan's deep, velvety voice grazed over her skin like a silky promise.

"Yes?"

"Are you done torturing me?"

She looked up at him and grinned. "I've discovered that this new Vicki has a bit of a vindictive streak. I thought I'd pay you back for taking so long to realize that I've been here waiting for you, wanting you, all these years."

Jordan's head fell forward. "So you're not done torturing me."

"But I realize that the longer I make you wait, that's the longer I have to wait, too. And I don't want to wait any longer."

His head popped up. His eyes grew intense, their smoldering depths lighting her skin on fire as he stared into her eyes.

"I'm sorry it took me so damn long to see what's been standing right in front of me," he said. "But I'm about to make up for it."

Jordan's gaze remained locked with hers as he lifted the back of her head and lowered his mouth to hers. The first touch of his soft lips sent Vicki's head on a cosmic spin. It was sweet and sexy and everything she'd expected of him.

Yet so much more.

His kiss was mesmerizing—the taste, the texture, the urgency... It all combined to drive her mad with desire she could feel down to her toes. With gentle insistence, he applied pressure to her lips, his delicious mouth urging her to join him. She did, wrapping one hand around his neck and caressing the back of his head. She licked at the seam of his lips until his mouth opened, then she thrust her tongue inside, claiming his mouth as if it had always belonged to her.

Jordan released a low groan as he turned her more fully toward him and cradled her against his body. He began a slow journey down her sides until he cradled her waist. As his mouth continued to ply her with strong yet gentle kisses, his fingers inched their way along her torso, moving gradually up her belly until they neared her breasts.

Vicki stuck her chest out, dying to feel his hands on her, but he held back, his hands stopping just short of the place where she wanted them the most.

"Is this payback?" she panted.

"I just don't want to move too fast."

"You're not moving fast enough." She caught the hem of his sweater and pulled it over his head. Then she trailed her fingers down his muscled chest, her nails leaving faint streaks.

The guttural moan that crawled from Jordan's throat was the very definition of agony.

"Do that again," he said.

"Not until you do it to me," she returned.

Her nipples hardened from mere anticipation, the achy peaks reaching for him, waiting for him to touch her. Jordan pushed her shirt over her head, taking her bra with it and flinging them both to the floor. Vicki climbed on top of him, straddling his lap. She hooked her arms around his neck and tilted her head back as his lips and tongue swept up and down her throat.

"Oh, my God, you taste good," he whispered, his warm breath heating her blood.

The rasp of his tongue against her skin set off a mass of powerful sensations along her nerve endings. He cupped her breasts, his palms squeezing them, massaging them. He rolled her nipples between his fingers, pinching the rock-hard nubs before flicking his thumb across them.

Moisture pooled between her thighs as desire surged throughout her bloodstream. Every fantasy she'd ever held, every night she'd lain in bed, wishing, dreaming, praying that this one day would become her reality... It all coalesced into this delicious, momentous moment in time. It was so beautiful, so incredibly earth-shattering, Vicki wasn't sure she could handle it.

Jordan dipped his head low and lapped at her nipple, and she decided she could handle it just fine.

A moan tore from her throat as he sucked the rigid peak into his mouth. She undulated in his lap, rubbing her swollen sex against his hardening erection.

That was when Vicki decided there were too many layers between them.

She needed him stripped bare, his naked body displayed for only her eyes to see. She tugged at his belt.

"Take this off," she said.

"Soon." He returned his mouth to her breasts. He molded one mound in his palm, cupping the underside, holding it up so that his lips and tongue could have full reign over her nipple.

"Jordan, please," she cried.

Mercifully, he finally decided to put them both out of this sweet misery. He grabbed the condom he'd tucked into his pocket before levering himself up and pulling his pants down his legs as Vicki took hers off, too. Together they quickly rolled the condom over his hard flesh, and then, taking it in his hand, Jordan guided his erection inside of her.

Vicki's entire being seemed to scream with pleasure. The delicious give as her body stretched to receive him made her wetter, hotter, more turned on than she had ever been in her life. She welcomed his hot, solid length into body, sliding slowly along his erection until she was fully impaled.

Jordan dipped his head forward and sucked her breast into his mouth, his teeth nipping and biting, his tongue swirling and lapping at her nipple, before moving over to the other one. Vicki curled her fingers around the top of the love seat and held on tight while she rode his lap. Down she moved, taking his entire length inside of her and rolling her hips before she pulled back up.

She rode him hard and fast, then easy and slow, changing the pace, driving them both wild. The groan that tore from Jordan's throat reverberated around the glass-enclosed room.

"I...I have to," Jordan said seconds before he clamped his hands against her waist and guided her up and down. He pumped his hips in rapid thrusts, pounding inside of her until Vicki exploded in a haze of hot white light.

She fell against him, her breaths coming in short pants.

She'd waited half her life for this. Never had she imagined it would surpass even her wildest fantasies. But it had. *He* had. Jordan Woolcott was everything she'd ever dreamed of and more.

As she lay against his naked chest, Vicki knew with certainty that what she felt was no longer the dreams and fantasies of a lovesick schoolgirl. What she felt was love.

Jordan looked up at the back porch's ceiling, staring blindly as the thick snowflakes continued to shuttle down the slanted glass. He ran his fingers lazily up and down Vicki's back, trailing lightly along her smooth, moist skin. He could spend the next week in this very spot, with her naked body spread out on top of his.

Yet even as he luxuriated in having her here with him, something uncomfortable pulled in Jordan's gut.

Was he moving too fast?

Vicki and Allison could not be more different, but Jordan couldn't deny that this scenario felt like déjà vu. He'd been swept away by Allison, caught up in a whirlwind romance that had him married and expecting a baby all within a few months.

With Vicki it hadn't even been months, only a few short weeks. And the feelings he'd started to develop for the woman cradled in his arms went so far beyond anything he'd felt for Allison that it wasn't even worth comparing.

Was he setting himself up for another fall?

"No way," Jordan whispered. Vicki would never do to him what Allison had done. Forget the new, sexy hair and makeup. Strip all of that away and she was still Vicki on the inside.

And *that* Vicki was the one he found himself falling in love with.

Jordan's chest tightened at the word, but how could he deny it? He'd been in love before; he understood what that intense, all-consuming feeling felt like.

He was there, neck deep in it. And he didn't want to get out anytime soon.

"You're thinking really hard," Vicki murmured against his chest.

"You're awake," he said.

"Barely," she said before yawning. She twisted so that she could look out the glass walls surrounding the deck. "It's still snowing."

"Hasn't stopped for hours," Jordan said.

She looked up at him from where she lay on his chest. "Have you checked on Mason?"

"Kind of hard to do that with a hundred pounds of satisfied woman draped over me."

"A hundred pounds?" She laughed. "You've already scored, Jordan, there's no need for flattery."

She started to rise, but Jordan clamped his palms on her naked backside and pulled her against him. He grew so hard so damn fast it hurt.

"Where do you think you're going?" he asked.

"To check on the baby."

"He's almost a year and a half, Vicki. He's been sleeping through the night for months." Jordan brought his hand around and slipped it between her legs. "You can stay right here. I'm still trying to atone for my sins, remember?"

He slipped one finger inside of her and quickly added another moving in and out; he nearly came when she began to undulate against him in rhythm to his thrust. Capturing her mouth, Jordan removed his fingers and held his erection steady so that she could glide her body on top of it. Their twin moans of pleasure echoed against the walls as he slid his hard length into her hot body.

They started slow, but Vicki soon quickened the pace, flattening her palms against his chest as she pumped her hips up and down. Her head flew back, exposing her neck and breasts to his lips. Jordan pulled a nipple into his mouth and sucked hard. He couldn't get enough of her, and he didn't want to.

After several long, deep thrusts, he felt her body shudder around him. He followed quickly on the heels of her orgasm, his body jerking with the power of his release.

"My God," Vicki breathed against his chest. "You've totally changed the way I see lawyers."

Jordan's head dropped back with his breathless laugh. "How did you see lawyers?"

"Serious and conservative. Definitely not the kind to let loose in the bedroom the way you do." The edges of her lips tipped up. "You probably felt the same way about me, didn't you?"

"You have been a surprise," he said. "A good one, but a surprise nonetheless."

"What were you thinking about…you know…before?"

"Before what?" he asked.

Her cheeks turned beet-red. It was the most adorable thing he'd ever witnessed, especially when he took into account where they were and what they'd just done. "Come on, Vicki," he encouraged. "I want you to say it."

She rolled her eyes. "Before we made love," she said. "For the second time. I want to know what you were thinking before we made love for the second time."

"I was trying to think of how I could convince you to do it a second time, and then maybe a third."

"You were not," she said with a laugh, pushing up from where she'd been draped on top of him. Jordan instantly missed her weight and warmth.

She grabbed the afghan that he kept on the deck furniture and wrapped it around herself. A tiny part of him died as she covered up her nakedness. If he could, he would keep her naked for the next week.

"Tell me," she said. "What were you thinking?"

He blew out a sigh as he realized that she wasn't about to let this go.

"I was thinking of how fast this is all moving." He paused for a moment before continuing, "And of how it all turned out the last time I allowed things to move so quickly with a woman."

In a soft, slightly accusatory voice, Vicki said, "You're still comparing me to her."

"It's hard not to make comparisons," Jordan said. "She was my last serious relationship." He moved over to her and pulled her onto his lap. He didn't miss the way she stiffened against him. "But also know that things are different with you, Vicki. Because *you're* different." Jordan pressed a kiss to her bare shoulder. "I can't help this fear. It's been a part of me since Allison walked out, but I'm determined to fight through it, because you're worth it."

"*We're* worth it," she said. "I don't care what it takes, I'm going to prove to you that I'm better than Allison."

"You don't have to prove anything to me. These issues I have over what happened with Allison are just that—they're *my* issues. I don't want you to feel that you need to compete with my ex-wife. You've already won that battle." He paused for a moment before continuing, "I'm going to admit something that I've been too ashamed to admit to anyone."

Several moments crept by before Vicki prompted him. "What is it?" she asked.

In a voice that was barely a whisper, Jordan said, "I don't think I ever really loved her. I was enamored with her, some might even say enthralled, but if Allison had not gotten pregnant with Mason, I doubt our relationship would have lasted more than a couple of months." Jordan shook his head. "When I think of my parents' long, loving marriage, I feel ashamed that I made such a mockery of the institution by marrying a woman I wasn't in love with."

"You thought you were doing the right thing. Giving Mason a two-parent home."

"And just look how that turned out. I probably scarred him for life."

Her expression softened. She cupped his jaw in her palm. "To quote the great Dr. Seuss, 'Oh, the things you can find if you don't stay behind.' The mistakes you made with Allison, the hurt she caused you, it's in your past, Jordan. Leave it all behind and look toward the future."

"I'm going to try my best to take that advice," he said. He pulled her more firmly against him. "Who would have thought Dr. Seuss would come to the rescue yet again tonight?"

"You'd better pay attention to those books when you read to Mason. Dr. Seuss was filled with those little nuggets of wisdom. Whenever things start to get overwhelming, I read it and remember that I'm continually striving to make my business the best that it can become."

Jordan trailed his finger along her temple and down her cheek. "You're amazing, you know that? You have the ability to change my entire perspective with just a few words. I don't know if I can ever find a way to thank you for everything you've done, Vicki."

A wicked smile lifted the corner of her mouth. "If you think long and hard enough—" she wiggled on his lap "—I'm sure you can come up with something."

Jordan barked out a laugh. He pressed a swift kiss to her lips. "I think I may have found it," he said as he flipped her onto her back and inched his mouth down her body. "Give me just a second. I'll show you."

## Chapter 9

"You mind sharing whatever it is that put that smile on your face?"

Vicki jumped to attention at her mother's question. She knew the heat creeping up her face was turning her fair skin red, but how in the heck was she supposed to prevent that when thoughts of the night she'd spent in Jordan's arms invaded her mind every waking minute?

"I'm not sure it's something a mother would be all that comfortable hearing from her daughter," Vicki replied.

Christine Ahlfors's eyes narrowed as a smile drew across her lips. "Who is he?" her mother asked.

"Just because I'm smiling a little more than usual today, you automatically assume there's a man behind it?"

"Yes," her mother stated. "Now, tell me who he is?"

"How many centerpieces will you need for the senior citizens' Christmas luncheon?" Vicki asked.

"Don't even try changing the subject on me," her mother said.

Vicki arranged the poinsettia in the brass pot and set it in the center of the table in her mother's informal dining room.

"Vicki!" Her mother screeched.

She whipped around. "What?"

"Tell me who he is," she practically whined.

With a sigh, Vicki finally relented. "Jordan Woolcott."

She watched as her mother's mouth formed a perfect O. He eyes grew just as round. "Really," she said. "After all these years."

It was Vicki's turn to stand with her mouth agape. "Was it that obvious?"

"Honey, I'm your mother. Do you really believe I could miss those longing looks you would send Jordan's way whenever he was around? I'm just happy he finally caught a clue." Her mouth curved with a coy grin. "As far as catches go, he's a good one."

"He has some issues," she said.

"The election?"

"And the ex-wife."

"Ah, yes." Her brows arched. "She is a bit of baggage, but she hasn't really been around, though, has she?"

"No, but she left her mark on Jordan," Vicki said. She fingered the poinsettia's silky petal. "To say he's gun-shy about trusting another woman is an understatement."

"He just needs a good woman to show him the right way. At least he's finally opened his eyes to the possibilities. I'm grateful for that."

"So am I," Vicki said with a grin. She kissed her mother's cheek. "I have to go. I've got several arrangements to complete for the Williamses' holiday party and a lot of work to get done on the float. The kids have been working on it everyday, but I need to be there to make sure it's all going according to plan."

Her mother caught her by the wrist. "Vicki, you know it's not too late to pull out of this float competition, don't you?"

Vicki's heart deflated. "Really?" she asked. "Are we back to this? What is it, Mom? Are you afraid that I'm going to embarrass the family or something?"

"Of course not," her mother said. "I just don't want you to be hurt if this doesn't turn out the way you think it will."

"Oh, so you think I'm going to come in last place? Is that it?"

"Vicki, you know that's not the case." The sting of her mother's chastising tone was softened by the gentle smile on her face, but it didn't do much to assuage the disappointment Vicki felt at the realization that her mother still didn't believe in her. Would her family ever take her seriously?

"I have to go. I'll see you later," she said, giving her mother a kiss on the cheek.

Three hours later, Vicki began to wonder if there wasn't something to her mother's concerns. As she stared at the planks of particleboard littering the ground around the base of the float, Vicki had to stop herself from crying.

"Are you okay?" Jasper Saunders, one of the high school students she mentored through Mass Mentors, asked.

"No," Vicki answered. "This is not good."

"It's just a setback, Ms. Vicki. They can probably cut you more particleboard in a day."

She looked over at Jasper and smiled at his attempt to make her feel better. "What have I told you about calling me Ms. Vicki?" she asked. "It makes me feel older than I really am."

He grinned. "Sorry." He hitched a thumb at the door. "Since we can't do any more on the float today, do you mind if I go? A few of us are heading to the mall to celebrate being off for winter break."

"Sure," Vicki said. "Have fun. I'll text you when I get the new particleboards."

Once she was sure Jasper had left the building, Vicki thought long and hard about indulging in a much-needed cry. But she wasn't going to do that. This was a setback—a big one, but not insurmountable.

She unrolled the float's design plans and cursed. She acknowledged that she was the one who'd made the mistake in the calculations. The particleboards she'd had custom cut for her float were short by several inches.

"A math whiz, you are not," Vicki said.

If she had the pieces shipped to her, it would cost her another two days that she couldn't spare. She would have to drive down to the lumberyard in Cambridge where she'd ordered them and hope that they could cut her all new boards today.

"You can still do this," Vicki said. But she was not relying on her own math skills to get it done this time.

It was a good thing she was dating a self-proclaimed math nerd.

If anything could brighten her sullen mood, it was thoughts of Jordan. She took out her phone and explained her dilemma to him. Twenty minutes later, Vicki heard his car pulling up.

"Where's Mason?" she asked, immediately noticing that he didn't have the toddler in tow.

"Grandma Nancy insisted on taking him to Boston to see some ice-skating show at TD Garden arena."

"Oh, I saw the commercial for that. He's going to love it."

"He loves being spoiled by his grandmother, and she loves spoiling him. It's a win-win." He motioned to the float. "What's going on here?"

"I'm in over my head," Vicki admitted. She explained the mishap with her measurements. "I called the lumberyard while you were driving over and they said if I emailed the correct measurements they could have new boards cut by this afternoon, which makes me the luckiest girl in the world. But it still sets me back by at least a day. It's time I can't afford to lose, but there's nothing I can do about it."

Jordan covered her shoulders with his palms and pulled her toward him, placing a gentle kiss on her forehead. "You've got this," he said. "Don't worry about it. We'll make up whatever time you lost today."

There he went again, making her heart melt. Vicki found herself falling more and more in love with him every day, and this was just one of the reasons why. He always knew the exact thing to say to set her mind at ease.

Jordan pulled out a tape measure and started assessing the dimensions of the float base. Vicki typed the numbers he called out into her phone and emailed them to the lumberyard.

"See how easy that was?" he said.

"Painless," she said. "Now to get down to Cambridge before the lumberyard closes for the day."

"Do you want some company on the drive?"

"You have time to drive down to Cambridge with me?"

"I'll make the time," Jordan said, pulling her in for another kiss, this one leaving her knees weak.

They drove to Cambridge together and picked up the newly cut boards for her float, but instead of returning to Wintersage, Jordan took her on the Jordan Woolcott personal tour of the town where he'd gone to both college and law school. They visited several of his old haunts. Vicki laughed until her sides hurt as he regaled her with stories of his days as a hotheaded law student who thought he knew everything.

"I've been put in my place by quite a few professors in this town." He palmed the massive burger he'd ordered at Doyle's, a historic pub in Jamaica Plain, just south of Cambridge.

"I can totally see you as a know-it-all," she said.

"Thanks," he said with a sarcastic grunt as he bit into the burger.

Vicki reached across the table and patted his arm. "That's okay. You're reformed."

"You may be the only person who thinks so." He laughed, wiping the corners of his mouth. "I consider myself a work in progress."

"I'm sure if any of your old professors saw you now, they would be extremely proud."

With a grin, he threw the words she'd used the other night back at her. "You've already scored, Ms. Ahlfors, no need for such flattery."

By the time they arrived back in Wintersage, Nancy and Mason had returned from their outing. Vicki couldn't help but feel a bit self-conscious as she entered the house she'd spent untold hours in as a teen, when she and Janelle would come over for sleepovers. It felt different being here as a guest of Jordan's instead of Sandra's.

The moment she entered the house, Nancy's face lit up.

"Well, hello," she said, taking Vicki by the hands. "You look fabulous, honey. I meant to tell you at Sandra's wedding just how much I love the new haircut. It accentuates those cheekbones that I've always been so jealous of."

"Thank you," Vicki said. She'd always adored Nancy.

Jordan's mother's brows arched as she looked from Vicki to Jordan. "So," she said, leaving the word hanging.

"Very subtle," Jordan said.

"I was trying to be," Nancy said. "Did I succeed?"

"No." He kissed her on the cheek. "How did Mason enjoy the ice-skating show?"

"He loved it." She pointed a finger between Jordan and Vicki. "Someone needs to tell me right now how long this has been going on. And, if I may be so bold, tell me exactly *what* is going on."

Jordan barked out a laugh. "Aren't you just dying to know?"

"Jordan!"

"Thanks for taking Mason on his outing today," he said. "We'll see you later."

Nancy followed them to the door. "Vicki, you're reasonable. I just want to know how serious things are between you two."

"We're leaving, Mom," Jordan called as he carried Mason outside.

Vicki turned to her. "I'll explain everything when we meet to discuss the final plans for the Kwanzaa celebration," Vicki said.

Nancy grabbed both of her hands and squeezed them, letting out an excited squeal. "I don't know who finally knocked some sense into his head, but it's about time it happened. I'm so happy for the two of you."

Vicki stood there with her mouth agape. For years she'd thought she'd done a good job of hiding her feelings, only to find out that both her mother and Nancy had seen it all along.

It was starting to look like the only person who *had* been clueless all this time was Jordan.

"Vicki? Vicki!"

Vicki's head shot up. She looked across the table to find her brother Terrance staring at her, his expression a mixture of annoyance and concern. Of her three brothers, she had been closest to Terrance, but probably because he was the closest to her in age. Vicki never quite knew if it was by design or not, but their parents managed to space their four children out equally, having them all two years apart.

Spence, the eldest at thirty-four, was two years older than Jacob, who was two years older than Terrance. Being the only girl and the baby had not been easy for Vicki. She was convinced her intimidating older brothers were the reason she hadn't asked out on more dates in high school.

"What is it, Terrance?" she asked, breaking off a small piece of the grilled salmon her mother had served for Sunday dinner. Even though all four of the Ahlfors children were no longer living in the family home, they all came together for dinner at least twice a month.

As usual, talk about Ahlfors Financial Management had dominated much of the conversation. Her father's company had recently scored a big client; it was as if Christmas had come early for the men at the table. Vicki had allowed her mind to drift as her father and brothers strategized how best to capitalize on this boon to the business. Apparently she'd tuned them out to the point that she hadn't heard Terrance calling her name.

"I asked how things were coming along with the toy drive?" her brother said. "We'll have to start distributing the toys soon, won't we?"

Her spine went rigid. "Terrance, I told you weeks ago that I wouldn't be able to work on the toy drive this year."

His eyes widened with shock. "You haven't done anything?"

"I told you I couldn't," Vicki stressed. "I've taken on several new clients at Petals and they all had big projects for the holidays."

"Oh, come *on,* Vicki. You've got to be kidding me. All this time I thought you were handling things."

"So there's no toy drive this year?" her father asked. "Isn't the local paper coming to do a story on it?"

Everyone around the table looked to her. Vicki put her hands up. "Don't blame me," she said. "I specifically told you all that I wouldn't be able to take on as many projects this year."

"But the toy drive is your thing," Terrance said.

"No, it's not. It's *your* thing," Vicki countered.

Her brother had first come up with the idea for AFM to sponsor an annual toy drive, but that was where his input ended. For years Vicki had planned and organized the drive, collecting the toys and coordinating with local charities and children's hospitals to see that they were distributed. The only time Terrance made an appearance was when it came time for the local media to do a human-interest story.

And was her name ever mentioned? Of course it wasn't!

It had never been about praise and acclaim for her. The driving force behind why she'd happily coordinated the event in the past was because she loved seeing the kids' faces when the wrapped gifts were placed in their hands. It broke her heart knowing that, for some, it was probably the only gift they would receive for the holidays.

And now some of those kids wouldn't even get *that* gift.

"I can't believe you dropped the ball like this, Vicki," Terrance said.

"*I* dropped the ball?"

"Yes! How will it look when the paper comes and we have to tell them there's no toy drive? You should have—"

"Everybody calm down," Spence interrupted in his calm voice. "This is easily solvable." He pulled his wallet from his pocket and tossed a credit card on her placemat. "Go to the toy store tomorrow and just buy a bunch of toys. See, problem solved."

"It isn't that simple," Vicki said, tossing the credit card back at him. "I don't have time to go toy shopping."

"What else do you have to do with your time?" Jacob said with a snort.

Vicki slammed her fork down. "Kiss my ass, Jacob."

"Vicki!" her mother yelped.

"I'm tired of the way everyone in this family thinks that they have the right to decide how I'm going to spend *my* time."

"I understand that you're upset," her mother said, "but can you please watch your language at the dinner table?"

Vicki huffed out a humorless laugh. "Seriously? With all that's been said in the past ten minutes, my saying *ass* is what bothers you?"

"There's no need for the sarcasm," her father said.

"I agree with Vicki," Terrance said. "If Mom's going to point out something, she should point out her daughter's selfishness."

"Selfishness!" Vicki saw red. She stared her brother down. "For the past five years you've strutted around this town accepting praise for that toy drive when you know damn well you don't lift a finger to put it on. If this toy drive really mattered to you, you would have started looking for an alternative from the moment I told you I couldn't do it."

"I'm busy."

"And I'm not?"

Terrance rolled his eyes. "Here we go again with the hardworking florist. Remind me again how much time it takes to shave thorns off rose stems."

Vicki put her hands up. "I'm done. I don't need this." She pushed away from the table and tossed her cloth napkin over her barely touched food.

"Vicki, please sit down," her mother begged.

"So I can be subjected to this? I don't think so. Besides, I have work to do," she said. "Unlike *some* people, as a small-business owner I don't have the luxury of taking the weekends off."

The last thing Vicki observed as she stormed out of the dining room was how much all the men in her family resembled each other when all their mouths were left hanging wide-open.

Without much thought to where she was going, she got behind the wheel of her car and headed below the bay, driving straight to Jordan's. She didn't even think to call to see if he was at home. It didn't matter at this point. If he was not there, she would wait in his driveway until he arrived. She needed to see him. She craved his steadiness right now. She needed someone who was willing to take care of *her* for a change.

Jordan was in his front yard when she pulled up to the house. A trio of wired lit reindeers now decorated the lawn.

A huge smile broke out over his face the moment he saw her, and just like that, everything in Vicki's world seemed right again. She got out of the car and ran right into his arms, leaning her head against his chest and wrapping her arms around him.

"Hey," he said, smoothing a hand down her back. "What's going on?"

"I just need you to hold me." She wiped her eyes on his soft lamb's-wool jacket. They stood there for several moments, quietly holding on to each other.

"You have new holiday decorations," Vicki remarked.

"I wanted to surprise Mason. He enjoyed the ones at Bright Lights at Forest Park so much."

Vicki looked up at him. "You're such a wonderful father."

He grinned. "I'm trying."

"Where is he?"

"Sandra agreed to watch him. I wanted to get some work done."

"I'm sorry," Vicki said. "I knew I should have called before just coming over."

He reached down and took her chin in his fingers.

"Never feel sorry for coming here. You're always more than welcome to stop by whenever your pretty little heart desires."

He sure knew exactly what to say to make her pretty little heart beat faster.

"Work can wait," Jordan continued. "What do you say we go inside and pop open a bottle of wine, and you can tell me what prompted this particular visit. I can tell that whatever it is, it has you upset."

She nodded and followed him into the house. Ten minutes later, ensconced in the steadiness of his arms as she sat with her back against his chest on the sofa in the great room, Vicki told him about the argument she and her brothers had had over Sunday dinner.

"I'm just fed up with them never taking me seriously, and always taking me for granted. It's at the point where they barely ask anymore. It's just automatically assumed that Vicki will take care of everything."

"You probably don't want to hear this, but it's not entirely their fault," Jordan said. "You share some of the blame here."

She looked up at him over her shoulder. "Excuse me?"

"Besides now, of all those times they demanded you take care of something, how many of those times did you tell them no?" he asked. "Especially when you knew you didn't have the time?"

"That's not fair. I've always gone out of my way to *make* the time."

"That's my point," Jordan said. "Face it, Vicki. You've made it too easy for your family. The reason they automatically assume you're going to handle everything is because you always do. They don't have to worry that something won't get done because you go out of your way to make sure that everyone else is taken care of."

"You say that as if there's something wrong with being helpful."

"That's not what I'm saying at all." He turned her around and wrapped his arms around her, settling his hands at the small of her back. "What I'm saying is that you need to stop being everything for everybody. I've had to learn that the hard way," he said.

"So you're a pushover, too?" she asked.

He chuckled. "Not exactly."

He motioned for her to scoot to the other side of the sofa. Vicki knew what was coming next. She moved to the other end and placed her feet in his lap. Jordan took her right foot between his hands and began massaging her sole with the pad of his thumbs. She damn near melted all over his sofa.

Vicki was still amazed whenever she took the time to consider how easily they had fallen into this comfortable place. In her previous relationships—not that there had been many—it had taken months to find the same level of familiarity and contentment that had taken her and Jordan only weeks to discover.

"What did you mean when you said you've had to learn your lesson the hard way?" Vicki asked, retrieving the glass of wine from the coffee table.

"My problem is that I have a hard time delegating responsibility," Jordan said. "You know the saying 'if you want something done right, do it yourself'? Well, that's been my motto for way too long. Take the election, for example. I started out as a volunteer on Oliver's team, and then when his campaign manager had to resign, I stepped into that role. I didn't like his pollster's methods, so pretty soon I was doing that job, too."

"The man who wears many hats," she remarked.

"Too many hats," he said. "If it's something I really believe in, I tend to take ownership over it. And when things don't work out to my expectations, I'm extra-hard on myself."

She tilted her head to the side and studied him. "That's why you won't let this election go, isn't it?"

"Probably." He shook his head. "I still don't understand how Oliver could let it go so quickly, though."

"What I don't understand is what it is about Oliver Windom that attracted you to his campaign. Don't get me wrong, he seems like a good guy—at least what I know about him from his campaign appearances during the election—but what made him a better candidate than Darren Howerton in your eyes?"

Jordan's fingers stilled for just a moment before he continued massaging her foot. Thank goodness he hadn't stopped. Vicki would be just fine having him pay such attention to her aching soles for the next hour.

"Oliver seemed different," Jordan began. "He's not the same old politician. He has fresh ideas. He would bring something new to the legislature."

"And you don't think Darren is capable of doing the same?"

"I have nothing against Darren. Our families have known each other for ages. Hell, Darren Jr. and I went through Wintersage Academy together. But Darren Sr. is of the same ilk as the previous state representative."

"So you decided to back Oliver because he was different."

"Actually, one of the driving forces behind why I chose to back Oliver is because he agreed to support Mass Mentors."

"Well, I can't argue with that reasoning. It's such a

special program," Vicki said. "It's been a blessing not only to the kids who are a part of it, but to the businesses that support the program, as well."

"I didn't even know about Mass Mentors until last year when an old college friend asked me to do a job-shadowing thing for a day. He's one of the cofounders."

"Really?" she asked, her brows arching in surprise.

Jordan nodded. "Instead of continuing on to law school, he started Mass Mentors to expose underprivileged youth to opportunities beyond what they would find in their neighborhoods. How could I not get behind something like that?" He put a hand to his chest. "I know my family has been blessed. It was never a question of whether or not I would go to college, or how it would be paid for when I got there. Some of these kids have the brightest minds I've ever seen, Vicki. They just have never had anyone to show them their full potential."

"You don't have to convince me of the merits of Mass Mentors. I've seen how it has changed lives. And, unlike yours, my family wasn't always in this position, Jordan. Remember, I didn't move to Wintersage Academy until my sophomore year, after AFM finally took off. If my father had not busted his butt to build that company, I could have been one of those kids in the Mass Mentors program."

"You do understand," he said, sliding his hand up her pants leg and caressing her calf.

"Yes. It's an important part of the community. Just think of how great it would be if it were in more places in Massachusetts."

"That's just it. One of the items on Oliver's agenda once he got to the state legislature was to work for funding for the program so that it could be launched statewide. *That's* the reason I worked so hard to get him elected."

Vicki reached over and stilled his hand. She waited until Jordan looked up at her. "What makes you think Darren wouldn't work just as hard to get the program funded?"

His forehead creased in a frown, as if the thought had never occurred to him.

"God, I'm stupid," Jordan said. He exhaled an anguished sigh. "I became so hung up on finding the discrepancy to prove that my polling was right that I forgot what was really important. The goal should be to make sure Mass Mentors gets funded, no matter who is in the state representative seat."

"That can still be your goal," Vicki said.

"Except that I've pissed everybody off because I let my own damn ego get in the way."

"Go to the Howertons, Jordan. Talk to Darren about Mass Mentors. Explain what the program is about, and how it played into your decision to support Oliver's candidacy. Darren is a reasonable man."

"Reasonable enough to back a program I support, even though I still have investigators looking into whether or not he stole this election? And what if he did steal it, Vicki? That question hasn't been answered yet."

"Do you really believe that?" she asked softly.

"My gut tells me that I've got those investigators on a fool's errand," he said. "But I still believe in my polling data."

"Then you have to go with what you believe," she said, "or you'll question it forever."

Vicki set her wineglass down and scooted over to him, resting her head on his chest. She could hear his steady heartbeat beneath her ear. As the seconds flowed into minutes, the heartbeats began to thump at a faster pace. His fingers trailed lightly along her cheek, the faint caress seductive in its gentle promise.

"When is Sandra bringing Mason home?" Vicki asked.

Jordan lifted his wrist to check his watch. "Not for another hour."

"Hmm," she murmured. "I know you mentioned that you had work to do, but can you think of anything else you'd like to do with that hour?"

The soft rumble of his laugh reverberated along her skin. He lowered his head and whispered in her ear.

A cluster of wickedly erotic sensations traveled up her spine.

"I think that's the best idea I've heard in a long time," she said as she wrapped her arms around his neck and lost herself in his kiss.

# Chapter 10

Jordan picked up a package of baby spinach and tossed it into the shopping cart. The "homemade" dinner he was planning to prepare tonight for Vicki consisted of prepackaged salad, canned vegetables and a frozen lasagna. He gave himself a fifty/fifty shot at not messing it up.

He never claimed to be a cook. The closest he usually came to cooking was warming up whatever leftover takeout was in his fridge. If his housekeeper, Laurie, were to see him in an actual grocery store, she would probably fall away in a dead faint. But he wanted to do something special for Vicki, even if his brand of "special" came already prepared. He decided to stop in at the bakery section to pick up an extrarich chocolate cake to make up for the lackluster meal.

"It's a good thing Vicki likes us for more than Daddy's cooking, huh, buddy?" he said to Mason, who was devouring the animal crackers Jordan had yet to pay for.

After adding a tomato, red onion and cucumber to his basket, he left the produce section in search of salad dressing. He had no idea if there was any at the house. The take-out restaurants always included more than enough with his order.

As he rounded the endcap stacked high with the canned artichoke hearts that had won the privilege of being this week's special hot-item buy, Jordan nearly ran his cart right into Darren Howerton, Jr.

The tension that stretched between them as they stared at each other in the middle of the grocery store was palpable.

"Jordan," Darren Jr. said, his voice stoic.

"How's it going, Darren?" Jordan replied, trying to infuse a bit of lightness into his reply. It wasn't all that long ago that he and the man standing before him had been friends. Jordan didn't want to lose that friendship over this election.

"How do you think it's going, Jordan?"

"I know things are a little awkward—"

"A *little* awkward?" Darren Jr. asked. "You accused my dad of cheating. I'd say things are more than just a *little* awkward."

"I never explicitly said it was Darren Sr. who cheated," Jordan said in his defense. "I said it was the campaign."

"Ah, yes. The campaign. My *father's* campaign. You can play whatever semantics game you want to, Jordan, but actions speak louder than words, and the minute you started up that petition you made your thoughts about my father's integrity loud and clear."

"Explain how he managed to win," Jordan challenged. "Oliver was leading in the polls up until election day. Explain to me how your father pulled off that defeat."

"I don't have to explain anything," Darren Jr. said, his mouth twisting with derision. "The election results speak for themselves."

Jordan released a weary breath. He was suddenly very tired.

"Look, Darren, despite what you may think, I didn't start that petition without giving it some serious thought. But something was not right with those election results. I would never have petitioned the outcome if I didn't think there was some credibility to my theory."

"You want to know what I think, Jordan? I think you're full of crap."

With that Darren Jr. turned and walked away, leaving his cart of groceries in the middle of the aisle.

Jordan's head fell forward. It suddenly felt as if the weight of the entire world had climbed onto his shoulders and sat there, weighing him down.

He was no longer convinced that this fight was worth it.

Hell, Oliver refused to take it up, and it was his seat in the state legislature that was on the line. If it wasn't worth it to Oliver to fight, why in the hell was he alienating lifelong friends over this? What did he expect to gain? Was it worth it just to prove that his polling data wasn't faulty? Did any of that even matter anymore?

It was as if Jordan was running on autopilot as he went through the checkout line and drove home. He put the lasagna to bake and the wine to chill, but his mind was occupied with thoughts of his run-in with Darren Jr.

The only bright spot in his gloomy afternoon was Mason's bath time. His son enjoyed himself so much in the tub that Jordan couldn't help but delight in it. But when Vicki arrived not long after he'd dressed Mason in his pajamas, Jordan still hadn't shaken off his moroseness.

"Hey there," Vicki greeted as she entered the house. She lifted Mason from his arms and planted a kiss on his cheek. "How are you two handsome guys doing?" She turned her attention to Jordan and frowned. "Okay, really, how are you doing? You look like someone rolled over your dog, or, in your case, your favorite attaché case."

"Good one," he answered with a wry smile. She always managed to get a laugh out of him.

Motioning her to follow him into the kitchen, he shared his earlier encounter with Darren Jr. in the condiments aisle at the grocery store. While Vicki strapped Mason into his high chair, Jordan retrieved the lasagna from the oven and served them both healthy portions, all with salad and sweet corn. He waited for Vicki to take her seat before pouring them both a glass of wine.

As he mashed up a bit of lasagna noodles on Mason's Thomas the Tank Engine plate, Jordan brought his story to a close with Darren Jr.'s dramatic grocery store exit.

Vicki paused with the fork halfway to her mouth. "He left the shopping cart in the middle of the aisle?"

"Yeah. I was nice enough to return the ice cream to the freezer."

"Wow." She put the fork down and picked up the wine instead. She took a sip, then brought her elbows onto the table and rested her chin on her folded hands. "Now that I think about it, I'm not all that surprised by his reaction, Jordan. You knew you would alienate people when you started that petition."

"Maybe I should just call the whole thing off."

"And you think *that* will help?"

"I can't piss anybody off any more than I already have."

"Really? So you think calling a stop to it now, before bringing the investigation to a conclusion, is going to endear you to anyone?"

"No," he said with a frown.

Vicki reached over and covered his hand with her own. "You demanded a recount because you believed there was an issue with the election. Do you still feel that way?"

"I do," he said. "But the longer this drags on, the worse it's going to get, Vicki."

"The damage is already done, Jordan. Calling a halt to the investigation will only leave you with a bunch of unanswered questions. Whether or not the answer is the one you're expecting, you won't be satisfied until you see this through to the end." She squeezed his hand. "See it to the end."

Jordan tugged her hand to his mouth and placed a gentle kiss in the center of her palm. "You are the personification of the voice of reason, Vicki Ahlfors."

"In the past that trait has led to some unflattering comments, usually by your sister when I've talked her out of doing something outrageous. Today, I take it that my voice of reason is a good thing."

"It's a very good thing," he said.

As he smiled into her eyes, Jordan couldn't help feeling that this was exactly what he wanted his life to be like for the next fifty years. Sitting at the dinner table with Mason and Vicki every night, sharing their day, planning out their future; at the moment, he couldn't think of a single thing he wanted more. Never had a woman fit more perfectly in his world. He wanted her to stay here. Permanently.

He'd always been a man of action. He needed to figure out just what he had to do to make that happen.

"Oooooh. I recognize that glow," Sandra said in a singsongy voice as she leaned against the counter where Vicki was working on the centerpieces for the Woolcotts' Kwanzaa celebration. Sandra rested her chin on her fist, and said, "It's the 'I just got laid' glow."

"Really, Sandra? Must you be so crass?"

"How is that crass? You're the one who's wearing the glow." She picked up a red-and-black Peruvian lily and pointed it at Vicki. "Let the record show that I said weeks ago that this was a good thing. Lord knows Jordan needed it."

Vicki was pretty sure her face was the color of a fire hydrant. If anyone knew how to embarrass her, it was her friend here.

Sandra's cell phone rang, halting her commentary on the positive effects a healthy sex life would bring to both Vicki's and Jordan's lives. When her face immediately beamed, Vicki automatically knew who was on the other end of the line.

Her own cell phone dinged with the arrival of a text message. She snatched the phone from the counter, hoping to see Jordan's name. Instead, it was a message from Angela Darrow, a fellow florist who had a thriving design studio and nursery in North Andover, a town just west of Wintersage. She and Angela were far away enough that they didn't compete for business, but close enough that, if necessary, they could help each other out.

Angela had a huge project—a decorating job for a

wedding with a winter-wonderland theme—and had asked to borrow Vicki's snow machine. In exchange for the machine Vicki had purchased last year when she'd decorated for the homecoming dance at Winter-sage Academy, Angela was going to loan her the five-foot-high cornucopia she had in storage. She had no idea why her friend had a cornucopia that was almost as tall as she was, but it would be the perfect focal point for the Woolcotts' Kwanzaa celebration.

As she headed west to North Andover, Vicki decided to stop in at Jordan's to check in on Mason, who had developed a cold over the past couple of days. When she'd left Jordan's last night, the baby had been so congested she could hear the rattle in his chest with every breath he took.

As she turned into the cul-de-sac where Jordan lived, Vicki spotted an unfamiliar black BMW in the driveway. She slowed her car, but continued toward the house. Vicki's stomach dropped at the sight of the woman standing on the porch with Jordan.

Allison Woolcott.

She slammed on her brakes, not even thinking to look to see if there was a car behind her. Vicki just sat there for several long moments, paralyzed by the scene in front of her. Allison stood mere inches from Jordan, one hand resting on his shoulder. She wore stylish dark blue jeans tucked into calf-length boots, and a shapely white coat that showed off her drop-dead-gorgeous figure.

Every inadequacy Vicki had ever harbored came roaring back. There wasn't a haircut or eye shadow palette in the world that could ever make her measure up to the woman standing on the porch with her hand on Jordan. Some women were born with that amazing beauty and the personality to match. Allison was one of them; Vicki was not.

Janelle's earlier warning came back to haunt her.

*What if Allison decides to come back?*

Jordan's ex had not been around in months. Vicki was certain that she was out of Jordan's and Mason's lives forever. Yet, here she was, looking as if she fit perfectly with Jordan.

Just as she was putting her car into Reverse, Jordan looked her way. Their eyes caught and held through the windshield, but Vicki didn't dare to stay another minute. She didn't want to see guilt or pity or sorrow in his eyes. She didn't want to witness Allison gloating.

Vicki backed into his neighbor's driveway and drove away. She didn't even consider confronting them like some jealous girlfriend, and she damn sure wasn't going to shed a tear over this.

She and Jordan had made no promises to each other. What they had was too new; she wasn't even sure if it could even be classified as a real relationship.

"It sure felt like one," Vicki whispered.

Still, it paled in comparison to what Jordan had with Allison. The two of them had a history—a rocky one, but nevertheless significant. They had been married; they had a *child* together, for goodness' sake.

How could she ever compete with that?

It was simple: she couldn't. She wouldn't even try.

Holding her head up, Vicki didn't bother to so much as glance in her rearview mirror. She continued driving, proud at how she was able to hold her emotions in check.

She stayed in North Andover longer than necessary, helping Angela decorate the reception hall and then treating herself to a nice dinner at a local steak house.

That was right, she could dine alone and be just fine with it.

It was after nine o'clock by the time she drove through the gates of her subdivision. When Vicki pulled up to her house, she spotted Jordan's car in the driveway. Maybe she should drive right past it.

What in the heck was she thinking? This was *her* house.

She pulled up next to his car and took her sweet time gathering her things before opening the door and sliding from behind the steering wheel.

"Let me explain about Allison," Jordan said the moment she got out of the car.

"You don't owe me an explanation, Jordan."

"Apparently, I do, especially since you wouldn't answer my calls or text messages."

Vicki hoisted her purse higher on her shoulder, folded her arms across her chest and leaned back on the driver's-side door.

"Okay," she said. "If you feel you have something to explain, go right ahead."

"I called Allison," he started.

His words slammed into her like a fist to the gut. *He'd* called his ex-wife?

"And she came running back? Just like that?" Vicki asked, proud that she could maintain the air of nonchalance she certainly wasn't feeling at the moment.

"No, she took two weeks before she even responded. I called her because I wanted to talk to her about her family's medical history."

Her spine stiffened. She had not expected to hear that. "Medical history?"

"Yes," Jordan said. "I called her the day after we brought Mason to urgent care. I had to fill out that patient information form and it had all these questions about both our medical histories. I realized then that I didn't know anything about her family's medical history."

He held his hands out, pleading with her to understand.

"Allison and I were together for such a short period of time. We never discussed whether diabetes runs in her family, or if there's a history of high blood pressure, or any of that. I need to know those things for Mason's sake."

"Of course you do," Vicki said. She suddenly felt like the biggest idiot in the world.

"I can only imagine what you thought when you came over and saw us together this afternoon," he continued. "I tried to call and explain, but you wouldn't answer your phone."

"I was an idiot. I'm sorry."

"I think the idiot title belongs to me. I should have told you that I'd called her."

"You don't owe me anything, Jordan. We haven't made any kind of declaration to each other. I'm sorry I made you feel as if you had to give me an explanation. Whether or not you see Allison shouldn't matter one way or the other."

He stared at her for some time before he shook his head and reached over to take her hands in his. "You don't get it, do you?" he asked, rubbing his thumb along the backs of her fingers. "I *want* it to matter, Vicki. I'm making my declaration right now. I want this to mean more."

He took a step forward and brought one hand up, cradling her jaw.

"I'm falling for you so much faster and harder than

I've ever fallen for anyone before. You need to know how much you've come to mean to me."

She tried to speak, but her heart was lodged in her throat.

"I'm in this, Vicki. You've told me what you want, and I'm telling you that I'm *in* this. Are you with me?"

Her head bobbed with her vigorous nod. "Yes," she managed to choke out. "I'm in this with you."

His eyes slid closed as he lowered his forehead to hers. "Thank you," he whispered. "These past few hours of not knowing whether or not I'd completely messed things up with you have been some of the most tortuous of my life." He opened his eyes and peered into hers. "I meant what I said, Vicki. You never have to worry about another woman, especially Allison. I'm with *you*. You're all I need."

His words washed over her like a soothing balm, restoring her confidence after the beating it had taken earlier today.

"I'm sorry I doubted you," she said. "If you follow me inside, I'd like to make it up to you."

His mouth tipped up in a smile. "With pleasure."

## Chapter 11

Vicki could feel the excitement building in her veins as she opened the final box of carnations. The mixture of exhilaration and accomplishment swirling in her belly grew more wonderfully turbulent with each stem she stuck into place. She was so overwhelmed by the time she pinned the final flower to the float that she had to stop herself from bursting into tears.

She'd done it. She'd actually done it.

Petals wasn't a huge floral shop with corporate sponsors and a dozen employees working around the clock, just a one-woman shop with a handful of dedicated teens who believed in the work they were all doing.

At this point she didn't even care if Petals placed in the competition. Just the fact that her float would travel the streets of Wintersage on Saturday was enough for her.

"You lie through your teeth," she whispered to herself, a grin curling up the corners of her mouth.

She wanted to *win*. She'd come this far. Now she wanted it all.

A high-pitched whistle had her spinning around. A huge smile broke across her face when she spotted Jordan standing in the doorway. He started toward her.

"If this float doesn't come in first place this weekend I may just have to launch another investigation into voter fraud."

"I think one investigation is enough," she said, wrapping her arms around his neck and pulling him in close. She gave him a loud smack on the lips, then went in for a deeper kiss. God, she loved kissing him.

"This looks amazing," Jordan said. "You are going to shock your brothers speechless on Saturday."

"If they even bother coming," she said. "I haven't spoken to them since the Sunday dinner when I told them off."

"They'll be there," Jordan said.

"I hope they are," she said. "I can't wait to see their faces when they see my float. And if I win? My gloating will be so obnoxious they won't want to be around me."

His head flew back with his laugh. "There is not an obnoxious bone in your body."

"Just let this float take first place on Saturday. You'll see."

He shook his head, his mouth still twitching with mirth. "So now that the float is finished, is the Woolcotts' Kwanzaa celebration the only thing left on your plate?"

"Yep. I've completed all of the centerpieces. I don't have anything else to do for your parents' party until the morning when we set up."

"So you're free?"

"Until the parade on Saturday," she said, suddenly suspicious of the wicked gleam in his eyes. "Why?"

"Because I just filled your calendar for the next thirty-six hours. We're going to Vermont."

"Vermont? Jordan, I can't go to Vermont."

"You just said you were free until Saturday."

She opened her mouth to speak, but then closed it. He had her there.

"*You* can't go to Vermont," she countered. "You have Mason."

"He's already being spoiled to pieces by Grandma Nancy and Grandpa Stu."

A slow smile spread across Vicki's face. "We're really going to Vermont."

He nodded. "There is a suite at the Equinox Resort in Manchester with our name on it. We leave right now and return to Wintersage tomorrow evening. You'll be back in plenty of time to get a good night's sleep before the parade on Saturday." He leaned in and nipped at the skin just beneath her ear. "And you're going to need it, because you won't be getting any sleep while we're in Vermont."

The spot between her thighs instantly grew damp.

"You are so bad." She cupped his jaw and placed a tender kiss on his lips. "But you're also incredibly sweet."

"I haven't always been this sweet. You're a good influence." He kissed her neck. "Now let's go and get you packed up so we can hit the road."

They quickly made it to her house and in less than an hour were heading northwest on 495. Light snow flurries peppered the windshield as they climbed into the higher elevations of southern Vermont's Green Mountains.

When they pulled up to the luxury resort's grand entrance, Vicki couldn't hold in her gasp. The towering white columns stretching to the stately structure's second floor added such elegance, while the rocking chairs on the promenade that wrapped around the massive exterior created a cozy feel.

A bellman retrieved their bags from the car, and Jordan checked them in while she toured the spacious lobby with its simple yet refined furnishings. Moments later, Jordan claimed her by the hand and guided her to the Green Mountain Suite on the resort's top floor.

He held up his index finger. "One minute," he said, before inserting the key and opening the door just wide enough to peek inside. When he turned to face her, a secretive grin had made its way to his lips.

"After you," he said.

Eyeing him suspiciously, Vicki entered the suite and, once again, was so blown away that she let out a sharp gasp.

Never mind the sheer luxuriousness of the massive space. What truly stole her breath were the dozens of roses and multitude of candles decorating the downstairs room.

"I hope you don't mind that I had to use another florist," Jordan said. "It would have ruined the surprise if I'd ordered the flowers from you."

"I don't mind," she said with a laugh. She turned to him and wrapped her arms around him. "I don't know what to say, Jordan. This is just… It's amazing."

"*You're* amazing," he said before leaning forward and gracing her lips with the sweetest, most decadent kiss. "I want you to forget about everything tonight. The float competition, your family, the business. All of it. I want you to just concentrate on what we have here.

"You've come to mean so much to me, Vicki. I don't know why I've been so blind, but I thank God every day that my eyes have been opened."

Her heart swelled to the point that Vicki thought it would burst clear out of her chest. Wrapping her arms around his neck, she tugged his head toward her and kissed him with all the love filling her soul.

They stumbled into the great room, leaving a trail of clothes in their wake. Within minutes they were both naked and sprawled out on the rug in front of the fireplace.

The blaze turned Jordan's chest a brilliant shade of bronze. As he hovered over her, Vicki relished in the beauty of his fit body. He worked a white-collar job; how he maintained such a fabulous physique was beyond her.

He pulled a condom from the wallet he'd tossed on the sofa. His intense gaze burning with passion, he rolled the latex over his erection, then hooked his arms beneath her knees and pulled her to him. Vicki reached down between them and fisted his erection, rubbing her palm up and down the solid length before guiding him into her body.

Her eyes fell shut and her back bowed off the floor as he filled her. She would never, ever get enough of this feeling, the moment when his welcoming thickness first entered her. Nothing she'd ever experienced in life could match the pleasure she felt when his erection stretched her body to its limits.

As he pumped his hips, Vicki surged with him, the ebb and flow of their bodies creating a beautiful, sensual dance. She settled her palms against his chest, caressing them up and down his glorious skin. The cadence of his heartbeat matched her own, nearly bringing tears to her eyes as she realized the depth of their connection. They were linked together on so many levels, body and soul.

Jordan dipped his head to her neck and glided his tongue down the gentle slope, trailing it along her skin to the shallow valley between her breasts. He traced the underside of each breast before pressing delicate kisses to the tips.

The light teasing was too much for Vicki to withstand. Thrusting her chest out, she cradled his head in her hands and held him to her, pleading with him to relieve the ache his wicked tongue had created.

"Suck them," she breathed. "Please, Jordan."

His deep chuckle reverberated against her skin, but seconds later he put her out of her misery, closing his lips over her left breast. He massaged her right nipple, pinching and plucking it before bringing his mouth over and laving the tip with several long, wet licks. Then he sucked. Hard.

At the same time his hips thrust. Harder.

The sensations collided in her brain, shooting sparks from all of her pleasure centers and turning her entire body into a numbing mass of ecstasy.

Jordan continued his outrageously satisfying assault on her senses. His hips and mouth worked in tandem. The harder he sucked, the deeper his rigid hardness plunged inside her. Vicki didn't know which to focus on, the magic his mouth was creating or the erotic pleasure that hummed throughout her body with every delicious slide of his solid erection.

Just as she felt the climax building in her belly, Jordan quickened his pace, plunging in and out, driving his hips against hers in rapid succession until her entire being seemed to explode into a million pieces.

And still Jordan continued to thrust, his hardness driving deeper and faster until his body stiffened above her and a groan tore from his throat.

He collapsed on top of her, the feel of his delicious weight something to be cherished. Vicki wanted nothing more than to remain in this very spot for the next twenty-four hours.

"Damn, you're good at that," Jordan said between shallow breaths.

"You're not too shabby yourself," she said with a laugh.

He braced his hands on either side of her head and started to push himself up, but Vicki stopped him, clamping her hands on his shoulders and her legs around his waist, holding him to her.

"Where are you going?" she asked.

"I want to salvage the plans I had in place. Believe it or not, my intent was to wine and dine you before we got to this part of the evening."

"I'll bet you're happy I'm easy."

His grin matched hers. "That means that I can expect more of this *after* I properly wine and dine you, right?"

"You can count on that."

It soon became apparent just how much trouble Jordan had gone to in order to wine and dine her. Dressed in plush bathrobes provided by the resort, they settled in for a candlelit dinner at a table overlooking the impeccable gardens and, just beyond them, the majestic mountain range.

After feasting on a superb meal of Maine lobster and mouthwatering filet mignon, they shared a decadent chocolate lava cake from one of her favorite bakeries in Boston. The fact that he'd both remembered her mentioning the cake from a silly conversation they'd had during one of their earlier dates, and gone to the trouble of having it brought from Boston, touched something deep inside of Vicki.

Following dinner, Jordan insisted she sit by the fire and enjoy her second glass of wine while he took care of "something special" upstairs. Several minutes later, he guided her up to the suite's impressive bathroom, with windows overlooking the mountain landscape.

Vicki was wholly overwhelmed by the fantasy he'd created. Dozens of thick pillar candles blazed brilliantly around the bathroom. There were even more roses scattered around, including dozens of petals floating on the surface of the steaming water in the huge sunken tub. Another bottle of wine stood chilling in a wine bucket.

Her hand to her throat, she turned to him and said in a soft voice, "I can't believe this, Jordan. No one has ever done something this remarkable just for me."

He trailed a single finger along her cheek. "I wanted you to feel as special as you really are," he said. "It is nothing less than you deserve."

Vicki's chest tightened with the sweetest ache, and emotion clogged her throat.

God, she loved this man.

It had happened much quicker than she ever thought possible, but in that moment it was impossible to deny it.

She loved him. And she wanted him to know it.

Cradling his jaw in one hand, she rested her forehead against his and stared into his eyes.

"I'm in love with you, Jordan Woolcott. I don't know if that was in your plans. I don't even care if you don't feel the same way yet. But I need you to know that I am in love with you."

"Vicki, how could you ever think that I don't feel

the same way?" he asked. "What do you think this is all about? Just saying the words wasn't enough for me. I wanted to show you how much I love you."

Everything inside of her melted at his achingly sweet words. He drew his lips over hers in a kiss that left her breathless, then stripped her out of her robe and helped her into the perfumed bathwater. Discarding his robe, he climbed in and settled against the rim of the tub. Vicki molded her back to his chest, savoring how good it felt to feel his smooth skin against hers.

Jordan traced dewy circles along her arm, listening as she went through the schedule of events for Saturday.

"Are you nervous about the parade?" he asked.

"A part of me is more than ready for it, but there's still a part that is so afraid that I'm going to make a fool of myself."

"Don't," Jordan said, pressing a kiss to her damp shoulder. "No matter where you place in the competition, you need to remember that you've done something that very few people have the courage to do, Vicki. You put yourself out there."

"You're right," she said. "Just a few months ago, I never would have contemplated doing something like this. I guess it's all a part of the process."

"For growing your business?"

She shook her head. "For finding myself."

She turned and looked up at him. "I've been hiding the real me for so long, Jordan. I've always been so cautious, afraid of what people would say if I stepped out of those tight boundaries that I've always been pressured to remain in. I was too afraid of how my parents and brothers would view me, of what Sandra and Janelle and everyone else who's become accustomed to sweet, sensible Vicki would think if I ventured too far away from this role I've been confined to my entire life."

"So what do you think about the person you've found?"

A small smile tipped up the corner of her lips. "I like her."

"I like her, too," he said. "She's so much stronger than she realizes."

"I'm starting to realize it," she said. "It took me a while, but I now see that winning this float competition was never my real goal. The most important thing in all of this is finally proving to myself that I'm strong enough and capable enough to do whatever I set out to do."

"You amaze me," Jordan said, the reverence in his voice making her skin tingle. "You have nothing to prove, Vicki. You're amazing. That's all there is to it."

She lifted herself slightly so that she could reach his lips, then she settled back against his chest and asked, "What about you?"

"What about me?"

"Are you done proving whatever you set out to prove when you started that petition? Are you ready to accept the results of the election, even if it comes out that you were wrong?"

Jordan exhaled a deep breath. "I don't have much choice, do I?"

"Yes, you do," she said. "You can continue on the way you have for the past month. You can allow it to fester and drive yourself crazy." She looked at him over her shoulder. "Or you can accept it and move on."

Bracing her hands on the edge of the tub, Vicki lifted herself up and turned to face him, straddling his thighs. She cupped his jaw in both hands.

"You said that the most important thing about Oliver Windom's campaign is that he agreed to help Mass Mentors. If you explain to Darren exactly why you supported Oliver and why you are so passionate about the program, he will listen to you."

"You don't think I've burned that bridge?"

"Not only is Darren a sensible man, but he's a *good* man, Jordan. I know you believe that Oliver is a breath of fresh air because he's younger and cut from a different cloth than the older generation, but don't sell Darren short."

"I probably won't do anything until I hear from the investigators that I hired, but you've given me something to think about."

"Good," Vicki said. She settled onto his lap and dipped her head, running her tongue along his moistened neck. "Now let me give you something else to think about."

Vicki hugged her arms across her chest as she tried her hardest to appear cool and collected on the outside. On the inside, she was a ball of chaotic nerves.

When she'd driven up to the staging ground for the parade, stunned was the only way she could describe how she felt as she stared at the elaborate floats. Stunned and overwhelmed. The participants had stepped their games up to a new level this year.

There was a float dedicated to significant milestones in New England's revolutionary history, including the Boston Tea Party and a musket made out of black lilies to signify the famous "shot heard around the world." Another float showcased the eight U.S. presidents born in the New England area. There were several seaside-themed floats, staples in the parade every year.

One of the most elaborate was dedicated to the region's professional football team. For a minute, Vicki feared the team's star quarterback was on the float. Thank goodness that wasn't the case. It would have been the automatic winner by sheer popularity.

Her Christmas from Around the World float wasn't as large as some of the others, and it didn't have the animatronics and other mechanical marvels, but for a one-woman shop, Vicki couldn't help but be proud. As she looked at the excited faces of the kids from Mass Mentors who had put such hard work into the float and who would be riding on it during the parade, she knew that no matter the outcome, every sacrifice she'd made for this competition had been worth it.

"I think you've got this," came a voice from behind her.

She turned to find Jordan and Mason a few feet away.

"Hey there, you two," she said.

The toddler looked as adorable as ever, dressed in black corduroy pants, a white button-down shirt, a red sweater vest and a Santa hat on his head. His father looked downright edible, showing off his casual side in fashionable dark blue jeans, a black cashmere sweater and a black leather jacket.

"You think I have a shot, huh?" Vicki asked, leaning over for a kiss as she took Mason from his arms. "Maybe if this little one here was the grand marshal."

"I can't deny that he would help, but I think you've got this even without this charmer riding shotgun." Jordan trailed a finger along her cheek before capturing her chin in his hand and tipping her head up. "I'm so proud of you. You did an incredible job."

"I had a lot of help from my team."

"But it was your vision, and it is spectacular."

Her heart swelled with gratitude. "Thank you," she said.

The parade coordinator blew a whistle and directed the tractor drivers to line up the floats according to the numbers that had been assigned to them. The parade would start at 2:00 p.m., which meant they had just under an hour to enjoy some of the other festivities of the annual extravaganza.

Vicki and Jordan brought Mason to Santa's Workshop, which was held in the lobby of Town Hall in the middle of the square. Because Mason had already taken pictures with Santa during the Bright Lights at Forest Park tour, they were able to bypass the line of kids waiting to snatch a portrait with St. Nick.

While Vicki helped Mason play some of the games that had been set up for the kids, Jordan ventured out to several of the food vendors, returning with miniature lobster sliders and three gingerbread men for dessert. Vicki took one bite of the sandwich and pushed the rest toward him. She was too nervous to eat.

The minutes ticked by at lightning speed, and sooner than she'd anticipated, she, Mason and Jordan were heading out of Town Hall to stake out their spot on Main Street for the parade.

Despite her anxiety, Vicki still managed to soak in the pure joy of the day. It was cold, but the sky was clear, and the exuberance radiating from the crowds was palpable. She waved at a little girl who was sitting on her father's shoulders, waiting for the parade to start. She remembered doing the same when she was that age. The thought brought a smile to her face.

As they walked in the direction of the Silk Sisters'

yellow Victorian, near where they planned to watch the parade as it rolled down Wintersage's main thoroughfare, Jordan's footsteps slowed. Vicki looked over at him and followed the direction of his eyes.

The Howerton clan stood a few yards away—Darren Jr. and Sr., Janelle and her husband, Ballard.

"Great," Jordan muttered.

Seeing them there only added to Vicki's pending anxiety attack. The float competition was enough to rattle her nerves for the day; she didn't need tension over the election adding to it.

"This doesn't have to be a big deal," she said to Jordan, urging him forward.

As they neared the Howertons, Darren Sr. walked right up to Jordan and put out his hand.

"I want you to know that I don't harbor any hard feelings toward you, son," he said.

Darren Jr. snorted and shook his head. Apparently, he didn't share his father's graciousness.

Jordan accepted Darren Sr.'s outstretched palm. "You know that none of this has been personal, right?"

The older man shrugged. "It's hard not to take it personally, but you did what you thought you had to do. I know for a fact that you haven't found anything untoward with my campaign yet, and I can assure you that you're not going to find anything." A smile came upon his lips. "I don't gloat often, Jordan, but I am looking forward to telling you 'I told you so.'"

With that, Darren Sr. turned and greeted several people who had come to speak to him.

Darren Jr. took his place, stepping up to Jordan and saying, "I won't be satisfied with 'I told you so,'" he said. "When you realize that you were wrong, I expect you to apologize not just to my father, but to his entire campaign, Jordan."

The tension returned with a vengeance as the amity they'd experienced moments ago with Darren Sr.'s diplomatic greeting evaporated. Vicki noticed the muscle in Jordan's cheek jump as he held his face rigid.

"I guess we'll have to wait and see what my investigators find," he said.

"They won't find anything," Darren Jr. bit out through clenched teeth, and then he turned to join Janelle and Ballard, who were standing a few feet away.

Vicki hadn't even realized that the parade had already started. She turned to find the Boston Tea Party float moving its way up Main Street. Her Christmas from Around the World was fifteenth in the line of twenty floats, so between the slowly moving tractors and marching bands, she still had a bit of time before the Petals float would pass.

Vicki stood on her tiptoes, trying to see which float was coming up next. That was when she spotted Terrance and Spence walking toward her. Her parents followed them.

Great. Just what she needed to send her spiraling into a full-blown panic attack.

But then she noticed the smiles on their faces.

"We haven't missed your float, have we?" Her mother greeted her with a hug.

"No," Vicki said. "There are four more floats ahead of it."

"Good," her father said before placing a kiss on her cheek.

She stared at her brothers. "Wait, you two came out here to see my float?" she asked. "You haven't been to the extravaganza in years."

"We came out here to support you," Terrance said.

"Yeah, and that call from Jordan had nothing to do with it," Spence said, cutting his eyes at Jordan. "The threats were totally uncalled-for, dude."

Vicki turned to Jordan, her mouth agape. "You threatened my brothers for me? That's the sweetest thing I've ever heard."

Terrance snorted and hooked a thumb toward them. "These two were made for each other."

Vicki kissed her brother's cheek and said, "Thanks for coming *and* for making the toy drive a success. I heard it went off without a hitch." Then she wrapped her arms around Jordan and Mason. "Thank you," he said.

"This means a lot to you, and so does your family. They needed to be here to show you some support."

She really could not love him any more than she did at this very moment. Jordan gestured toward the street with his chin. "You may want to turn around."

She turned, and there, gliding along the streets of Wintersage for everyone to see, was her labor of love. Her kids from Mass Mentors, who had all chosen to wear costumes mimicking Sinterklaas, the Dutch version of Old St. Nick, started to whoop and holler when they spotted her.

Vicki laughed along with them, wiping tears of mirth and joy from her eyes. Her mother came up to her and wrapped her arms around Vicki's shoulders.

"The float is absolutely gorgeous," Christine Ahlfors said. "I'm sorry I ever doubted you."

"It's okay, Mom," she said, returning the hug.

"I think it's time AFM joins the holiday extravaganza," her father said. "Maybe Petals will work on our float next year."

"I don't think you can afford me," Vicki said teasingly.

Twenty minutes later, they all joined her at the stage where the extravaganza's committee was preparing to announce the winner of the competition. When Petals won third place, a huge roar lifted from her cheering section. Vicki was pretty sure it would take no less than a month before she was able to wipe the smile off her face.

She accepted her white third-place ribbon and walked off the stage. Janelle was waiting for her just to the right of the stairs. She held her arms out.

"Congratulations, honey," she said, squeezing her in a long hug. "I'm so proud of you."

Vicki's throat tightened with emotion. "Thank you."

"Someone else wants to congratulate you, too." Janelle held up her phone and a slightly pixelated image of Sandra appeared. She and Isaiah had been forced to miss the extravaganza due to a meeting with a major furniture retailer in New York who was interested in carrying Swoon Couture Home in their stores.

Sandra squealed with delight and blew kisses, promising to give her a proper congrats when they met at the Quarterdeck Monday night.

The crowds dispersed now that the winners of the float competition had been announced. Vicki and Jordan decided not to return to the spot where they'd watched the parade near the Victorian. She was still stoked after placing in the competition, and she didn't want to spoil it with the strained atmosphere of being around the Howertons.

Instead, they took Mason to see the live reindeer that had been brought in special for the extravaganza, then

Jordan took him on the Polar Express train ride that meandered around the town's main square.

By early evening, Mason was worn-out. He'd fallen asleep with the adorable Santa hat still on his head. Vicki gently pushed his stroller back and forth as she sat on a bench with Jordan, her head resting on his shoulder.

"It turned out to be a pretty good day," Jordan murmured against her temple.

"I can't complain," she said, smiling. Her smile dimmed a smidgeon as she stared out at the children running around the square, playing a game of tag. "I could have done without seeing that confrontation between you and Darren Jr.," she said.

"We all could have done without that," he said. "At this point, I just want this entire thing with the election to come to an end."

"The sooner, the better," Vicki said.

Jordan's phone rang. Vicki moved from where she'd been resting against him so that he could retrieve it from his pocket.

He blew out a breath. "It's my investigator."

Vicki's heart started to pound against the walls of her chest.

Jordan swept his thumb across the touch screen. "What do you have for me, Mike?"

He sat there in silence, just listening for several minutes.

"Are you sure?" he asked in a voice drenched in disbelief.

Vicki's heart started to beat faster. It pounded more erratically as a look of dread claimed Jordan's face.

Finally, in a hoarse voice, Jordan said, "Thanks for your hard work."

"What is it?" she asked the second he ended the call. "Did the investigators find proof of ballot tampering?" Her stomach was a ball of nerves as she waited for his answer.

His throat worked as he swallowed, and then he nodded. "Yes," he said, his voice still raspy. "There's proof of tampering."

Vicki's heart sank. Her eyes fell shut. This was going to kill Janelle.

"But it wasn't Darren's campaign," Jordan continued. Vicki's eyes flew open. "It was Oliver's."

## Chapter 12

Jordan brought the mug of eggnog to his lips but set it back down without taking a sip.

"You don't like it?" Vicki asked.

Jordan looked over to where she sat on the floor, her legs tucked underneath her. She was surrounded by Christmas wrapping paper, ribbon and empty cardboard boxes. She'd spent the hour since they had arrived home from spending Christmas Day at both his and her parents' wrapping the empty boxes so that Mason could unwrap them. It was his son's new favorite pastime.

"There's nothing wrong with the eggnog," Jordan said. "I'm just not in the mood for it."

She frowned. "Jordan, I hate seeing you like this."

"Don't worry about me, Vicki. I'm okay," he told her, even though they both knew it was a lie.

He felt like such a callous ass. Vicki had spent the entire day trying to lift him out of his funky mood, but if the Christmas spirit hadn't gripped him yet, Jordan doubted it would happen at all.

Vicki gracefully rose from the floor and carried the freshly wrapped boxes over to Mason, who was encircled by the crumpled paper and bows from the half dozen boxes he'd just finished unwrapping.

"Prezzie," his son called, excitedly clapping his hands.

Vicki set the boxes before him, then started toward Jordan. She looked divine in her cream-colored silk shirt and matching wool pants. How she'd managed to keep the outfit spotless, even through feeding Mason his Christmas dinner, was beyond comprehension. She was amazing.

She wasn't just amazing, she was more than he deserved, especially with all his brooding. Yet here she was. And not for the first time today it made him feel like the luckiest man in the world.

Jordan held his arm out, inviting her to snuggle up alongside him on the sofa. She joined him, folding her legs underneath her and resting her head on his chest.

"I'm sorry I'm ruining your Christmas," he said, pressing a kiss to the crown of her head.

"Who says you're ruining my Christmas?" She twisted around until she lay across his thighs, and rested her head on the sofa's arm. "You haven't ruined anyone's Christmas, Jordan. I know it's been rough since you discovered the truth about the ballot tampering. It was a shock to your system, one that will definitely take longer than just a couple of days to get over."

She reached up and cupped his jaw. "I don't want all of that election mess to overshadow the things you should be focusing on today. Family. Love. All of us being together." She pointed at Mason. "Just look at your son over there. He is having the time of his life."

Jordan couldn't help but laugh as he observed Mason once again tearing into the wrapped boxes, his two-teeth smile wide as he ripped through the colorful paper. A silver bow clung haphazardly to the side of his head, and another had found a place to rest on his knee.

"That boy is a character, isn't he?" he asked.

"I don't know if I've ever seen someone so happy to receive an empty box on Christmas."

A smile tipped up the corner of his mouth, yet Jordan still couldn't shake the melancholy that continued to grip him. If only he could coax his mind into thinking of something other than the treachery his investigator had uncovered. But betrayal was a hard pill to swallow, and Oliver Windom's perfidy was even harder to take, because Jordan had believed in him so damn much.

At least he now understood why Oliver had been so quick to concede the election, and why he'd been so against Jordan's demands to contest the results. The moment Mike, his investigator, had revealed what he'd found, the pieces had begun to fall into place.

Winning had never been Oliver's endgame. The entire campaign had been a scheme cooked up by Oliver and Morris London, one of the political strategists who had been a part of the campaign before Jordan had climbed aboard. Oliver's entire reason for joining the race for state representative had been to skim money off the top of the campaign finance fund.

They had known that Darren Howerton was a strong candidate who would be tough to beat. Their plan had been to run a race that would gain enough support to attract a significant amount of campaign dollars, but to remain just inadequate enough not to win.

Jordan had put a kink in the chains when he'd joined and quickly taken over as campaign manager. He'd turned a satisfactory campaign into a well-oiled political machine, applying complex polling strategies and raising Oliver's profile among voters. He had no idea he'd been thwarting Oliver's plans to get rich quick by stealing campaign dollars.

After interviewing county election commissioners in several of the districts where Oliver had polled the strongest yet ended up losing on election night, Jordan's investigator had begun to notice a pattern. As he had dug deeper, he'd discovered that in all of those districts a disproportionate number of absentee ballots had mysteriously gone missing.

It turned out that Oliver had paid employees in the county clerk's offices in the districts where he'd had the best polling numbers to destroy absentee ballots in hopes of tipping the odds in Darren Howerton's favor.

Oliver hadn't wanted to serve the people of Massachusetts. He'd only wanted to serve himself. And Jordan had fallen for it hook, line and sinker. For the second time in his life, he'd put his full trust in someone who'd turned out to be the total opposite of the person he'd thought them to be.

Was he fundamentally flawed when it came to judging people?

"Stop thinking so hard," Vicki said.

Jordan stared down at the woman sprawled so invitingly across his lap. She was the one person whose character he would never have to question. She had been a steady rock over these turbulent couple of days, as he'd looked into his investigator's findings to confirm that they were true.

His Christmas had not turned out quite the way he'd

planned, but if there were a Christmas miracle to be had, it would be that Vicki's steadiness would be there to see him through for many more days to come.

"I love you," he said.

With a smile tilting up the corners of her lips, she cupped his jaw and smoothed her thumb back and forth across his cheek. "I will never get tired of hearing you say that."

"Good, because I plan to say it a lot." He stroked her lips with his fingertips. "You mean so much to me, Vicki. You're like a piece of me that I didn't know was missing."

"Thank you for opening your heart enough to let me inside," she whispered.

Jordan dipped his head and captured her lips in a kiss.

"Prezzie!" Mason screamed, thumping an unwrapped cardboard box on the floor.

"Uh-oh." Vicki laughed as she pushed up from Jordan's lap. "Time to feed the beast. You may have to go to the store to get more wrapping paper. We're going to run out soon."

"Check under the tree, toward the back," Jordan said. "I think there may be a gift still there."

"Are you sure?" Vicki said, walking over to the tree and gently moving a couple of ornament-laden branches around.

Jordan's breath began to escalate as he nervously waited for her to find the box.

"You're right," she said, pulling out the flat rectangular box. She brought it over to Mason and stooped down in front of him. "Looks as if we forgot one of your presents from Santa."

Mason grabbed the box from her hand and quickly

started to tear the paper. Jordan's pulse pounded harder with every rip.

"Let me help you with that," Vicki said once all the paper was gone. She lifted the top off the box and pulled out the toddler-size T-shirt. "There you go," she said, handing the shirt to Mason.

"Why don't you read it for him?" Jordan said.

She looked at him with a curious gleam in her eye, then took the shirt and held it out in front of her.

She gasped.

"Jordan," she said. "Is this for real?"

She turned the shirt to him. It read, Will You Marry Us?

Jordan rose from the sofa and walked over to them. He dropped on the floor next to them and took the shirt from her, pulling it over Mason's white undershirt. He turned the baby to face her.

"I figured you wouldn't be able to say no to this face," Jordan said.

Vicki covered her mouth with both hands. Tears began to stream from her eyes. She reached over and wrapped her arms around his neck.

"There is nothing I want more than to marry you." She looked down at Mason. "The both of you. Becoming a part of this family, making you two *my* family, is the greatest gift I could ever hope for."

Exuberant chatter floated around the ballroom where the Woolcotts' Kwanzaa gathering was being held, as guests celebrated the start of the weeklong observance set aside to honor the values of African culture. In keeping with the traditions of the holiday, they feasted on the *mazao,* or crops, of fresh fruit, nuts and an array of harvest vegetables, along with a bounty of fragrant African dishes.

The entire room was awash in red, green and black, with the giant cornucopia Vicki had brought in serving as the focal point. Guests presented gifts to the cornucopia, which would be given out on Imani, the seventh and last day of the celebration.

Vicki felt Jordan's eyes on her as she listened to John Bancroft, a longtime associate of Ahlfors Financial Management, talk about the recent trip he and his wife had taken to Jamaica.

"It sounds heavenly," Vicki said, smiling at the man, who felt it necessary to describe every single detail about the all-inclusive resort where he and his wife had vacationed.

Out of the corner of her eye she noticed Jordan standing several yards away, his intense gaze searing and seductive.

"I would love to hear more about the fake volcano at the hotel's pool, but I see one of the centerpieces has a flower out of place. As the decorator, I just can't have that."

"Of course, of course," the man said.

Vicki quickly made her exit and headed straight to Jordan.

"Having fun?" he asked as he wrapped one arm around her waist and pulled her against him.

Vicki lifted her face to receive his kiss. Keeping her voice low, she whispered, "If you want to go to Jamaica for our honeymoon, I know where you can slide down a fake volcano and into a pool made to look like lava."

"The only thing I plan to slide down on our honeymoon is you," he said against her lips.

The shivers that cascaded along her body had no

business being there in the midst of a ballroom filled with all their family and friends.

"You're trying to get me in trouble, aren't you?" she asked.

"Me? Of course not," he said, the wicked gleam in his eyes belying his words. His expression sobered, and Vicki didn't have to think too long to figure out why.

"Let me guess," she said. "Darren Howerton just walked in."

Upon learning of Oliver Windom's cheating on the evening of the holiday extravaganza, Vicki and Jordan had gone over to the Howertons to break the news to Darren Sr., only to learn that the man had gone down to Boston to spend the holidays. Tonight was the first time they'd seen him since discovering the truth about the election results.

Jordan let out a deep breath. "I don't want to wait another minute to apologize," he said.

Vicki took his hand and squeezed it.

"It takes a man with integrity to admit when he's wrong," she said. "And you have as much integrity as anyone I know."

Jordan's eyes filled with gratitude. He crushed his lips to hers in a swift, sweet kiss. "I love you so much."

"I love you, too," she said against his lips.

Hand in hand, they started for Darren Sr., who was speaking to Jordan's father, Stuart Woolcott. Vicki saw the moment when Darren Jr. spotted them heading for his father. He started walking toward them, as well. They all arrived to the two older gentlemen at the same time.

Jordan cleared his throat to get their attention. Darren Sr. and Stuart both turned.

"I hope you don't mind my interrupting, but I owe

this man an apology," Jordan said. He looked directly into Darren Sr.'s eyes. "By now, I know you've heard the results of the investigation I started. I didn't want to apologize over the phone, because it's something you deserve to hear face-to-face. I am truly sorry for the accusations I made against you and your campaign, Darren. I put my trust and support in the wrong candidate. All I can do is ask that you forgive me."

The older gentlemen stood there for a moment without speaking. Finally, he said, "I want to know why, Jordan. Why did you back Oliver's campaign?"

"I was intrigued by several of his ideas," he began. "But mostly, I agreed with Oliver's support for Mass Mentors, a mentorship program that was started by a former classmate of mine."

As Jordan explained the program to Darren Sr., Vicki stepped in to mention that it was kids from Mass Mentors who'd helped to create her float.

"This sounds like something that should be statewide," Darren Sr. said.

"I think so, too," Jordan agreed. "Oliver pledged to fight for funding for the program. It's desperately needed."

"Supporting our state's underserved youth has always been a priority for me," Darren Sr. said. "You should have come to me with this idea, Jordan. I would have supported it."

"I'm sorry I didn't," he said. "But I'm here to help now. If you'll allow it, I want to work with you on this."

"I would love to have your input," Darren said, clamping Jordan on the shoulder with one hand and offering the other to shake. As the two shook hands, the tension of the past month seemed to melt away.

"I'm proud of you, son," Stuart said, shaking Jordan's hand, as well.

Stuart and Darren Sr. both left to join the others at the head table, leaving Jordan, Vicki and Darren Jr. together. Jordan turned to his former schoolmate and Darren Jr., too, held out his hand.

"I appreciate you doing that," Darren Jr. said.

"When I'm wrong, I say I'm wrong," Jordan replied. "And I was wrong to accuse your father of cheating. I regret that I put my trust in someone as untrustworthy as Oliver Windom. If I'd known the kind of person he was, I would have left his campaign and come to work on Darren's."

"We would have welcomed you," Darren Jr. said with a grin. "It was miraculous to see how quickly you turned Windom's campaign around. It was because of you that he nearly pulled off a win." He shook his head. "I don't know if you would ever consider leaving law, but if you ask me, you've got a career as a political strategist waiting for you."

Jordan chuckled and stuck his hand out again. "I appreciate you saying so."

After a vow to get together over dinner soon to talk about the Mass Mentors program, Vicki and Jordan headed for their table toward the front of the ballroom.

Stuart Woolcott was at the microphone, welcoming everyone to the Woolcotts' annual Kwanzaa gathering. He took a few moments to explain the cultural holiday and the meaning behind the seven principles of Kwanzaa.

"It is befitting that we are all here today with family and friends as we celebrate Umoja, this first day of Kwanzaa. *Umoja* means unity. May we all continue to be united throughout the years to come." He held up his glass and toasted everyone in the room.

Jordan clinked his glass against hers, a secretive smile on his face. Then, tugging her by the hand, he started toward his father.

"Jordan," Vicki said in a loud whisper, but he continued walking.

He stepped up to the microphone his father had just vacated.

"Can I have everyone's attention please?" Jordan spoke into the microphone. "Seeing as we are here celebrating unity tonight, this is probably the most appropriate place for me to do this."

Setting his champagne glass on the table next to them, Jordan got down on one knee.

A collective gasp rent the air.

He pulled a ring box out of the pocket of his tailored tux and looked up at her.

"I asked you last night, but here I am, formally asking in front of all our family and friends. I want to unite my life with yours. I want you to become my wife. Will you marry me, Vicki?"

She nodded, tears streaming down her face. "Yes," Vicki answered. "Yes, I will marry you."

An excited roar sounded around the room.

"I knew it!" Sandra shouted. She ran over to them and gathered Vicki in her arms. "I knew this was going to happen the minute I saw the way Jordan looked at you at my wedding." She kissed both Vicki and Jordan on the cheek. "I am so happy for the both of you, and for Mason, too. He is getting the perfect stepmother."

Vicki's heart swelled. "Thank you," she said.

She turned and accepted hugs from Janelle and then from her parents. Her brothers all teased Jordan good-naturedly before showering Vicki with congratulatory kisses.

When she turned back to Sandra and Janelle, they both wore conspiratorial smiles.

"What?" Vicki asked, unable to squelch her suspicions.

"Give us one minute," Sandra said. "We have a surprise for you."

A few minutes later, she and Janelle returned to the ballroom carrying a flat garment box. They set it on the table before her.

Eyeing them cautiously, Vicki opened the box and gasped.

"What? How?"

It was her mother's wedding gown.

"You mentioned at the Quarterdeck a few months ago that you would love to get married in your mother's gown," Sandra said. "Last week, when I saw the way your eyes lit up just at the mention of Jordan's name, and the way his did the same whenever someone said *your* name, I knew a proposal couldn't be far off."

She took Vicki by the shoulders and brought her in for a hug. Janelle joined them.

"And to think I used to complain about not having sisters," Vicki said.

"So did I." Sandra laughed.

"Me, too," Janelle added.

"I think God knew what He was doing when He brought us all together," Vicki said. "You two will forever be my sisters."

# *Epilogue*

"By the power vested in me by the State of Massachusetts, I now pronounce you Mr. and Mrs. Jordan Woolcott. Sir, you may kiss your lovely bride."

Vicki turned to Jordan and couldn't hold back her wide smile as he leaned in and kissed her. And kissed her. And kissed her.

He kissed her for so long that her father loudly cleared his throat, causing the wedding guests to erupt in laughter.

"Congratulations, Mrs. Woolcott," Jordan said, his grin as wide as hers.

"Congratulations to you, too," she returned.

She kissed him again before they started down the small aisle in the tastefully decorated chapel. They led everyone to the chapel's small gathering hall next door. On the outside it looked like a rustic seaside cottage, but the inside had been made to look like a winter wonderland, with white gossamer draping from the ceilings and sparkling white lights casting an ethereal glow on every surface.

The gathering was small, with only the members of the Woolcott, Ahlfors and Howerton families, along with a few close friends, in attendance. It was exactly what Vicki had envisioned her wedding day to be like, and exactly the man she'd always dreamed she'd marry.

"I have never been happier in my entire life," she said.

"I take that as a challenge," Jordan said, pressing a kiss to her lips. "I plan to spend the rest of my life making you happier than you were the past day."

"I look forward to it," she said.

Sandra and Janelle, who had both stood as attendants, came over to them. Sandra carried Mason, who was dressed in an adorable baby tuxedo.

"Isn't he the *most* cutest baby in the world?" Vicki asked.

"He is," Janelle said. "But I think mine will give him a run for his money."

Sandra and Vicki both looked at her and started screaming, grabbing the attention of everyone in the room. Sandra handed Mason off to Jordan so that she, Vicki and Janelle could join in a group hug.

Jordan laughed at their shenanigans. "I think the Silk Sisters will have to add a baby portion to the business."

"I think that's the perfect idea," Vicki said.

At Janelle's announcement, the mood became even more festive. As the food and drinks flowed, Vicki soaked it all in. At this moment, her life felt complete.

Yet it was just getting started.

"It's time to throw the bouquet," Nancy Woolcott

called, handing Vicki the small bouquet of white calla lilies that had been made specifically for tossing.

Vicki turned her back to the crowd, but not before taking a mental note of where her three brothers stood. Angling her aim, she tossed the bouquet over her shoulder, right at Terrance, Spence and Jacob, making sure there would be more weddings to come in Wintersage.

* * * * *

*Just in time for the holiday season!*

## HOT *Christmas* NIGHTS

**Fan Favorite Authors**
FARRAH ROCHON
TERRA LITTLE
VELVET CARTER

FARRAH ROCHON
TERRA LITTLE
VELVET CARTER

HOT *Christmas* NIGHTS

Raise your temperature
this season with these new
sensual holiday stories...

These new novellas offer perfect holiday reading! Travel to Tuscany, Las Vegas and picturesque Bridgehampton with three couples who are about to experience very merry seduction against the perfect backdrops for everlasting love.

"The heat from the two leads practically sets the pages on fire, but it's the believable dialogue and well-defined characters and storyline that make this novel a must-read."
—*RT Book Reviews* on Farrah Rochon's
*A Forever Kind of Love*

*Available now wherever books are sold!*

**H HARLEQUIN®**
™ www.Harlequin.com

KPHCN1601014R

The first two
stories in the
*Love in the Limelight*
series, where four
unstoppable women
find fame, fortune
and ultimately…
true love.

# LOVE IN THE LIMELIGHT

*New York Times*
bestselling author
## BRENDA JACKSON
&
## A.C. ARTHUR

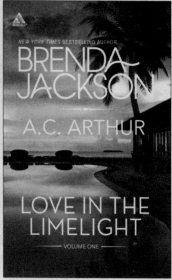

In *Star of His Heart*, Ethan Chambers is Hollywood's most eligible bachelor. But when he meets his costar Rachel Wellesley, he suddenly finds himself thinking twice about staying single.

In *Sing Your Pleasure*, Charlene Quinn has just landed a major contract with L.A.'s hottest record label, working with none other than Akil Hutton. Despite his gruff attitude, she finds herself powerfully attracted to the driven music producer.

*Available now wherever books are sold!*

**HARLEQUIN**®
™ www.Harlequin.com

KPLIM11631014R

# REQUEST YOUR FREE BOOKS!

## 2 FREE NOVELS
## PLUS 2 FREE GIFTS!

KIMANI™
ROMANCE

### Love's ultimate destination!

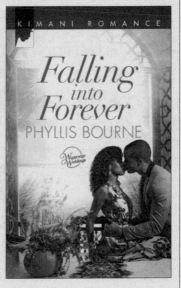

Taf. 20

Trésor                                     profondeur

Tresor de Priam découvert à 8½ mètres de profondeur

Taf. 193

No. 3491 No. 3492 No. 3493 No. 3494 No. 3495 No. 3495 a

No. 3495 a No. 3495 b No. 3495 c No. 3495 e No. 3495 f No. 3495 g

$\frac{39}{100}$ grandeur naturelle

Trésor de Priam
découvert à 8½ mètres de profondeur

Taf: 202

N° 3601

N° 3602

N° 3603

N° 3603 b

903 a

59/100 ... aturelle

Trésor de Triau découvert à 8½ mètres de profondeur

Taf: 192

N: 3484    N: 3485    N: 3486

N: 3487    N: 3488    N: 3489

N: 3490

N: 3490 a    N: 3490 b    N: 3490 c    N: 3490 d

grandeur naturelle

*Le gr...*

$$\frac{59}{100}$$

Taf. 209

Trésor de S.

*bandelette de Tête cony 1 4 m 35 bis*

*iam grandeur*

bandelett[e]
de 55 C[en]
avec 6[...]
auxque[ls]
[s]uspen[...]
idoles [...]
à tête de chou[...]
tout est en or et en gr[os]

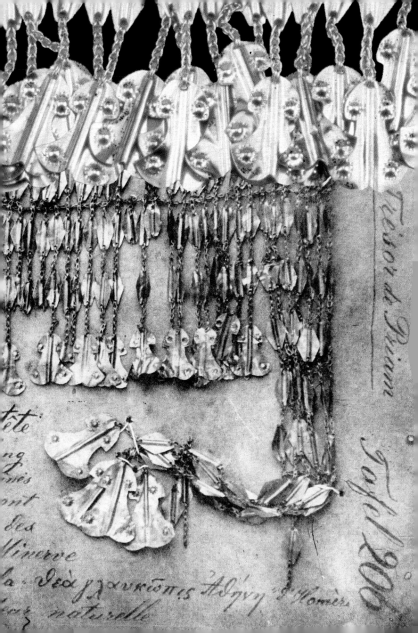

# CONTENTS

# GOLDEN TREASURES OF TROY
## THE DREAM OF
## HEINRICH SCHLIEMANN

Hervé Duchêne

DISCOVERIES

HARRY N. ABRAMS, INC., PUBLISHERS

"He combined business acumen and scientific zeal with the soul of a conquistador, whose personal El Dorado, stubbornly imagined, patiently unearthed, was the unexplored substratum of the Hellenic world. His poverty-stricken youth, his swift rise to fortune, his successful excavations—these are the stuff of fiction. If we did not possess the evidence of this triumph of one man's will, it would be difficult to believe."

Salomon Reinach
*Revue Archéologique,* 1891

## CHAPTER I
# A ROMANTICIZED BEGINNING

The ancient Greek poet Homer (opposite) was Heinrich Schliemann's sole guide on his voyage of exploration. It was Homer's *Iliad* and *Odyssey* that led the amateur archaeologist to the discovery of Troy.

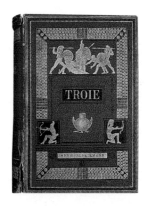

Until quite recently biographers of Heinrich Schliemann (1822–90) faced a straightforward task. They had only to follow the man's own autobiography, scrupulously edited by himself and his wife, Sophia, or his commissioned biography. To illustrate his story they could draw on the personal reminiscences dotted throughout the writings (in many different languages) of the man who discovered Troy. They could mention Schliemann's taste for retsina (a Greek wine), his passion for bathing in the sea, and his habit of sending his shirts from Athens to London for laundering and ironing. They could recall Sophia Schliemann's stomach-aches and the moods of her Greek parents. As for the charges of improper practice, of manipulation, and of mythomania leveled at this controversial figure, they could safely be ignored. They were the

B raving academic scorn, the self-educated Schliemann had become a distinguished archaeologist. He had discovered Troy and Mycenae. His prestige in Europe, and particularly in Britain, was enormous. "I remain the hero of the hour," he wrote to his wife. "I am daily the guest of lords and dukes.… The painter [Sydney] Hodges is hounding me to pose for a life-size portrait [opposite]. He wants to exhibit it at the Royal Academy, and clearly thinks it will be a great feather in his cap to have painted Schliemann."

work of malicious minds, part of the eternal conspiracy of the intellectual establishment against the businessman.

By presenting his own story as a series of adventures, as the victorious struggle of an amateur archaeologist against the academic establishment, Schliemann fostered the birth of a myth: that of a pioneer spirit, a seeker of gold, a hero of fiction. A contemporary of the composer Richard Wagner, he staged his own life as if he were the leading actor in a second version of the *Ring*. Its prelude evokes a humble childhood peopled with legends inspired by German Romanticism and Greco-Roman myth. In three acts played out over the course of sixty-eight years, it portrays the businessman realizing his childhood dream of reawakening the Greece of the great poet Homer, and walking in the steps of the heroes of the epic poems the *Iliad* and *Odyssey*. The first act was apprenticeship. The second led to fortune. The third was inspired excavation.

T he dream of uncovering the ruins of Troy was nurtured in the young Schliemann, so he later wrote, by an image of the city in flames [opposite], which he found in a children's history book. Homer's *Iliad* tells of the Greek siege of the fortified city on the coast of modern-day Turkey. According to Homer the Greeks finally succeeded in penetrating the walls through the "peace offering" of a wooden horse, which was, in fact, filled with Greek warriors.

Schliemann's point of departure was simple—a refusal to read the Homeric poems as mere stories. Flying in the face of accepted opinion, he perceived in them the building blocks of history. He gave them a geographical setting, that of the sites uncovered by excavation: Ithaca, Troy, Mycenae, Tiryns. He thus revived the Aegean world of the second millennium BC and became the father of pre-Hellenic archaeology. It was a field ablaze with objects such as the "Mask of Agamemnon" and the artifacts now collectively known as the "Treasure of Priam"—objects whose very names Schliemann fondly hoped would recall the heroic age.

SAC DE TROYE

## Fame and Controversy

It is now a century since the death of this multilingual, self-taught man, who attained glory as an archaeologist despite the scientific community's hostility. The man and his discoveries still stand center stage. Today, in the age of Indiana Jones, Schliemann is the leading character of a novel, a play, and an opera. Irving Stone described his adventures in *The Greek Treasure*; Bruno Bayen's French play about the archaeologist, *Episodes Ignorés*, was staged in Paris in 1982; and the composer Betsy Jolas has just written an opera based on the play.

The man still stirs controversy. In 1972 the Stasi (the East German secret police) launched an inquiry into an unauthorized lecture delivered by a visiting American professor, William Calder III. Undaunted at the prospect of raising a storm, Calder had been rash enough to make some distinctly iconoclastic remarks as he stood by a Christmas tree in the vicarage where Schliemann was born a century and a half earlier. According to Calder the discoverer of the Homeric world had consistently blurred fact and fiction. The adventurer had lied to achieve his ends. A fog of doubt clouded his greatest successes. This

*Episodes Ignorés* (poster above), a play about Schliemann, ends with the disappearance of Berlin's Trojan collection in 1945. The "Treasure of Priam" eventually resurfaced in Moscow. The first meeting of Russian and German experts took place in 1994, under the aegis of the Pushkin Museum's director Irina Antonova (below).

two-sided view of Schliemann spurred renewed investigation of Berlin's most illustrious honorary citizen. And there remained one final indignity for Schliemann: the Berlin Wall had fallen, and the golden hoard of King Priam —donated by Schliemann in 1881 to the city of Berlin— now emerged from the cellars of Moscow's Pushkin

Schliemann's birthplace (left) in Neubuckow no longer exists. Heinrich did not live there long; in 1823 his father, Ernst Schliemann (below), became pastor of the village of Ankershagen. The black sheep of a long line of Lutheran ministers, Ernst (below) was a man of wavering loyalties and dissolute morals. Inheriting his father's energy, Heinrich felt a mixture of hatred, admiration, and exasperated affection for him. "Just the thought of being such a man's son," he later wrote, "fills me with fury."

Museum, after it had been assumed to have vanished without trace in the turmoil of the Second World War. Mystery thus continues to shroud Schliemann.

## A Grocer's Apprentice

Nothing in his early life suggested that Johann Ludwig Heinrich Julius Schliemann would one day become the founder of pre-Hellenic archaeology. He was born on 6 January 1822 in the little village of Neubuckow in Mecklenburg, northeastern Germany. He spent his first eight years in the even smaller hamlet of Ankershagen, between Waren and Penzlin, where his father, Ernst, was the Lutheran minister. Ernst quickly gained local notoriety by having an affair with one servant girl and marrying another soon after his wife's death from childbirth in March 1831. Learning of the scandal, his superiors forced him to abandon his ministry the following year. In his journal Heinrich describes his father as a mad dog, a tyrant as

cruel as Nero, a violent and hypocritical figure.
Entrusted to the care of his uncle, a pastor at Kalkhorst,
the boy entered the Neustrelitz vocational school in 1833.
Yet after three years he broke off his studies, helping to
support his debt-ridden family as apprentice to a grocer
in Fürstenberg. When not sweeping the store he sold
herring, butter, sugar, alcohol, and cooking oil.

According to Schliemann the only Greek he heard in
those days were a few lines from the *Iliad* recited by a
drunken miller: Homer in exchange for a stiff shot of
whiskey! To hear the *Iliad*, Schliemann willingly dug into
his pockets, pleased with this first business deal. In 1841
he was forced to leave his job at the store when he
injured himself while shifting a heavy barrel. By now he
dreamed of leaving for the New World, but his father
refused to let him go. That summer Heinrich took a
course in accounting at Rostock. Still finding himself
drawn to the high seas, he signed on with a Hamburg
merchant vessel bound for Colombia and Venezuela.
The ship foundered off the Dutch coast, and Heinrich
almost enlisted as a soldier in Amsterdam—before
becoming an office boy in a trading house. But the
young man quickly realized that the world is governed
by those who can manipulate words and figures, and
he was soon expert at juggling them. Exercising his
memory as he ran his errands and spending his leisure
hours learning languages, Schliemann mastered English,

Above: Faces of
the Trojan War
(Agamemnon, Achilles,
Nestor, Odysseus,
Diomedes, Paris, and
Menelaus). According to
Homer it was Paris, son of
King Priam of Troy, who
triggered the Trojan War
by stealing the beautiful
Helen, wife of the Greek
King Menelaus. Below:
The Trojan Aeneas fleeing
his burning city with his
father and his son.

French, Portuguese, and Italian in the space of a few months.

## Childhood Memories

But this picture does not always fit the mythic tone of Schliemann's own published childhood memories, which he slanted to support his later claim of a lifelong archaeological vocation. "The pickax and spade for the excavation of Troy and the royal tombs of Mycenae were already being forged and sharpened," he wrote. Heinrich regaled his six brothers and sisters and his friends Louise and Minna Meinke with tales of hidden treasure. Ankershagen was rich in such fables. A young woman bearing a silver chalice was said to emerge from the village pond at midnight. Not far from there, a robber baron had buried his son in a golden cradle; the whereabouts of his fortune remained a mystery. The family garden was haunted by the ghost of the previous tenant. A medieval castle nearby hid a thousand secrets in its cellars. Heinrich swore he would give Minna, his playmate and sweetheart, a share of his future spoils. True to his word, he remembered her in his will.

His father, who was neither a scientist nor an archaeologist but was passionately fond of ancient history, told his son of the tragic fate of Herculaneum and Pompeii, followed by their miraculous reappearance from beneath volcanic ash under the excavators' picks. The child also learned every exploit of Homer's warriors. One picture in particular spurred him to dream of rediscovering the remains of Troy. "My joy may be imagined, therefore, when I received from him [his father], in 1829, as a Christmas gift, Dr. Georg Ludwig Jerrer's *Universal History*, with an engraving representing Troy in flames, with its huge walls and the Scaean Gate, from which Aeneas is escaping, carrying his father Anchises on his back and holding his son Ascanius by the hand," he wrote in 1880. Despite his father's skepticism, Heinrich was convinced that the Trojan city would one day rise again. "If such walls once existed," he speculated,

"I think back with great fondness to our garden in Ankershagen, with its flowers, pears, cherries, plums, gooseberries, and the big lime tree where I carved my name. I remember too our church spire, from which I looked out over the world. I remember the verses my father wrote on the wall of our garden gazebo." How much truth is there in this recollection, penned by Schliemann in the course of an exercise in conversational Greek? In his autobiography Schliemann enticed his readers with childhood fables: "The gazebo was said to be haunted by the ghost of my father's predecessor, Pastor von Russdorf. Behind it was a pond." The family house (above) is today a museum to the hero.

"they cannot possibly have been completely destroyed: vast ruins of them must still remain, but they are hidden away beneath the dust of ages."

## Testing a Childhood Dream

The preface to Schliemann's *Ithaque, le Péloponnèse, Troie* (published in 1869) recalls another facet of this Trojan dream: "For Christmas 1832 I gave my father an account, in bad Latin, of the principal events of the Trojan War and the adventures of Odysseus and Agamemnon." His father's influence was decisive: "From the moment I could talk, my father told me the great exploits of Homer's heroes: I loved these stories; they held me spellbound; they fired me with enthusiasm."

Some today question this picture of childhood devotion and the ambition it is said to have kindled. As far as we know, Jerrer's *Universal History for Children* (with the famous engraving of Troy) is mentioned for the first time by Schliemann in a letter written in 1875, when he was fifty-three! And the presence in his library of an 1828 edition of Jerrer's book doesn't necessarily indicate the date of its acquisition. A handwriting expert asserts that the signature inside—"Heinrich Schliemann"—is not that of a child. The suggestion that this appealing tale was fabricated is strengthened by the fact that Schliemann actually borrowed the material for the Ankershagen legends—which had supposedly fueled his childhood daydreams—from a collection of tales first published in 1857. But the part played by the author's imagination in reconstructing his past counts for less than his concern to link this childhood to his passion for the Homeric world and his urge to disinter it.

Sigmund Freud pondered the Schliemann case. From his readings about Schliemann's excavations, he borrowed the image of successive levels of excavation to evoke the repository of our psychic impressions. In 1899 the psychoanalyst wrote to his friend Wilhelm Fleiss: "In discovering Priam's treasure this man found happiness, for only the fulfillment of a childhood desire can engender happiness." With the twin successes of the businessman and archaeologist in mind, Freud had noted in an earlier letter: "Happiness is the deferred realization

Sigmund Freud worked in Vienna surrounded by objects from antiquity (above). In 1899 he wrote: "I have bought Schliemann's *Ilios* and was fascinated by the story of his childhood."

Signs and symbols (opposite) intrigued Schliemann, who wrote an article in 1892 on the meaning of the swastika. In common use as far away as India, this emblem, suggestive of a wheel or of walking feet, seemed to him to be related to a primitive conception of solar movement.

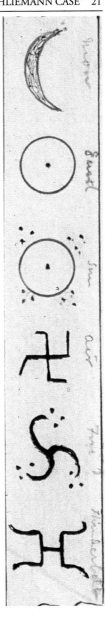

of a prehistoric desire. That is why wealth plays so insignificant a part in it." That same year Freud congratulated himself on successfully concluding the analysis; he had reawakened a primordial episode buried in the unconscious of one of his patients. "It was as if Schliemann had once again uncovered the supposedly imaginary ruins of Troy," he wrote.

The archaeologist's life, therefore, can no longer be reduced to the handful of autobiographical facts he offers. The truth about the man and his achievement is emerging as unpublished archives surface, particularly those of the Gennadius Library in Athens. The mass of surviving documents is on a par with this outstanding personality: more than sixty thousand letters received or sent, hundreds of financial statements, and eighteen travel and archaeological notebooks—in all, thousands of pages written in ten different languages. A comparison of these sources with other recollections (his own and those of family and friends) is not to Schliemann's advantage. But the private person's subterfuges do not detract from the value of his discoveries. It matters little whether inventing a destiny for oneself implies weakness or genius. Heinrich Schliemann belongs to the race of great discoverers. We have only to follow his trail.

It took Schliemann just twenty years to achieve material success. The spoils of financial speculation would later help him to secure the treasures of knowledge—the gold of Troy. In the meantime, however, Schliemann donned an adventurer's guise. Leaving Amsterdam he established himself as a trader in Saint Petersburg, then traveled to California. His financial coups, like his stories, were partly the offspring of lies. Whether actually experienced or simply invented, his adventures would undergo a metamorphosis and become—in his autobiographical self-portrait—the logical stages of apprenticeship.

## CHAPTER II
# INTERNATIONAL WHEELER-DEALER

Schliemann in 1860 (opposite); his German passport at the right. In the space of a year, Schliemann claimed to have more than doubled his investments. "Smug German grocer" was the French writer Maurice Barrès's acerbic comment.

REISE- PASS.

Wir Bürgermeister und Rath der Stadt Rostock ersuchen alle Civil- und Militair-Behörden hiedurch, nach Standesgebühr ziemend, Vorzeiger dieses Herrn Johann Heinrich Ludwig Julius Schliemann

Beschreibung.

### Linguistic Flair in the Service of Commerce

On 1 March 1844 Schliemann was hired by the Amsterdam firm of B. H. Schröder & Company. As office boy he looked after the ledgers. His pay was initially skimpy, but he was hardworking and his zeal increased as his wages rose. He claimed to have begun the study of Russian with the help of a grammar book, a dictionary, and a translation of French writer François Fénelon's *Aventures de Télémaque*, an account of the voyage of Odysseus's son Telemachus. "So I betook myself to the study of it without a master, and, with the help of the grammar, I learned the Russian letters and their pronunciation in a few days. Then, following my old method, I began to write short stories of my own composition, and to learn them by heart. As I had no one to correct my work, it was, no doubt, extremely bad." Schliemann also paid a student (who spoke no Russian) to listen to him read. Six weeks after beginning his Russian studies, he was able to write a letter, in Russian, to Vassily Plotnikoff, the agent for Moscow's leading indigo traders. At public sales in Amsterdam, he negotiated discreetly with their emissaries.

Schröder (left), his Amsterdam employer, was the first to appreciate Schliemann's potential. Displaying the fullest confidence in him, the company dispatched him to Russia. Schliemann was grateful for this mark of esteem. Passport in hand, he left to explore Saint Petersburg and the Nevsky Prospekt (below). Schliemann began to teach himself Russian with a translation of François Fénelon's *Aventures de Télémaque* (map, below left).

## Schliemann in Saint Petersburg

At the end of January 1846 Schröder & Company sent Schliemann to represent the firm in Saint Petersburg. The ambitious twenty-four-year-old successfully carried out his duties. On the side he did business on his own account, at first confining himself to indigo. "My business went so well," he wrote, "that in the beginning of 1847 I was inscribed in the Guild as a wholesale merchant." His only defeat was a sentimental one. Encouraged more by his improved social status than his bank account, he asked for the hand of his childhood sweetheart. It was too late; she was already married. "It had indeed happened to Minna and me as it often happens to us in our sleep, when we dream that we are pursuing someone and can never catch him, because as often as we reach him he escapes us again."

Despite his skills it took Schliemann several years to be

Schröder & Company's representative in Russia was at first a model employee, even taking care to husband his superiors' funds. He wrote to them: "I do not wish to occasion any expenditures until you have seen that the results of my efforts in the defense of your interests are truly worthy of compensation." But soon he was refusing to "work for one-half per cent in this magnificent Petersburg [below], the most expensive city in the world, where every step costs its weight in gold."

accepted into the closed circle of major Saint Petersburg merchants. But he had already opened a Moscow affiliate of his trading business. His reputation grew. "Here [in Saint Petersburg] and in Moscow I am considered the most clever, crafty, and competent merchant," he wrote to his father.

## Accidental American

In 1850 Schliemann left Russia for California. According to his autobiography, he spent two years there. "Not having heard of my brother, Ludwig Schliemann, who in the beginning of 1849 had emigrated to California, I went thither in the spring of 1850, and found that he was dead. Happening, therefore, to be in California when, on the 4th of July, 1850, it was made a state, and all those then in resident in the country became by that very fact naturalized Americans, I joyfully embraced the opportunity of becoming a citizen of the United States." In reality, however, Schliemann did not set sail for the New World until December 1850 and reached California only in the spring of 1851. As for American citizenship, he obtained it years later, in 1869. Similarly, despite the assertions in his travel diary, he probably never met the president of the United States or the "famous General Grant" or the governor of Panama. Some observers have seen in these fabrications just the start of Schliemann's later archaeological falsifications. Others have spoken of "psychopathic tendencies." Most certainly Schliemann lied and misled, but it is also possible that his intimate jottings —which initially were not intended for publication—

Schliemann's first wife, Katerina (above). This unflattering study probably mirrored the mood of a disillusioned husband, who wrote to her shortly after they were married: "How utterly reality, that grim specter, has destroyed my joyful hopes of yesteryear! You do not love me, and that is why you refuse to join in my happiness and remain indifferent both to my joys and my sorrows. You oppose me at every step, at every turn; worse, you accuse me of crimes that exist only in your imagination. Even thinking of it sets my hair on end and makes me shudder."

After the divorce Schliemann remained devoted to the children borne him by his Russian wife. His daughter Nadja (left) in 1863.

were no more than an exercise in style. His notebooks, a compendium of unusual or commonplace thoughts about the countries he visited, are a private world, the theater of his written apprenticeship in foreign languages. Schliemann, traveling always alone, dreamed of parallel lives, of escape from reality. Working by turns on his English and his Spanish, he told himself stories—both of his own adventures and ones he dreamed up.

His account of the fire that gutted San Francisco in the night of 4 June 1851 lends weight to this theory. At the time Schliemann was actually in Sacramento. Even if he had been in San Francisco, he could not have witnessed the disaster, which had, in fact, taken place one month earlier—in May. The date is of minor importance. More revealing are Schliemann's words, which are a first-person adaptation, down to the minutest detail, of an article in the 6 May *Sacramento Daily Union*. Improving his English by writing, Schliemann sought less to mystify unlikely future readers than to appropriate an event by telling it to himself.

The year 1854 opened brilliantly for Schliemann. "In expectation of future war," he wrote, "the prices of every kind of merchandise are soaring, and I made a large profit on a little coal deal concluded in a matter of half an hour." The Crimean War made his fortune. In 1855, a year after the Battle of Balaklava and the Charge of the Light Brigade, James Robertson took this photograph (below) of a port under blockade —so favorable to the trader's interests—by Anglo-French and Turkish forces.

San Francisco ablaze (left). Schliemann claimed that he was asleep in the Union Hotel at the time. The noise outside awoke him and he saw the fire from the top of Telegraph Hill: "It was a frightful but sublime view, in fact the grandest spectacle I ever enjoyed." The truth is, he did not witness it. He simply dreamed up the account.

## Prospectors' Banker

In California Schliemann was unable to take over the land claim staked by his brother, who had died of fever at the age of twenty-seven. But his money bore fruit in Sacramento. He helped gold prospectors purchase supplies—by lending at a rate of twelve percent per month! His enterprise prospered. In September 1851 he joined forces with a San Francisco banker backed by the Rothschilds in London, and bought gold dust for cash at seventeen dollars an ounce. For eight months the precious metal—an average of eight thousand dollars worth each month—was ferried to San Francisco aboard the Gregory Express Company's steam trains, which returned to the gold fields with the cash.

Schliemann in his turn fell victim to fever, once in October and again in mid-January 1852. A third attack, at the end of March, prompted his departure. His partner accused him of cheating on the contents of the gold sacks and of setting up his own network on the side. On 7 April Schliemann sold his share to his associate. An announcement in the *Sacramento Daily Union* recorded the change of ownership. Schliemann left California much richer than when he had arrived.

*Your Obedient Servants,*

# H. SCHLIEMANN & Co.,

Bankers, in the Brick Building Cor. J and Front Streets.

## Dead Languages and Travel

In May 1852 Schliemann left New York and eventually returned to Saint Petersburg. On 12 October 1852, in the Orthodox Cathedral of Saint Isaac, he married Katerina Petrovna Lyshin, the daughter of a Saint Petersburg lawyer. It was an unhappy marriage, which produced three children: Sergei, born in 1855, Natalie, born in 1859 (she died at the age of ten), and Nadja, born in 1861.

The Crimean War of 1854–6, pitting Russia against Turkey (in alliance with Britain and France), made Schliemann's fortune. He delivered supplies, military equipment, and strategic materials (saltpeter, sulfur, lead) to the czar's armies. Only business, he told friends, made his life bearable. But business also brought its share of

Letterhead (opposite below) and advertisements in the *Sacramento Daily Union* are reminders of the days when Schliemann, from his brick office building, functioned as banker to adventurers and gold panners (below). As he told friends, "I always get up at 5 o'clock in the morning, take at 5 1/2 my breakfast in the Orleans Hotel and open my office at 6 o'clock to shut it at 10 o'clock in the

anguish—as on the day in 1854 when our hero believed he had lost everything. The Anglo-French blockade of Russia's ports made it necessary to land all goods in Prussia and then ferry them overland to their destination. On 4 October the neutral city of Memel in Lithuania (site of Schliemann's warehouses) was gutted by fire. Fortunately the flames spared his goods and, by an apparent miracle, his investment remained intact. Ironically, his profits were swollen by the fact that "capitalists were afraid to do much business during the Crimean War." By the end of the fighting, his earnings had more than doubled in a year.

evening.… My bank is from early till late constantly jammed, crammed, and rammed full of people from all nations and I have to speak all the day long in eight languages."

With Russia once more at peace, and with his fortune made, he began to learn modern Greek in 1856, using a translation of Bernardin de Saint-Pierre's romantic novel *Paul et Virginie*. He apparently feared at first that "this language would exercise too great a fascination over me and estrange me from my commercial business." But within several months he had mastered ancient Greek as well, and both the *Iliad* and the *Odyssey* were familiar reading. He took lessons from a Greek theological student, Theokletos Vimpos. The two men became friends, and fate was later to intertwine their lives. In the summer of 1858 Schliemann resumed his study of Latin, broken off when he left school in Ankershagen, and soon mastered its difficulties. This passion for the ancient world was not a pretense. "I believe a man can live without business activities," Schliemann wrote his father, "and before settling down I would like to visit the countries of southern Europe, particularly my beloved Homer's homeland, where I'll speak the new Greek language the way I speak German." This is the first indisputable reference to an interest in Homeric poetry and the land that gave it life.

Left unscathed by the economic crisis of 1857, Schliemann was tempted to liquidate his business assets. Deciding, in the end, against this step he began to travel, going first to Sweden and Denmark. Next he traveled through the East, keeping up a travel diary in six languages. For the return trip from Constantinople to Saint Petersburg, he took the Danube route. His crossing of the Dardanelles provided him with a first glimpse of the Troad—the area surrounding the ancient city of Troy. But the plain that had witnessed the battles of the *Iliad* excited the traveler less than his journey up the Nile, or the desert between Cairo and Jerusalem, or his visit to Petra (in modern Jordan). Admittedly, Schliemann had to cut short his trip. As he wrote, "After Syria I visited… Athens, in the summer of 1859, and I was on the point of starting for the island of Ithaca when I was seized with fever.… I therefore hurried to Saint Petersburg."

Above all, however, he needed to defend himself against charges of fraud brought against him by Stefan Soloviev, one of his debtors who had declared bankruptcy.

The businessman in Saint Petersburg (opposite) in 1860 and a bill of the same year recording the import of an American cotton consignment. Schliemann was eager to learn modern Greek and, as was his habit, he refused to study grammar, apart from declensions and verbs, relying chiefly for his progress on the recitation of selected passages. He was proud of his fluent written and spoken command of the language of Homer: "I am perfectly acquainted with all the grammatical rules without even knowing whether or not they are contained in the grammars; and whenever a man finds errors in my Greek, I can immediately prove that I am right, by merely reciting passages from the classics where the sentences employed by me occur." Once settled in Greece Schliemann cultivated a conversational Greek in the Homeric manner —which could surprise his contemporaries. Philologists (language experts) who have studied his doctoral dissertation at the University of Rostock agree on the quality of his Latin as opposed to the peculiarities of his Greek.

238
1860.
Note of Cotton imported by
Mr Henry Schliemann of
St Petersburg
pr "John R____ C°
Cotton ———— 288. 056 ———— Tons 125
84

Apparently in good health once more, Schliemann set off again in August, bound for Spain. But the outcome of Soloviev's suit remained uncertain for a long time and Schliemann had to resume his business activities. The secret of his success was importing on a large scale—and his unwillingness to trust middlemen. "I never confided the sale of indigo to clerks or servants, as others did, but always stood myself in my warehouse, and showed and sold it personally and wholesale to the indigo dealers." The indigo merchant had by now diversified into other fields: oil, tea, and cotton—once again a profitable business, as a result of the blockade of southern ports during the American Civil War in 1861.

Two years later Schliemann won his lawsuit on appeal. In December he began dissolving his Saint Petersburg business: "I found myself in possession of a fortune such as my ambition had never ventured to aspire to." His archaeological destiny beckoned.

**"**At last I was in a position to fulfill the dream of a whole lifetime—to visit at my leisure the theater of the events that had so powerfully interested me. I accordingly left in April 1868 …and visited one by one the sites where the poetic memories of Antiquity are still so fresh.**"**

Heinrich Schliemann
*Ithaque, le Péloponnèse, Troie*, Preface, 1869

CHAPTER III

# IN SEARCH OF A DESTINY

A 19th-century engraving (opposite) showing Muslim graves on top of the so-called Tomb of Achilles. For Schliemann, *Odyssey* in hand, this was indeed the Greek hero's resting place. A scene in Yokohama (right) from the time of Schliemann's visit.

## A Barbarian in Asia

"I have an immense urge to see the world," Schliemann wrote in a letter of May 1864. His Asian voyage, beginning that December and lasting six months, took him from India to China and Japan, and ended in San Francisco. This journey—decisive for his intellectual development—represented a double break: from the Russian business world and from his wife, with whom his relationship had long since deteriorated. The journey also charted his future course. In 1867 he began his first

The Great Wall of China (below) impressed Schliemann. "It silently protests," he wrote, "against the corruption and decadence that has fallen on the Chinese Empire."

book, *La Chine et le Japon au Temps Présent* (*China and Japan Today*). Written for a Saint Petersburg paper, it was based on the wanderer's travel journal; Schliemann also kept up a voluminous correspondence during the voyage. Private jottings, letters, and press accounts were all grist for his embryonic work. His later archaeological writings would evolve in the same fashion.

Enthusiasm rarely deserted Schliemann and he willingly set himself an exhausting schedule. In one day, in a series of forced marches, he reached and marveled at the Great Wall of China. He was as thrilled by the spectacle of nature as he was moved by the beauty of monuments and the diversity of foreign customs. His romantic soul delighted in descriptions of trees, flowers, and birds. He was awed by the Himalayas: "The prospects were too vast, too sublime. I simply stood there, overwhelmed by the beauty of the landscape."

Businessman Schliemann continued to watch his

*China and Japan Today*, brought out in French by a small Paris publisher, was the fruit of Schliemann's travel diary (above). The explorer was spellbound by Chinese theater (below).

expenses. He bought only second-class tickets on the Indian railways. He complained if the food was bad and haggled over hotel rates. Nor did he forget his own financial interests. He used letters of recommendation and of credit to purchase consignments of indigo and tea; he visited a silkworm farm. At Yokohama in Japan he railed against the exchange rates: "The Japanese government has in its wisdom devised this refined form of corruption in order to impose the most crying injustices on foreign trade."

His travels also brought the pleasures of writing: "One is always so happy, contented, and focused while writing," he observed. "And in company one always has a thousand and one interesting things to impart, which invariably—as the fruit of long research and long reflection—amuse everyone."

## Sorbonne Student

Schliemann reached France in the first days of 1866, at the conclusion of an around-the-world trip. "I have…settled down in Paris," he wrote, "to study archaeology, henceforth with no other interruption than short trips to America." But this decision did not deter him from going to Moscow in March and traveling through Bavaria and Switzerland until mid-October. Initially he nurtured some hopes of attempting a reconciliation with his wife, then resigned himself to their separation. He speculated in real estate in a Paris whose layout had been newly configured by Baron Georges-Eugène Haussmann in the fading years of the Second Empire. By the start of the academic

In Paris Schliemann moved into a private townhouse at 6 Place Saint-Michel. He attended the Sorbonne (facade, below), and made friends with the great historian Joseph-Ernest Renan (below left).

year Schliemann, by now a wealthy property owner, was a student at the Sorbonne, taking courses in Asian languages, embarking on Egyptology, and studying Sanskrit. He had a first taste of Greek and Arab philosophy, of classical poetry, of contemporary French literature, and of comparative grammar.

He then broke off his studies and departed on a business trip to the United States, where he invested in railroads and bought land in Cuba. In a diary packed with figures

and business addresses, Schliemann praised the American spirit of enterprise, although he worried that freeing the slaves would reduce their productivity by a third. He recorded various visits: to schools, factories (particularly meat-packing plants), and cemeteries. He was haunted by the face of death, but even more so by the memory of his vanished brother, whose grave he never found.

At the end of January 1868 Schliemann returned to his studies at the Sorbonne, as well as to lectures at the Collège de France and meetings of scientific societies. In April he considered resuming his business activities in

Emile Burnouf (below) played a major part in Schliemann's intellectual development. An academic specializing in comparative mythology and author of the first French-Sanskrit dictionary, Burnouf was also a renowned Hellenist. From 1867 to 1875 he directed the French School at Athens. At one point Schliemann thought of leaving his Trojan gold to France; Burnouf served as intermediary, meeting with the French authorities, but an agreement was never reached. Burnouf's friendship with Schliemann began with the fifty letters that Burnouf sent him, along with flattering articles, and active help in the Trojan digs. It was Burnouf's task to record the depths at which each object was unearthed.

Russia in order to be near his children. In a letter to his son he outlined a journey intended to take him to Saint Petersburg via Switzerland, Italy, Greece, Turkey, Odessa, Kiev, and Moscow. But on learning that his Saint Petersburg associates had again initiated legal proceedings against him, he decided to delay his return to Russia. Nevertheless he set off—but southward. The ruins of ancient Rome and Pompeii had roused his curiosity.

## Tourism and Archaeology

It all began with a pleasure jaunt. On 5 May Schliemann turned up at Rome's Piazza del Popolo as an "ordinary tourist," aware that he lacked the knowledge necessary to carry out scientific activities. The traveler's journal conveys the swift awakening of his passion for archaeology. During his four weeks in Rome Schliemann divided his time equally between the monuments of antiquity and more modern sights. He approached the former through the intermediary of historical figures who intrigued him, such as Cleopatra or Nero. His fascination with the tyrant impelled him to explore the Domus Aurea, Nero's palace. He admired the Temple of Castor and Pollux. Yet there was a distinct touch of naïveté to his enthusiasm. He even believed, for example, that he had seen the fig tree where Romulus and Remus, the legendary founders of Rome, were abandoned!

Twenty days in the Bay of Naples introduced the apprentice archaeologist to the realities of antiquity. He visited Baia, Stabies, Cumae, and Capua, and above all Pompeii. He made two expeditions to the last site, attended a series of lectures, and marveled at the paintings uncovered during excavation and put on display at the Naples Museum. He was impressed by a meeting with Giuseppe Fiorelli, who was directing the dig and concentrating—and this was an innovation—on

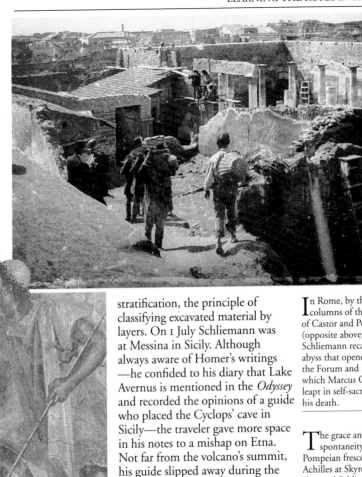

stratification, the principle of classifying excavated material by layers. On 1 July Schliemann was at Messina in Sicily. Although always aware of Homer's writings —he confided to his diary that Lake Avernus is mentioned in the *Odyssey* and recorded the opinions of a guide who placed the Cyclops' cave in Sicily—the traveler gave more space in his notes to a mishap on Etna. Not far from the volcano's summit, his guide slipped away during the night. Schliemann had to climb on alone. He reached his hotel, under his own steam, the next day!

His journey to the Greek mainland began with a stop at Corfu on 6 July. After visiting Ithaca Schliemann met a fellow German in Athens on 25 July, the architect Ernst Ziller, who had been working

In Rome, by the columns of the Temple of Castor and Pollux (opposite above), Schliemann recalled the abyss that opened under the Forum and into which Marcus Curtius leapt in self-sacrifice to his death.

The grace and spontaneity of Pompeian frescoes (left: Achilles at Skyros) charmed Schliemann. He also admired the excavations (above) undertaken by Giuseppe Fiorelli. He marveled at Fiorelli's ability to bring the doomed Pompeians back to life by injecting plaster into the impressions left by their bodies.

Schliemann spent several days in Constantinople (modern Istanbul, left), awaiting the return steamer after his second visit to the Troad.

Diploma from the University of Rostock (opposite above), conferring a doctorate on the author of *Ithaca, the Peloponnese, Troy*. Seven hundred copies of the book were printed.

in the Troad. The meeting with Ziller was decisive. When he learned of the excavations under way and of the various theories about the site of ancient Troy, Schliemann set sail for the Dardanelles. While waiting for his ship, he busied himself visiting the plain of Argos—including Tiryns and Mycenae—where he hoped one day to uncover the tomb of King Agamemnon.

### Ithaca, the Peloponnese, Troy

In Paris that September Schliemann wrote *Ithaque, le Péloponnèse, Troie* (*Ithaca, the Peloponnese, Troy*), which was published in French at the author's expense at the beginning of 1869. It was the central component of an archaeological dissertation that earned him a doctorate from the University of Rostock in Germany.

The book was a blend of literary references and travel notes. Its tone was often lyrical. It shows us the traveler sleeping on Ithaca, a bank of stones for a bed and

VIRUM PRAENOBILISSIMUM

# HENRICUM SCHLIEMANN

TRADITO LIBRO ARCHAEOLOGICO
DE ITHACA INSULA PELOPONNESO ET TROADE

## PHILOSOPHIAE DOCTOREM ARTIUMQUE LIBERALIUM MAGISTRUM

ORNATUM ESSE

### PUBLICO HOC DIPLOMATE

CONFIRMAT

Homer's poems for a pillow. It tells us that the islanders warmly thanked their visitor for a public reading. There, "every hill, every rock, every fountain, and every olive grove breathe Homer and his *Odyssey*, and we are carried at one leap into the most resplendent era of Greek chivalry and poetry." He had borrowed this gust of enthusiasm from an English tourist guidebook; likewise the breathless (but fictitious) account of an attack by dogs in the south of Ithaca.

The fact remains that Schliemann carried out his first digs on the island of Ithaca and tested his methods there. Attempting to find Odysseus's palace on Mount Aëtos, he sought to locate the events of the Homeric epic in the landscape around him, to match the written record to the topography. The results were disappointing, but the novice was not discouraged. He now dreamed of identifying the sites described in the *Iliad* and *Odyssey*, confident that he had recognized "the mistakes of nearly all the archaeological explorers concerning the site once occupied by the Homeric capital of Ithaca, Eumaeus's stables [where Odysseus once stayed], the isle of Asteris, ancient Troy, the tombs of Batieia and Esyetes, Hector's tomb, etc." Unearthing a handful of urns, Schliemann

"We climbed Mount Aëtos [on Ithaca] on its western slope, which was a little less steep than the two other approaches. Many traces of an old pathway were visible, apparently leading from Odysseus's palace to the little port now known as Saint Spiridion." Schliemann was mistaken in thinking he had rediscovered the palace of Homer's hero on the mountain. He had explored the site of ancient Alalcomenae, an archaic-era settlement, traces of whose Cyclopean walls have survived (engraving of Ithaca, below).

naively exclaimed: "It is quite possible that these five little urns of mine contain the bodies of Odysseus and [his wife] Penelope or their descendants!"

Despite its defects, *Ithaca, the Peloponnese, Troy* attracted the interest of a university review board. The theory Schliemann proposed was indeed innovative. In a return to the traditions of antiquity—and in the face of contemporary opinion—he intended to seek Homeric Troy on the hill of Hissarlik in the territory of the Ottoman Empire (modern Turkey). Since Jean-Baptiste Lechevalier's initial exploration of the Troad, carried out in 1795, researchers had confined their activities to a nearby site at the Turkish village of Bunarbashi. Schliemann proved that this was a dead end. Whatever the experts believed, the writers of antiquity had not placed the Greco-Roman city of Ilium—the heir of Homer's Troy—at Bunarbashi, whose topography did not match the descriptions in the *Iliad.* Digging there had brought no conclusive results.

Unsung hero of the Hissarlik digs: the American Frank Calvert (above). He was the first to realize that the hill was "largely artificial, and had been formed by the ruins and debris of temples and palaces built one on top of the other over long centuries."

However, Schliemann only became slowly convinced of the possibility of Trojan ruins on the Hissarlik site. His travel diary shows that he himself also situated them initially at Bunarbashi. He began to suspect their presence on Hissarlik only after an encounter with the American Frank Calvert, who was preparing to leave the Troad. Calvert, the son of the United States vice-consul in the Dardanelles, was an amateur archaeologist and owned some of the land at Hissarlik. He had made promising preliminary probes there. *Ithaca, the Peloponnese, Troy* paid homage to this shrewd pathfinder. But while endorsing Calvert's opinion, Schliemann reserved the lion's role in the book for himself—presenting himself as standing alone against the scientific community, with a combination of lucidity, boldness, and intuition. However, it would be more accurate to suggest that Schliemann, having welcomed the ideas of other men, then managed to forge his own brand of certainty by giving himself time to think in Paris. His conviction was rational. He came to it while writing his book, after extensive reading, and correspondence with his American counterpart. The Hissarlik hypothesis was to prove a shrewd assessment.

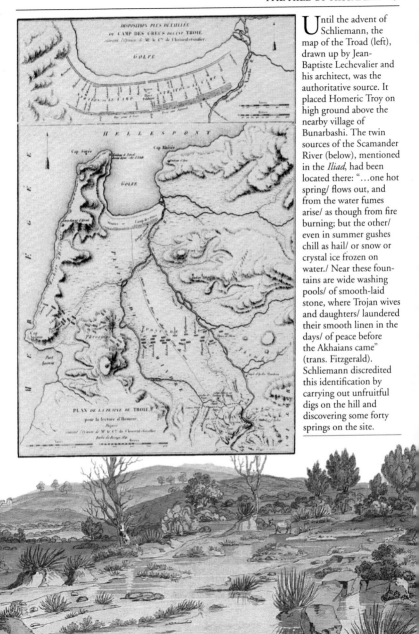

Until the advent of Schliemann, the map of the Troad (left), drawn up by Jean-Baptiste Lechevalier and his architect, was the authoritative source. It placed Homeric Troy on high ground above the nearby village of Bunarbashi. The twin sources of the Scamander River (below), mentioned in the *Iliad*, had been located there: "…one hot spring/ flows out, and from the water fumes arise/ as though from fire burning; but the other/ even in summer gushes chill as hail/ or snow or crystal ice frozen on water./ Near these fountains are wide washing pools/ of smooth-laid stone, where Trojan wives and daughters/ laundered their smooth linen in the days/ of peace before the Akhaians came" (trans. Fitzgerald). Schliemann discredited this identification by carrying out unfruitful digs on the hill and discovering some forty springs on the site.

"If my memoirs now and then contain contradictions, I hope that these may be pardoned when it is considered that I have revealed a new world of archaeology. The objects which I brought to light by thousands are of a kind hitherto never or but rarely found. It was an entirely new world for me; I had to learn everything by myself and only by and by could I attain the right insight."

Heinrich Schliemann
*Troy and Its Remains*, Preface, 1875

# CHAPTER IV
# HOMER'S LAND, PROMISED LAND

Sophia Schliemann (Heinrich's wife, opposite), adorned with jewels from the "Treasure of Priam." The urn (right), which Schliemann believed was decorated with an owl's head, graced the title page of his *Trojanische Alterhümer* (*Atlas of Trojan Antiquities*).

The conversion of the new initiate to archaeology was accompanied by a change in civic status: In 1869 Schliemann became an American citizen. In the same year he divorced his Russian wife and married again, in Athens. With the support of his friend Frank Calvert he began to explore Hissarlik in April 1870. For the next twenty years, in the course of seven intermittently conducted digs, he laid bare the remains of Troy and with it the "Treasure of Priam," revealing superimposed layers of ruins dating from successive eras of habitation. He extracted thousands of objects, swiftly trumpeting his discoveries and demonstrated a truly scientific interest in earthenware and in stratification. The man was a pioneer.

At a time when Delos, Olympia, and Delphi still awaited the

archaeologist's pickax, he began a series of "campaigns" that would bring Greek civilization back to life. Thanks to his bold research the Greek past, which until then could be traced back no further than the traditional date of the first Olympic Games in 776 BC, was now firmly located in the second millennium BC.

In 1874 Schliemann began excavating in the northeast Peloponnese; two years later he uncovered the gold of the Mycenaean tombs and the "Mask of Agamemnon." His dream was approaching fruition. Schliemann believed he had demonstrated that the Homeric texts did indeed reflect historical reality, and he used those texts to interpret the unknown Greece he was bringing to light. He thus claimed to have established a clear relationship between the architectural remains of the second millennium BC and the world described in the *Iliad* and the *Odyssey*. The approach had its weaknesses, for it blurred the line between real experience and events described in Homer's epics. But with Schliemann archaeology became a science; digging was now elevated to the status of an experiment designed to validate a theory.

Schliemann (opposite) —a United States citizen. Below: The Trojan plain and 1873 excavations. "If I may say so, the hill is now more impressive-looking than ever," wrote Schliemann. "The trenches and banks of rubble give it the look of some great fortress. The onlooker standing on the walls of the site sees below him a kind of immense caldron, at whose bottom sits the burned city with her walls and her house foundations as distinct as if marked out on a chart. From such a vantage point he can gain precise knowledge of the peculiar nature of the structures."

**Sentimental Education**

Schliemann spent much of the year 1869 in the
United States. As an American citizen he traveled to
Indianapolis to take advantage of local legislation
facilitating divorce. His own divorce became final in
June, and three months later he married Sophia
Kastromenos, daughter of a Greek cloth merchant. He
had selected the seventeen-year-old girl from a photo
album put together by his Saint Petersburg friend
who had taught him Greek, Theokletos Vimpos, an
Orthodox priest and uncle of the bride. Schliemann
wrote to him: "I believe that a woman whose character

Reaching New York
on 27 March 1869,
Schliemann began the
process of naturalization
(below). United States
citizenship came with
startling swiftness: His
new papers reached him
two days later. On 1 April
he was in Indianapolis,
where the obstacles to
divorce were easily
surmountable. Four days
later he applied for his
divorce and a hearing
was set for 30 June. He
bought a house (left)
for $1,125 and invested
a further $12,000
in a factory. These
investments were meant
to show the judge that
he had settled in the
country. Yet in April he
had already made plans
to marry in Greece,
launching an
investigation into the
character of his intended
and bombarding Sophia's
uncle with questions.

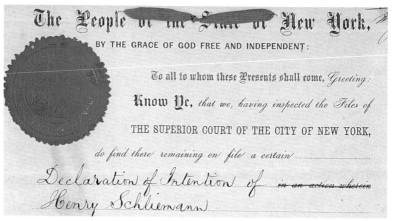

The People of the State of New York,

BY THE GRACE OF GOD FREE AND INDEPENDENT:

To all to whom these Presents shall come, Greeting:

Know Ye, that we, having inspected the Files of

THE SUPERIOR COURT OF THE CITY OF NEW YORK,

do find there remaining on file a certain

Declaration of Intention of in an action whereis

Henry Schliemann

agreed wholly with mine, and imbued with my own love for the sciences, could respect me. And since she would remain my disciple her whole life long, I dare to hope that she would love me firstly because love is born of respect, and secondly because I shall endeavor to be a good teacher and shall devote all my free time to helping her in her quest for philological and archaeological knowledge." Like Pygmalion, Schliemann dreamed of shaping his creation in order to unite knowledge and beauty. But things were not to be so simple. After a honeymoon in Paris, the Schliemanns returned to Athens in early February 1870. There a disappointment awaited them. Official Turkish permission to dig at Hissarlik—which they had requested before leaving for Paris—had not materialized. Heinrich left for the Greek Cycladic Islands, alone. This excursion put the finishing touches on his archaeological training and rounded out his knowledge of the major sites. He

Above: The Acropolis of Athens at the time that Heinrich and Sophia (below) were wed.

The Cyclades (the island of Syros, left, at the turn of the century) were Schliemann's destination when he left Athens on 27 February 1870. He stopped in Delos, soon to be explored by the French School at Athens. Directed by Emile Burnouf, the School was in the Lemnian House (below), on the site of the present Hotel Grande Bretagne. Schliemann reached Santorini only shortly before the French archaeologists. In April 1870 the latter were to find traces of houses dating from the second millennium BC. This unsuspected prehistoric past and the super-imposition of geological strata on the site excited Schliemann's curiosity. Like the tourists in the area (who were already numerous), he must have admired the pumice beds and the eastern port of Nea Kameni (opposite above, 1866 engraving).

visited Syros, Delos (where excavations did not begin until 1873), Paros, Naxos, and Santorini. Renewed volcanic activity on Santorini in 1866 had spurred increased scientific research there. Uniting the skills of volcanologists and archaeologists, work proceeded under the aegis of the French School at Athens. The material uncovered by excavation embarrassed the experts, for it bore no resemblance to anything so far encountered. Geological evidence appeared to place it in the first half of the second millennium BC, which seemed implausible. No comparative yardstick yet existed—but Schliemann's Trojan and Mycenaean digs would soon provide one.

Still waiting for news of his authorization to dig in the Troad, Schliemann postponed plans for another month. He organized family outings to Attica and the Peloponnese. Then, unable to wait any longer, he set off for the Dardanelles on 10 April. Although still without permission to excavate, he began a preliminary probe on the northwest corner of

Hissarlik to determine the depth of the topsoil. Sinking a sixteen-foot shaft, he uncovered a series of Roman and Hellenistic walls. Digging was halted at the end of the month when the owners of the site objected.

Sophia took no part in this work. She was absent the following year as well, giving birth in Athens to a baby girl, Andromache. Yet Schliemann wrote in his diary: "My dear wife, an Athenian lady who is an enthusiastic admirer of Homer, and knows almost the whole of the *Iliad* by heart, is present at the excavations from morning to night." However, she was indeed present during the 1872 season, throughout the month of June. Life on the work site was not without danger. Schliemann mentions the accidental destruction by fire of their house in March 1873: "Last night my wife and I and the foreman Photidas had the narrowest escape of being burnt alive." A letter written in April informs us that Sophia was the victim of an attempted robbery. Yet she remained with her husband until May, when she returned to Athens to bury her father.

## Rediscovery of Troy

*Trojan Antiquities,* accompanied by an *Atlas,* came out in January 1874. "This book," wrote Schliemann, "is a kind of journal of my excavations at Troy. Every section was

Sophia Schliemann gave birth to Agamemnon in 1878, seven years after the couple's firstborn, Andromache. Reciting lines from the *Iliad,* the proud father pressed Homer's epic against the newborn infant's forehead. On the christening day, it is said—to the fury of the officiating Orthodox priest— Schliemann measured the temperature of the holy water!

written by me on the spot as our work progressed."
The book was essentially a reprinting of the articles
he regularly dispatched to the *Times* in London.
Schliemann had a flair for communication and for
argument and used the press to fan the interest sparked
by his archaeological investigations. But there were
major obstacles to his research in the field. He did not
obtain official permission to excavate until September
1871, after three trips to Constantinople and thanks to
the generous intervention of an American diplomat.
Nothing could be taken for granted. The following
year Schliemann was informed that his previously
negotiated right to keep half his finds was being
withdrawn.

The first campaign began on 11 October 1871 and was a
disaster. Torrential downpours brought work to a stop at
the beginning of November. Schliemann's initial staff
and supplies were ludicrously small. The first day he
hired eight laborers. The next day there were thirty-five,
and from then on they averaged eighty. They had to
remove debris in baskets. Schliemann possessed only
eight wheelbarrows and four bull-drawn carts. Eager to

Marking the progress
of the Trojan digs
(preceding pages and
below), the *Illustrated
London News* published
a series of engravings
based on watercolors by
William Simpson, the
magazine's correspondent
on the spot. Clearly
visible as it emerges from
the rubble is the steeply
sloping paved road,
more than twenty feet
wide, which led to the
southwest entrance of the
prehistoric citadel. Two
pages from Schliemann's
working notebook
(opposite above) contain
the archaeologist's
sketches and written
record of his daily finds,
including ceramic
pitchers like that
shown opposite below.

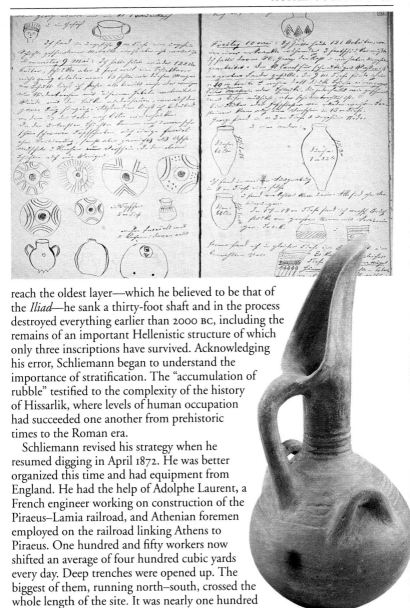

reach the oldest layer—which he believed to be that of the *Iliad*—he sank a thirty-foot shaft and in the process destroyed everything earlier than 2000 BC, including the remains of an important Hellenistic structure of which only three inscriptions have survived. Acknowledging his error, Schliemann began to understand the importance of stratification. The "accumulation of rubble" testified to the complexity of the history of Hissarlik, where levels of human occupation had succeeded one another from prehistoric times to the Roman era.

Schliemann revised his strategy when he resumed digging in April 1872. He was better organized this time and had equipment from England. He had the help of Adolphe Laurent, a French engineer working on construction of the Piraeus–Lamia railroad, and Athenian foremen employed on the railroad linking Athens to Piraeus. One hundred and fifty workers now shifted an average of four hundred cubic yards every day. Deep trenches were opened up. The biggest of them, running north–south, crossed the whole length of the site. It was nearly one hundred

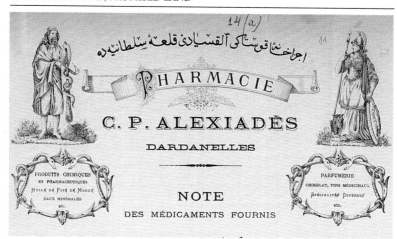

14 (a)

اجراخنا قوشتاكى آلقسّيادى قلعة سلطانيه ده

11

**PHARMACIE**

**C. P. ALEXIADÈS**

**DARDANELLES**

PRODUITS CHIMIQUES
ET PHARMACEUTIQUES
HUILE DE FOIE DE MORUE
EAUX MINÉRALES
etc.

PARFUMERIE
CHOGOLAT, VINS MÉDICINAUX
Spécialités Diverses
etc.

**NOTE**

DES MÉDICAMENTS FOURNIS

and thirty feet wide and over fifty feet deep. When malaria struck down workers on the site in mid-August, however, operations came to a halt.

But already Schliemann sensed victory. "Now, as regards the result of my excavations," he exulted, "everyone must admit that I have solved a great historical problem, and that I have solved it by the discovery of a high civilization and immense buildings upon the primary soil, in the depths of an ancient town, which throughout antiquity was called Ilium and declared itself to be the successor of Troy, the site of which was regarded as identical with the site of the Homeric Ilium by the whole civilized world of that time." For the archaeologist this triumphant report was vindicated on several grounds. Hissarlik's location corresponded to that of King Priam's citadel in the *Iliad*. A section of wall that Schliemann had uncovered might well be linked to the fortifications built at Ilium by Lysimachus, a lieutenant of Alexander the Great and later king of Thrace—but not to Priam. Finally, the confusion of foundations and walls guaranteed the existence at Hissarlik of at least three prehistoric levels. At this point Schliemann identified the deepest of them as being from the period of the Trojan War, which ancient historians dated to around 1250 BC.

The decoration of certain articles of pottery

Sickness was a permanent threat on the work site. Schliemann regularly swallowed quinine powder to prevent malaria. Above: Prescription from a Dardanelles pharmacy. Below: A Trojan vase with vaguely human features.

intrigued the excavator, leading him to a series of mistaken hypotheses. Some decorative motifs appeared to him to be the signs of a Trojan alphabet. He also developed theories about a series of anthropomorphic vases, seeing in them "the Ilian Minerva crowned with an owl's head and surmounted by a kind of helmet." He believed that a two-handled drinking cup he found illustrated a type of jug celebrated in the *Iliad*—the *depas amphikypellon.* But his readiness to see proof of the truth of the Homeric poems in every object he unearthed led Schliemann astray. Today the vessel in question is dated considerably earlier, between 2600 and 1800 BC.

While a demanding taskmaster on the site, Schliemann showed great concern for his workers' health. Appointing himself makeshift medical officer, he administered quinine, rubbed herbal ointments into cuts, and prescribed sea-bathing for a range of ailments. And in his conduct over the architectural fragment known as the "Sun Metope," the major find of 1872, he proved as determined to protect his own interests as to

Sophia and Heinrich can be seen wandering through the site in the watercolor below. "I am most anxious that local Christians or Turks be prevented from stealing the paving-stones from the tower road. To that end, I have spread the rumor that Jesus Christ visited King Priam, approaching the monarch along this very road; and to lend this story greater weight I have set a large picture of Christ in the earthen wall on the northwestern side of the tower road."

7 M.

4. m.

7. M.    7. M.

4 ½

8. M.

7. M.

## A Passion for Artifacts

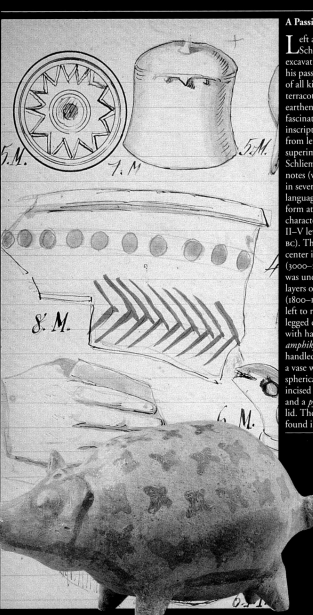

Left and overleaf:
Schliemann's
excavation report reveals
his passion for pottery
of all kinds—vases,
terracotta articles,
earthenware—and a
fascination with
inscriptions. Objects
from left to right are
superimposed on
Schliemann's working
notes (which he made
in several different
languages). The female
form at the left is a shape
characteristic of Troy
II–V levels (2500–1800
BC). The idol in the
center is from Troy I
(3000–2500 BC). The pig
was unearthed in the
layers of Troy VI–VII
(1800–1100 BC). Overleaf,
left to right, are: a three-
legged draining jug
with handle; a *depas
amphikypellon* or two-
handled drinking cup;
a vase with tall neck,
spherical body, and
incised geometric design;
and a *pyxis*, or box with
lid. These pieces were
found in Troy II–V levels.

ΣΑ
ΕΣΑΙ
ΑΒΟΥΚΟΑ

ΟΥ
ΕΡΡΑΝΦ

Σ ΚΑΤΑΠΛΗΘΟΣ ΕΙΣ ΟΙΝ ΣΥΡΑ
ΤΩΝ ΕΥΉ ΎΙΣΘΑΙΣ ΚΑΔΡΕΙΣΟ
ΙΑΝΔΡΑΣ ΤΟΥΣΣΥΝΘΗΣΟΜΕΝ
ΕΡΟΝ ΥΠΗΡ ΛΕΝ ΚΑΙ ΣΤΗΛΩΝ
ΕΝ ΤΩΙ ΤΩΝ ΣΑ ΜΟΘΡΑΚ
ΣΑΠΟΚΑΟΙΣ ΤΑ ΜΕΝ
ϹΝΟΥΣ ΤΗΝ ΣΥΝΘΕΣΙΝ
ΜΟΛΟΓΙΑΣ ΤΟ ΑΝΤΙ ΓΓΑ
ΟΙΚΗΣΟΝΤΕΣ Η ΡΕΟΝΗΣ
Ο ΠΕΙΘΟΥΜΙΛΗΣΙΟ
ΘΟΥΔΙΟΠΕΙΔΗΣ Β
ΤΙΦΑΝ ΡΙΣΑΣΤ

... Dorf Jerischehir u. Kal.fatli, ...

Topf 1/2 grösse

Schale 1/2 grösse

4. M.

7. M.

gefunden würde!

6. M.

M.

M.

5.

hold down the rising price of wine and his soaring expenses. The *metope*—a sculpted panel—from the Temple of Athena, which had dominated Ilium during the Hellenistic period, was found in the area of Hissarlik owned by Frank Calvert. Calvert had authorized Schliemann to dig there on condition that they share the objects unearthed. When they discussed the details of a future division of the spoils, Schliemann proposed simply paying his colleague and friend for what he found. After much haggling he undertook to pay Calvert one thousand francs (about two hundred dollars) for the *metope*—a fraction of Calvert's original asking price. Calvert at last wearily gave in, but when he later learned that Schliemann was quoting the value of the

"Helios here, so to speak, burst forth from the gate of day and sheds the light of his glory overall," Schliemann wrote of his spectacular find below. The "Sun Metope" belonged to the Temple of Athena. This Doric structure, probably built at the time of the Greek ruler Lysimachus (c. 355–281 BC), was adorned with a sculptured frieze on which triglyphs and *metopes* alternated. The themes they depicted may have echoed those of the Athenian Parthenon —the battles of the gods of Olympus and the sack of Troy.

*metope* at one hundred and fifty times what he had paid, Calvert rebelled and demanded compensation. Schliemann refused—on principle! "A bargain is sacred," he said. "One does not go back on it or change it: such is the world's custom."

## The "Treasure of Priam"

Schliemann's third campaign lasted from February to June of 1873. He was in a self-critical mood, regretting the destruction he had caused in sacrificing more recent structures on the Hissarlik site. He realized that he had been mistaken in assuming that Troy was built on virgin soil—as if it had known no history prior to the Greek expedition. The yield from the earliest prehistoric layer was too skimpy to have been Homeric Troy. The second stratum reflected a more advanced civilization. Its remains were impressive: a fortress some 325 feet in diameter, with dwellings inside the perimeter. Within a few weeks Schliemann cleared a gate and part of the defensive walls of this second settlement. To his Homer-obsessed way of thinking, he had discovered the Scaean Gate—the entranceway to Troy—and he decided that the domestic structures within them were the remains of the palace of the *Iliad's* Trojan ruler, Priam.

He likewise gave the two hundred and fifty gold objects he found there the collective name of the

Reproduction of the golden pin found by Schliemann in the northwestern trench, under the great Hellenic wall attributed to Lysimachus. The engraving above shows the progress of digging in May 1873. *Iliad* in hand, Schliemann identified the remains as the Palace of Priam, northwest of Troy's Scaean Gate. At the top of the mound, from left to right, are the archaeologist's wooden house, his workshop, and a stone house. Behind lie the Trojan plain and Hellespont, today's Dardanelles.

VII

VI

V

IV

III

II

I

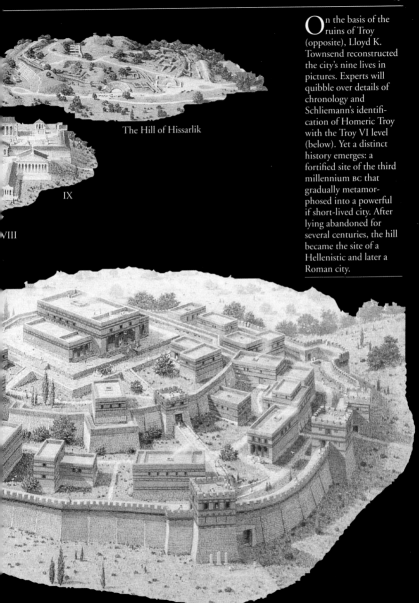

The Hill of Hissarlik

IX

VIII

On the basis of the ruins of Troy (opposite), Lloyd K. Townsend reconstructed the city's nine lives in pictures. Experts will quibble over details of chronology and Schliemann's identification of Homeric Troy with the Troy VI level (below). Yet a distinct history emerges: a fortified site of the third millennium BC that gradually metamorphosed into a powerful if short-lived city. After lying abandoned for several centuries, the hill became the site of a Hellenistic and later a Roman city.

"Treasure of Priam." The clandestine transfer to Greece of these jewels and vases raised a storm. To avoid legal proceedings Schliemann struck a bargain with the Turkish legislature and government. In exchange for fifty thousand francs, the Turks agreed to relinquish their claim to the "Treasure of Priam." Schliemann then considered that he had met his obligations and was henceforth the owner of the objects. In Paris and Berlin, however, their authenticity was questioned. So much blatant publicity had made archaeologists suspicious of this man, decidedly not one of their own. But in England a number of scientific societies invited Schliemann to address them—which pleased him immensely. In the presence of Prime Minister William Gladstone, Schliemann and his wife became honorary members of the Society of Antiquaries in Burlington House. In December 1877 he displayed the "Treasure of Priam" in London.

The exhibition was a great success. But it soon appeared that Schliemann dated his finds incorrectly. Far from being contemporary with the presumed date of the fall of Troy—around 1250 BC—they were a good millennium older, as would be demonstrated by the comparative stratigraphy (study of layers) of the Trojan and Mycenaean sites.

Even Schliemann's account of the discovery of the "Treasure of Priam" at the end of May or in mid-June 1873 carries a whiff of deceit. He tells us that at great danger to himself (the wall under which he was digging threatened to collapse and bury him at any moment), he used a knife to dislodge precious objects, gold, and jewelry. He had taken care to move his workers out of harm's way, allowing them an extra rest period. He then relied on the help of his "dear wife," constantly ready to wrap the booty in her shawl and move it to safety. Untrue. An exchange of letters

Experience and scientific caution were Schliemann's gift from Wilhelm Dörpfeld (opposite below), the young German architect and archaeologist who began work on the Trojan site in 1882. Schliemann (left) poses beside some partially unearthed *pithoi*. He decided against fully exposing these six huge jars, deterred by a sort of religious fear. But the local inhabitants shattered them, convinced that rich treasure lay inside. Reconstructing the necklace (below)

demanded enormous skill. Its various components were among the 8700 gold objects found in a silver vase.

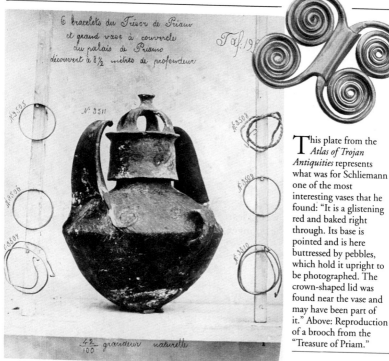

6 bracelets du Trésor de Priam
et grand vase à couvercle
du palais de Priam
découvert à 8½ mètres de profondeur

Taf. 198

N° 3511

42/100 grandeur naturelle

This plate from the *Atlas of Trojan Antiquities* represents what was for Schliemann one of the most interesting vases that he found: "It is a glistening red and baked right through. Its base is pointed and is here buttressed by pebbles, which hold it upright to be photographed. The crown-shaped lid was found near the vase and may have been part of it." Above: Reproduction of a brooch from the "Treasure of Priam."

shows that Sophia was not present at the time her husband says the discovery occurred. And when exactly did it take place? Intent on blurring his trail, Schliemann inevitably contradicts himself in his various excavation reports. The passage in his diary relating to the treasure is dated 17 June—"in Athens." Schliemann later falsified this, substituting "Troy" for "Athens." Other clues have lead some to believe that the "Treasure of Priam" might in fact be forgeries or a miscellaneous grab bag thrown together from a series of finds made at different areas of the site throughout the months of March and April 1873. But these theories have yet to be proved.

Anxious for the support of a scientist of unquestionable qualifications, in 1882 Schliemann hired—for a generous salary—a young architect and archaeologist, Wilhelm Dörpfeld. He had known the twenty-nine-year-old German for several years and admired his talents as a draftsman. In 1876 Dörpfeld had illustrated an article on the royal necropolis of Mycenae for a colleague of Schliemann's. The reputation of the technical director of the digs at Olympia, first undertaken in 1875, was now an accomplished fact and Dörpfeld's organizational skills and rigorous approach were widely known. Schliemann had earlier criticized Dörpfeld's painstaking level-by-level approach to the exploration of the sanctuary at Olympia as "doing everything backwards." He felt that one should plunge immediately into the depths, "only then will one find things." But Schliemann now abandoned his earlier criticisms of Dörpfeld (who had just been named architect of the celebrated German Archaeological Institute in Athens). Willingly retreating from his past strictures, Schliemann would learn from the experience and the technique of the younger man. Thanks to Dörpfeld, he realized that the archaeologist is something more than a seeker of gold.

Interior of the prehistoric citadel (foreground) and its southeast entrance, as depicted in *Ilios: the City and Country of the Trojans* (below). The wheelbarrow at right sits on a lintel of the gate. In front of the man taking notes can be seen the transverse walls and gateways. In the background, at a higher level, Roman *propylaea* —buildings forming an entranceway—dominate the tangle of structures.

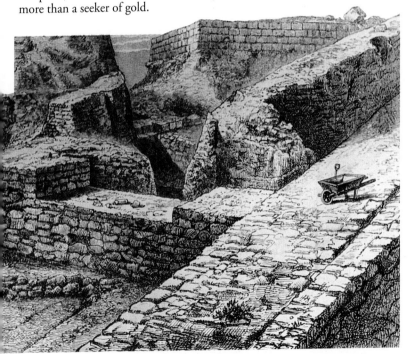

Taf. 6

1368  1369  1370  1371

1372  1373  1375  1377
1378  1374  1376

1379  1382
1381  1383  1384
1380  1385

1387
1386  1388  1389
1390

Terracottas aus 7 metern Tiefe ½ natürlicher Grösse

834  835  836  837  838  839  840

841  842  843  844

845  846 847 848 849 850  851  852  853  854  85

856  857  858 859 860 861 862  863  864  865

866.  867  868  869

Verschiedene Gegenstände aus 1 und 2 metern Tiefe ⅟₄ natürlicher Grösse.

## Mycenae and the Bronze Age Warriors

In February 1874 Schliemann began excavations at
Mycenae. A century earlier a French diplomat, Louis-
François-Sébastien Fauvel, had described one of the
beehive tombs outside the citadel (largely emptied of its
contents by pillagers in ancient times). Even before the
English artist and traveler Edward Dodwell, he had
sketched the Lion Gate outside the acropolis at Mycenae.
In 1840 the newly formed Greek Archaeological Society
had begun to clear the gateway guarding the entrance.

Once again Schliemann's intuition was guided by a
reading of the ancient texts. Taking at face value the
Homeric description of "Mycenae rich in gold," he
followed in Agamemnon's footsteps. He re-read the
"travel guide" written by the 2nd-century Greek
geographer Pausanias, who had visited the region in
search of its bygone grandeur. One of Pausanias's
passages on the funeral monuments of those heroic
times had long kindled Schliemann's interest. Already in
1869, in *Ithaca, the Peloponnese, Troy,* Schliemann had
suggested a revolutionary interpretation of the passage.
It led him to seek the royal tombs inside the perimeter of
the Mycenae acropolis, not outside. Philologists treated
him with sarcasm and accused him of being illogical.
The *Times* in London was equally amused, asserting that
"no one will find tombs within the citadel walls, unless

Previous spread: Pages
from the *Atlas of
Trojan Antiquities.*
Clearing the Lion Gate
at Mycenae (above)
of rubble put the
monument at great risk.
Somewhat rashly,
Schliemann complained
of the sluggishness of the
Greek Archaeological
Society, which had failed
to send an engineer to
shore up the various
structures. Left: English
traveler Edward
Dodwell's view of the
beehive interior of the
"Treasury of Atreus."

the man who destroyed Troy dug graves there under cover of night." Nor were the Greek newspapers indulgent toward the adventurer who was poisoning their country's already difficult relations with the Ottoman Empire. They called on the authorities to rein in this ambitious man, widely suspected of being a forger. The relevant Greek government ministry grew anxious. It ordered the prefect of Nauplia, just south of Mycenae, to keep his eye on the work; then it called off Schliemann's operations entirely.

They resumed only after two years of bargaining. Schliemann appealed to all his friends, from Prime Minister Gladstone to Sophia's uncle (and their matchmaker), now archbishop of Mantinea, and from Emile Burnouf, director of the French School at Athens, to the increasingly numerous Greek archaeologists who supported his cause. Schliemann had offered the Greek

Greek geographer Pausanias's *Description of Greece* (above, title page of a 1551 Florentine edition) served, like the *Iliad* on Hissarlik, as Schliemann's guide to the discovery of Mycenae. Pausanias had himself visited Mycenae at the height of Roman imperial power. Here again, the archaeologist sought to equate the monuments he unearthed with a great text from antiquity.

Archaeological Society money to pay for the demolition
of the Frankish Tower—symbol of Turkish occupation
—on the Acropolis. This gesture of support for Greek
freedom helped secure official permission to resume
digging. With a hundred laborers, the excavations lasted
from August to December 1876.

The operation was carried out under the auspices of
the Greek Archaeological Society and the direction of a
young Greek archaeologist, Panagiotis Stamatakis.
Schliemann's relations with this representative of the host
government were stormy. Each did his best to make life
impossible for the other. On the site, Sophia's exchanges
with her young countryman were far from cordial.
Schliemann wrote his excavation reports in English to
prevent Stamatakis from deciphering them. Stamatakis
criticized the haphazard placing of Schliemann's digs.
Schliemann was intent on locating all the monuments
that Pausanias had seen and named after the heroes of the
*Iliad.* To his wife he entrusted the exploration of the so-
called Clytemnestra's Tomb. He explored the approaches
to the "Treasury of Atreus" and sank several shafts near
the Lion Gate. Both his objectives and his methods drew
fire. But criticism died after the discovery of a grave circle
inside the citadel. For Schliemann, the controversy over
Pausanias's text seemed to be resolved. The man in the
field had won out over the desk-bound scholar.

His ambition remained unchanged: to
bring Homer's world back to life by fitting
the texts of the epic poems—taken
as historical guidelines—to the
archaeological remains. When the
first golden masks emerged from the
five shaft graves he had uncovered,
Schliemann was convinced that he
held King Agamemnon's mask in his
hands. "I have the greatest joy," he
cabled King George I of Greece, "to
announce to Your Majesty that I have
discovered the tombs which tradition,
transmitted by Pausanias, has designated
as the tombs of Agamemnon, Cassandra,
Eurymedon, and their companions, all

slain at table by Clytemnestra and her lover Aegisthus....
In the sepulchers I have found immense treasure in
archaic objects and pure gold. By themselves alone these
treasures are enough to fill a great museum, which will
be the world's most wonderful and which for centuries
to come will draw thousands of foreigners from all
countries to Greece." In all, over thirty pounds of golden
artifacts were consigned to the Bank of Greece.

These golden objects would soon be the pride of the

Inside the citadel efforts
were finally focused on
the grave circle (bottom
left of plan). Opposite:
One of the four masks
found in the fourth tomb
of the grave circle (16th
century BC).

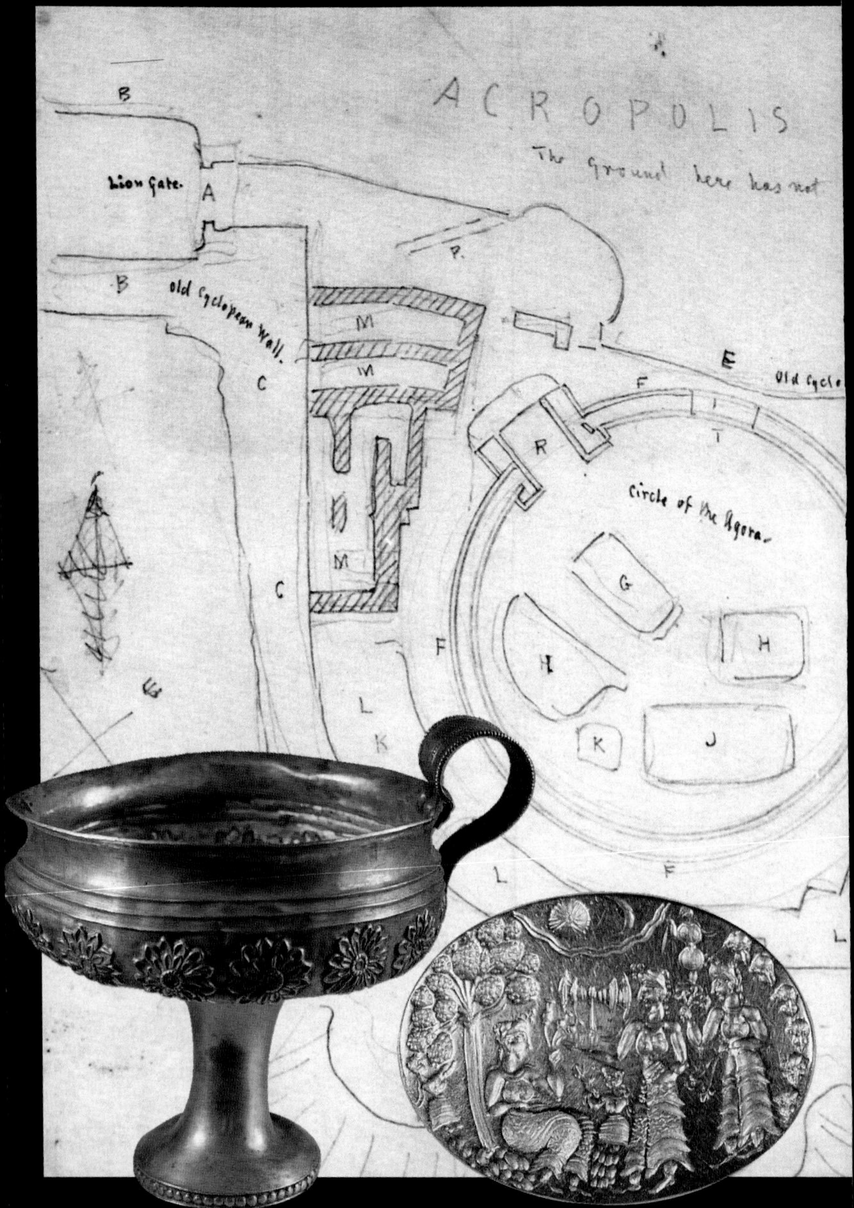
ACROPOLIS
The Ground here has not
Lion Gate.
A
B
B
Old Cyclopean Wall.
C
C
M
M
M
P.
E
Old Cyclo
F
R
Circle of the Agora.
G
H
H
K
K
J
L
L
F

The sketch plan shows handwritten notations:

Sketch plan of "D" Schliemann's
Excavations
in the Acropolis
of Mycenae.

MYCENÆ

...cavated

Temporary Wooden House
G

...ing wall.

E

C

...ound & has not been excavated.

O

old walls.

18½
13½   N.

...opean Walls.

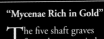

## "Mycenae Rich in Gold"

The five shaft graves from the grave circle explored by Schliemann —designated on the map by the letters G, H, I, J, K —yielded golden masks, weapons, and other objects. From left to right: Chalice decorated with fourteen *repoussé* (carved in relief) rosettes (grave J); gold seal (grave H) with ritual scene—two female worshipers presenting their offerings to a seated goddess, holding poppies beneath a vine branch; and cypress box (grave K) covered with twelve gold plates depicting hunting scenes and spiral motifs. These masterpieces have been dated to the first or second half of the 16th century BC. Overleaf: Two funeral masks— at right, the so-called Mask of Agamemnon— and a dagger blade inlaid with running lions.

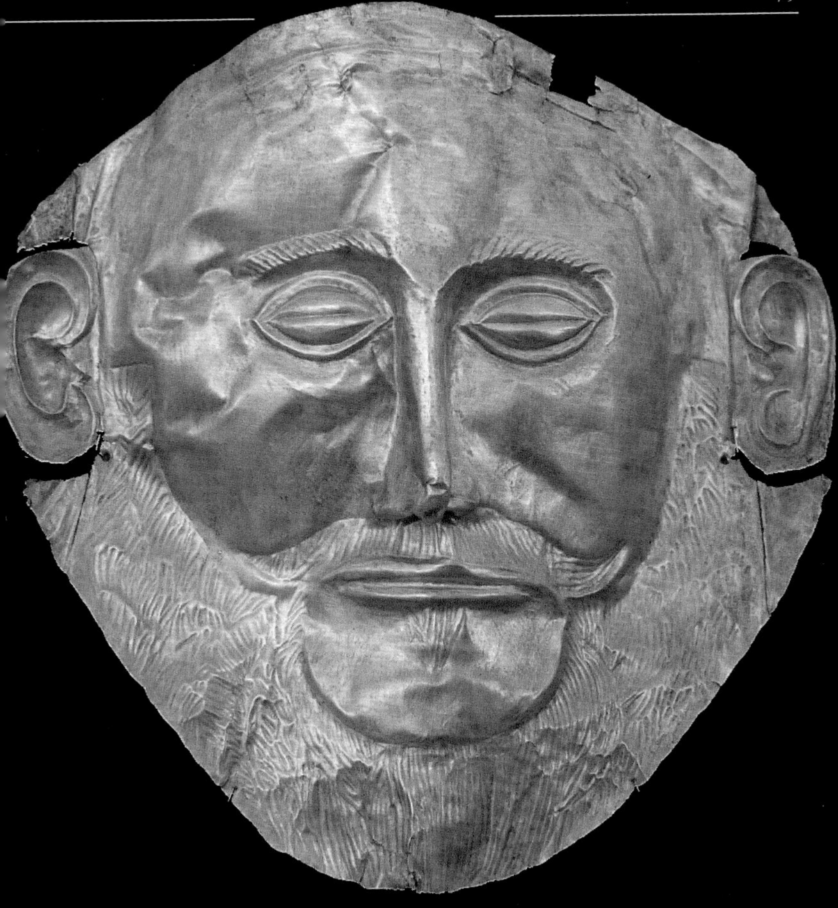

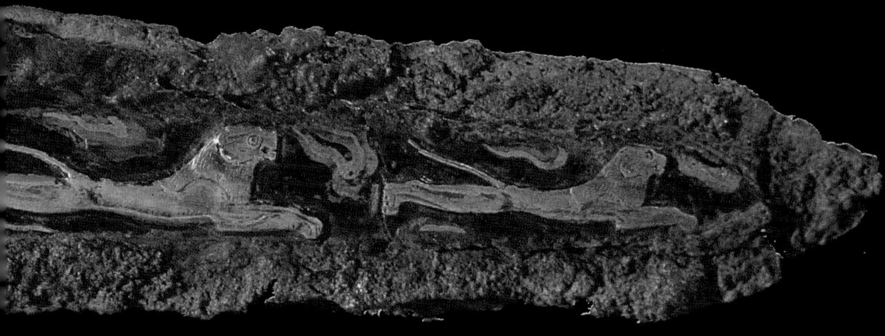

MYCENÆ
TROY
MYKENE

COLLECTION
Dr KETSCHOU

Dr. H. SCHLIEMANN and J. T. WOOD

WILLIAM SIMPSON

*Mycenae* (opposite: the original cover) was first published in English. Schliemann used the contents of three major photo albums as the basis for the engravings illustrating the book. The British archaeologist Sinclair Hood purchased the original albums from an Athens bookseller in 1955. The photographs were the work of the Romaïdes brothers and showed the objects before restoration, just as they were found. One funeral mask was so badly crushed that it was simply a shapeless mass. Among the 296 documents found in the albums (apart from Schliemann's own notes and sketches) were original plans and watercolors reproducing monuments and discoveries. They were executed by various Schliemann collaborators, such as Vasilios Drosinos or Dimitrios V. Tountopoulos. Left: Title page of the portfolio of watercolors of Mycenae by William Simpson.

Athenian Polytechnikon, the future National Archaeological Museum. But the objects in ivory and silver and earthenware were equally spectacular. In 1882 Schliemann wrote proudly, "so great is the press of foreigners who have come to see these treasures that there are already ten times more hotels in Athens than before my excavations." Early in 1878 *Mycenae* appeared. This stout, well-illustrated volume reproduced and enlarged upon the reports sent the previous year to the London *Times*.

Although the new book was a blend of myth and fact, its author did not confine himself to the revelation of the newfound masterpieces. The book opened a new field in

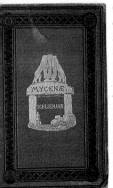

Greek studies—Mycenaean civilization. Before Schliemann Mycenae had been simply a name, its role in recorded history confined to a minor participation in the Persian Wars and destruction by Argos in 468 BC. Apart from the references in Homer and the much later tragedy by Aeschylus, almost nothing was known of the citadel in heroic times. Schliemann's excavations were an introduction to this vanished world, which had reached its apogee during the Bronze Age, between 1600 and 1125 BC. The discoveries provided a cultural model that would reappear in Argos and throughout Greece.

However, the graves unearthed by Schliemann are older than he believed. We now know, in the light of discoveries made during the 1950s, that they were in use between 1600 and 1510 BC. In the 13th century BC they were ringed by a circular structure integrated into the citadel precincts, as if Mycenae's rulers sought to emphasize their reverence for the tombs. Finally, the funeral ritual they reveal—burial —fails to correspond to the practices described by Homer, whose heroes were burned on funeral pyres after their death. In identifying the graves with the Mycenaean warriors of the Trojan War, Schliemann was wrong.

Schliemann's excavations paved the way for a new examination of the funeral customs of the Mycenaean world. The *tholoi* (beehive-shaped graves) are no longer necessarily identified as royal graves. In November 1951 a new grave circle, comparable in size to the one exhumed by Schliemann, was cleared. Older, and less rich in objects, it was in use between 1650 and 1550 BC. Thus the royal Mycenaean dynasty seems to have displaced a primitive oligarchical system. The new rulers remained attached to the aristocratic values of hunting and war, as the many weapons deposited in the graves (below, ornamental dagger) testify.

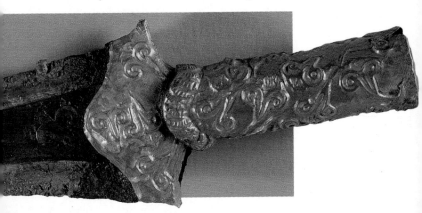

## Archaeologists Gather at the Site

After a visit to the site, the obligatory pose for the camera at the entrance of the *tholos* known as Clytemnestra's Tomb (this page). Opposite: Archaeologists gather before the Lion Gate. According to one of his biographers, Leo Deuel, Heinrich Schliemann is standing at the summit, one hand on the sculpted portal. Wilhelm Dörpfeld is on the left, above, sitting in a breach in the ramparts. On the ground, Sophia Schliemann (far right) sits on a stone block at the entrance to the citadel. Overleaf: The grave circle after Schliemann's excavations and consolidation efforts. Inset is an engraving based on Plate V of the first of the photo albums purchased by Sinclair Hood. Schliemann annotated this general view of the grave circle and of the five tombs investigated. The original photo is signed Tountopoulos.

"We could describe Schliemann's excavations on the hill of Hissarlik and consider their results without speaking of Troy or even alluding to it; even then, those discoveries would retain their value; even then, they would have added a whole new chapter to the history of civilization, the history of art."

Georges Perrot
*Journal des Savants*, 1891

CHAPTER V
# THE ARCHAEOLOGIST AS MODERN HERO

A sixty-year-old man and a thirty-year-old woman: the Schliemanns (opposite), painted by Eugene Broerrmann. Schliemann's tomb (right) in the First Cemetery of Athens.

Fresh sites beckoned the pioneer of Mycenaean archaeology: Ithaca and Orchomenos in Boeotia. But the results were less spectacular. Seeking to authenticate events recorded by history, Schliemann turned next to the battlefields where Greeks and Persians had once clashed, digging at Thermopylae in 1883 and at Marathon in 1884, but again without success. He started excavations at Tiryns but lost heart when his plans to explore Knossos collapsed. Gold had become elusive.... Schliemann then went to Central America and Cuba, followed by Egypt. He returned to Egypt with a friend who had assisted him on his last digs in the Troad, the doctor Rudolf Virchow. One last dream haunted Schliemann: discovering the tomb of Alexander the Great in the Egyptian city he had founded, Alexandria. Like the fallen king Sisyphus, who was doomed to forever roll a rock uphill, the archaeologist was tirelessly ranging the world in his quest to reawaken the past.

## The Archaeologist's Personal Palace

In 1878, returning to Ithaca with the *Odyssey* as his guide, Schliemann entrusted the architect Ernst Ziller with the task of creating for him an Athens home befitting his name and reputation. The Iliou Melathron, or House of Ilium, with its polychrome mosaics and walls decorated with frescoes glorifying Schliemann's excavations, was

inaugurated two years later with a grand ball. Some dignitaries were shocked by the nakedness of the statues on the building's roof, and Schliemann playfully had them clothed in brightly colored robes. The guests then urged him to undress them. He did so himself, to the delight of the Athenians.

Wined and dined all over Europe, the gentleman-archaeologist was now at the height of his fame. He admitted to having a huge income of which he annually spent half, the bulk of it on archaeological research. In 1875 he had even explored the Isle of Motya off Sicily—in search

of a Phoenician settlement—and Alba Longa, where he sought to solve the mystery of Rome's origins. The following year he prudently refused to dig at the Etruscan city of Chiusi, since he felt that it presented no problem for him to solve and he would find nothing there that was not already to be found in museums. Schliemann's great achievement was to have inaugurated "investigative" archaeology. He was, however, beginning to realize that the objective he had always set himself—fitting the architectural remains to the written texts—had its limits. In 1880 he investigated

For his house in Athens, Iliou Melathron (above), Schliemann hired the architect Ernst Ziller (opposite), a specialist in neoclassical construction inspired by the Italian Renaissance. Schliemann had met him ten years earlier in Athens while Ziller was taking part in excavations in the Troad. Buying furniture for his Athenian residence by catalogue (left), Schliemann was now spending money right and left.

Today hemmed in by modern buildings on noisy, polluted Venizelos Avenue, Schliemann's Athenian residence has lost much of its former charm. But the Muses still gaze down from the loggia ceiling (opposite) and the mosaic floors of the entranceway depict Mycenaean jewelry. Lines from Homer, Hesiod, and Pindar adorn the marble-covered walls in letters of gold. The ballroom, an extension of the dining room, is decorated with a large fresco (below). The bedrooms, library, and Schliemann's study were on the second floor.

the necropolis of Orchomenos, a city the *Iliad* describes as "rich in sheep" and whose "Treasure of Minyas" is mentioned by Pausanias. The dig revealed nothing spectacular; the relation of ancient tradition to the realities on the ground thus could not be taken automatically for granted.

Schliemann remained a controversial figure. Jealous of his finds academics rejected his beginnings and the unorthodox intellectual itinerary he had followed. To publicize his activities he chose the forum of popular magazines rather than specialist journals. And the attacks from academic circles were personal rather than scientific. Ulrich von Wilamowitz-Möllendorf, the leading German Hellenist of the day, heaped scorn on the Schliemanns. The retired businessman's wealth was thrown in his face; it raised suspicions about the origins of his discoveries. There was dark talk of disguised purchases or forgeries. And it was true that Schliemann exploited his fortune in the cause of his own fame, hiring journalists and scholars to write articles in his praise. This hunger for publicity undercut his prestige in the public's eyes. In 1881 Adolf Furtwängler, respected curator of the Berlin Museums, delivered this damning verdict: "Schliemann is hugely celebrated here. Nevertheless, he is and remains half-mad, a man of confused ideas who has no idea of the value of his discoveries." The explorer of Troy and Mycenae would never be admitted to the Berlin Academy—an honor

The self-educated Schliemann valued marks of distinction and intellectual recognition (above: diploma from the German Anthropological Society). In the archives of the Gennadius Library in Athens are an additional eighteen diplomas awarded the scientist by scientific institutions in Europe and the United States. Top: The site of ancient Orchomenos by Edward Dodwell.

reserved for university figures. But on 7 July 1881, with great pomp, he was awarded honorary citizenship of the city of Berlin: "By dedicating his practical activity to the service of an ideal," the award noted, "he has become a model for his fellow-citizens." Schliemann had just presented his Trojan collection, until then on display in London, to the German people. His friend Rudolf Virchow had advised that he make the move.

Schliemann and Virchow (below left) wrote one another regularly from 1876 to 1890. Their recently published correspondence is a mine of information. The London letter, dated 14 July 1884, informs Virchow about Schliemann's movements and the state of his health. The letter from Boulogne, on the north-west coast of France, is a miniature treatise on the Tiryns excavations.

## Tiryns: The Earliest Mycenaean Palace

As early as 1876 Schliemann had looked for the Palace of Tiryns in the Argive—the area around Argos, where he sank several exploratory shafts. According to the *Iliad* Diomedes had reigned there. The master of eighty warships, Diomedes was a respected chieftain whose sway extended as far as Epidaurus and Hermione. But, absorbed by Mycenae and later by new investigations in the Troad, Schliemann would not resume work on the citadel site until March 1884.

When he did eventually return to work at Tiryns, he again joined forces with Dörpfeld, who played an important part in the investigation. Two campaigns, each lasting several weeks, laid bare the earliest example of a Mycenaean palace. For Schliemann these remains made it possible to envisage the living conditions of Homeric kings. He believed that the courtyard of the *gynechaeum*, or women's quarters, overlooked by a line of rooms, and the banquet hall in Ithaca where Penelope and her suitors met in the *Odyssey*, found a parallel here. The existence of massive fortifications lends credence to the legend that seven Cyclops—one-eyed giants—were employed to build the walls.

In 1941 the archaeologist Arne Furumark published a landmark study of Mycenaean pottery. But Schliemann had been the first archaeologist to appreciate the significance of such production (above, color plate from *Tiryns*).

Following the Mycenaean tombs, the picture of Greek princely society finally became clear with the appearance of Schliemann's new book, *Tiryns*. Published simultaneously in German, English, and French, the book was an archaeological publishing event. It reached the booksellers in November 1885, just four months after the last blows of the archaeologist's pickax, but, like the excavation itself, the book suffered from hasty execution. An architectural overview served as preface, written by Friedrich Adler, Dörpfeld's father-in-law and former teacher. The latter, entrusted with illustrating the book, also wrote two major chapters, one on the construction and design of the palace, the other on the 1885 digs. An Asia Minor expert, Ernst Fabricius, wrote the notes for the objects unearthed during the last digging season. Schliemann himself prepared the catalogue of the most ancient finds and reconstructed the history of the site. In a brief overview he also suggested

We owe the adjective "Cyclopean," used to characterize the massive stone-block structures at Tiryns (below), to the Greek geographer Pausanias. In 1884 Schliemann and Dörpfeld cleared part of the ogive-(pointed arch) built southeastern great hall. Once again, controversy erupted. Schliemann was accused of mistaking Byzantine-era remains for a palace dating from the second millennium BC. "Schliemann's luck has deserted him," complained the *New York Times*. "He has found no gold nor any object of any value whatsoever."

the possibility of a Phoenician presence in ancient Greece and analyzed the legend of the birth of the "sun god and hero" Hercules at Tiryns.

Lacking comparative evidence, Schliemann was unable to comment on one outstanding find, but he realized its importance and had it reproduced on the cover of the book. It was a fragment of a mural depicting a man leaping onto a bull's back. Fifteen years later the British archaeologist Sir Arthur Evans would interpret it in light of the bull-jumping frescoes at Knossos. As it would later transpire, comparisons between the Homeric world and the Mycenaean palaces had little meaning, while Crete's influence on the Mycenaean world was much more obvious and decisive. Schliemann, intent on verifying Homer's reference to "the city where Minos, confidant of great Zeus, reigned in nine-year cycles," would be unlucky in Crete. As he states in one of his letters, he would have liked to "investigate the prehistoric palaces of the kings of Knossos in Crete," a project he thought would take "a week with a hundred men." This never materialized. During Schliemann's last stay at Knossos in 1889, negotiations with the site's owners failed at the eleventh hour. The owners claimed that the price they sought was justified by the presence on their

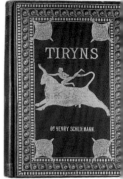

For the cover of *Tiryns* (above) Schliemann ordered a watercolor sketch (opposite) of an intriguing fresco fragment discovered near the *megaron*, or main hall. The significance of the find became apparent only when Sir Arthur Evans, in the first years of this century, unearthed a similar bull-jumping scene in the east wing of the palace at Knossos.

The design of the krater (a wide-bodied jar often used for mixing) below—depicting warriors and a hound escorting a chariot—has been gradually pieced together.

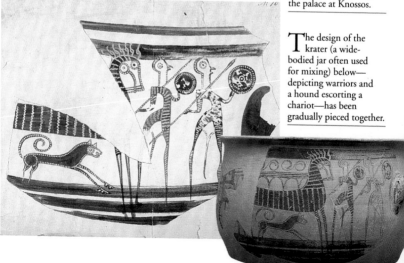

land of twenty-five hundred olive trees. Schliemann counted less than nine hundred. Deciding that he had been lied to, he refused the deal. King Minos's palace slipped from his grasp; its discovery was to fall later to Sir Arthur Evans.

## Ilios: the City and Country of the Trojans

In ancient Greece the poet was known as a "rhapsode," in other words one who "stitches together" fragments of song, sometimes of diverse origins, in order to compose an original story. Schliemann used this technique in the writing of *Ilios: the City and Country of the Trojans,* which appeared in 1880. Here Schliemann was overseeing a collective enterprise, organizing and conducting the efforts of a multidisciplinary team.

Running to a thousand pages in all, and with an introduction by Virchow, the book outlined the history of the seven settlements uncovered by Schliemann at Hissarlik. Twelve appendices, drawn up by five authors, including Frank Calvert, tackled as many different themes on Troy and its surroundings: ancient inscriptions, relations with Egypt, the role of metals in the prehistoric era, Hera Boöpis and the cattle cult, Hellenistic Ilium, and contemporary medical practices. The book, combining letters, reports, and analyses, is an astonishingly modern apologia for a scientifically based archaeology, calling on experts from many fields:

*Tiryns* pays tribute to Kikolaos Yannakis, Schliemann's loyal foreman on Hissarlik who was accidentally drowned in 1883. The excavation (like the book that resulted from it) was a team effort. Another fruit of this collective editorial endeavor was *Ilios: the City and Country of the Trojans.* Unusually for a scientific work, it began with the principal author's autobiography, which explained how the exploration of Troy was the fulfillment of a childhood dream. In his conclusion, Schliemann reported his financial holdings. Responding to detractors who accused him of squandering his money, Schliemann reassured them that a family man would never dream of ruining his children through archaeological follies: "My excavations do not cost me more than 125,000 francs per year; so that every year I am able to increase my capital by a sum equivalent to my expenses. I thus hope to leave to my children a fortune which will permit them to continue their father's scientific activities without eating into their capital."

epigraphy, ceramics, geography, geology, botany, chemistry, and medicine.

The archaeologist was still seized with a passion for business. Worried by the imminent prospect of the liberation of slaves in Cuba, he went there in 1886 to look after his sugarcane estates. Still on business, he visited Paris, Berlin, and then London. At a meeting of the Hellenic Society on 3 July he took the opportunity to answer those who accused him of burying the ancient wall of Tiryns beneath the debris of his excavation, and of misjudging the antiquity of the site. Dörpfeld was present. The two men were able to convince their listeners.

Heinrich and Sophia (left) adding the finishing touches to displays at the opening of the Trojan exhibition in Berlin in 1881. Schliemann (who with German Chancellor Otto von Bismarck and the military strategist Helmut von Moltke was one of the rare honorary citizens of the city) commented: "I am prey to varied emotions. Today is perhaps but a semicolon in one paragraph of my life. Yes, this is true, and this thought comforts me in the tumult of recent events." Schliemann (above) would soon be off to Egypt.

## Egyptian Mirage

Schliemann was surprisingly self-effacing as a patron of the arts. He did not attend the opening on 18 December 1886 of the Trojan Rooms at the new Berlin Ethnological Museum. For the past month he had been on a solo cruise up the Nile to Luxor. Schliemann was dreaming of Cleopatra and of Alexander. He was also studying the question of lighting in the Pharaonic temples. He collected pottery shards and stone objects. Above all he sought points of convergence between the Aegean world and Egyptian civilization. A stirrup-handled Mycenaean vase depicted on a wall of Ramses III's tomb caught his attention. It was similar to those he had uncovered in Argos—which meant he could now date those objects with great accuracy: for Ramses III was known to have reigned from 1198 to 1166 BC.

In 1887 Schliemann received permission to dig at Pylos in the Peloponnese, where he now hoped to bring to light the palace of Nestor, king of Pylos, according to Homer. But that winter he returned to Egypt. In February 1888 he excavated a few steps of a great staircase and the foundations of a palace in Alexandria. Against all the laws of probability, Schliemann was determined to believe that this could only be Cleopatra's palace! His single-mindedness drove him to falsify information. He exhibited a marble portrait said to be of the Egyptian queen, but he produced no proof that he had actually found it there; in fact, he probably purchased it. We know today that this Roman copy of a Greek original represents Corinna, rival of the 5th-century BC poet Pindar—not

the mistress of Pompey and Caesar.

Schliemann then returned to the Nile, where Virchow joined him. Schliemann was disappointed to not be able to proceed with the excavations he had planned near the Nebit Daniil Mosque in Cairo in hopes of finding Alexander the Great's tomb. He returned to Athens after learning that a Mycenaean stirrup-handled vase had been found in a Fayum grave in Lower Egypt dating back even earlier than the previous vases to the years 1304–1237 BC, the reign of Ramses II. He was convinced that Egyptian soil would give the dedicated seeker the answers to the riddles of Greece. The pharaohs' dates provided a sound chronological framework for the Greek objects found buried in their graves. Comparative archaeology was emerging.

Bötticher's book on Hissarlik (above). Left: Fascinated as ever by death, Schliemann sent Virchow this photo from Egypt of a mummified head that had intrigued him.

## Return to Troy

But first Schliemann's detractors had to be confronted. One of them, Ernst Bötticher, a retired artillery officer, was publishing books and pamphlets to prove—on the basis of material gathered during excavations—that the structures on the hill of Hissarlik had been designed for an exclusively funerary purpose. Bötticher's thesis was well received at the International Congress of Anthropology held in Paris in the summer of 1889. It was developed further by Salomon Reinach—a former member of the French School at Athens, a member of the Académie Française, and curator of the Museum of Saint-Germain-en-Laye outside Paris—in his article "Chronique d'Orient" ("A Tale of the East") in the magazine *Revue Archéologique*. Schliemann fought back. To win the scientifically minded public to his cause, he hired a university professor, Carl Schuchhardt, to write the history of his excavations and discoveries. The book was published in Leipzig in 1891. To confound his adversaries in the field, Schliemann then convened the first of two conferences in Troy itself. In December 1889, with Dörpfeld at his side, he welcomed Bötticher to Hissarlik. He had also invited,

as witnesses, Georg Niemann, a professor of the Viennese Academy of Fine Arts, and Bernhard Steffen, an officer on the king of Prussia's staff who had published plans and maps of Mycenae. Bötticher departed unconvinced; the two witnesses were converts to Schliemann's cause even before their arrival.

But the conference had a positive result: The Turkish government granted Schliemann fresh authorization to dig. Work resumed on 1 March 1890. A second Trojan conference also brought a number of experts together. Their observations and work confirmed their host's own conclusions. Meanwhile, there was great amusement abroad over "Schliemannopolis"—the barracks that their host had built to house them for the occasion.

On the work site (where small carts were now being used to haul out the rubble) there was a double objective. The first was to lay bare the remains of the second prehistoric settlement on Hissarlik, known as Troy II. This—among the seven successive Troys identified by

Under the leadership of Schliemann and Dörpfeld, new excavations began at Hissarlik in March 1890. Several witnesses were invited to the conference convened by Schliemann to mark the occasion (below, posing for the official photo). Behind Frank Calvert (seated, front row left) stands Schliemann. On his right are Wilhelm Grempler and Virchow. The conference issued a declaration in support of Schliemann's opinions against the positions sustained by Bötticher.

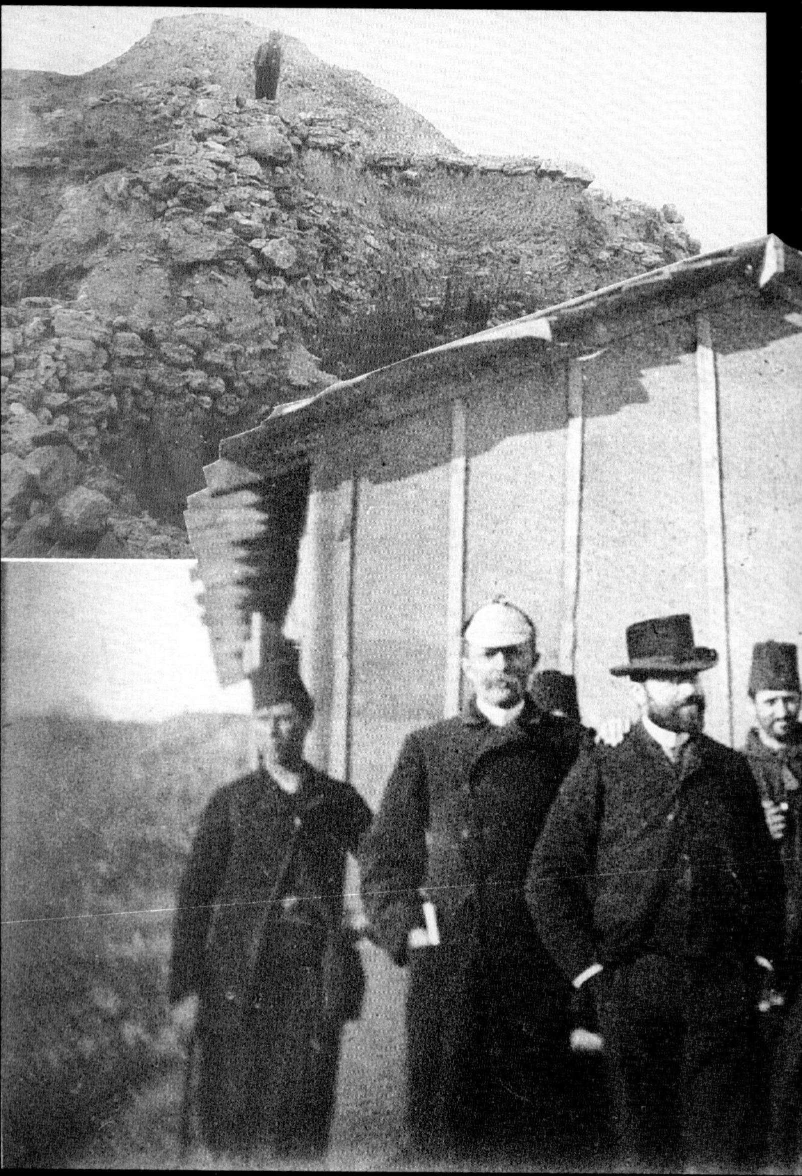

Schliemann welcomed
Major Bernhard
Steffen to Troy in
1889 (above). The
archaeologists invited
to the second Trojan
conference, in 1890, were
housed on the site, in
the barracks erected at
"Schliemannopolis"—
as Georges Perrot called
it. The photo at left,
captioned by Virchow,
includes "Zaptich [in
deerstalker], Dörpfeld,
Mr. Babin, Scherkasse
[in fez], Mrs. Babin,
Telamon, Schliemann,
Christophoros, and
Ghalib Effendi."

the digs and numbered in ascending order from the oldest to the most recent—was the level that Schliemann believed to be the Homeric city. The second objective was to begin new digs outside the ramparts of Troy II. Schliemann exhumed a marble head he took to be that of Emperor Caligula in the Roman levels of the excavation. It fell to Dörpfeld to make a major discovery: the foundations of a rectangular hall with a centrally placed hearth. Pottery fragments linked to this structure were comparable to those found in the Mycenaean shaft graves. This level also revealed a new prehistoric site,

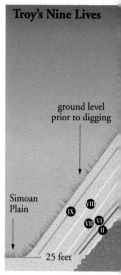

## Troy's Nine Lives

ground level prior to digging

Simoan Plain

25 feet

Dörpfeld continued Schliemann's excavations after 1893 (left and overleaf, his Trojan excavations of 1894). By the end of his investigations Dörpfeld had identified nine levels of occupation. In his view, Homer's Troy was Troy VI. Like Herodotus he located its fall around 1250 BC— a date disputed since antiquity. Eratosthenes, director of the Alexandria library in the 2nd century BC, believed it happened in about 1150 BC.

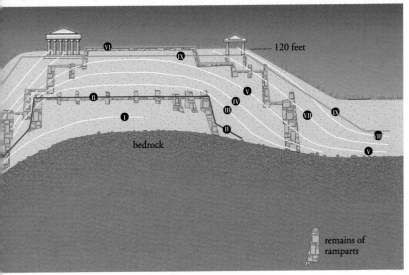

120 feet

bedrock

remains of
ramparts

designated Troy VI. For Dörpfeld this complex—much bigger than its predecessors and heavily fortified—was the city celebrated in the *Iliad*.

At this point (in 1890) Dörpfeld did not yet know the full extent of Troy VI, where he began excavation after Schliemann's departure. But he had already managed to date this sixth level, and thus undermine his friend Schliemann's earlier theories. The "Treasure of Priam" (in Troy) and "Mask of Agamemnon" (at Mycenae) were not contemporaneous, as Schliemann had believed. A thousand years separated them. Indeed, a kind of pottery present only in the sixth Trojan layer and in the Mycenaean sepulchers proved that Troy VI was contemporaneous with the grave circle at Mycenae. The much older Troy II (the Troy of the "Treasure of Priam") could not be the city where Helen had dwelt and Odysseus and his companions slaughtered and plundered during the Trojan War.

It cost Schliemann dear but he acknowledged his mistake, even stressing it in the conclusion of his last report. Urged by Dörpfeld to reexamine the whole Homeric question, he planned to undertake a new investigation. On 22 July he wrote to Prince Otto von

Troy I: a fortified site, 3000–2500 BC.
Troy II: 2500–2200 (it was at this level that Schliemann found the "Treasure of Priam").
Troy III: 2200–2050.
Troy IV: 2050–1900.
Troy V: 1900–1800.
Troy VI (1800–1300): To Dörpfeld this was Homer's city, although it was destroyed by an earthquake. Troy VII (1300–1000): a city ravaged by a violent fire, repopulated by the survivors, perhaps invaded around 1200, then abandoned. Troy VIII: reoccupation around 700 BC.
Troy IX: Hellenistic and Roman city.

When he discovered the imposing remains of Troy VI (left, view of the northeast tower), Wilhelm Dörpfeld, director of the German Archaeological Institute in Athens, thought he had stumbled upon confirmation of Schliemann's brilliant intuition. Below: Dörpfeld lightheartedly posing neck-deep in a huge storage jar.

Bismarck: "My workers and I are utterly exhausted. I shall be forced to suspend operations on August 1. But if Heaven grants me life I intend to resume work with all the energy at my disposal on 1 March 1891." Death would thwart his plans.

## Schliemann's Legacy

Schliemann had long suffered from an earache, which became unbearable in the autumn of 1890. Virchow

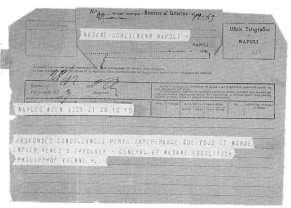

S chliemann's body was taken from Naples to Athens by Dörpfeld and by Sophia's elder brother. At her husband's death, Sophia received countless expressions of sympathy (left). One of the first to offer tribute and condolences was German Emperor Wilhelm II. The funeral took place in the afternoon of 4 January 1891 in the presence of King George I of Greece, the Greek prime minister, the United States ambassador, and a host of Greek and foreign scientists. A huge crowd joined the procession. Dörpfeld read his friend's funeral eulogy. It ended with these words: "Rest in peace. You have done enough."

made him promise to consult a specialist in Germany. In early November he went to Halle, where Dr. Hermann Schwartz examined him and decided to operate. As soon as he was dismissed from the clinic, Schliemann left for Leipzig to confer with his publisher; in December he journeyed to Paris. But the pains persisted and grew worse. Now deaf, Schliemann decided to return to Greece. He stopped en route in Naples, intending to see Pompeii again. On Christmas Day he collapsed, comatose, on a street near the Piazza Carità. On 26 December 1890 he died at the Grand Hotel in Naples, without emerging from his coma. He was buried in Athens at a funeral attended by throngs of onlookers on 4 January 1891.

Troy continued to baffle experts even after the archaeologist's death. Dörpfeld carried on Schliemann's work and brought to light all of Troy's successive lives —nine in all. According to him Troy VI was Homer's city, destroyed around 1250 BC by Agamemnon's soldiers. An American archaeologist, Carl Blegen—who also dug at the palace in Pylos—challenged this theory during the course of new excavations begun in 1932. He became convinced that Troy VI was destroyed by an earthquake. In his opinion the city sacked by the Greeks of the *Iliad* was Troy VII, or more precisely Troy VIIa (VIIb being merely a resettlement of the ruins of its immediate predecessor).

But this interpretation is shaky. All that can be said with any certainty is that Troy VIIa was destroyed by fire at a date when the Mycenaean world may already have collapsed. The English historian Moses I. Finley has noted that Homer's Trojan War must be lifted out of the history of Bronze Age Greece. That is, according to Finley, the *Iliad* was not the oral transmission of a historical reality. According to recent thinking Homer's epic was a poetic invention that re-created a model past, one that allowed 9th- and 8th-century BC Greek communities to forge their identities "in the shadow of the heroes."

Since 1984 a team from the University of Tübingen in Germany, led by Manfred Korfmann, has been carrying out excavations in Troy. These now make it certain that Ilium—the city which according to ancient tradition was the heir to Troy—did indeed stand on Hissarlik. But the hill was merely the fortified citadel. Ilium itself had

Schliemann's tomb lies in the First Cemetery of Athens, south of the Olympeion and the Ilissos. The archaeologist himself had chosen the site, which boasted a magnificent view. His monument (opposite) was completed in 1892, based on plans drawn up by Ernst Ziller: a small Doric temple on a raised pedestal with a frieze (below) depicting archaeological operations.

occupied a much greater area, proved by the recently unearthed remains of a defensive wall built one quarter of a mile south of the area explored by Schliemann. Troy I, hitherto dated at around 3000 BC, is apparently less ancient than conjectured, more probably dating from about 2500 BC. Finally, the site was already occupied in the fourth millennium before the birth of Christ. Troy's history was thus much more complex than had been supposed.

The Hissarlik site as it is today (above). This aerial photo shows the southeastern end of Troy. In the foreground are the fortifications of Troy VI and one of its guard towers. Behind them lie the foundations of a residential building.

## In Praise of the Archaeologist

Schliemann did no more than draw near to the truth. He was fully aware of this, after striving his whole life long to close the gap between his dreams and reality. Eager for wealth and social recognition though he was, his overriding desire was to quench his thirst for knowledge. In his quest for his own and our civilization's origins he was prepared to accept any sacrifice. On the brink of death he was magnanimous enough to accept the refutation of the theories he had defended. Thanks to his determination, he extended the frontiers of Mediterranean archaeology and pushed back the boundaries of time. Before him, Bronze Age Greece was virtually nonexistent. His discovery of Mycenaean civilization gave birth to the study of Aegean protohistory.

Schliemann's excavation techniques have been widely criticized. They caused irreparable damage, but they were, after all, the methods of the day. Nevertheless, he realized that he needed to modernize his methods and eventually acquired the services of a specialist in stratification of the caliber of Wilhelm Dörpfeld. Himself a competent student of pottery, Schliemann was careful not to overlook the smallest on-site clue. His excavation notes were models of conscientiousness; he compiled meticulous excavation reports and carefully labeled the tiniest artifacts. And he was swift to make his findings public. His *Atlas of Trojan Antiquities* was one of the first books to reproduce photographic plates, making it possible for every reader to decide from the evidence on hand. If such practices were faulted, it was because they were ahead of their time.

A fanatical student of historical geography and a tireless traveler, Schliemann was a pioneer prospector. He left two final lessons for his successors: Archaeology is a matter of teamwork—increasingly technical and demanding the participation of experts from diverse scientific disciplines. And, archaeology has to be a profitable activity, constantly dependent on museum connections and oriented toward the general public. Properly conducted, it encourages tourism and fosters the economic interests of the host countries. And such tourism in its turn promotes new vocations for archaeology. After all, it was his own visit to Pompeii that changed the whole course of the life of the businessman from Ankershagen.

ATLAS TROJANISCHER ALTERTHÜMER.

PHOTOGRAPHISCHE ABBILDUNGEN

ZU DEM

BERICHTE

ÜBER DIE

AUSGRABUNGEN IN TROJA

Dr. HEINRICH SCHLIEMANN.

LEIPZIG

"It is now an idle question whether Schliemann, at the beginning of his researches, proceeded from right or wrong presuppositions. Not only has the result decided in his favor, but also the method of his investigation has proved to be excellent.... Who would have undertaken such great works, continued through so many years—have spent such large means out of his own fortune—have dug through layers of debris heaped one on the other in a series that seemed almost endless, down to the deep-lying virgin soil—except a man who was penetrated with an assured, nay an enthusiastic conviction? The Burned City would still have lain to this day hidden in the earth, had not imagination guided the spade."
Rudolf Virchow

# DOCUMENTS

"I [Poseidon] walled the city [of Troy]
massively in well-cut stone, to make
the place impregnable"
Homer, *Iliad*
Book XXI, lines 521–23
(trans. Fitzgerald)

# A Who's Who of Homer

*Schliemann was guided through his expeditions by the words of the great poet Homer, who lived in Greece in the 8th century* BC. *The characters of the* Iliad *and the* Odyssey *fueled the archaeologist's imagination as well as his life's work.*

T he Trojan horse in a 19th-century engraving.

## The *Iliad* and the *Odyssey*

*The* Iliad *was probably composed around 750 BC, and it tells of the war between the Trojans and the Greeks. The war began over the abduction of Helen, wife of the Greek king, Menelaus, by the handsome Trojan prince, Paris. Historians today date the Trojan War to about 1250 BC. According to Homer, the Greeks finally succeeded in penetrating the enormous walls of Troy (on the coast of modern-day Turkey) by leaving a huge wooden horse outside the gates, presumably as an offering. When the curious Trojans wheeled the "gift horse" into their citadel, Greek soldiers piled out of it and thus penetrated the city.*

*The* Odyssey, *most probably written some years after the* Iliad, *is the story of Odysseus's ten-year return from the Trojan War back to his native Greece.*

*The main characters in Homer's epics are a fascinating group; their histories are summarized below.*

ACHILLES: Credited with being the Greek's best fighter. In a piratical foray en route to Troy, Achilles's share of the booty is a pretty young woman named Briseis. But Agamemnon, as the expedition's commander in chief, demands her for himself, infuriating Achilles, who broods in his tent while the Trojans defeat the Greeks in battle after battle. He is eventually roused from his tent when his best friend, Patrocles, is killed; spurred to action Achilles avenges Patrocles and helps lead the Greeks to victory.

AENEAS: Actually the hero of a great Roman epic, Virgil's *Aeneid*, Aeneas, a native of Troy, nonetheless features in Homer's *Iliad* as well.

Schliemann claimed that he was inspired as a child to discover Troy by the image in a children's history book of Aeneas fleeing his burning city with his aged father on his back and his young son by the hand [see page 18].

AGAMEMNON: King of Mycenae, brother to the wronged King Menelaus, and the richest and most powerful of the Greek kings, for these reasons chosen to head the expedition to Troy. His greed and pride precipitate a row with Achilles that nearly wrecks the Greek cause. While he is away his wife, Clytemnestra, takes a lover, then has Agamemnon murdered when he returns.

When Schliemann discovered a gold funerary mask at Mycenae, he is said to have exclaimed, "I have gazed upon the face of Agamemnon!"

AJAX: Next to Achilles, the best Greek fighter. Actually Ajax may have lived earlier, but his exploits were so extraordinary that bards gave him a role in the Trojan story.

HECTOR: Priam's son and Troy's finest warrior. Hector leads the besieged Trojans to victory in a series of skirmishes beneath the city's walls. In one of these actions he kills Achilles's closest friend, Patrocles. This forces Achilles to action; he challenges Hector to single combat and, after chasing him around the walls of Troy, kills him. In a touching scene in the *Iliad*, the old and defeated King Priam goes to the enemy camp and begs the Greeks to return the body of his son.

HELEN: Paris's seduction and abduction of the dazzlingly beautiful Helen, wife of King Menelaus, triggers the Trojan War. Despite her infidelity, Homer treats her gently in the *Iliad*, and in the *Odyssey*, she and Menelaus are reconciled.

MENELAUS: King of Sparta and brother to Agamemnon. His wife, Helen, runs off with a young Trojan prince, so Menelaus appeals to Agamemnon for help in seeking revenge. Agamemnon responds by organizing the expedition to Troy.

NESTOR: King of Pylos and probably the second-ranking man on the Greek side. Older than the other commanders, and presumably wiser, he persists in giving long, windy advice to his fellow warriors.

Schliemann hoped to find Nestor's palace in Pylos, but never began excavations.

ODYSSEUS: King of Ithaca, and the most complex and interesting of the *Iliad*'s heroes. A favorite of the later Classical Greeks because—though not the strongest man around—he triumphs by his wits. Homer's *Odyssey* is about Odysseus's ten-year adventure trying to get home after the fall of Troy.

Schliemann thought he had found the Palace of Odysseus in Ithaca.

PARIS: Also Priam's son, a handsome young man who, in his youth, was inveigled into judging which of three goddesses was the most beautiful. He chose Aphrodite, who, as a reward, arranged for Paris's seduction of Helen, the world's most beautiful woman, precipitating the Trojan War.

PRIAM: King of Troy. An old man, unable to fight himself, he senses that his city is doomed, that he and his sons will die, and that his wife Hecuba and all the other Trojan noblewomen will be carried off into slavery.

Schliemann called the gold that he found at Troy the "Treasure of Priam."

Adapted from *The Lost World of the Aegean*
Maitland A. Edey
1975

# Schliemann's Writings

*Schliemann's extensive travel diaries and excavation journals have their own particular flavor—a blend of scientific considerations, calculating personal "confessions," and anecdotes. Here we see what daily life could be like on an excavation site.*

B elow: an 18th-century drawing of Homer reciting his verse. Opposite: Odysseus strapped himself to the mast of his ship so that he would not be tempted by the beautiful music of the deadly sirens.

## The Journey to Ithaca

*In 1869 Schliemann published* Ithaca, the Peloponnese, Troy *in the form of a travel diary. The book conveys the first excitement and enthusiasm of the novice excavator (and earned him a doctorate from the University of Rostock). Here Schliemann seeks the Palace of Odysseus in Ithaca.*

On 10 July, after swimming in the sea and drinking a cup of black coffee, I set out with my workers at five in the morning. At seven, bathed in sweat, we reached the top of Mount Aëtos.

First I had the four men uproot the undergrowth and then start digging at the northeast corner where, I surmised, the famous olive tree once stood—the tree of which Odysseus made his nuptial bed and around which he built his bed chamber [*Odyssey*, Book XXIII, lines 216–27, Fitzgerald trans.];
"An old trunk of olive
grew like a pillar on the building plot,
and I laid out our bedroom round
that tree,

lined up the stone walls, built the walls
    and roof,
gave it a doorway and smooth-fitting
    doors.
Then I lopped off the silvery leaves and
    branches,
hewed and shaped that stump from the
    roots up
into a bedpost, drilled it, let it serve
as model for the rest. I planed them all,
inlaid them all with silver, gold and
    ivory,
and stretched a bed between—a pliant web
of oxhide thongs dyed crimson."

But we found nothing beyond
fragments of tile and earthenware, and
two feet down we reached bare rock.
There were admittedly many crevices in
this rock, which the roots of the [olive]
tree could have penetrated; but all hope
of finding archaeological objects there
had disappeared as far as I could tell.

Next I ordered them to dig in the
adjacent earth, for I had found two

rocks there of considerable size, which
seemed once to have formed part of a
wall; and after three hours' work my
men uncovered the two lower layers of
a small building some ten feet wide and
fifteen feet long; the door opening was
three feet in width. The stones were
well cut and measured thirteen inches
square; they were joined together by a
quantity of snow-white cement, pieces
of which I have kept. There was a thick
layer of this cement even beneath the
lower bed of stones. The presence of
this cement convinces me that the
building was erected at least seven
centuries after the Trojan War, for I
have never seen cement in buildings of
the heroic age....

While my laborers were busy with this
excavation, I examined the whole site of
Odysseus's palace with the most careful
attention. Having discovered a large
stone, one of whose ends seemed to
describe a gentle curve—perhaps the

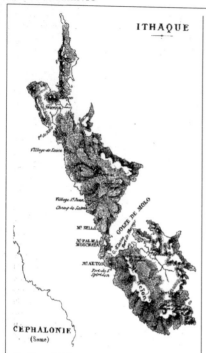

ITHAQUE

CEPHALONIE
(Same)

Map of Odysseus's kingdom from Schliemann's *Ithaca, the Peloponnese, Troy*. Opposite: A view of Ithaca, c. 1820.

hundredth part of a circle—I detached the earth from the stone with a knife, and found that the [whole] stone formed a half-circle. Continuing to probe with the knife, I swiftly realized that the circle had been completed on the other side by small stones set one on the other and forming a kind of miniature wall. I first sought to disengage this circle with my knife, but to no avail: the earth, mingled with a white substance I recognized as burned bone-ash, was almost as hard as stone. I therefore had to dig with a pickax, but I had barely progressed four inches before I shattered a fine but very

small vase filled with human ashes. I then continued to dig with the greatest care, and uncovered some twenty vases of curious shape and each one quite distinct from its fellows. Some lay on their sides; others were upright. But unfortunately, due to the hardness of the earth and my lack of appropriate tools, I broke most of them as I extracted them, and was able to recover only five in good condition. The biggest of them is but four inches high, with a mouth less than half an inch across; another had an opening two inches across. Two of these vases had quite handsome paintings of men when I removed them from the earth. These paintings disappeared almost as soon as I exposed them to the sun, but I hope to revive them by rubbing them with alcohol and water.

All these vases were filled with the ashes of burned human bodies.

In this small domestic graveyard I also found the curved blade of a sacrificial knife, five inches long, and rust-covered, but otherwise well preserved; a terracotta idol depicting a goddess with two flutes at her lips; then the remains of an iron sword, a boar's tooth, several small animal bones, and finally a handle made of woven bronze wires. I would have given five years of my life for an inscription—but alas, there was none!

Although the age of these artifacts is difficult to determine, it seems certain to me that the vases are much older than those from Cumae at the Naples Museum, and it is quite possible that in my five little urns I hold the bodies of Ulysses and Penelope or of their offspring!

Having excavated the circular pit to its depths, I measured it: on the south side it was thirty inches deep, and on

the north thirty-six inches, while its diameter was four feet.

There is nothing more thirst-provoking than the rough job of digging in 120 degrees in the sun. We had brought with us three huge water-jugs and a large bottle containing four liters of wine. The wine was quite enough [for our needs], since the product of Ithaca grapes is, as I have already said, three times stronger than Bordeaux wine; but our supply of water was soon exhausted, and we were twice obliged to replenish it.

My four workmen completed their excavation of the post-Homeric dwelling just as I finished unearthing the little circular grave-pit. I had been more successful than they; but I bore them no ill-will, for they had worked

hard, and another thousand years may go by before the site is once again blanketed with dust.

[By now] It was noon, and we had eaten nothing since five that morning; we therefore sat down to lunch beneath an olive tree between the two enclosing walls, some fifty feet below the summit. Our meal consisted of dry bread, wine and water whose temperature was around eighty-seven degrees Fahrenheit. But I was eating the fruit of the soil of Ithaca, and eating it in the courtyard of Odysseus's palace, and perhaps on the very spot where that king wept as his favorite dog Argos died of joy on recognizing his master again after twenty years' absence.

Heinrich Schliemann
*Ithaca, the Peloponnese, Troy,* 1869

# In Search of Love

*After his first disastrous marriage, Heinrich Schliemann was determined to find himself a more compatible mate. In his novel about the archaeologist, writer Irving Stone describes Schliemann's "interview" (based on Schliemann's own accounts) with a prospective bride, thirty years his junior.*

Henry Schliemann hired the largest sailboat available but it seemed pitifully small and frail to Sophia [who was afraid of the sea]. The trip out of the harbor was calm, and she had hopes of coming through the afternoon without disgracing herself. But the moment the boat left the protected bay and entered the open sea the sun vanished behind a cloud, a wind sprang up and the sailboat began to pitch to and fro. Sophia became queasy….

"Miss Sophia," he began in an earnest, affectionate tone, "why do you want to marry me?"

"Oh no," thought Sophia, "not at this moment! When I am about to lean over the railing."

There was no escaping his intense gaze, or the tense posture of his head on his neck as he awaited the all-important answer to his question…. She answered as honestly as she could:

"Because my parents have told me to."

She saw Henry Schliemann turn pale. For an instant she thought he was the one to be sick. Then anger thundered into his eyes; she had never seen them blazing this way before. Outraged color flooded upward on the lean cheeks. His voice was hoarse.

"I am deeply pained, Miss Sophia, at the answer you have given me, one worthy of a slave; and all the more strange because it comes from an educated young woman. I myself am a simple, honorable, home-loving man. If ever we were married, it would be so that we could excavate together and share our common love of Homer."

The seas had grown rougher. The sailboat was surrounded by white-caps. … Nauseous as she was, she had better set this strange and unpredictable man straight.

Heinrich and Sophia Schliemann, c. 1880.

"Mr. Henry, you should not be shocked by my answer. The marriage of every girl in Greece is arranged by her parents, who conscientiously try to find her the best possible husband. That is what my parents have done and I accept their judgment. It is a quality you should value in me: if I am a good daughter, it means I will be a good wife."

Only partly appeased, Henry demanded in a quieter but still stern voice:

"Is there no other reason why you are willing to marry me? Surely there must be something in your decision besides blind obedience?"

...Making a desperate effort to formulate her thoughts, she murmured to herself:

"But what other answer is he looking for? I have already said that I admire and respect him for the strength of his convictions about Homer. I have already indicated that I have faith in his writings. For what other quality does he want me to admire him, when he has told us that these pursuits are his whole life? That he wants a Greek wife to help him to fulfill his dreams. I have missed something. And how can I think when all I want to do is die?"

Then...she said to herself:

"But of course! The quality for which all the world admires him, and because of which every family in Greece with a daughter to marry has been pursuing him. He is a millionaire! With more money than anyone we've ever heard of! And he achieved it all by himself, without formal education, without family or backing. He has a right to be proud of himself."

She looked up at Henry Schliemann once again, putting all the admiration and pride into her voice that she could muster, paying him the world's ultimate compliment:

"Because you are rich!"

Henry's face became stony.

"You want to marry me, not for my value as a human being, but because I am rich! I am no longer in a position to converse with you. I have decided not to think of you any more."

He turned away, calling curtly to the crew:

"Put back into port."

Irving Stone
*The Greek Treasure*, 1975

## An Anniversary Letter

*Despite their rather rocky start, Heinrich and Sophia were eventually married. On the eve of their twenty-first wedding anniversary, Heinrich wrote his wife a letter.*

...Today, as I look back at the long time I have spent with you, I see that the Fates have spun us many sorrows and many joys. We are accustomed to look at the past through rose-colored spectacles, forgetting the past woes and remembering only the pleasant things. I cannot praise our marriage enough. You have never ceased being a loving wife to me, a good comrade, and an unfailing guide in difficulties, as well as a loving companion and a mother like no other. I am so delighted with the virtues with which I see you adorned that I have already agreed to marry you in the coming life.

Letter to Sophia Schliemann from Heinrich Schliemann
23 September 1890
Excerpted in David Traill
*Schliemann of Troy*
1995

# Mycenae

*At Mycenae, relations between the Schliemanns and Panagiotis Stamatakis, the official representative of the Greek Archaeological Society, were far from smooth. Not over-endowed with tact, the couple behaved unfairly to one of the most gifted Greek archaeologists of his generation. Here is the Greek scientist's version of events as he reported them to his superiors.*

Drawing of the Lion Gate, Mycenae, 1877. Opposite: Sophia Schliemann surveys the Mycenaean excavations.

The morning of Thursday 24 August, when I arrived at the site I saw that excavation had begun on the underground chamber. I had told Mr. Schliemann that I could not supervise this new enterprise and consequently could not authorize it. He replied in a hostile manner, as is his custom, that he was going to clean out the entrance to the underground chamber and that if I was not equal to the task, Ministry would send more officials. I replied that the Ministry had granted permission for an excavation with fifty to sixty workmen, not with ninety workmen, and not with workmen paid by the cubic meter. He answered that he had permission to have as many excavations as he wished and under whatever terms he wished and that my only task was to receive the finds. I pointed out that my mission was not merely to receive the finds but also to have general supervision over all the work at Mycenae and to prevent any contravention of the law or of the Ministry's instructions. I added that since he had such an opinion of my mission, he should communicate this to the General Ephoria of Antiquities and if it approved the work undertaken, then that was fine. Otherwise, the sites being excavated would be reduced to one so that the collection of the finds could proceed in a proper manner and the workmen could be carefully supervised to prevent them from stealing objects, as it was rumored a few days ago in Argos they were doing, and so that the finds could be properly recorded every day.

The following day at the excavations outside the underground chamber there appeared a line of walling of squared bricks and beside this another wall at a greater depth. In my absence, Schliemann instructed the workmen

to destroy both these walls. When I got there later and learned this, I told the workmen not to destroy the walls before they had been carefully examined and if they appeared insignificant, then they would be destroyed, but if they were important, they should be preserved. While Mr. Schliemann was absent, the workmen followed my instructions. The next day, however, Saturday, Mr. Schliemann came to the site very early, bringing his wife along with him. He instructed the workmen to destroy the walls they had struck against. In case I should try, when I arrived later, to prevent further destruction, he left his wife in charge of the workmen as guardian of his instructions, while he proceeded to the acropolis. When I arrived a little later, I asked the workmen why they were destroying the walls when they were prohibited from doing so. Schliemann's wife answered that I had no right to give such instructions, that her husband was a scholar, that the walls were Roman and that it was appropriate to destroy them because they were impeding the workmen, that I had no idea about such

matters, and that I ought not to trouble Mr. Schliemann with such instructions because he was easily provoked and might break off the excavations. I replied that Mr. Schliemann was not entirely free to do as he wished with the ancient objects, as he had done at Troy, and that he had been given a permit to conduct excavations at Mycenae in conformance with the law. Mr. Schliemann, from the very beginning of the excavations, has shown a tendency to destroy, against my wishes, everything Greek or Roman in order that only what he identifies as Pelasgian [prehistoric] houses and tombs remain and be preserved. Whenever potsherds of the Greek and Roman period are uncovered, he treats them with disgust. If in the course of the work they fall into his hands, he throws them away. We, however, collect everything—what he calls Pelasgian, and Greek and Roman pieces.

Panagiotis Stamatakis
Report to General Ephoria of
Antiquities, Athens
Excerpted in David Traill,
*Schliemann of Troy*, 1995

# What Happened to "Priam's Gold"?

*After promising them at various times to Greece, Russia, the United States, England, and France, Schliemann finally bequeathed his Trojan treasures to his native Germany. They were to be exhibited in the Berlin Museums in a special gallery bearing Schliemann's name. The treasures were on exhibit for several decades but were put away for safekeeping during World War II. By the end of the war, however, all the gold had disappeared.*

## A Discovery in the Basement

*The fate of "Priam's Gold" was one of the great mysteries of the war.*

One day in September 1987, Grigorii Kozlov, who had recently become the curator of the new Museum of Private Collections in Moscow, a branch of the Pushkin Museum, was asked by a colleague to make photocopies of some papers. In 1987 this was still a formidable task. Copying machines were rare in the Soviet Union, and there were none in the Pushkin Museum. But Kozlov had worked in the Ministry of Culture and had friends there, and he thought he could use his connections to get access to a copier.

…When Kozlov reached the fourth floor, where the Department of Visual Arts was located, he saw piles of papers and books strewn about in complete disorder. At first he thought there had been an accident of some sort. Then he saw a former colleague, G., walking toward him with a heap of old documents under his arms.

"What's going on?" Kozlov asked him?… Kozlov's friend told him that the chief of the Department of Museums had decided to clean out old papers and other "junk." They had already thrown away tons of documents, he said, and then he asked Kozlov to help him carry a batch to the basement, where they would be destroyed. Kozlov took part of the load and followed him…. Finally they stopped, and G. knocked on a door that was opened by a woman wearing dirty white overalls and a gauze mask and rubber gloves. She was carrying a long knife.

"Ach, they've brought more," she said to someone inside. The room was dimly lit by a couple of unshaded lightbulbs hanging from the ceiling, and the air was full of dust. Another woman, similarly attired, was standing at a big metal table heaped with bundles of old documents, cutting the strings and throwing the papers into a pile on the floor. At the other end of the room there was a shredding machine. The woman who had opened the door showed the men where to put their loads. In the dim light Kozlov noticed that a sheet of paper lying on the floor near his foot had the words "State Pushkin Museum" at the top. He picked it up and began to read. G. was in a hurry and left Kozlov alone with the two women.

"May I see the papers?" Kozlov asked them....

"Sure," answered the older one. "Take a knife and cut the strings. Your help is welcome."

Kozlov was having trouble breathing in the dusty air, and he made a mask of his handkerchief. As he opened the bundles, he glanced quickly over each paper. On the sheet he had picked up from the floor, he had noticed something that made his heart skip a beat. Near the name of the museum was written in red pencil the word "restitution." The word conjured up an event that he had until recently thought he knew all about: the Soviet Union's return to East Germany in 1955 of the masterpieces taken from the Dresden Gallery at the end of World War II. The "rescue" of the Dresden Gallery had been the major cultural event of the war as far as the Soviet Union was concerned, and its restitution ten years later was a milestone in the relations between the two countries....

Could there be artworks removed from Germany that were still hidden in storerooms in the Soviet Union—great and famous masterpieces that the world believed destroyed or lost?

Now cutting the strings and sorting quickly through the brittle papers in the cellar of the Ministry of Culture, Kozlov hoped to find answers to some of his questions. He could see that the documents were important. After half an hour of digging in the dusty heaps, he found what he wanted: minutes of the Soviet-German negotiations for the return of the Dresden Gallery pictures and papers dealing with their exhibition in Moscow before they were sent back to Germany. Koslov kept on sorting through the papers, hoping for more information. Then he turned up something that made him gasp: a handwritten document entitled "List of the Most Important Art Works Kept in the Special Depository of the Pushkin Museum." Another document, entitled "Unique Objects from the 'Large Trojan Treasure,' Berlin, Museum für Völkerkunde," was signed by Nora Eliasberg, acting chief curator of the Pushkin Museum, and dated March 28, 1957. Kozlov had in his hands evidence that the famous Trojan treasure excavated by Heinrich Schliemann in 1873, which had mysteriously disappeared from Berlin in 1945, had not been destroyed but had been hidden in the Soviet Union for more than forty years.

The "Trojan Treasure" listed in Nora Eliasberg's inventory was more than simply one of the greatest archaeological discoveries in history. From the moment Heinrich Schliemann announced to the world that he had found the treasure of King Priam of Troy, the ancient gold and silver objects had exerted a special hold over the popular imagination. Had Priam himself poured wine into this small gold goblet? Had Helen of Troy worn these diadems and adorned her fingers with the gold rings?

Schliemann was a rich German businessman and amateur archaeologist obsessed with proving that the Trojan War had been a real event, not just a legend handed down by generations of bards to the blind Homer. He believed that Priam and Helen, Hector and Agamemnon were real people. The discovery of the golden hoard was his proof....

In 1881 Schliemann presented the treasure to the German nation, "in perpetual possession and inalienable custody," and museum officials promised that it would be on view in Berlin for all time. It remained there for sixty years, first in the Ethnographic Museum and then in the Museum for Pre- and Early History.

In 1939, as war became imminent, officials of the Berlin State Museums

were told to safeguard their precious possessions, and all the exhibits of the Museum for Pre- and Early History were packed up and trundled down to the basement. Objects made of precious metals and those that were considered irreplaceable, including most of the objects from Troy, were packed into three crates. An inventory list was stuck into each crate, and they were sealed. In January 1941 most of the museum's exhibits, including the three crates, were moved to the vault of the Prussian State Bank to protect them from air bombardment. Later that year they were moved again, to one of the new fortresslike antiaircraft towers that Albert Speer's workshop had designed to protect the capital of the Reich. Two of these steel-and-concrete behemoths, which were considered impregnable, were earmarked as repositories for Berlin's cultural treasures. The Museum for Pre- and Early History was assigned two rooms on the north side of the tower near the Zoological Garden—the Zoo Flakturm.

The Zoo tower, occupying almost an entire city block, was the largest of the Flakturm. From its roof, the Luftwaffe directed the defense of Berlin, firing off 128-mm guns with a deafening boom. Ammunition was stored deep below ground and brought up in steel elevators. The museum's exhibits remained in the tower until 1945, by which time the surrounding area had been reduced to rubble. The zoo had been destroyed and most of the animals killed. A team of veterinarians chopped up the carcasses of the dead elephants to be processed into soap and

A bust of Sophia Schliemann wearing the headpiece from the "Treasure of Priam."

bonemeal, and hungry Berliners were said to be cooking crocodile tails and sausage made of dead bears.

In February 1945 the directors of the Prussian State Museums were ordered to evacuate all their collections to an area west of the Elbe River that had been designated as an American and British occupation zone if there were to be a surrender. The Germans didn't want their treasures to fall into Russian hands. But the museum directors thought it would be so dangerous to move the collections on highways, railways, or waterways subject to enemy bombing that they were unwilling to obey the order. Hitler himself was consulted, and in March a "Führer's Order" was issued. The art was moved.

Marshal Georgy Zhukov, deputy supreme commander of the Red Army and leader of the assault on Berlin, launched the final battle for the capital on April 16, 1945. By this time, most of the art treasures had left the city, headed for several salt mines. Many ended up in Merkers, where they were found by General Patton's Third Army. Several thousand crates filled with artworks and archaeological objects, including fifty from the Museum for Pre- and Early History, were discovered in Grasleben by the U.S. First Army. But the three crates containing the Trojan gold had a different fate.

Dr. Wilhelm Unverzagt, director of the Museum for Pre- and Early History and a loyal Nazi, had obeyed Hitler's order to transport his collection out of the city—except for the three precious crates. He didn't want them to leave Berlin, and as the Red Army attacked the Zoo tower he remained with the crates, sleeping on top of them at night. The din of battle was made more horrible by the groans of the wounded from the hospital that had been set up in a nearby room. Corpses and amputated limbs piled up. Terrified civilians who had fled the bombardment were crammed in so tightly that they could hardly move. The city was in flames.

The devoted Unverzagt remained in the tower after everyone else had fled. On the first of May, the day after Hitler's suicide, it was surrendered to the Russians. They swarmed in, clattering up and down the staircases looking for loot. Unverzagt stood his ground until a senior officer appeared. He told him about the treasure packed in the crates and asked for his help. The officer posted guards at the door of the room. A few days later, Colonel General Nikolai Berzarin, the Soviet commander of the city, came to inspect the tower and assured Unverzagt that the crates would be taken to a safe place. At the end of May, the three crates containing the Trojan gold were loaded onto a Studebaker truck. Unverzagt never saw them again.

The fate of Priam's gold was one of the great mysteries of the Second World War. Scholars had been attempting to track it down for over four decades by the time Grigorii Kozlov picked up the piece of paper on the basement floor that indicated that the treasure was locked away somewhere in Moscow's Pushkin Museum, a refugee from yet another siege and the sacking of a great city.

Konstantin Akinsha and Grigorii Kozlov
*Beautiful Loot:*
*The Soviet Plunder of*
*Europe's Art Treasures*
1995

# "Priam's Gold" on Display

*For almost fifty years the golden artifacts that Schliemann gave to the city of Berlin were thought to have been lost, stolen, or even melted down. In fact, however, they were taken, along with other treasures, by Soviet troops in the last days of the war and brought to Russia. In 1994 the Pushkin Museum announced that it was holding the "Treasure of Priam" among its collections. German officials came to Moscow and inspected the golden objects at the museum, where the "Treasure of Priam" will be exhibited for the first time since the war. Its future is unknown.*

## Treasures at the Pushkin

*Vladimir Tolstikov is head of the Department of Art and Archaeology of the Ancient World at the Pushkin State Museum for Fine Arts in Moscow. Mikhail Treister is senior researcher and curator of the same department.*

The collection of Trojan antiquities that is now at the Pushkin Museum has a complicated and dramatic history. From the very beginning some of the objects were removed from Troy by Heinrich Schliemann illegally, without the permission of Turkish authorities. Later the collection was given by Schliemann as a gift to the German nation and housed in Berlin. At the start of the Second World War the most valuable pieces of the Berlin collection (thirteen of the original nineteen hoards, known as Treasures A to S) were packed in boxes and hidden away. Only recently has the public learned that in 1945 these crates were collected by Soviet troops and shipped to Moscow. Most of the bronze vessels and axes that were part of the Berlin collection are now in the Hermitage Museum in Saint Petersburg; while other pieces, such as the group known as Treasure C (which were in fact stolen by Schliemann's workers), found their way to the Archaeological Museum in Istanbul after the thieves were apprehended. And still another group, mainly beads, was given by Sophia Schliemann after her husband's death to the National Archaeological Museum of Athens.

Only a few scholars have been allowed to examine the objects at the Pushkin Museum since their resurfacing, among them the prominent Bronze Age scholar Machteld Mellink from Bryn

Mawr, Donald Easton, an English expert on Schliemann, and Manfred Korfmann from Germany, head of the "Troy Project," who has been leading excavations at Troy since the late 1980s. However, the very first to examine the pieces as they emerged from storage were representatives of Berlin's Museum for Pre- and Early History, who visited the Pushkin in October 1994. The Berlin team was astonished at the excellent preservation and storage of the objects, all of which still have their German accession numbers. The original packing material was not kept, but the objects had been carefully weighed, packed into new crates, and hidden away for almost fifty years. In the late 1940s some Soviet archaeologists were fortunate enough to catch a glimpse of the treasures, but the new generation of Russian scholars had no idea of the whereabouts of the world-famous archaeological finds. Although there were often rumors....

Treasure A, also known as Priam's Treasure, includes gold and silver vessels (among them the famous "sauceboat"), earrings, bracelets, and beads. But the finest pieces are two gold diadems composed of chain links and thousands of tiny golden leaves. The larger diadem was immortalized in the famous photograph of Sophia Schliemann [see page 44].

American philologist David Traill once suggested that "Priam's Treasure" might be a fraudulent collection of items, amassed from different sites. Our evidence, however, points to the authenticity of the pieces. Important to this argument is the composition of the treasures, which matches what we know about the economic situation of pre-historic Troy—the wealth of its people and the materials available to its artisans—and makes improbable the forgery theory.

The most plausible date for the objects is around the middle third quarter of the third millennium BC, which corresponds well to the date of the burned level of Troy IIg. (Manfred Korfmann dates this to c. 2600–2450 BC based on stratigraphy of the settlement and carbon dating.) By around 2500 BC Troy, located at the crossroads of maritime and overland trade routes between Europe and Asia, had become a center of prosperity, attracting the finest artisans of the ancient world.

We are still uncertain of the specific functions of the various pieces; they may have belonged to temples, rulers, goldsmiths, or served several different roles in Trojan society.

What will happen with the collection after the Moscow exhibition? The question of whether it will stay in Moscow or be returned to Germany has not yet been resolved, although a joint Russian-German commission on restitution has been meeting since 1993. Meanwhile the Russian parliament has issued a moratorium on the return of cultural treasures, which is understandable, given the numerous losses of Russian monuments and art works during the war.

Although the future of the Trojan Treasures is not known, it is clear that the objects are of tremendous cultural and scientific importance to the world and must be made accessible to the international community of scholars as well as the general public.

Vladimir Tolstikov and
Mikhail Treister
1996

# Distinguishing Fact from Fiction

*In his lifetime Heinrich Schliemann was called a liar, a forger, and a cheat; while few today dispute his enormous contributions to archaeology and our knowledge of ancient Greece, the abuse continues to fly. Has criticism of Schliemann been carried too far?*

T erracotta idol from Mycenae.

### A Case for the Prosecution

*David Traill has scrupulously analyzed Schliemann's diaries, letters, and publications, finding in them a litany of discrepancies.*

It is of course his lying and penchant for fraud that are of greatest importance when we consider Schliemann's career as an archaeologist. The prevalence of lies in Schliemann's writings and the peculiar quality of many of them suggest that his lying was pathological. Consider for instance, his "eyewitness" account of the fire of San Francisco or his interview with President Fillmore, both in his 1851–2 diary. There is also the bizarre entry in the 1869 diary, in which he insists that he will have nothing to do with the "horrors" of "false certificates and perjury" to obtain a New York divorce on the very day on which he obtained his American citizenship by these means. Here too Schliemann's behavior improved as he grew older. The influence of Virchow from 1879 onwards and Schliemann's efforts to please and emulate him were no doubt factors in this improvement.

Schliemann almost certainly fabricated the story concerning his original impetus toward archaeology. The evidence points overwhelmingly to the conclusion that Schliemann had no childhood dream of excavating Troy. What was it then that prompted him to devote the last twenty years of his life to Homeric archaeology? The answer may surprise and disappoint, but it is quite clear. He fell into it. In the spring of 1868 he planned to return to St. Petersburg to see his children. His route was to take him via Italy, Greece, and the Black Sea. Ithaca and

Troy were to be stops on the way, since he had missed them on his previous Grand Tour. Discussions at the learned societies in Paris had stimulated his interest in Homeric sites but the thought of actually excavating them seems not to have even occurred to him at this stage. The news that he would face renewed litigation in St Petersburg forced him to abandon his visit to Russia. This allowed him to take a much more leisurely trip than he had originally planned....

How then are we to assess Schliemann's excavations? The greatness of his achievements and their enduring significance are beyond dispute. But given his propensities, the question naturally arises, how much can we believe? His archaeological reports clearly provide, *for the most part,* a reliable record of his excavations. That is not in dispute. On the other hand, the comforting formula that he told lies in his private life but not in his archaeology is no longer tenable. Neither can we say that he told lies in his published work but not in his diaries. There are a great many lies in the diaries. We need to be skeptical at all times, but especially when it comes to the most dramatic finds.

Consider Priam's Treasure. Sophia did not witness the discovery in May 1873 as Schliemann reports. She was in Athens at the time. Schliemann's earliest account placed the findspot in a room in the so-called Priam's Palace. Later the findspot was moved to the city wall "directly next to Priam's Palace." But all the plans place it just *outside* the city wall. This coincides with the testimony of Yannakis [Schliemann's foreman at Troy]. The earliest accounts imply a discovery

date of 31 May. Later this was changed to 7 June. Several pieces that appear in photographs of Priam's Treasure also appear in photographs taken in 1872 of the previous two years' finds. The gold jewelry is not mentioned in the earliest accounts of the discovery. Should we accept Schliemann's account as essentially true with a few honest mistakes, or was Priam's Treasure actually a more modest find of bronze and silver pieces enhanced by the season's unreported gold pieces and even some earlier finds? The building just within the Scaean Gate, which he identified as Priam's Palace, was not very impressive. Was the treasure a dramatic attempt to authenticate it?

In 1882 very few of the season's more valuable finds ever reached the museum in Constantinople. It is clear from Schliemann's correspondence with Virchow that he was carefully keeping his best finds hidden from the Turks. Accordingly, when he came to write up his report, he could assign his finds to whatever part he wanted. He reported that the overwhelmingly bulk of the more interesting pieces came from what was now the most impressive building in Troy II: "Temple (later Megaron) A." This looks like another instance of Schliemann "bundling" his best finds in much the same way he seems to have done in 1873 and for similar reasons.

In his later excavations, Schliemann resorted less frequently to dishonesty. It is hard to imagine, for instance, that there are many serious distortions in his reports on Orchomenos and Tiryns. On the other hand, in 1890 he smuggled all the best finds—the stone axes, the silver vase, and the marble heads—past the Turkish supervisors and off to Athens. He thereby deceived Hamdy Bey [Director of the Imperial Museum in Constantinople], who courteously allowed him to take the pottery, which legally belonged to the Turkish government. Even at the end of his life he could act in an unprincipled manner towards those who helped him and he had no qualms about paying the workmen who brought him finds clandestinely. His success and the ineffectiveness of the supervision are all the more remarkable in that the Turks knew from 1873 onwards that Schliemann was a wily and unscrupulous manipulator, who needed to be watched very carefully.

What then of Mycenae? The extraordinary wealth of Shaft Graves III, IV, and V has never been adequately explained. A noted expert on the finds comments on the "startling discrepancies in quality and organization of design." May not the great wealth and "startling discrepancies" of these tombs be

attributable to more "bundling" by Schliemann? It is clear that Schliemann came across quite a few tombs and burials long before he reached the shaft graves. There were rich finds of bronzes in some of these tombs. There may well have also been gold pieces, smuggled past Stamatakis [the Greek archaeologist appointed to watch over Schliemann at Mycenae] to Schliemann by the workmen for payment and then saved for the grand finale: Shaft Graves III, IV, and V. At Troy in 1882 Schliemann paid local villagers to make clandestine excavations in the surrounding area. In 1876 he was well aware that there were rich tholos and chamber tombs in the vicinity of Mycenae. Some of the pieces that seem too late for the shaft graves, like Nestor's Cup, may come from clandestine excavations commissioned by Schliemann. A simple microscopic examination should be able to determine whether there are any modern forgeries among the pieces that occur in multiple copies or, like some of the gold masks, are suspicious for other reasons. If, however, Schliemann added to Shaft Graves III, IV, or V authentic objects that had in fact been found elsewhere it is hard to see how this can now be proved conclusively. Stylistically, a number of pieces seem too late for these graves. Should we trust Schliemann's account of them because it cannot be disproved? Or should we be skeptical because it is hard to reconcile their attribution to these graves with evidence from other excavations?

Archaeologists, historians, and excavators gathered along the Cyclopean walls of Tiryns.

Schliemann was an extraordinary individual. In his life and character there is much to admire and much to deplore. It is hard, and probably misguided, to develop a consistent attitude towards him. His egotism, mendacity, and often cynical behavior inevitably alienate our sympathy. In light of his difficult childhood, however, his flaws become more understandable and one can only admire the unquenchable resolution to improve himself by sheer hard work. A picture emerges of a profoundly contradictory and elusive personality. He strove to become a hero. Although questions remain, and indeed are becoming more insistent, Heinrich Schliemann, thanks to his astonishing success, is likely to remain the emblematic archaeologist of all time.

David Traill
*Schliemann of Troy:
Treasure and Deceit*
1995

## In Defense of Schliemann

*Nigel Spivey reviews David Traill's book on Schliemann, finding the biography too harsh a study of the man.*

Traill…has been pursuing the traces of Heinrich Schliemann like a blood-hound for over a decade. Articles accusing Schliemann of diverse crimes have appeared in specialist journals, and were collected in a volume from Illinois called *Excavating Schliemann* in 1993. The present book is a piece of interim vulgarization of the case so far. Cruelly, it is issued by Schliemann's own British publishers, John Murray. Cruel, because David Traill's broad aim—

though of course he murmurs otherwise—is to discredit Schliemann's life and work.

He does this chiefly by insinuation. Traill's fraud-squad investigation into Schliemann is virtually a one-man project, but its launch in 1972 was by the Classical historiographer William Calder III, who programmed a method of attack: demonstrate that Schliemann was duplicitous in his personal and his business life; then infer a "patho-logical mendacity" carried over to Schliemann's archaeological career. Accordingly, much of Traill's chase has been devoted to inaccuracies and falsehoods in Schliemann's diaries, starting with Schliemann's colorful account of the San Francisco fire in 1851—an event at which he is unlikely to have been present, and seems to have written up vicariously from newspaper reports—and then sniffing out evidence of business malpractice, a shifty divorce, and some Walter Mitty-style inventions of meetings with American presidents and such like. So the argument advances: if Schliemann short-changed customers in the days when he was trading gold-dust and indigo, if he lied to his friends, his wives, and himself, then why should we believe his reports of finds at Troy and Mycenae and elsewhere?

Like so many investigations of fraud, however, Traill's enterprise gets so far and then fizzles out. Schliemann was certainly a dodger, and Traill establishes in a manner which is probably definitive the extent to which Schliemann romanticized the first half of his life. The son of a drunken and disgraced Lutheran pastor, Schliemann ostensibly redeemed family honor on two scores. First, he made himself more than respectably rich; second, he achieved academic distinction. Whether he was originally fired to gain that distinction as a boy by seeing pictures of Troy ablaze is, as Traill establishes, highly doubtful. And whether he got rich as a means to the end of academic honor is also unclear. Plainly he adored the sort of trite lionization that academics can muster when they try—the honorary degrees, the medals and so on—and plainly he felt desperately insecure in the world of scholarship, never apparently understanding that since the time of Galileo, scholarly dissension has been permissible. And sometimes he crassly muddled the two worlds of business and academia, as when he offered cash to journal editors for the publication of his articles. But on the whole, Schliemann achieved his double redemption. That he sedulously scripted an already adventurous life into a resounding epic we can surely forgive. His diligence earned at least the right to be pompous.

Beyond this, Traill is hard pushed to make anything stick. That Schliemann compressed, juggled, and generally dramatized his excavation reports can be proven to a point. But insinuations of actual forgery are no more than that. "Priam's Treasure" can be shown to be assembled from different stages of excavation, but it is not forensically demonstrated that Schliemann commissioned fake jewelry to bolster its appeal. Likewise, all that Traill can do with his suspicion that some of the finds from the shaft graves of Mycenae may be forged is tell us that the authorities at the Athens National Museum have so far refused to test the authenticity of the gold mask and other celebrated objects. This falls a long way short of a serious allegation. From the kangaroo court erected by Traill's court, Schliemann ultimately walks away free.

The book is engaging nonetheless. And if nothing else, it prompts some tangential reflections on the rhapsodic capacities of other archaeologists whose careers owe much, indirectly, to the extraordinary public interest raised by Schliemann's pursuit of Homer's heroic world. Do we imagine that Schliemann belongs to a crude age of folly, in his naive efforts to weave marvelous stories about disinterred objects? Then we deceive ourselves. In 1966, Carl Blegen entitled his excavations at Mycenae *Pylos: "The Palace of Nestor."* In 1988, Italian archaeologists on the Palatine Hill in Rome spoke of finding "The Wall of Romulus." It was early this year that the world was rashly telegraphed that the tomb of Alexander had been located in the Egyptian oasis of Siwa. And it was only a year or two ago that the first plaintive sagas began to be woven, by the sort of archaeologists who wear white coats, of the life and times of the "Ice Man" lately recovered from the Austro-Italian borders. These are random instances of a force which bears upon all composers of history: the breeze of inspiration from Clio, a muse. She wants more than a catalogue of relics. She demands stories, heroes, spilt blood, and enchantments. We should consider Schliemann's faults in this perspective: a case of Clio's derangement, nothing more, and nothing less.

Nigel Spivey
*Times Literary Supplement*
1995

# Further Reading

WORKS BY SCHLIEMANN
Schliemann wrote in several languages. The following works by him are noted in their original edition:

*La Chine et le Japon au Temps Présent*, Librairie Centrale, Paris, 1867

*Ithaque, le Péloponnèse, Troie. Recherches Archéologiques*, Reinwald, Paris, 1869

*Trojanische Alterhümer. Bericht über die Ausgrabungen in Troja* (with atlas), F.A. Brockhaus, Leipzig, 1874

*Mycenae: a Narrative of Researches and Discoveries at Mycenae and Tiryns*, John Murray, London, 1878

*Ilios: the City and Country of the Trojans*, John Murray, London, 1880

*Orchomenos: Bericht über meine Ausgrabungen*, F.A. Brockhaus, Leipzig, 1881

*Tiryns: the Prehistoric Palace of the Kings of Tiryns*, Scribner's Sons, New York, 1885; John Murray, London, 1886

*Troja: Results of the Latest Researches and Discoveries on the Site of Homer's Troy*, John Murray, London, and Harper & Bros., New York, 1884

*Troy and Its Remains*, John Murray, London, 1875

THE CORRESPONDENCE OF SCHLIEMANN
Hermann, J., and Evelin Maaß, *Die Korrespondenz zwischen Heinrich Schliemann und Rudolf Virchow*, Akademie Verlag, Berlin, 1990

Meyer, Ernst, ed., *Briefe von Heinrich Schliemann*, Walter de Gruyter, Berlin, 1936

ON THE LIFE OF SCHLIEMANN
Calder, William M., III, "Schliemann on Schliemann: A Study in the Use of Sources," *Greek, Roman, and Byzantine Studies* 13, pp. 335–53, 1972

—— and Justus Cobet, *Heinrich Schliemann nach Hundert Jahren* (text of a lecture delivered at the symposium marking the 100th anniversary of the death of Schliemann), Klostermann, Frankfurt am Main, 1990

—— and David Traill, *Myth, Scandal, and History: The Heinrich Schliemann Controversy and a First Edition of the Mycenaean Diary*, Wayne State University, Detroit, 1986

Deuel, Leo, *Memoirs of Heinrich Schliemann*, Harper & Row, New York and London, 1977

Lehrer, Mark, and David Turner, "The Making of an Archaeologist: Schliemann's Diary of 1868," *Annual of the British School at Athens* 84, pp. 221–68, 1989

Lilly, Eli, ed., *Schliemann in Indianapolis*, Indiana Historical Society, Indianapolis, 1961

Ludwig, Emil. *Schliemann: The Story of a Gold-Seeker*, Little Brown, Boston, 1931

Moorehead, Caroline, *The Lost Treasures of Troy*, Weidenfeld & Nicolson, London, 1994

Payne, Robert, *The Gold of Troy: The Story of Heinrich Schliemann and the Buried Cities of Ancient Greece*, Robert Hale, London, 1959

Poole, Lynn and Gray, *One Passion, Two Loves: The Story of Heinrich and Sophia Schliemann, Discoverers of Troy*, Crowell, New York, 1966

Schuchhardt, Carl, *Schliemann's Excavations: An Archaeological and Historical Study*, Macmillan, London, 1891

Stone, Irving, *The Greek Treasure*, Doubleday, New York, 1975

Traill, David, *Schliemann of Troy*, John Murray, London, 1995

Turner, David, "Heinrich Schliemann: The Man Behind the Masks," *Archaeology*, Nov/Dec, pp. 36–42, 1990

Weber, Shirley H., ed., *Schliemann's First Visit to America, 1850–51*, Gennadius Monographs, no. 2, Harvard University Press for the American School of Classical Studies at Athens, Cambridge, Mass., 1942

OTHER WORKS
Blegen, Carl, *Troy: Excavations Conducted by the University of Cincinnati, 1932–8*, 4 vols., Princeton University Press, 1950–8

——, *Troy and the Trojans*, Thames and Hudson, London, and Praeger, New York, 1963

Cook, J.M., *The Troad: An Archaeological and Topographical Study*, Oxford University Press, 1973

Cottrell, Leonard, *Realms of Gold: A Journey in Search of the Mycenaeans*, New York Graphic Society, 1963

Edey, Maitland, ed., *Lost World of the Aegean*, Time-Life Books, New York, 1975

Finley, Moses I., *The World of Odysseus*. Viking, New York, 1954

Fitzgerald, Robert, trans., *Homer's Iliad*, Doubleday, New York and London, 1974

Furumark, Arne, *Mycenaean Pottery*, Stockholm, 1941

Greek Ministry of Culture, *Troy: Heinrich Schliemann's Excavations and Finds*, Athens, 1985

Wood, M., *In Search of the Trojan War*, Dutton, New York, 1989

H. DUTHEIL

GODARD

# List of Illustrations

# Index

## Acknowledgments

The publishers wish to thank the following for their help in preparing this book: Patrice Androussov, M. Bogdanov, Elias Eliadis, Alexandre Farnoux, Pierre de Gigord, Georges S. Korrès, and André Sidéris.

## Photograph Credits

Alinari-Giraudon 38a. All rights reserved 14, 16a, 18a, 18b, 19, 26b, 27, 28a, 31b, 35a, 37r, 42, 50b, 51b, 62, 66b, 72, 92r, 98ar, 99a, 100ar, 100–1, 104, 116, 120. Patrice Androussov, Paris 26a, 41a, 48a. Archiv für Kunst und Geschichte, Berlin 44. Archives, Berlin Academy of Sciences 93, 100al. Association des Amis du Peintre Zuber, Paris 33, 34–5. Berko Fine Paintings Collections, Knokke-le-Zoute/Brussels/Paris 86. Bibliothèque Nationale, Paris front cover, 15b, 32, 36b, 42–3, 49a, 51a, 73al–73ar, 74–5, 137. Bibliothèque du Saulchoir, Paris 94–5. Bildarchiv Preussischer Kulturbesitz, Berlin 1b, 3b, 5b, 7, 8a–9a, 15a, 16b, 22, 46a, 46–7, 49b, 55b, 56b, 58bl–r, 59b, 60–1b, 63a, 67b, 68r, 98b, 102–3, 106–7, 113. British Library, London 1–9, 45, 52–3, 66–7, 68l, 70, 71, 84 inset, 92a, 111. British Museum, London 117. Dagli Orti, Paris back cover, 38–9, 74, 76bl–r, 77b, 78–9, 78a, 79a, 81b. Editions Gallimard Jeunesse 24b, 104–5, 122. Editions Gallimard, Paris 114. Elias Eliadis, Athens 13, 81a, 87, 88b, 88–9, 90, 90–1a, 90–1b, 96a, 108r, 109b, 112, 119, 130. E. Engelmann, New York 20–1. French School, Athens 50a. Gennadius Library, Athens (Elias Eliadis collection) 21r, 23, 28b, 31a, 48b, 55a, 56a, 58–9, 60–1, 89b, 96bl, 97, 108l. German Archaeological Institute, Athens 64, 82, 83, 84–5, 94, 102a, 103, 123, 132–3. Giraudon 12. Klaus Göken 63r. Mitchell Library, Glasgow 54, 57, 95. Nebraska State Historical Society 28–9. Jorgos Phaphalis, Athens 11, 96br, 99b, 126. Pierre de Gigord, Paris 40. Réunion des Musées Nationaux, Paris 116. Roger-Viollet 24–5, 34, 36–7, 39a, 40–1, 43a. Royal Institute of British Architects, London 76–7, 80. Schliemann Museum, Ankershagen 17, 24a, 118. Lloyd K. Townsend 64–5. M. Emele and L. Spree, Troia-Projekts, Tübingen 110. Ullstein Bilderdienst, Berlin 68–9.

## Text Credits

Grateful acknowledgment is made for use of material from the following: Akinsha, Konstantin, Grigorii Kozlov, and Sylvia Hachfield, *Beautiful Loot: The Soviet Plunder of Europe's Art Treasures*, Random House Inc., New York, 1995; © Konstantin Akinsha and Grigorii Kozlov; reprinted by permission of Random House Inc. (pp. 124–7). Edey, Maitland A., and the editors of *Time-Life Books*, *The Emergence of Man: The Lost World of the Aegean*, Time-Life Books, New York, 1975; © 1975 Time Inc.; All Rights Reserved (pp. 114–5). Spivey, Nigel, "A case of Clio's derangement," *The Times Literary Supplement*, n. 4815, 14 July 1995 (pp. 134–5). Stone, Irving, *The Greek Treasure*, Doubleday & Company, Inc., New York, 1975; © 1975 Irving Stone (pp. 120–1). Traill, David A., *Schliemann of Troy: Treasure and Deceit*, St. Martin's Press, Inc., New York, 1995; © 1995 David A. Traill; reprinted by permission of St. Martin's Press, Inc., and John Murray Ltd, London (pp. 121–3, 130–4).

Hervé Duchêne, a former member of the French School
at Athens, is Professor of Ancient History at the
University of Burgundy in Dijon. A specialist in Eastern
Mediterranean port and commercial archaeology, he has been
involved in excavations at Delos and Thasos in Greece,
working in the footsteps of the archaeologists of the
past one hundred years. In *Notre Ecole Normale*
(Belles-Lettres, 1994) he brought fellow-archaeologist
Salomon Reinach's journals to the world's attention.

Translated from the French by Jeremy Leggatt

For Harry N. Abrams, Inc.
Editor: Sarah Burns
Typographic Designer: Elissa Ichiyasu
Design Supervisor: Miko McGinty
Assistant Designer: Tina Thompson
Text Permissions: Catherine Ruello

Library of Congress Catalog Card Number: 95–79942

ISBN 0–8109–2825–6

Copyright © 1995 Gallimard

English translation copyright © 1996 Harry N. Abrams, Inc., New York,
and Thames and Hudson Ltd., London

Published in 1996 by Harry N. Abrams, Inc., New York
A Times Mirror Company

Printed and bound in Italy by Editoriale Libraria, Trieste